Praise for *What I Kn*

"A beautifully written, compelling ta   n
psychological thrillers with complex c   ,
this book is a must-read."

—*Big Indie Books*

Praise for *Retrograde*

"With all the suspense of a finely wrought mystery, this remarkably assured first novel tells the story of a marriage unexpectedly—and unwittingly—revisited, testing the boundaries of love and memory—and it does so with prose exquisitely calibrated to reflect the subtleties of these two characters' thoughts and feelings in all their strangeness and familiarity."

—Ellen Akins, author of *Hometown Brew, Public Life, Little Woman* and *World Like a Knife*

"Hausler's ability to describe the precarious state of the emotions involved is consistently convincing. . . . A strongly written tale about resurrecting a marriage under the most unusual and mysterious of circumstances."

—*Kirkus Reviews*

"This disturbing, haunting and powerful story explores the minutiae of the relationship between the couple as they start to live together again . . . The ending is a masterpiece of the power of 'less is more' in storytelling—but if you want to know what it is, then you will have to read this wonderful novel."

—Linda Hepworth, *Nudge Books*

"Hausler's debut novel was an incredibly beautiful look at love put through the test of time. *Retrograde* is very much about the nature of love as it features many of the ups and downs of a difficult relationship. From touching dates and admiration to petty fights and full blown arguments, Hausler's breakout has it all."

—Melissa Ratcliff, *Paperback Paris*

also by Kat Hausler

RETROGRADE

WHAT I KNOW ABOUT JULY

A NOVEL

KAT HAUSLER

Meerkat Press
Asheville

ISBN-13 978-1-946154-80-4 (Paperback)
ISBN-13 978-1-946154-81-1 (eBook)

Cover and book design by Tricia Reeks

Printed in the United States of America

Published in the United States of America by
Meerkat Press, LLC, Asheville, North Carolina
www.meerkatpress.com

For Sergej

*Sometimes I wonder if you're mythologizing me
like I do you*

—of Montreal, "The Past Is a Grotesque Animal"

ONE

The stalker was literally the only one of Simon's fans he never thought about sleeping with. No, not *literally*. His little sister Franzi was always getting on his case about that. You're not *literally* dying. Like she'd know. But anyway. Obviously, some of his fans were ugly, some were men, some were too young—pedophile-bait rather than jailbait—and there were the girls who spent his whole show making out with their greasy boyfriends without ever looking up. But not the stalker. *She* wasn't even bad looking. Not that his standards were very high, which worried him since his therapist acted like he was some sex addict with zero ability to commit. The stalker never even glanced at her phone while he was playing. He didn't mean to look, but there was something magnetic about the intensity of her gaze. As bad as he felt when a woman *didn't* show interest, this was worse. His drummer Micha had been the first to call the short brunette with awful taste in lipstick and an endless array of band shirts "the stalker," even though only Simon felt threatened by her.

She hung around before and after shows. Venue managers made nudge-nudge references like she was some exotic pet Simon kept, and that was probably what she wanted, having her name linked to his as often as possible. As if they even used her name. It was something ordinary like Julia, but she always acted like Simon should know who she was. And he did, some little warning light flashing when he saw her maneuvering through the crowd toward him: *Watch out, stalker!*

It was this maneuvering and positioning of herself that put him off, even more than her postcards piling up in the mail room of Poor Dog Records. He didn't know her, or if he did, it was only because she'd forced her acquaintance on him. He assumed she lived in Berlin since she'd made every show in town since their first album came out. She sometimes turned up in nearby cities and had once even accosted him in Munich with a story about visiting relatives. It creeped him out to think of her traveling all that way for him. With someone else, that amount of devotion would've stroked his volatile ego enough for a positive response, but seeing her stupid knowing smile in the front row that night had almost cost him his rhythm. What gave her the right?

Micha laughed himself silly at the slightest hint that Simon was afraid of her, and now Tanja had gotten wind of it. She played bass, and teased Simon and anyone she could get her hands on with the mercilessness of an older sibling. Micha had pointed out that, in addition to her obvious talent, Tanja offered certain demographic benefits. Tom, their first bassist, had quit before they recorded anything after a coke-fueled fight over his girlfriend, and Simon had gone on to have a crushing relationship and even more crushing breakup with the willowy blonde who'd replaced him. Nadine had left the band when they'd been just popular enough for people to notice. Since Tanja wasn't into men, Simon couldn't start anything with her. She smoked like a chimney but didn't touch drugs. She was a godsend. The other advantage was her ruthless careerism. Despite the tough, sarcastic impression she made, or perhaps because of it, she'd soon coerced and charmed the band onto a bigger label.

"I don't plan on dying young," she'd said. "I need something in the bank for when I'm an old hag." She worked at a temping agency doing everything from data entry to dishes, but had only the usual Berlin savings account, a shoebox full of change.

"*When* you're an old hag?" Micha had asked. They'd gotten close enough to be mean to each other almost right away.

Simon liked Tanja, which Dr. Froheifer said was a healthy development in his relationship to women. Of course, he didn't buy into everything she said. It had taken him a few sessions to notice she had a doctorate in literature, not psychology, but that was what you got for picking your therapist based solely on proximity to your apartment. Between touring, recording and making overpriced lattes at his day job, he didn't see her that often. He should've had the stalker analyze him. She got more face time.

Mostly, though, he went back and forth between worrying that what Dr. F said was true and he'd never be cured, and coming up with reasons why it couldn't be. Like the sex thing. He didn't actually have sex that often. In fact, he never did except after a show. That averaged out to less than with Nadine, though they'd had their ups and downs, and not just in bed. Right now, he happened to be single, which meant he had to divide a perfectly normal amount of sex among different women. He also happened to be incapable of picking up anyone outside of a concert venue.

That was another of Dr. F's suggestions: meeting someone "the normal way." He'd tried saying it *was* normal to meet potential partners at work, but she'd made it into this whole power thing. In actual fact, it was just easier. On his days offstage, he made good coffee and bad small talk if he had a shift at Café Astral, read or listened to music in Volkspark Friedrichshain if he didn't. A beer with Micha and Tanja was a big night out for him. And when he was himself, Simon Kemper without a guitar or mic, surprise, surprise, women didn't throw themselves at him.

Sure, he got occasional darting glances. But they always seemed to be asking how far gone he was, whether the downcast eyes and five o'clock-yesterday shadow were intriguing or signs of unemployment, addiction, a life of crime.

Now that Hare vs. Hedgehog was playing bigger venues, people sometimes came up to ask if it was really him. But instead of leading to new love interests, his minor celebrity status only created more distance. He felt slow and clumsy in the harsh light of day, and never managed to say anything clever. They probably thought he wanted to be left alone. He did and didn't. They never even asked for autographs, just identified him and drifted away to tell their many loved ones about the slightly famous misanthrope they'd run into. The anecdote would be more interesting than the actual encounter.

It was different at a show. Beforehand, they'd sidle up with breathy compliments and talk of great parties later. He didn't party much anymore, or at all, really, but admitting that made him feel old. The beauty of these pre-show invitations was the idea that there was some cachet in being seen with him. He loved to play the person they saw him as.

Afterward, he'd scribble signatures on tote bags, t-shirts and skin, and get photographed with countless devices and overheated fans whose heartrate tripled when he put an arm around them. It was easier when you knew you were wanted.

He specialized in the very bold and very timid. When he was exhausted, and he almost always was, he liked athletic girls with taut ponytails, fierce smiles and more self-assurance than he'd had on the best days of his life. When he had the energy, though, he chatted up the skittish ones who stammered in search of replies and gulped when he touched their arms. It felt like charity, bestowing his favor upon those too meek to demand it. But in his heart of losery hearts, he knew he had more in common with these helpless wallflowers who'd never know they were attractive, not even when they were in bed together, not even when they did nervous, breath-holding imitations of sleep as he whispered, "You're beautiful," as hopefully and hopelessly as if he were talking to himself.

The stalker was neither of these types. She put a steady arm around his waist when she demanded a picture, and acted like she'd known him before he was famous—if you wanted to call it that. In a way, she had, since she'd been at their first show after their first album came out, but that wasn't the same. She only knew concert-him, which—even if he liked this persona better than his actual personality—wasn't the real him. And what was she to him? Her face had the impersonal familiarity of a pop-art celebrity, Mao Zedong or Marilyn Monroe. He didn't feel like he'd always known her, but like he'd always known what she was: a standard feature of his surroundings, like the sticky bars and foul, graffitied bathrooms of clubs—unpleasant, but expected.

It remained unclear whether she was trying to flirt, or so deluded she thought they were friends. Once she hung around so long a bartender told her how talented her "boyfriend" was. Simon said, "I don't even know her," but she laughed like it was an inside joke. Being rude to her might backfire since she posted on their website several times a day and was probably all over whatever social network could most effectively spread the word that he was an asshole. The only thing he could think to do was leave with the nearest fan. If the stalker was disappointed, she never let on.

~~~

The fall before their second album, they had a local show he knew the stalker would be at, not only because she hadn't missed one in the two years since their self-titled, but also because he'd spotted her in nearby Potsdam the night before.

She touched his arm as he carried in his guitar. "Hey, it's been a while."

He kept walking. He'd managed to avoid her in Potsdam by going home with a saner fan named Ilse. Before that, they'd toured Austria, which seemed to be out of her range.

"Siiimon, it's me! It's the new haircut, right?"

He couldn't remember what her old one had been. She had a nothing hair-style, brown and to her shoulders. He'd never had a reason to look closer. Or maybe he'd never had the chance. It was hard to contemplate someone so busy demanding a reaction from you. "Hey, Julia."

"No, silly, it's 'July,' remember? A lot on your mind, huh? Need a hand?"

"No, thanks." He headed for the concert hall, which wasn't open to the public yet, and tried to tell the bouncer with his eyes that she was part of that public and *not* with him. Behind them, he heard Micha snickering and then, miraculously, Tanja saying doors weren't open yet. He didn't stay to hear the stalker's reply.

It's my fault, he told himself while he unpacked his guitar. If I told her to fuck off . . . But more than his fear of confirming to himself and the world what a jerk he was, he was afraid nothing would happen. That he'd realize how helpless he was, caught in one of those dreams where you scream and scream but nobody can hear you; you can't even hear yourself.

He told himself he wasn't upset. She was a minor annoyance like the smoker's cough he was only now getting rid of after months without cigarettes. His voice, his career and so on. Having to smoke on the sly at rehab had forced him to cut back until quitting became a possibility. Plus, the facility was in the middle of nowhere, so he'd been unable to restock. But like that annoying cough, which had convinced him every now and again that he was on the fast track to death, the stalker sometimes got under his skin, and he hated her for it. Dr. F would've said what he really hated was himself for letting her get to him. It was so obvious he didn't need to hear it. And yet she did get to him and he did hate her for it.

He wrote down the set list. He'd long since memorized it, but rewriting it relaxed him, helped him feel ready. Then tuning, the kind of precise concen-tration that was the only real albeit temporary cure for anxiety. Other than drinking, drugs, sometimes sex, and those moments of innocent happiness so rare he dismissed them as hearsay.

Tanja finished tuning her first string before she said, "She's still there."

"Who?" You could always hope. There must've been somebody who'd sound like good news. Nail-biting, fidgety Ilse had said this morning that she couldn't make it, which he'd taken as: didn't want to. He'd only gone home with her to escape July. She'd spent half the night apologizing for things he didn't care about—she'd only recently gained this weight; her place wasn't usually this messy; the neighbors weren't usually this loud—but by morning she'd become purposeful and confident, rushing him out so she could lock up, no mention of phone numbers. A dead end.

Who else, then? Nadine would be even worse news than the stalker. His mom had always been supportive, especially since he'd gotten help for his supposed habits, but she had yet to come to a show. Franzi was busy saving the world or studying. There weren't many people in his life, let alone *shes*.

"The stalker, obviously. I'll set up the mics if you wanna talk to her."

"I don't. Where's Micha?"

"Getting takeout. Why not put her out of her misery?"

"Because I don't *want* to." He hated sounding like a bratty kid stomping his foot and insisting he didn't *want* to go to bed, but he didn't, not with July. It wouldn't be like with other fans; it would mean something. She'd make sure it did. But she couldn't make him like her.

Tanja laughed, coughed and hacked onto the floor.

"Maybe lay off the cigarettes?" The smirk he managed to keep off his face was all over his voice.

She spat again. "Didn't I tell you? I'm down to a pack a day. Birthday resolution. Anyway, she's your problem."

He sighed. What wasn't?

~~~

"Listen," he said, even though she was fixated on him the second he came out. It was like when you got stuck talking to a boring party guest and couldn't find anyone else to say hi to. "We need to get warmed up, so . . ."

"So?" She put a hand on her hip. Like many of her poses, it seemed staged. It was strange how fake you could find someone without having any idea what their real looked like.

"We don't have time for anything else. Sorry." He hated himself for always acting like he owed everyone an apology.

"No problem, see you later." She didn't seem disappointed, but it was all part of her just-stopping-by-to-see-a-friend act that made him crazy.

He hurried backstage. She should've felt insecure, rejected. Star-struck, at least. He didn't consider himself a star, but she must, or why bother stalking him? Nadine's nasty stoned voicemails about how gray and toxic he was weren't the only reason he'd changed his number. The stalker's perky "Hey, Siiimon!" had been equally draining. The kind of energy-suck he didn't need tonight. That bigtime music critic was supposed to come, meaning they were likely to play a shitty show. He saw Tanja's leather jacket on a music stand and thought about looking for the flask she kept in an inner pocket "for an emergency." Which this definitely wasn't. He needed to calm down. Breathe. He put two fingers under his chin to feel his pulse. *Duh-duh, duh-duh.* Still alive. He needed air, not alcohol. He had trouble eating before a show. His nerves upset his stomach, and that limited the amount he could drink. A cigarette would've been just the thing, but he wasn't going to let her throw him off track.

Tanja came back huffing and puffing, and he thought she really should quit before they had to find yet another bassist, but who was he to talk? He'd written their first album in rehab. Not the kind for famous people, but rural, public-health-insurance rehab for back-country addicts and losers like himself. The most shameful part was that he hadn't even had a problem with drugs. He'd had a problem with reality. There was a reason he'd been the only patient without withdrawal symptoms. But now he was healthy, never taking anything, not smoking, drinking less, just a tad anxious. It was a chicken-egg situation, drinking or smoking or swallowing something to kill the panic, the panic bigger when it came back. The cure worse than the disease. The disease worse after every cure. Sometimes he thought about giving up even alcohol, going vegan. Yoga, religion, the whole shebang. But he knew he'd feel insincere, like he always did.

"She gone?"

"Hope so. Should we get warmed up?"

"When Micha's here. Chill." She ran a hand over the top of her stiff, oily mass of hair. He could never tell whether that coiffure was the result of a cosmetic product or complete lack of them. She didn't smell like anything but smoke, so he liked to think she bathed.

"I'm chill," he said in his least convincing, most Woody-Allen-neurotic voice, then cleared his throat. "I'm still getting used to not smoking. I feel jittery."

"Yeah, I quit once, and it sucked. But don't fuck up your voice. The singer's not replaceable."

"Evening, Ladies." Micha came in with a bag of takeout he and Tanja would wolf down like those kids who grew up in the wilderness, and Simon would pick at, while they philosophized about random shit like they weren't about to go onstage. He hadn't heard the door open. It made him nervous to think someone could sneak up like that, but he knew that was only his anxiety seeking an outlet. Dr. F had said so last month when he admitted to being terrified to sleep alone after watching a movie where a monster comes out of the kid's closet. There was always something. Right now, it was the stalker, but if it weren't her it would be the monster or terminal illness or dying alone and being eaten by cats. Which was a stretch since he didn't even have *a* cat.

"I saw the stalker," Micha said. "She's one of your nicer weirdos. Although serial killers' neighbors always say later on how nice and quiet they were."

"I wish she'd be quieter." Simon took the döner kebab Micha handed him, but no matter how much he chewed, the bread and meat stuck in his throat.

Tanja snorted, and beer came out of her nose. That had taken Simon a while to get used to, and he still wondered whether her nasal passages were hooked up wrong. But he shouldn't have said anything. Now wasn't the time to talk about something stressful, not with them.

That was one thing he missed about Nadine. She'd been a good listener and had a calming effect on him when they were getting along. He could admit now that he hadn't quite been in love with her—whatever that was—but she'd had such an aura of gentleness before he got to know her better. Then she'd kissed him while Micha was off setting up the merch stand, and even though a lot of him thought, oh, cool, there was one part that already thought, no, not *her*.

It was never going to work, of course: seeing each other every day; writing songs, practicing and touring together. It had gone well at first because everything stayed the same except they were sleeping together, which saved time he'd otherwise have spent picking up fans or worrying about STDs dodging around condoms, and was more intimate than anything else he'd experienced.

Micha would've told them to break it off if he'd noticed in time, but he was a little slow on the uptake. They'd had a few great weeks and a few good months before things got worse. Then he'd woken up breathless in the middle of the night in a shitty motel room the three of them were sharing and realized he couldn't do it. He and Nadine had been bickering at a constant low flame ever since they got serious, but it wasn't that. He couldn't do anything right. Her voice would freeze over, flat and cold as she asked how he could be so thoughtless, whether he'd introduced her wrong at a show, forgotten to pick up something at the store or misunderstood what she said. There was no way he could live up to her expectations. What would happen when the glow wore off and she figured out how he really was? In what Dr. F would later call the defining characteristic of his romantic encounters, he'd felt sure that everything Nadine liked about him was fake, put on for her benefit. It was an exhausting charade, and he was cracking under the pressure.

According to Dr. F, that was only his insecurity making him think no one could love him for who he was. But the feeling had been pretty convincing at the time. When he tried to avoid Nadine after that tour, her iciness had burst into flames of unexpected rage. They'd broken up and gotten back together a few times, the layer of affection over their resentment stretched a little thinner each time. Rehab should've been a clean break, but he'd come out lonely with nowhere to go, and found her nostalgic and welcoming. By the time their album came out, this last brief honeymoon phase was already a memory.

He was the opposite of Micha, who went with the flow, saw a woman as long as she was interested, then forgot her. His motto was "We'll see." But Simon couldn't wait and see. He lived in the eye of a perpetual storm. One false move could wipe out what little stability he had.

"My advice?" Tanja was saying. "Just say yes."

"Huh?"

"She loves the chase. If she doesn't have to stalk you, what's the point?"

"Whoa, who invited Freud?" Micha asked.

"Yeah," Simon said, "it could work like that, or the exact opposite. Like if I encourage her at all, she'll stalk me even more. What if she finds out where I live?"

"You don't have to invite her over; just hang with her."

"You really think it'll help?"

She finished chewing, crumpled up the paper and rubbed the crumbs off her hands. "Can't hurt."

~~~

He'd been too nice the first time they talked. But it had been Hare vs. Hedgehog's first chance to present their debut album—opening for a band a smidge less obscure than they were—and he'd been so nervous he would've made small talk with Hitler to get his mind off things. The album had only been out a few days, and he'd only been out of Springtime Healthy Living a few months. The stalker approached him before the show and said she'd loved seeing him solo and was so excited to finally see the band live. Which left him wondering which of the minuscule sets he'd played before the band could've left such a lasting impression. Was she a friend of a friend, someone he should know? No, he had so few friends. If she seemed a little familiar, it was probably because the audiences at his solo shows had been small enough for him to make out each individual face in the crowd. If you could call it a crowd. At least they were only the opener tonight and wouldn't be to blame if no one showed up.

"So how's it feel to be out?" she was asking.

"Out of where?"

She laughed in a put-on, coquettish way, and he felt the first twinge of the discomfort he would come to associate with her. "Of rehab. Don't tell me you're high again already?"

"No." Stay friendly. She'd bought a ticket and wanted to make conversation. It wasn't real to her. "I actually really don't like to talk about that."

"Oh, right." Her hand on his arm was unwelcome, but less so than further discussion of the topic. "I feel you. Let's forget I ever brought it up, and just keep looking ahead."

"Yeah, cool." He backed out from under her touch. As she talked about listening to the new album online, he wondered why she hadn't been to any other H vs. H shows, if she liked his solo work so much. They'd been playing concerts long before the album came out—before he ruined things and then ducked out to rehab, forcing everyone to pity instead of blame him. Maybe she thought pretending she liked his early work would give her more cred. He knew the kind. At times he *was* the kind. Either way, her reference to rehab was a dead giveaway that she'd been hanging out on their site. Their last post before announcing the album and show had been a sappy picture of Micha hugging him, captioned "Welcome Back, Simon!" He was dying to go back and delete his cringey comments about feeling grateful and pure after rehab, but that would only call attention to their having existed in the first place.

He thanked her again, trying not to seem surprised that someone liked him that much. At the time, that seemed desirable, flattering, not a source of recurring panic.

What else had she said? Something random like, "Have I put on too much weight?" even though she wasn't heavy.

He said, "No, you look good," which must've been the compliment she was fishing for. More than anything about her appearance, he realized, it was her way of speaking that made her seem familiar—not because he recognized her voice or mannerisms, but because, from the beginning, she'd talked like they knew each other. Many fans imagined that kind of personal connection to members of their favorite bands, but July was the first he'd interacted with, and no amount of interaction seemed to convince her that they were strangers.

"Thanks. You look better without the beard."

"Thanks." Another reference to that "Welcome Back" picture—he'd shaved right after. Sort of a weird thing for a fan to say, but the goodness of *having* a fan still outweighed the weirdness of said fan.

He didn't say anything to get her hopes up. Just that he hoped she'd enjoy the show. To be honest, he might also have said he'd love to hear what she thought. But that was all.

Of course, she turned up at their little folding table afterward, and since they'd spoken before, there was this whole recognition vibe. But all she said was "Great show." Other strangers said that, too. There was no reason for her to feel special.

~~~

Once he agreed to Tanja's stupid idea, he felt his pulse even out and the blood come back into his icy hands. Having a plan meant his brain could check the whole thing off until the next danger signal. He was used to tricking himself this way, and even though he saw through it, it almost always worked. For a while.

Sometimes he thought about joining one of those cults where they brainwash you into an unnatural calm in exchange for all your material assets—but what if it didn't work? Like he'd be sitting there chanting his secret mantra in a paper hat, and not be taken in. Besides, he hadn't even seen Franzi or his therapist, let alone his parents, in ages. Who had time to get brainwashed? He asked Micha to get him a drink so he wouldn't risk seeing July, tried picking at his food again, tried breathing the rancid air in the courtyard, and then settled in to half-hear the opener from backstage.

He felt vague through the first couple songs of his set, like when he slept late and woke up heavy to a slower world. But it was a gentle feeling, better than that hard, painful beat of his heart when he couldn't tell whether he was still breathing.

This was one of the ways in which concerts could be good: the clarity of his role, the knowledge that the audience wanted him to play, had come especially for that purpose. It was one of the few situations involving other people where he knew what he was supposed to do. Sometimes when he'd gone off to play outdoors at rehab, other patients would sneak up to listen, and who could blame them because Springtime Healthy Living was one of the most boring places he'd ever been. What bothered him hadn't been their presence, but the sense that the actual entertainment value was in laughing at him, a crybaby singing to himself about his pathetic feelings. There were a couple prematurely aged fortysomethings who made a real sport of interrupting him with sarcastic clapping and jeers—fat Tammy and her roommate with the constant nosebleeds—and he couldn't help feeling like they were just saying what everyone else was thinking. Even the youngest patient, a teenager with a bloodied face and a gaze like the Mona Lisa, always just shy of looking at you, seemed to be smirking whenever he caught her listening. Most of the others who turned up had only watched quietly, but you never knew. Except here, tonight, in times and places like this, he did.

He must've left the blah-blah with the audience too long, because Micha took it upon himself to ask how they'd liked the opener, how they were feeling. Clapping, whoos and the rest. Was it loud enough? It was the biggest crowd yet for a show they were headlining. Of course, a crowd always looked bigger in a venue the size of an apartment. Not his, obviously. Someone's apartment who had a steady paycheck.

He kept his eyes on the unlit back of the crowd, where all the faces were facets of one big shadow. It was a habit he'd developed in school when struggling to make eye contact during presentations. Plus, the stalker would never stand back there, so there was no risk of their eyes meeting.

His stomach flipped at the thought, like he'd forgotten something important. Early on, when playing in front of people meant an automatic panic attack, he'd showed up at a competition without his guitar. They would've lost their slot if it weren't for this saint from the last band in the lineup who let Simon use his. Hare vs. Hedgehog had come in second to the saint's band. Seeing one of the few non-assholes on the planet win had helped with Simon's nauseating sense of failure.

A joke. Now would be the time for a joke. Nothing occurred to him. But experience had taught him that the right audience would laugh at anything.

"That's how you are," he said once the applause died down. "How do you think *I'm* feeling?"

Stray laughs, a general uncomfortable chuckle. "Like shit?" some guy in the back yelled. Simon laughed into the mic even though he hated people like that: people with ready answers and few enough inhibitions to shout whatever popped into their heads. People who didn't need a mic to get others listening.

He let them wait another few beats. "Exactly."

Now the real laughter came, relief, the audience thinking misery was just a joke: his misery, theirs, all the misery in the world.

"I love you, Simon!" yelled a voice he chose to believe sounded nothing like the stalker's.

"I love me, too." He was already playing the next song.

Time sped up, but that was okay once you got started. There was always that immense hurdle you had to fling yourself over or bust through, but then you could play without thinking about it, a record spinning along until someone hit stop, stretching that last distorted note to the breaking point before you fell silent. They played two encores and the audience kept clapping and stomping even after the venue put the lights up. Backstage, he closed his eyes and allowed himself to know things were good.

"You're weird," Tanja said.

"What?" He opened his eyes and tried to remember what he'd said. Pretty standard fare. But her last band had been hardcore. They must not do the same quirky angst bit indie fans went in for.

Micha tossed Simon a bottle of water that hit him in the gut.

"Hope you've got some better conversational gambits for later," Tanja added.

"Conversational what?" Micha asked.

"Shit." Simon hadn't forgotten but wished everyone else had. There was still a narrow sliver of hope, though. The stalker could get lost in the crowd. Tired. Something could come up. She could, for whatever reason, not be waiting for him.

As the saying goes, "Hope dies last." His outlived chugging water, stepping back out into that crisp autumn air tinged with dumpster, and arriving at the merch table to smile for the smartphones and scribble on the records their hipster fans always surprised him by buying. His hope survived any number of compliments and cute fans he hoped might stick around in case he was free after all.

As the crowd thinned, he even dared to laugh when Tanja joked about him getting stood up, though he was pouring sweat and close to tears. It was the strain of being in front of people so long: all those eyes like so many magnifying glasses between him and the sun, their scorching focus frying him. On top of everything else, he was starving. Ravenous. Ready to kill and eat one of his fans. Forget cute girls: His big fantasy was grabbing some takeout and a cab, falling asleep in front of the TV.

All of a sudden, he felt that palpable, magnetic dread that makes horror-movie heroines look behind the curtains. There she was, a drink in each hand, parting the crowd like somebody who didn't have to wait in line. He wasn't a deer in headlights, but there was nowhere to run.

He felt the chill of the glass, the warmth of her hand in unnecessary contact as she handed him a drink. "Caipirinha's your favorite, right?"

He didn't have a favorite, but often drank a caipi to cool down after a show, and her knowing even such a small thing bothered him. He muttered something about not drinking on an empty stomach, but he was back in that dream where nobody could hear him. The stalker was already talking to Tanja about their new t-shirt. Somehow, she knew a friend of Tanja's had designed it. Maybe there was nothing weird about that. Tanja might've put it on their website to help her friend. But it was the *way* the stalker said it. Possessive, entitled, like it was only natural for her to know that and any number of other things.

"I know a great tapas bar near here," she was saying as he tried to unfreeze his face from the grotesque grin it was stuck in. Of course she didn't have to think about where to go. She had been the whole time. "Simon, you're hungry, right?"

"Yeah." The whole conversation was far away until Peter or Paul or whatever his name was, the singer of their opener, came over to thank him, making Simon feel grounded, a bastion of success.

"You guys were great," he told the singer.

"Oh, you caught it? We weren't sure."

"We were back at the bar," Simon lied. "Amazing stuff." Peter or Paul had written some great songs, but he'd been too tired or discouraged to come out from behind the curtain, or maybe afraid of hearing something better than his own music. He sometimes wondered whether it would ever be enough. Fame, critical acclaim, wealth, what have you. Love. Whether he'd ever be sure enough of himself to have something left over for others.

"Mind if we take a picture for our blog?"

"I'll take it," the stalker offered before Simon could say anything. He didn't mind about the picture, but it was none of her business. He put one arm around the singer's shoulder and the other around Tanja's. Tanja pulled Micha in, and they all smiled for a couple shots on Peter-Paul's phone and a couple on the stalker's.

"What're you guys up to now?" Peter-Paul asked, and the stalker butted in again to invite his band to the bar. Simon tried to roll his eyes at Tanja or Micha, but they were backing up the stalker with that we're-all-friends-here bullshit that always turned his stomach, but only because he could never pull off such hale and hearty sociability himself.

"I'll get my stuff." But the Neanderthal watching the backstage area didn't want to let him past even though he'd seen him play. Simon forced himself to stay calm. He only ended up looking like an ass when he tried to stand up for himself.

"Forget something?" The stalker handed him the pass he'd left on the table. She and Tanja laughed like they'd just been talking about silly old Simon. Let them. He'd only stay long enough to eat. He had to eat either way, so who cared where he did it? Then he'd say he had food poisoning and leave. No, bad idea. With his luck, the stalker would call an ambulance and ride to the hospital with him. He'd say he wasn't feeling well.

~~~

The bar was as nearby as she'd claimed, with an inconspicuous exterior he'd never have noticed. The kind of hidden gem everybody but him always knew about. The interior had that slight aftertaste of smoke that comes more from overfilled ashtrays than anyone lighting up, and he took rare pleasure in being a nonsmoker. A melancholy copla was playing, its every other word *corazón*.

The stalker spoke to the waiter in Spanish that sounded good to Simon, although he only knew what his coworker Soledad taught him, and usually forgot it by the end of each shift. The waiter put his arm around the stalker and said something that made them both laugh. Was that supposed to make him jealous? But like Dr. F always said, it wasn't all about him. He'd heard that chorus repeated one or ten too many times.

Another waiter came and helped push together several tables under the stalker's supervision. Simon took the opportunity to engage Peter-Paul and the three other members of his band—painfully earnest young men with shaggy hair and t-shirts from bands as obscure as their own—in a conversation about their influences so he'd be surrounded when the crucial seating moment came.

"Perfect, thanks," the stalker said when the tables were arranged.

Simon sat between Peter-Paul and the one with a full beard who might've been the drummer.

"You'd be surprised how much Beethoven I listen to," Peter-Paul was saying.

"I can see that," the stalker butted in from across the table. "The intense rhythms."

"Really?" he asked with that coy modesty Simon knew so well, questioning every bit of praise in the hopes that another scrap will be thrown.

Simon picked up a menu and tried to tune out the stalker. He was getting to the point where the hunger would turn into exhaustion and he'd have no appetite, just weakness and inability to control his facial expression.

"Do you listen to much classical music, Simon?" the stalker asked. No, call her July. His nightmare was that all his nasty thoughts would one day escape.

"Not as much as I should." He felt like a fraud among these more knowledgeable but less successful musicians. But then he felt like that most places.

"The last time I heard Beethoven was in *A Clockwork Orange*," Tanja said.

Simon admired that, the way she owned everything about herself. The others laughed and started talking about Kubrick. Simon must've missed that lesson everyone else had had about turning a conversation to your advantage. But his areas of expertise were harder to own. If he started talking about Thomas Mann, they'd think he was a pompous ass. Or, as Dr. F would say, *he'd* think he was a pompous ass. Or it was all some meta-projection, projecting onto his therapist what he thought he was projecting onto other people. The thought made his head hurt like those pictures of mirrors facing each other.

"What?" He could tell from the silence that someone had asked him something.

"Your favorite movie," the beard repeated, but the waiter arrived so he had a moment to think while he ordered tapas at random and a couple liters of wine for the table. To show how sociable he was. Having the time of his life. Stick around for a drink, everybody.

"I really like *Nosferatu*." He felt the ebb and flow of shame. He did, but only said so to look cool and artsy, like someone who appreciated silent films. The fact that he did appreciate silent films didn't make trying to score points with them any less insincere. Still, it seemed to work.

"Yeah, rad," Tanja said. "That actor's so fucking creepy—he was made for the part. What's his name again?"

"Schreck," said know-it-all July. "Perfect name for such a frightful person."

They all laughed like she'd said something original, and then the confusion of distributing glasses, carafes of wine and water, and the array of small plates bridged any gap in subject matter. Micha started talking about the time he'd hitched to Spain, which was one of those helpful stories that could shrink or expand to fill any conversational space and never failed to remind listeners of their own adventures. Relieved not to have to entertain anyone, Simon emptied and refilled his glass of water, sipped his red wine and began systematically working through his tapas before anyone could suggest sharing.

"See, they thought we were out to turn tricks, and they didn't understand a word of English, let alone German, so at the stoplight . . ." Micha was saying. Simon had heard it all before but didn't mind. He was surprised to catch himself in a moment of goodness. The food was great, the wine was great for the price, and all he had to do was sit here, surrounded by people who liked him. July wasn't doing anything weird. It was like she didn't send postcards filled with minute lunatic handwriting to their label or post on their site more than they did. She was just someone at the table, like the beard. In this rare calm, he was able to look back and realize that, not only had nothing gone wrong, but they'd played well. Sure, he needed to work on his stage presence, but he felt confident that they'd get a good write-up. He couldn't remember the last time he'd felt so relaxed without outside assistance, and was surprised to find himself thinking: what a great night. Maybe this was how normal people with lots of friends felt.

Far from faking sick, he suggested more wine, espresso and dessert. He still felt a faint background hum of anxiety that July would trap him in endless conversation or hit him over the head and stuff him in a sack, but the longer the evening wore on without anything like that happening, the less the feeling mattered. Micha was telling everyone how they'd come up with the band's name working at the video store where a cartoon of *The Hare and the Hedgehog* was playing and Simon, not quite sober, had tearily insisted that it wasn't FAIR and he hated that hedgehog for cheating in the race. It was a stupid name but too late to change it, a stupid story but everyone laughed. Simon even felt a twinge of regret when the musician opposite the beard said, "Shit, it's after three; my girlfriend'll be so pissed."

"They couldn't find a sitter," the beard explained. "And you know what two-year-olds are like."

"Sure." He felt as fake as he had during the discussion of Beethoven. These earnest young men had not only sound knowledge of classical music, but also partners and children.

A couple bottles of wine went on the house, and Simon paid for the rest after some token resistance from the group. Peter-Paul said something about this new band he'd love Simon's opinion on in a last-ditch excuse to get his number, which Simon went along with, knowing Peter-Paul would either chicken out and never contact him, or spam him about shows. But he was flattered that someone considered him a useful contact. He dreaded the moment when July would take advantage of the situation to suggest they exchange numbers, too, then felt an unnerving gap in the evening when she didn't.

Peter-Paul's band split a cab, and Simon and July stood outside, waiting for Micha and Tanja to come back from the bathroom. His awareness of being less drunk than everyone else, not only in his group but the whole street, the whole city, was like heavy winter clothing, muffling his words and making his movements stiff and awkward. There was no in-between with July; her eyes were either riveted on his face or blank like they were now, turned toward the street without seeming to see it.

"You smoke?" he asked.

"No, and you shouldn't, either."

"I quit." Like she had any say in the matter.

"I know. I'm proud of you."

For an instant, the glow of those words outshone the absurdity of this imperfect stranger feeling anything at all on his behalf. Someone was proud of him! He felt warm all over, like the time he'd shocked himself and his family by slugging an older boy for picking on Franzi. His dad, never as heavy on the praise as his mom, had said, "Don't do it again, but it was the right thing to do." There were so few moments like that, when you believed in what you were and what you'd done. He almost started to tell that story, but something personal like that would only have been one more thing about him to own, like she was trying to own him quitting smoking.

"Kicked all your bad habits, didn't you?"

"Sure." Let her think she owned that knowledge, too. He'd never been a real addict, and all she knew was a couple vague references in his lyrics, things he'd detached from his inner self and put out for public consumption. Rehab had been a kind of plea bargain, with his concerned family as much as the justice system. The only thing he'd needed help quitting was his overwhelming dread of facing either the future or day-to-day life. A couple bowls of meth had only been a side dish to whatever emotionally debilitating substances his own brain had been pumping out.

"Good for you." She reached to pat his arm but stopped, her hand hanging in midair like it had come up against a physical barrier rather than the pained look he gave her. "It isn't easy, is it?"

This was getting to be a bit much. He weighed his words, careful not to provide any new facts for her to post online or treasure within the depths of her freakish heart. "I never was that bad off. You should've seen this one girl at rehab with me, totally messed up from crack and whatever bad guys she was hanging around."

Gaunt and quiet, she'd arrived with burnt and bloodied lips, bruises on her face and throat. He'd been the youngest patient until then, and it had hurt to think about what the rest of her life would look like if it was already that messed up. He couldn't remember her name or what she looked like, other than damaged, but over time he'd made her into a symbol of what he didn't want to be. Then again, he was more likely to end up like the old man who'd sat around in his underwear in the cramped room they'd shared, cursing or punching the wall when he was awake, whimpering in his sleep. Simon tried not to think about where his fellow patients were now. If they hadn't died in the meantime, they'd probably bounced back into another facility. He hoped there were exceptions like him who'd managed to get well and lead normal enough lives. But then he'd never really been unwell. Not the way they had.

He didn't expect July to understand, because she hadn't been there, hadn't seen the hollow eyes and rotting grins around the table, the fingers twitching on the placemats or crawling up the arms to tear open bloody scabs. He didn't expect her to understand how he'd felt, trapped between guilt about being there on a false premise to get the same treatment as those people, and fear of becoming like them. But least of all did he expect her to react the way she did: by bursting out laughing.

She gave him a dig in the ribs. When he didn't join in, she caught her breath and said, "Poor girl," but he could hear the residue of laughter on her voice. It was like he'd always thought; she had no empathy for anyone outside her immediate field of interest, and maybe not even there. He didn't get the impression that she spent a lot of time trying to put herself in his shoes. If she did, she wasn't very good at it, since she seemed to be sensing a lot of interest in her that wasn't and never would be there.

"Sorry," she said at last. "You sing about it sometimes, but I thought you didn't like to talk about rehab."

"I don't."

"Me, neither." She laughed again, a high-pitched whinny like she'd said something hysterical. Of course she didn't, because that part of his life was before she started inserting herself at every opportunity. He chuckled to keep her company until he realized she might think they were flirting.

A silence set in that he found totally unacceptable between people who weren't smoking or looking at their phones, but she didn't seem to mind. If that had been flirting for her, was this intimacy? It was so quiet he noticed the slight hiss of drizzle right away, that dry beginning of rain that could be wind scuttling dead leaves across the pavement or something sizzling on a hot stove.

"It's raining," they said at the same time, which meant they had to laugh even though nothing was funny.

"What's the closest station?" He knew but didn't want that silence back.

"Eberwalder's down there. But I live nearby. You could crash if you wanted."

Her casualness was staged. Why ask only him? A shiver of anxiety stirred under his drowsiness. It almost sounded nice. Nicer than getting soaked on the way to the tram and waiting twenty minutes in the unheated shelter. But things that seemed like good ideas at the time rarely turned out to be, and things you knew were bad ideas never did.

"No thanks. I've got a lot to do tomorrow."

"Like what?" Tanja, lighting a cigarette, arrived in a cloud of sulfur. Simon had no idea when she'd come out or how long Micha had been hovering in the doorway.

"Family stuff." He hoped against hope that July would misunderstand, think he had a wife and kids and a dog, the whole white-picket-fence menagerie. But a stranger who knew he'd quit smoking and didn't like to talk about rehab was a stranger who knew what his marital status was. Or wasn't.

"Cool," July said. "See you around."

At home, he found her number on a napkin in his coat pocket and threw it away. At least that was a normal fangirl thing to do.

The critic had raved about their show, so they talked about that instead of July. When they toured down to Basel, she didn't show up. Afterward, they stayed in Berlin to earn money at their day jobs and record their new album, which Simon called *Georg's Friend in St. Petersburg* as a Kafka reference he hoped to be admired for but not interviewed about, since he hadn't read "The Judgment" in years. He was feeling less anxious, maybe because he'd been a drug-free nonsmoker for a while, maybe because July was down to one postcard a month—he asked the mail room to throw them away—or because they were getting more good press.

Well, not literally press. But they were all over indie blogs. A couple dozen people bought their first album each month even when they weren't touring, and there was a steady trickle of legal downloads. It wasn't enough to live off, but it was something, and it was growing. Even if he didn't want to admit it, he believed Tanja when she said they were nearing a tipping point.

"Yeah, man," Micha said every time they had a beer in front of the club that let them practice during the day. "It's the second album where bands get successful."

Simon wasn't sure about that but couldn't think of any counterexamples and didn't want to. He felt good. It was early spring, unrealistically warm for Berlin, and he had a beer in his hand, two great bandmates and most of an album. Their big album, the magic one that would change everything.

~~~

The amazing, crazy, impossible thing was, they were right. By the end of May, *Georg's Friend* had gotten great write-ups in two local papers and thousands of legal, paid-for downloads. A lot of people bought both albums at once, hurrying to pretend they'd liked the band from the beginning. Reviewers praised Simon's "insightful" and "wounded" lyrics.

Since his esoteric boss Barbara had been savvy or lazy enough not to redecorate the business she'd inherited to match its new name, Café Astral's ceiling-high windows, cacti and exposed brick still drew a trendy crowd. Once while he and Soledad were descaling the espresso machine, he heard two lanky hipsters raving about the new album, although they "loved the rawness of his earlier work." Then a third hipster laughed and said, in that blasé drawl Simon couldn't stand but sometimes found himself imitating, "You guys know the singer liiike . . . made your flat whites?"

Ignoring Soledad's laughing fit, Simon fled to the storeroom to get fresh milk and bask in the warmth of his success. The last time he'd felt this popular was when Barbara liked his zodiac sign enough to offer him a job on the spot. And this was something he actually cared about.

Meanwhile, Micha had a new girlfriend he was smitten with and wrote terrible poems for, one of which Tanja found. For a few weeks, she referred to Mina as "my tall goldilocks" and "sunflower of loveliness" whenever she was alone with Simon. Mina might've been unattainable for chunky, balding Micha the year before, but maybe that was just Simon's cynicism. Or jealousy. He didn't feel like laughing about the poems when Mina showed up after every rehearsal and embraced Micha like they'd been parted for months, or when he saw Micha's face go soft as he read some cutesy message from her. And least of all when Micha announced that they were moving in together after the tour.

"Mazel tov," said Tanja. They were having a beer in the park and going over their set list for the next night. Or the others were having a beer and Simon was having a rhubarb spritzer because he was saving his drinking for when he needed it. Was that any healthier?

"How long have you known her?" He could tell from Tanja's loud intake of breath that he'd said the wrong thing. It sounded critical, like he was saying it was too soon. What was he supposed to say? Moving in with a woman you were committed to was such alien territory, he had no idea. Living with Nadine had been like camping out, knowing you'd fold up your tent and get in the car as soon as a storm broke.

"A couple months," Micha said. "But we spend every night together."

"Cool."

"We can shop for your wedding gown in Paris." Tanja was always saying much dickier things than Simon without sounding like a dick. Her tone was so consistent that no one took it seriously. She never talked about her own love life except in a boasting, juvenile way, and Simon wondered whether she was jealous, too. But it was probably just him. Other people knew how to be happy for each other.

~~~

"It's been a while," Dr. Froheifer said.

"I've been busy getting ready for the tour." Simon tried not to sound defensive, not rise to that dentisty accusation of putting off his checkup. His therapist was never going to admit to being passive-aggressive. It would only end up being his relationship to authority figures or something. But he'd come a long way, and knew he owed at least some of it to her.

"Wonderful. How are you *feeling* about everything?" She always put this special emphasis on feeling, like he had a different way of doing it from every other human on the planet.

"Fine." To save her the guesswork, he jumped right to his latest issues. "Micha has this new girlfriend." Then it was his discomfort with other people's good fortune, not because he didn't wish them well, but because they'd *think* he didn't. Because he couldn't meet anyone, and if he did, he'd ruin it. They were still digesting Nadine.

"When was the last time you saw a woman socially, not in a"—she cleared her throat, indicating that she was referring to sex, which made him blush because she was about his mom's age—"'romantic' way?"

"I hang out with Tanja after we rehearse, and Soledad and I talk all day at work." Soledad worked as many shifts at Café Astral as she could fit in while finishing her master's in film. When they weren't making fun of Barbara, she told him about movies she'd seen, dates she'd been on and random facts like that squirrels could swim or primeval humans had used laughter to say the coast was clear. Even though she had dark, dramatic curls and the cupid's-bow lips of a silent-film star, he'd never made a pass at her.

"Good, good, but what about outside of work?"

The longer he thought, the worse it looked, and the more he panicked and couldn't think of anyone. He'd seen Franzi's friends sometimes when she was still living with their mom, but she was at college in Hamburg now. He didn't have any friends outside the band and work, not ones he saw regularly. He wanted to bring that up, but made the mistake of saying what popped into his head: "We hung out with the stalker last fall."

It was the first time he'd explicitly mentioned her instead of dispersing her over various incidents as if she were as many different people. Talking about awful possibilities had a way of making them more real. As he'd feared, they spent the rest of the session on her.

"Name your demon. Why do you feel so anxious around her?" *Name your demons and they lose their power*; Dr. F loved to say that. She wanted to know if July presented a real threat, and if so, why he didn't he contact the authorities. Or was it simply the threat of someone getting close?

"I guess I feel like, if I encourage her, I'll never get rid of her."

"What gives you that impression?"

"She always acts like we know each other."

"Don't you?"

"Barely. But she's acted like I'm this old buddy of hers since day one. She's not like that with Tanja and Micha, just me." He hated the whiny note his voice faded out on.

"That's normal, isn't it? For fans to focus on the singer? You're the face of the band."

"Yeah . . ." He didn't know how to explain why this was different, didn't even know why it was.

"Do you feel like you don't deserve admiration? Like there must be something 'wrong' with someone who admires you?" Dr. F didn't just emphasize words with her voice; her fingers in their bulky turquoise rings were always tracing quotation marks in the air.

"I like it, or at least I don't mind when it's not her." Never admit to needing it. Then he'd get diagnosed a little lower on the patheticness scale. "I feel like I can't stop her. It's very invasive." He was tempted to put 'invasive' in quotes, draw her attention to its importance.

"Would you say you feel 'helpless'?"

He took a deep breath and nodded. He knew what was coming. They wouldn't stop at the stalker, but continue on to his helplessness in just about any situation. The worst part was knowing she was right.

~~~

Afterward, he felt a blend of relief and regret. Relief that they'd discussed the stalker, regret that it had kept them from covering other issues before the tour and would now forever be one of what Dr. F called the "construction sites" in his life. As he saw it, they were sometimes abandoned due to lack of funding, and sometimes unqualified workers caused near-fatal collapses. Very little ever got built.

The good thing was that she'd told him what to do: "If you have a legitimate reason for feeling uncomfortable, ask her to stop. If she won't, involve the police."

He felt both empowered by her advice and ashamed of needing it. Somehow, he'd lost control of the situation. Maybe it was enough to know he could have it back.

~~~

He showered because he always felt dirty after therapy, aware of the clammy hands that had touched the doorknobs, the crinkled magazines in the waiting room and the metal arms of the chairs. Then a soothing Smiths album, pasta with sauce from the jar for dinner, the not-quite-rancid dregs from a carton of orange juice. He pulled the beat-up duffle bag out from under his bed, pleased to see he still had travel cosmetics, complete with ample hand sanitizer, packed from the last tour. He called Franzi on speakerphone while picking out t-shirts that wouldn't look like he was trying too hard.

"That you, Simon? Hold on."

The noise in the background could've been a crowded street or a TV. Whether she stepped in somewhere or muted the set, he could suddenly hear the vast space of silence that always seemed to fill his phone calls, flow through the cables and radio waves, and stream out of the receiver, flooding his apartment like a vapor he'd need days to get rid of.

"Is it a good time?"

"Always. How are you?" It sounded like she was brushing her teeth, hopefully a sign she was at home.

"Good. A little nervous, you know, tour starts tomorrow. How is everything?" He heard her spit and mumble something. "That's good. Listen, do you wanna come to my show in Hamburg? It's—"

The faucet ran and then went off. "I *know* when it is, Simple Simon. Think I'd miss seeing my famous big brother?"

He laughed. The first time she'd discovered that nursery rhyme in English class, he'd hated it, wanted to burn every copy. But now it was one of those endearing bits of nostalgia that helped hold their patchy relationship as adult siblings together. Sometimes, he wished he were Simple Simon. Wasn't ignorance bliss? At the same time, overthinking things was part of who he was. He might not like his stupid face or untoned body, but it would scare the shit out of him to see anyone else in the mirror.

"How many tickets should I put on the list? Like if you wanted to bring . . . friends." She hadn't confided in him about her love life since he'd said Dirk was wrong for her. She'd agreed in in the end, but he could see how patronizing that had been, coming from someone who made so many bad choices himself. It was a shame, though. One more thing he couldn't talk about with one more person.

"One's fine."

"I'll put down two. I mean, it's free."

"You sound like Mom." He always liked the incongruous wickedness of her throaty laugh, like some alluring villainess. After their parents' divorce, their mom's thrift had taken on such astronomical proportions that *it's cheaper* or *it's free* could be used to justify anything.

"I heard that when a man gets to a certain age, he turns into his mother. What's new?"

"Same old, same old." Like he knew what that meant. "Wouldn't you rather catch up in person? Unless you don't have time."

"Of course I do." He felt bad that his only visit to Hamburg this year was for a show. It was only a couple hours away. But Franzi hadn't come to Berlin, either.

"Anyway, my life's not as exciting as yours."

"Nobody's is as boring as mine." Not that it was a competition, even if they were siblings. He just didn't want her to get the wrong idea.

"I look forward to hearing about your heinously boring life as an indie star touring Europe. But I gotta run. Places to go, people to see; namely, a romantic rendezvous. Don't snitch."

"I won't. Don't do anything I wouldn't."

They dragged out the laugh, then mumbled something and hung up, but not before the silence could slip out and flood his bedroom, flow from there into the kitchen and bathroom. But that was okay. She'd confided in him. And she was right; his life wasn't as drab as it felt. He might not have many friends or a partner, didn't party with celebrities. He played in a pretty good band, though, and was about to see more of the world than he ever had before.

It would be nice to catch up with her. Interacting with his parents was an intricate escape act that required all his skills as a contortionist to make it through dangerous topics unscathed. But he and Franzi could talk, and it would be like old times. Not old times the way they'd actually been, but the way you remembered them, a collage of bright little scenes pasted together without context.

He turned off the music, made himself a cup of chamomile tea, which was supposed to make you sleepy but never did, and put his guitar and bag by the door. As always, he was convinced he'd forgotten to pack something important, but told himself there was nothing he couldn't buy on tour. He slept in a thin half-dream state and woke to the nervous excitement he'd always felt before a new school year.

<p style="text-align:center">~~~</p>

He wished they were leaving right away. That wasn't even stalker-related. Her posts were as adoring as ever, so hopefully she wasn't mad that he hadn't called. He had no idea whether she was still writing to him because he'd told Poor Dog Records he didn't need to hear about fan mail. No one else sent any. Maybe she'd finally given up on getting a reply. He was never quite sure what she wanted from him—was it actual interaction, or only to keep him aware of her and maintain whatever link she saw between them? The obvious explanation was that she was obsessed with the band and in love with him, but he felt like there was something else going on, something too silly to say aloud, even at therapy. Like she wanted to own him, maybe even consume and absorb him into herself.

But, for the moment, he felt equipped to handle her and any number of things, even a little adventure. Why didn't he ever go anywhere? Money was only an excuse. If he really wanted to travel, he'd manage.

Short of leaving the country, the only thing to do with his newfound energy was empty his overflowing recycling bins and schlep his deposit bottles to the store. He hadn't showered, and everyone looked at him like this was his alcohol consumption from today instead of the past few months. Like they weren't all boxed-wine drinkers themselves. But he bought groceries and no beer, so at least the cashier knew he wasn't a drunk.

At home, he put eggs on to boil, then got the broom from its cobwebby corner and swept out his bedroom, bathroom and the small living room that turned into a kitchen almost right away. The trashcan looked like a sandbox by the time he was done, and he wondered why he hadn't noticed the furry layers of dust and tumbleweeds of hair before. What if he had a date? The worst part was, he *had* had dates here. If you wanted to call them that.

He wiped down the bathroom, enjoying the pungent lavender smell of cleaning spray. The bottle was full even though he'd bought it ages ago, and he had to press the trigger a few times before anything came out. Afterward, he washed his hands twice, remembered he was starving, and ran to the kitchen, where the water had boiled over. He made coffee in the pot that had succeeded a nicer one he'd smashed when high, toasted some bread, took out a package of questionable butter and sat down. But the thought wouldn't unthink itself.

What if he had a date? became: Why didn't he ever? He hadn't hooked up with anyone since their tour last year, and not even the last night of it, since they'd been with the stalker. Before that had been Ilse and scattered one-night stands, no one he'd cleaned up for. If he was brutally honest, the height of his romantic success was before rehab, before Nadine.

Relationships had never been his forte. The few girls he dated in college faded out within weeks, which he learned to do himself in the process. After graduating, he met Susi at one of his small no-cover shows. She was into his music at first, but later changed her tune to "get a real job." Rather than ask what was wrong with working at the grocery store, he handled things in his cowardly way, becoming less and less available until she ended what had never really started. Which gave him that much more time to meet old friends who already had great jobs or at least internships, keep drinking after they left, avoid his horde of roommates.

When he met a moderately successful musician at an open mic, he was sure it was his big break. He started playing second guitar in Andreas's sprawling, folksy band and smoking pot because everyone in the band did, and everyone in the audience, too. His inexperience had embarrassed him, but being stoned made him even more paranoid than usual that everyone hated him. Only a few weeks in, he picked the wrong side in an argument, with the result that he and a violinist he didn't even like got kicked out together. But he'd never really liked loudmouthed Andreas, either, with his gray ponytail, Celtic pendants and penchant for younger women.

He'd begun his brief career in a slowly failing video store and made friends with the other wannabe working there, a balding drummer named Micha. Still playing every gig he could get, he kept telling himself that music had never been a realistic plan, that he needed to grow up and figure something out. The problem was, he couldn't figure anything out. He'd been talented compared to other children, other students, but clearly had no talent for real life. He got tired of his successful friends, tired before he could develop feelings for a woman. Maudlin, he told himself Susi was right. Was he supposed to impress someone by barely holding down a job at Video World? That was the only thing getting him out of bed in the morning. Then his roommates had a meeting behind his back about how he never cleaned, cooked or hung out with them. Once they'd taken a vote, they told him to his face.

He'd asked Micha if he could crash at his place "for a couple days," mumbling some lie about relationship trouble because that sounded less pathetic than not being allowed to exist in the same space as five other grubby young people.

"Dude," Micha had said. "Don't you have any other friends?" But he let him stay.

As a cheap leisure activity, they started playing together and realized they weren't just losers calling themselves musicians to look cool. They were losers who *were* musicians. They hung up ads for bassists, found an emaciated cokehead named Tom, came up with a name and website and enough songs for a sampler. They weren't playing any real venues, but there was an endless supply of bars who'd let bands like them pass around a hat. They were musicians; really they were. Desperate to keep this little spark of optimism from going out, Simon had spent the money he saved on rent buying coke off of Tom, who was happy to share for a price. That didn't apply to Tom's girlfriend Rosa, caught at some unfortunate point between burlesque and goth but still sexy. Simon was high when she came onto him, but knew he shouldn't. He hadn't gotten hurt when Tom pushed him off stage in the middle of a show, but he hadn't felt like playing anymore, either, and anyway Tom had left.

Micha had said they could keep playing together but Simon had to move out, so Simon had exhausted all his friends from college, moving from couch to floor to airbed with a backpack full of dirty laundry, his guitars and amp on a dolly stolen from Ikea. Coke was too expensive to make a habit of, but he hadn't known how else to feel happy. The Rasta-capped dealers in Görlitzer Park only had skunky pot or meth in his price range, and he'd wanted something that wouldn't make him more antisocial. He'd told himself it was a rough patch, couldn't last long. He'd never bought much—couldn't afford to—but without any shows coming up, that easy, bright flash of energy was something to look forward to, at least until it triggered a gut-wrenching panic attack about his heart stopping.

He'd forgotten what it was like to have a room of his own. The feeling of being observed, of encroaching on someone else's well-earned space, was making him crazy, but he never passed the castings to get a room in another shared apartment. They always asked stupid questions like "If you were an animal, what would it be?" and he'd sit there thinking, *a wounded one, does that count?* and wanting more than anything to crawl into some dark place where he could lick his wounds or die.

He lost his job at Video World because business was bad and he was the worst employee. As he was nearing an even lower low point, they'd auditioned bassists and he'd insisted on Nadine, crystal clear in his certainty that she'd take them places with her glowing aura, until he came down and realized she was pretty and a good workman, not a creative composer.

There she was, though, his new friend and his luck. He found a short-term sublet and a job in another store, started feeling hopeful. But nothing was how he'd pictured it, least of all Nadine, whose gentle vagueness was half down to being stoned. Only after they were together had he discovered how terrifying her temper could be—but he preferred her shouting to the icy silence that could numb him for days. As their fighting edged toward a hideous crescendo, his last bowl of meth gave him heart palpitations, and he called Franzi to say he was dying. She told their parents he was a wreck, and the whole family rushed to Berlin—the first thing they'd done together in years. Franzi insisted he admit what he was addicted to.

"Crystal meth?" he'd said, uncertain like a kid in the back of class who missed the teacher's question. He hadn't smoked it more than five times, tops.

"*Meth,* Simon?! Have you completely lost it?"

He wondered what she'd expected, or what she would've preferred. Everybody had cried and scolded until he agreed to see a doctor. He wasn't on anything when Franzi said she was cutting off all contact until he got clean. He was only miserable, but no one had wanted to believe that. They thought they'd be enabling him if they did. As soon as he gave in and admitted to an addiction he didn't have, everyone had been kind, from Nadine to his snide stepmom Cindi. They were all so proud he could admit he had a problem. Like he'd ever denied *that*.

He'd continued his false confessions, and the DA dropped the possession charge in exchange for rehab and therapy. He spent six months in the middle of nowhere without so much as a glass of wine to soften things. His hosts said grace three times a day, his fellow inmates wailed and gnashed their teeth, and he fluctuated between exhaustion, restlessness, despair and apathy until he found something on the outskirts of peace and finished writing their first album.

Micha had been dubious when he got out. Nadine had believed in him, but she also believed in chem trails and aliens building the pyramids. Franzi was his sister again. His parents resumed not speaking to each other. The shitty studio where H vs. H recorded their first album gave it charming low-fi touches their only two reviews praised. An electronics chain trying to develop a more badass image hired Simon thanks to the beard he'd grown in rehab, which he shaved off a week later. Clubs started booking them as an opening act. Then he remembered it was his job to ruin things for himself. As if the gutting loss of Nadine weren't bad enough, Micha was pissed about having to replace her and having Simon crash at his place again. Tanja was ten times the musician Nadine was, but that wasn't the point. At least he had his own apartment now, even if it was kind of a dump.

Forget about a date, what if Franzi came to visit? Was she supposed to sleep on the floor? He ordered an air mattress and extra bedding online, finished his coffee and decided to go catch some of the golden light pouring through his windows because he'd never gotten around to installing curtains, and it was just a matter of time before anything you taped up came crashing down. Was that a metaphor? He got the first few letters of "curtains" onto his wrist before his only pen ran out of ink. Step one: Buy pens and paper. He didn't *need* to write anything this soon after releasing an album, but why waste an idea? Besides, a destination would make it easier to drag himself outside.

<p style="text-align:center">~~~</p>

The light was pale and bright, with a clarity that felt like putting on 3D glasses. Too real to be real. But there was plenty of it, skipping over the surface of the duck pond like a tossed stone, catching on the spokes of passing baby carriages. He sensed resentment on all sides. His was the only bench not occupied by a young upwardly mobile family, except the one where two shriveled old people were sitting, canes between their knees. It was hard to resent old people. He, on the other hand, looked, if not healthy, at least mobile enough to make it to a less family-oriented part of the park. He hated himself for forgetting his headphones, which would've at least provided a buffer.

It's not about you, he reminded himself. They're just looking for somewhere to sit. One of the high-end moms, one hand on her SUV-sized stroller and the other holding a toddler's, asked, "Do you *mind*?" and he almost fled, but decided to stand his ground.

"Not at all."

She parked her carriage at one end and her toddler even closer to Simon than was necessary to make him cringe, then gave the kid a bag of cheerios and herself an iPad in a pink leather case. Or maybe it was faux, to be PC.

He bent the spine of his new notebook and scribbled with his new pen until the ink ran smooth. He tried to pretend they were somewhere else, or he was. On the hill behind him, a family was having a picnic. And a fight, but they weren't letting on about that. Officially, the parents were lavishing all their attention on the twins in matching overalls searching the blanket for things to put in their sticky mouths. But what were toddlers supposed to say to: "Max, Philip, look at that racing bike. I had one like that when I was in good shape and we still lived in Stuttgart."

"To be honest, your mommy never rode that expensive bike much."

"Your daddy may not remember because he wasn't *around* much . . ."

Simon wrote: "We traded in our racing bikes / for a four-wheel drive / We haven't really talked in years / Just ask the kids to hold our hate." Was hate too much? He needed the rhythm of the single syllable but would've preferred a slant rhyme. He enclosed it in brackets. How could he fit talking about yourself in the third person into the next line? Soggy bits of cheerio disintegrated onto his notebook. He looked up and shook his head at the kid proffering the baggy. Manners weren't dead after all. He checked the mom for approval or dismay, but she was fixated on her tablet. Was she trying to keep up with work and unable to find a daycare? Or was she desperately bored and just wanted to read a little clickbait while her son rested his head on Simon's shoulder, undisturbed by the movement of his arm as he wrote? The wind carried over another shred of the taut conversation behind him.

"That was when your mommy had her own business and didn't spend *all* day—"

"Actually, that was only your mommy's hobby that never turned a profit or—"

"Your daddy never gave it a *chance* to turn a profit and your mommy should've gotten a loan from the Employment Agency instead—"

He could picture the very kind of shop, just like the ones north of here in the organic handmade heart of Prenzlauer Berg. Opening hours compatible with daycare. All the products nice, so nice the owner would've, and in fact already had, bought them for her own children. The heartbreaking effort to sell to customers of her own social standing, to pretend she didn't need to while needing more than anything to contribute something other than homemaking because she was educated and ambitious and could've run a real business if she hadn't married an engineer, if the tax system hadn't encouraged arrangements with only one breadwinner, if her husband hadn't earned so much and it hadn't made so much more *sense* for him to go back to work first after they had the kids, if, if, if . . .

He finished the song and exhaled, more or less satisfied. He'd tweak the wording, but it was all there, his sense of exclusion, the imagined tension of that marriage and the guilt of wanting something, anything for yourself. The only thing missing was how much more real the people around him sometimes seemed, the way there was so much yearning and arguing and struggling and daydreaming and loving and resenting going on here, and none of it was his, maybe never would be. Or was that just him feeling alone again? Another song for another day. This one was already long enough. It would run toward seven minutes, but they could afford that now. On a first album, if you wanted to make it past gloating about your street cred to an audience of ten, you had to write radio-length songs with hooks to sink into the listeners. Even live, you couldn't afford to go over five minutes. But now he could write what felt true. You had to sell out to afford integrity.

He wanted another coffee, but the baby started screeching somewhere inside the massive carriage, and he didn't want to look like he was leaving because of the eardrum-rupturing sound. The mom didn't look up, but rolled the carriage back and forth, used to it. The toddler didn't seem fazed, either. I could just take this kid and leave, Simon thought. Not like he wanted to. Was that a normal thing to think? What would he even do with a kid, not being a pervert or murderer or even in a cult? The police would scoop them up at the edge of the park. Anybody could see he wasn't a father. Why? What made him so sure the people strolling past didn't think he was part of this family? He didn't look successful enough. He wasn't poor anymore, but still thought of himself that way. Still dressed that way. Like we even know what *real* poverty is, in this country, Franzi would've said. But it was getting harder and harder to tell the difference between beggars and hipsters with their eccentric hairstyles and ragged clothing. What if he were a banker going for that look on a day off?

It was too hard to imagine. Instead, he got in line at the coffee stand. He couldn't be bothered to leave the park, not even to walk to Café Astral, where he could get a coffee on the house and see Soledad. It wasn't worth the risk of running into Barbara. She might be mad about him quitting again and tell him the stars were unfavorable for his tour. And today was a success so far. Was he happy? No, but blank.

And definitely not jealous of some absent businessman whose (not very polite) wife was still on that bench. It had more to do with being the only one alone in the park. The only one who was *always* alone. He knew as he thought that that it wasn't really true, but knew as he thought *that* that it was true in every way that counted. He carried loneliness within him like a child, careful of it, hampered by the extra weight. But instead of coming to term, it shrank and swelled as the opportunity arose, not a new life but a drain on his, a homegrown parasite.

Clichés like "I don't want to spend the rest of my life alone" were just another thing to hide behind. Words you'd heard so often you no longer processed their meaning, but stacked them in front of your feelings like sandbags, hoping they'd hold in the flood. He didn't need to be with someone; he just needed to know he could. But the mood would pass. That was one of the blessings of therapy, learning to dilute the urgency of his crises. The thoughts were true until proven otherwise, but he didn't have to think them all the time.

His mom kept suggesting he try the dating site where she'd met her boyfriend Reinhardt. He'd once filled out half a profile before giving up, disgusted with himself and anyone desperate enough to contact him. What did he have to offer, if he didn't even have enough wit to fill a few textboxes? And wouldn't it reflect poorly on the band that he couldn't find a girlfriend in real life? Stretching out this imagined shame the way he always did, he came up with excuses: the whole thing a comment on our times, inspiration for lyrics. But he was engulfed by an ennui he couldn't swim to the top of whenever he thought of filling out the form, grinning roguishly in a stupid selfie for the profile picture. Or worse still, having Micha take it and ask what it was for.

The line wasn't moving. At the head of it, he could hear the hard and soft sounds of Berlin dialect in a trivial argument—*g*'s exchanged for *j*'s, soft *s*'s transformed into hard, clipped *t*'s—and wished he had someone to roll his eyes at. Berlin was so famous for its "lip" they printed t-shirts about it, but he wished the tough old lady behind the counter would take her issues out somewhere else.

He left the line for a patio table at the restaurant next door, paging through his notebook so people would know he was busy and not alone for lack of a better offer. A lost cat poster stared at him from a tree trunk. "Where's Mei?" He was too far away to make out the rest. He could get a pet. Someone who wouldn't know any better than to love him. Although it looked like even a cat could leave you.

"Simon!"

Funny how much like dogs people are, pricking up their ears when they hear their names. He was the only person he knew who literally never ran into acquaintances. Maybe actually literally this time. For one thing, he didn't get out much. For another, he didn't know anyone. He swiped through his phone like anyone might want to get in touch with him. A shadow fell over his table, and he tried to decide whether to order a milchkaffee, latte or cappuccino, which suddenly seemed important, even though they were all coffee with milk.

"Siiimon," the voice insisted, and now he did turn, an obedient dog.

The I-know-her lights flashed on and then went dark again as true recognition set in. Why hadn't he stayed home? And why had he smiled like he was happy to see her?

"July, I didn't see you."

"Mind if I join you?"

Even if the waitress hadn't come right then, even if July hadn't sat down without waiting for an answer, it would've been impossible to say no. Less because of how she would've felt than because of how he would've felt about himself.

She ordered a milchkaffee and he copied her out of laziness, but regretted it. She probably couldn't wait to add it to her list of reasons they were soulmates. She already knew what he ordered at bars and was now noting his favorite coffee. Not that it was his favorite. Not that that was the point.

"How are you?" It was a safe thing to say. If they talked for a few minutes, she might be pleased enough with her chance encounter to leave him alone. If it *was* chance.

"Great! Looking forward to your show. You must be excited."

"I guess. Business as usual."

The waitress deposited napkins, spoons and two fat mugs of milky coffee.

"Not exactly," July said. "Taking your new album on the road for the first time, your biggest tour yet . . . "

"I guess."

"I guess this, I guess that." She laughed as she poured so much sugar into her coffee he could taste it in his. "Aren't you ever sure of anything?"

"Are you?" he asked before he could stop himself. This was the last thing he needed, getting roped into some philosophical discussion or amateur psychoanalysis.

"I'm sure of all kinds of things. I know what I like and what I don't, what's important to me and what isn't. Most importantly, I know what I want."

He kept his eyes on his coffee, afraid she was looking at what she knew she wanted. "It's simpler before you graduate." He remembered school as chaotic, but there were grades to let you know where you stood, deadlines for papers, dates for exams. The future coming up like an exit on the autobahn.

She laughed, stirred her coffee and drank, leaving a purplish smear of lipstick on her cup. "I'll take that as a compliment."

Trying not to look for faint lines around her eyes or protruding veins in her hands, he felt the situation slipping out of control. Mistake one: He'd said something that could be construed as a compliment. Mistake two: He'd set himself up to ask more questions.

"What do you do then?" The whole thing was creepier now. It would be less creepy if she were in high school, flooded with enough hormones to excuse her silly behavior and too young to actually believe they'd get together. If she were in college, you could chalk it up to vestigial silliness, trying to be a little wild before real life started. But she was a full-fledged adult who spent her free time posting about his band, going to almost all their shows and trying—unfortunately with some success—to hang out with him. There was nothing too weird about any of these things. Plenty of people had crushes on musicians. But it wasn't the same, not to him or to her.

"I'm a copywriter now." He must've looked puzzled because she added, "I write all those texts on toothpaste tubes and banner ads no one reads." That sounded just like her: something you had no interest in looking at, plastered over your line of vision, demanding your attention. "I've thought of translating, but I've gotten out of practice with Dutch. I know a little of a lot of languages, though. Sometimes I think about getting good enough to move to another country."

"How come?" he said instead of *please do.*

"There are things I'd like to leave behind, you know?"

"Sure." What could she possibly have to leave behind? As she continued talking, something crystalized for him: It wasn't that she did all those stalkery things; it was that she seemed to *only* do those things. To only be interested in his band. Not once in almost three years could he remember her bringing anyone to a show or talking about her life before she started listening to Hare vs. Hedgehog. The band—or he—was all she had. He had the urge to run as fast as he could, but she'd only turn up at his show. Besides, he didn't feel comfortable leaving her with the check. Were those excuses? Dr. F was right: It was in his power to get rid of July. It had to be.

". . . ultimately the flexibility. Who wants to be tied to a desk all day, am I right?"

"Yeah." He managed to squeeze out a laugh like the last toothpaste in the tube: flat, dry, not quite enough. He wasn't warm but could feel himself sweating. Or was he coming down with something, right in the middle of everything? As she continued talking, he nodded at intervals and pictured himself losing consciousness, helpless to free his hand from her grip. There was a movie like that, where the woman has a crush on some stranger, and then he's in a coma and she tells everyone he's her fiancé. But the sticky layer of sweat was only anxiety. He pretended to massage his wrists so he could feel the steady reality of his pulse.

Out of nowhere, or at least nowhere he'd been listening to, she broke through his fog of angst by asking, "Have you ever hated—I mean really *hated*—the person you are?"

Yes. Always. Or at least on a regular basis.

But before he could give away what might be the only thing they *did* have in common, she added, "That was a rhetorical question, of course. I mean, why would you? You're amazing."

He didn't know whether to feel flattered or offended that she considered him incapable of self-hatred. It almost made him question who he was.

"You didn't even let rehab get in the way of who you are."

"Oh, uh, thanks." He swallowed the "I guess" he nearly added, not wanting her to think they shared an inside joke.

"I wish I could be more like you."

He nodded but couldn't help asking himself whether she was right. Rehab hadn't gotten in the way of who he was, unless the miserable life he'd been leading right before was his true self. But it had changed him. Not so much physically, because there was no drug he'd tried more than five times, and yes, that was still *trying* in his book—not habitual use—and probably in Springtime's book, too, if they'd believed him. But being there had done a lot for him. From a practical standpoint, it had given him time to finish writing the album and a place to stay without imposing on anyone.

More than that, it was one of the few times in his life he'd been alone with himself. Not literally alone, because he'd had that paunchy roommate who wet the bed Simon's first night, all the "family" meals and the group therapy sessions where some people talked about wanting euphoria, others—like Simon—about just wanting to not feel bad, and the crack waif mumbled about needing to get "out, out, out," a sentiment they could all nod along with. But he hadn't been one of them, hadn't had to take notice of them or try to win their admiration or affection.

They were a grim backdrop, people to pity rather than empathize with. Since he'd never needed treatment for withdrawal and the only entertainment was a box of VHS tapes someone had probably left by the curb, he'd had all the time in the world to take walks by himself, play his acoustic guitar where he hoped no one would hear, and think. Life no longer loomed like a wave about to break over him; it had ceased to move at all, a still body of water at once placid and stagnant. There was nothing to worry about because there was, for a time, nothing.

July paused, so he gave a small nod that could've been construed as glancing at his coffee in case she hadn't said anything he could nod at. A few keywords he'd half-heard indicated she was talking about men, maybe trying to give him the impression that she was sought-after, a prize he'd be lucky to win.

"When I say he was crazy about me, I mean really, actually *crazy*."

That reminded Simon of someone he knew.

"I wasn't even that attracted to him, but it was flattering to have someone be that into me, you know?"

He nodded again, then regretted it. He knew and didn't want to. He felt his breathing stop and maybe his heart. He wasn't flattered; he was trapped. Not just now but indefinitely, until the unlikely event that she moved away or found someone else to stalk and ditched him as abruptly as she'd latched on.

He unlocked his phone, trying to think of some urgent summons he could pretend to receive, but nothing came to mind. "Be right back." He had to clear his constricted throat and repeat himself before she understood. All he needed was a minute alone.

In the bathroom, he regretted not taking his phone with him. He could've run away after all. Washing his overheated face, he reminded himself that all he had to do was finish his coffee. He breathed in as far as the air would go and told himself nothing bad would happen. In an hour or—hopefully—less, he'd be home alone, the irrational dread of this moment fading.

"Are you from Berlin originally?" he asked when he got back. Trying to make normal small talk was like stringing together sentences in a language he barely knew. But going to the bathroom had interrupted her monologue, and the last thing he wanted was a silence she might read as intimate. Every moment he didn't fill with innocuous small talk was an opportunity for her to say something inappropriate, something that grasped at his time and attention, at a stifling, ever-closer relationship and ownership of who he was.

"No, but I've been here a while."

"Yeah, me, too," he coughed up. He felt something like gratitude toward her for not noticing he was inches away from melting into a gibbering mess.

"You're from Hannover, right?"

"Yeah." Then the spring snapped back in the other direction, and he could barely contain his laughter. What a farce. Pretending to get to know each other when she already knew everything about him. What would he have to say to surprise her? "My girlfriend's a real Berliner, though."

"You don't have one," she said flatly. Her cheeks went red.

He watched the color spread to the rest of her face. "What?"

"Sorry. I misspoke. I meant, you have a girlfriend? I, um, that is . . ."

So she did have a weak spot. Couldn't he enjoy throwing her for a loop for once? But now that they were playing by his rules, he could afford to feel sorry for her. After all, wasn't he alone, too? He didn't even have anyone to stalk.

It didn't take her long to recover. "How come she never comes to your shows?"

He stalled by drinking his lukewarm coffee. "She does sometimes, but it's not very interesting for her because she's deaf."

"Deaf?" July shouted as if he were.

"You know, hearing-impaired. Can't hear the music."

It took him a second to realize she wasn't making random gestures with her hands. "I don't speak sign language." He searched for a name, but his mind was a dangerous blank. Then he spotted the blurry lost cat. "Mei can read lips." The poster wasn't in July's line of vision. "Her mom's Japanese," he added, in case the name seemed unrealistic.

"Do you speak *that*?" She'd gone from suspicious to accusing. Taking his girlfriend's side, resenting him for not speaking any of her languages, forcing her to communicate in his. Even in imaginary relationships, he was a bad partner.

"I wanna learn, but since she's from here, it's more natural for us to speak German. Speaking of Mei, gotta go." He waved to the waitress, paid and was on his feet before July could thank him.

He headed out of the park to keep from running into her again. But he wasn't stupid enough to go straight home. He'd take a detour through empty side streets to make sure she wasn't following him. He crossed three lanes but got stuck at a red light for the tram tracks. Too late, he remembered Dr. F's advice. But Mei had been more effective than anything else he could've said, and there was no reason to involve the police. July had only been in the park by chance. Hopefully.

"Siiimon! Wait!"

You don't hear her. She's not close enough to see whether you have headphones on. But he had a gruesome vision of her getting run over while chasing him, so he turned to look. She was waving and pointing. It took him a moment to recognize his notebook. Shame and hot discomfort surged through him. She'd read it. He knew she had. How could he have been so stupid? He wanted to knock her over and tear it out of her hand, but he was helpless, trapped on this island between trams, cars, bikes and buses.

When the lights changed, she crossed in slow triumph. He couldn't pretend not to see her now. She had him by the guts like Scorpion from Mortal Kombat, who'd always harpooned Simon's character and wrenched him across the arena because Franzi had memorized the combo for that move: *Get over here!* He should've known he wouldn't be able to dislodge July so painlessly.

"You shouldn't rush off like that," she smirked. "You might lose something important." She held onto the notebook as they crossed the other half of the street. "I love the new lyrics. I didn't realize you write by hand. That's so charming and old-fashioned."

"Thanks." The word got caught on the tumbleweed rolling up and down his arid throat. Was he imagining it, or was she being sadistic? It was obvious that she'd snooped, but she didn't have to say so. His stupid mistake had been just the opportunity she was waiting for. He couldn't tell whether reading her favorite lines aloud over his desperate shushing was her way of punishing him for having a girlfriend, or for inventing one. She can't know, he reminded himself. She isn't the Stasi with a network of informants and a tap on my phone. There's no way she can be sure.

"Thanks. Bye!" The cover of the notebook tore when he snatched it, but that didn't matter. He did what he should've all along: run. As fast as he could, around corners and across streets, the bells of angry bicyclists and horns of angrier drivers making the soundtrack to this chase scene. He only stopped when he thought he'd puke. The street was empty except for an old man shuffling along with an ancient dachshund. Simon gave him a hard look to make sure he wouldn't tear off a false beard to reveal July, then walked home, looked over his shoulder again and ran upstairs. The thought of seeing her again in a few hours was too unbearable to think. He felt free, a hunted rabbit that's escaped the predator one more time, lived to sleep another night before the terror of circling hawks and lurking foxes begins again. He wrote down that image before taping over the torn cover.

~~~

The evening was shot. And restricting this feeling to the evening and not the entire tour, eternity and the universe represented a certain level of damage control. Nobody was allowed to read his lyrics before they were ready. Not his parents or Franzi, not even Tanja or Micha who had a legitimate interest.

But *she* had. She'd gotten him so spooked he'd left them within her evil clutches. No, calm down. It wasn't that bad. Had she thought to take a picture? If not, they were only stored in her flighty little head, which was so full of creepiness there was no room for poetry. Although the lyrics didn't feel all that poetic anymore. Somehow, she'd done *that*, too.

He put on some music, but it coasted by him like the dull conversations of passing strangers, leaving him raw and alone in bed, his throat closing in the grip of invisible hands. He was letting this be too important. He put his knuckles under his chin to feel the steady heartbeats. All he had to do was breathe. In through the mouth, as much as his lungs could hold, then back out through the nose. Nothing had happened. In. Hold. Well, something had. Out. But—inhale, deeper—it wasn't as bad as he was making out. He'd run into someone he didn't like—out, emptying himself of this poison—and been sucked into wasting half an hour. That was all.

He sat up and gripped the bedframe. The breathing exercises were making him dizzy instead of relaxed, but the metal bar felt cool and reassuring. A stable thing, unaffected by panic. People less antisocial than he was had this happen all the time. You made small talk, and then an excuse.

Time to name his demons. She'd read his lyrics. Was that it? No, the second demon was him feeling trapped. He hadn't stayed out of politeness; he hadn't had a choice. Anyone else in there? Yes, the one so obvious you almost forgot it: She'd be at the show. Not to mention other shows. She was a parasite. Just thinking about her sapped his energy.

He heard the muffled vibration of his phone, already packed with the charger he always forgot and had to replace on tour. Probably Micha asking about dinner. He wasn't hungry, but there was something reassuring about the thought of a sane, normal question from a sane, normal person. He'd feel better once he told the others. He wouldn't mind their teasing as long as he managed to laugh with them.

Two messages: "Hey, Simon! I see you got a new number. Hehe." Some emojis that were supposed to look sassy. Was there no corner of his life she couldn't seep into? The next message read, "Hope you're not mad. Just figured you lost mine. Can't wait to see you play." This one had a heart and a picture of a guitar.

He had to stay calm. There were things you could do. You got someone's number blocked or changed yours. Like before. Or you ignored the messages until even the most desperate person in the world would be forced to admit defeat. Since he didn't want any trouble meeting Franzi in Hamburg or finding his bandmates in a foreign city, he decided to go with the last option. For now. The important thing was knowing he had options.

He messaged Micha: "Can you give me a ride?" He'd usually have taken the tram since the heavy equipment was already in the van, but what if July had located him within a couple blocks? Walking to the stop would give him away.

He wrote to Franzi, who was probably too busy to care. "I have a stalker, but she hasn't done anything illegal yet." For good measure, he asked Tanja to get him some of whatever she was drinking.

Micha said, "No prob, see you in half an hour." Franzi said, "Shit. Discuss in Hamburg?" and Tanja didn't reply but was hopefully getting him something strong. Alcohol's a drug, too, said that nag at the back of his mind. Don't jump out of the frying pan and into the fire. Don't prove everyone right for refusing to believe you weren't an addict. But he had more pressing worries. Anyway, he'd never had the real junky experience. He'd lost his job, apartment and most of his friends, but that hadn't been because of drugs. Other people were scratching themselves bloody and gibbering in the lobbies of banks.

He felt fake for writing about addiction, but that was his low self-esteem talking. Even his failures weren't good enough. Franzi had once said, "Johnny Cash never shot a man in Reno." It was one of those concise phrases you could summon up whenever you needed it, but it wasn't what he needed now.

With Micha's arrival imminent enough to keep it short, he called his mom. He could use some of her scattered, non-specific encouragement. As long as they skipped the worries. Busy signal. He tried his dad. Voicemail. Cindi answered halfway through, but he wasn't that desperate.

He checked again to make sure he hadn't forgotten anything, then read his emails: only notifications about posts on their site, which he deleted without seeing how many were from @JulyAllYear.

His phone vibrated again. "Busy, huh?" Hadn't she ever heard of not coming on too strong? Even if he were interested, this many texts without a reply was a bit much. He turned off his phone, picked up his guitar case and bag, and went downstairs. At least she didn't have his address. If she did, she'd be outside.

~~~

An eternity later, after a dozen neighbors had walked by and seemed to consider calling the police on the lurking vagrant until they saw his guitar, Micha pulled up. Simon put his hood on, ran out and got in as Micha picked up his phone.

"Whoa!" Micha dropped it in his lap. "You scared the shit out of me."

Simon locked the door and hunched down in his seat. "July's freaking me out."

"Don't let a few posts bother you. Everyone's weird online."

He tried to keep his voice level, be ready to laugh if that was the normal, healthy thing to do. "I'm not talking about online. I'm talking about her real, physical presence in the park. Appearing at my table. Snooping through my lyrics. Stealing my phone number."

"Shit." Micha waited for a break in traffic, then turned onto Danziger Strasse. "Think she knew you'd be there?"

"I don't know." Much as the teasing usually bothered him, much as he'd wanted someone to take him seriously, that wasn't what he wanted now. He wanted Micha's belly laugh, a stupid jibe, something to make it not count. "I was in Volkspark. A lot of people go there."

"During the week, it's mostly people who live nearby, which she doesn't, unless she was lying when she invited you over that time."

"You heard that?"

"She wasn't exactly whispering. What I'm saying is, people taking a walk go to the closest park. Why go all the way to *your* park on a random weekday, unless you're meeting people? Which she clearly wasn't."

"She, um, freelances?" He didn't like how convincing Micha sounded, since he was trying not to fall into the usual trap of thinking everything was about him. He'd struggled to admit to that weakness, because thinking the world revolved around you sounded like a problem for arrogant jerks, not cringing bundles of insecurity like himself. But, like Micha, he was thinking of it as his park, July a trespasser with no business there.

"The whole thing's starting to scare me." The last half of his sentence was drowned out by Micha honking when someone cut him off.

"To what?"

"Worry me."

"I see what you mean. It's too much."

"I can't tell if she hasn't noticed the obvious signs I'm not interested, or . . ."

"Or?"

"Or she's somehow . . . disturbed."

"Yeah. But you could take her. At least it's not some big, muscular type. At the end of the day, what's she gonna do?"

Simon didn't answer. At the end of the day, that was exactly what scared him.

Two

Obviously, July was waiting at the club. Her chat with the bouncer ended as soon as they pulled up. But Simon hid his face behind the neck of his guitar while Micha pushed him along like some guilty celebrity's lawyer herding him past the press.

Backstage, Tanja handed Simon a cup.

"Thanks, what is it?"

"Apple juice. You wanted what I was having."

"Thanks a lot. At a time like this . . ." He took a deep breath and tried to regain control.

"Keep your panties on; it's fortified. You guys just escape from a serial killer?"

He let Micha explain. Drinking didn't help but felt like the first step on the way to somewhere better. Like when he couldn't fall asleep, but his thoughts finally started to move without effort, a slow current eventually strong enough to carry him away. He needed to make himself light, not resist. That was a sign of a problem, needing a drink to cope. To cope with having coffee with a woman in broad daylight in a public park. The situation was so slippery, you could never catch hold of it and say: Here's where she did something inappropriate. She'd never threatened him, never done more than praise his music and collect trivial facts about him. But she was always there.

To his surprise, Tanja didn't tease him, either. "It's not the same, but a woman I used to know had this guy bothering her. What the police will tell you if you report it is to write down every time the person contacts you, every interaction you have."

"Did she get a restraining order?"

"Uh, not exactly. Come on, we've got a show to get ready for. Tim knows not to let her in, even if she's been chatting him up since before I got here."

"Tanja and I will unload the van. You stay here and, um, tune."

Simon was beyond grateful for the way they were looking after him, but felt worse after they left. The few minutes it took them to lug in the drums were time enough for him to see July in every dark corner, emerging from the closed stage curtains or behind a wall of sound equipment. In the hushed, shadowy space, she was a paranormal presence, so sinister the ridges of her fingerprints brushing the hairs on his arms could kill. He jotted down that image once the others were back and he could relax. He tried to make it only an image, not feel her fingers below his on the pages, her gaze in his eyes as he read his lyrics.

~~~

Nothing alarming happened before the show, but that only reinforced his sense of the calm before some unprecedented storm.

He didn't notice whether they played well, whether the audience warmed to them, whether more fans knew the words to songs from *Georg's Friend in St. Petersburg* or their self-titled album. He let the others do the talking. All he could think about was not looking at the first row where she'd be fixing him with her googly eyes like that snake in *The Jungle Book* that's always trying to hypnotize Mowgli and eat him. Maybe that's what it was all about. The primal terror of being devoured.

During the last encore, he found himself picturing his deaf Japanese girl-friend in the audience, reading the lyrics from his lips. It was a silly thought but emitted a little warmth.

At the merch booth, Tanja, Micha and a couple employees manned the orders with Simon behind them, out of reach but there to sign whatever they passed back. After a while, Micha gave him the keys and told him to go lie down.

"You don't look well," he said, but Simon felt okay. Just a little further away than usual, another layer of bubble wrap between the world and his fragile psyche. He lay in the dark cargo area of the van without even the instruments to keep him company, tried not to move lest he catch some hidden predator's eye. He thought of Poe's terror of being buried alive, and wondered if it might be something like this: darkness, keeping still, endless time and solitude a thousand times heavier than the earth above you.

He felt a great kinship with Poe, who'd been a bundle of neuroses and twisted thoughts if his writing was any indication, but also a romantic, a believer in complex passions and far-off paradises. Macabre, though. What was that one where the woman busts out of her tomb and then dies for real? He'd never have that kind of energy. If they messed up and buried him too soon, he'd just lie back and hope it was over quickly.

He must've drifted off, because he woke to sudden panic, the walls and floor shaking. This is it, his animal brain told him: You're going to die.

Then Tanja and Micha stopped shaking the van and opened the back door, stifling their laughter when they saw him.

"It was her idea," Micha said as Tanja said: "We couldn't help it."

She looked over her shoulder before asking, "How's Mei?"

"I'll get your things," Micha said before Simon could answer, or even remember. He was too tired to wonder why she'd asked, much too tired to admit he already knew.

<center>~~~</center>

They drove to Hamburg in the middle of the night, the autobahn almost empty, the silence heavy despite the radio. Some love advice show came on, and the lonely voices calling in merged with the impossible distance to the taillights ahead and flecks of warm light in passing houses to bring tears to Simon's eyes.

He nodded off, but only for a few minutes, because when he woke up, a new Mr. Lonelyhearts was talking about how he'd never been loved. Simon had to listen closely to make out what Tanja was saying.

"You think I fucked up?"

"About Mei? Yeah, big time." Micha laughed loud enough to wake Simon if he'd still been asleep. "Whether he has a secret girlfriend or made her up, he was obviously trying to get the stalker off his back. Saying you never heard of her is like being all, 'Et tu, Brute' and stabbing him in the back."

"Caesar said that, not Brutus."

"Did we wake you?" Micha asked.

"A falsely attributed quote would disturb my deepest slumber. What happened?"

Tanja turned off the radio. "You-know-who asked where you were. Micha said you'd left. Then she's all, 'Was he in a hurry to see Mei?' So, knee-jerk reaction, I'm like, 'Who?' and she's like, 'His *girlfriend.*' I figured, man, I missed the boat, so I ask Micha, 'Since when does Simon have a girlfriend?'"

"I saved your ass as best I could. I said, 'Sure, you know. Pretty blonde. Guess they're official now.' Then Ms. Encyclopedia-of-Simon says how come she's blonde if she's Japanese, and Tanja, who's talking to some fan, is all, '*Who's* Japanese?'" Micha made Tanja sound like some bumbling Looney Tune and she punched him, causing the van to swerve slightly. "I said she wasn't a *natural* blonde. Next thing you know, the stalker's asking how you get along with her *disability.* I was totally in the dark, so I said you barely noticed, and started packing up the merch, but she hung around for ages."

"Try not to worry," Tanja said.

<center>~~~</center>

The next morning, Simon ignored a dozen texts from July and scrolled down to one from Franzi. But she was at his door before he made it downstairs.

"Is my big brother hungover?" she asked as he leaned in to hug her.

"Nah, just tired. Where should we eat?"

"Depends who's paying."

"My label," he lied.

"There's a great café down the street. Everything's organic and fair trade."

"Yum."

He sent a group message so Tanja and Micha wouldn't worry.

"Tell me everything," he said, and felt the fullness of her life spill over into his emptiness as she talked about professors, students and local politicians, volunteering with refugees, working in the campus bookstore and—"Don't tell Mom and Dad because it's not a big deal or even any kind of deal!"—seeing someone.

"Congratulations." He almost wanted to say, "Me, too," but an imaginary girlfriend invented to keep a stalker at bay wasn't quite the same thing.

As she herded him along, she emphasized how unimportant Christian was, way too much for it to be true. They took a sidewalk table even though it was overcast and the café—"Fair Weather," ha ha—didn't have an awning. Probably all awnings were made by children in the Third World and you couldn't get them fair trade. But you weren't supposed to say Third World without quotation marks around it, so he was glad he hadn't made the joke aloud.

They shared their relief at no longer having to hear about their mom's online dating now that she'd settled down with Reinhardt. When the waitress came, they both ordered scrambled eggs and coffee. So Franzi wasn't vegan this time around.

"Better than Dad's troll," Franzi said. "Not to be a bitch . . ."

"Why not?" Neither of them made any show of liking Cindi, who was one of many reasons they rarely visited their dad. The last time, she'd asked Franzi in front of a roomful of dinner guests why she dressed "like a homeless lesbian."

"I need to talk to you about something serious," Franzi said after their food arrived.

"Are you in trouble?" Legal trouble or an unwanted pregnancy? He got ready to put on his tough big brother act and get her whatever help she needed. A paternity test, the best lawyer in Hamburg . . . Or the tenth-best, depending on what she'd done. He'd get their dad to foot the bill if she didn't want to.

"Not *that* kind of serious." She swept aside one of the ringlets that made her look like a mischievous ragdoll and him like a slob, and started rummaging in her purse. He had the queasy feeling she was about to pull out a pamphlet about the End Times or some guru. She'd only been "spiritual" in the past, but thrived on greater purposes.

Instead, she handed him a photo of a thin, dark-haired boy with a startled expression. His t-shirt was so big it covered his knees, and he was in some institutional-looking hallway.

"That's Yosef." She put her hand in front of her mouth as she chewed. "He's an unaccompanied minor. He came most of the way here on foot."

He didn't ask where from in case he'd look ignorant. He only read the paper when he had coffee out, but was betting on Syria.

"His family basically lives between ISIS and a rebel-controlled zone that the government bombs around the clock. They spent a fortune to get him here with smugglers. Now he's having trouble getting *them* here. Officially, Germany's supposed to ship him back to the first place he set foot on EU soil, whether that country wants him or not."

Before he could respond, she produced some pictures of miserable squalor, and was off to the conditions for refugees in Greece, Italy, Turkey, Libya. She talked about drowning in the Mediterranean, about childhoods spent without education or medical care.

He felt that clamping at the back of his mouth that indicated an allergic reaction to the terribleness of the world. While he pushed food past the road-block in his throat, she talked about anti-immigrant violence and support for the far-right AfD party skyrocketing.

She put the pictures back in her bag. "Every time there's a terrorist attack or debate about headscarves, everybody remembers they feel iffy about Muslims and immigrants in general. Nobody talks about how dangerous xenophobia is, even after hundreds of attacks on refugee housing."

"Yeah, these nationalist movements are scary. The AfD, Le Pen . . ." He trailed off, unable to remember the names of other politicians and wondering where she was going with this. At least it wasn't some cult.

"What hope do these people, especially kids like Yosef, have? He needs your help."

"My help?"

Instead of answering, she went into unnecessary detail about what happens to victims of barrel bombs and chemical warfare. He was glad he'd finished eating. She'd fought for animal rights, educational reforms and any number of other issues in the past, and he'd always thought somebody had to, but none of her pet causes had ever seemed so urgent. *He needs your help.* Did she want him to take in this kid?

She knew how irresponsible he was. How could he take care of a traumatized boy when he could hardly take care of himself? He would've hesitated if she'd asked him to adopt a rescue dog, but now, in spite of himself, he was starting to believe he *could* help. His mind wandered into a Hollywood montage as he tuned out all the graphic violence and saw himself shaking hands with the boy, making jokes in bad English, getting out of breath kicking around a soccer ball. Clapping a hand on his shoulder and introducing him as "my son." He saw his son excelling beyond anybody's expectations, giving a speech about how nobody but Franzi and Simon had believed in him.

"So how can I help?" he asked when she paused to finish her coffee. She might as well come out and say it.

She handed him a flyer and a pamphlet. "You're famous. Use it to help others.

This one's about helping people get their families over and this one's about integrating them once they're here."

"I'm not really famous, but I'm sure I can afford whatever he needs."

"Who? Oh. Yeah, sure, totally make a donation. Funding's a huge issue. But we also need people to care about the tens of millions who have to flee war and terror. Most of the people talking about refugees now are Nazis."

"What should I do?" The montage disintegrated into the made-for-TV movie preview it had always been. He was glad he hadn't said more. She thought he wanted to donate money, not adopt some random kid she'd been using to make a point. A kid who already *had* a family.

"Make some comments at your shows. Not just 'Refugees welcome' like everybody says to look good. Put the flyers out. Post a statement on your website. Link to this organization that helps families like Yosef's."

"You didn't have to make that huge pitch about a couple flyers."

"I know, Simple Simon." She pushed the rest of her eggs onto her fork with the crust of her toast. "But I wanted you to care."

"I do. I guess I didn't know I could help." AKA he'd never thought of it. He was as nauseated as the next person about civilians getting bombed or neo-Nazi attacks, but he'd never asked himself what he'd asked her: what he should do. For once, it wouldn't take much effort to do the right thing. He wouldn't have made a good father anyway. Yosef was better off without. "You can come early and put out the flyers, okay?"

"Thanks. You know, people in my initiative were talking about how we could get musicians or actors involved, and I was like, my brother's in this band. Three people had seen you play. You have more fans than you realize."

He waved for the check, hoping the waitress hadn't heard, and that she had.

"I want another coffee if you have time," Franzi said. "We can get it to go and zone out at the waterfront."

"Sounds good."

~~~

Walking past soulless hotels, boutiques with more staff than customers, and the occasional corner store looking like something someone had forgotten to sweep up, Simon asked, "What about school?"

"This all fits perfectly with my major."

"International Business?" He'd heard that from their mom, who was better at keeping up with the vicissitudes of Franzi's life than he was.

"International *Relations*. Mom always tries to make us sound more successful. She thinks you're bigger than Helene Fischer. It beats Dad thinking we should get real jobs, though. Anyway, I'm focusing on immigration policy. I might do law after."

"You're gonna become a lawyer?"

She laughed and pulled him across an intersection by his sleeve. The light was red, and the elderly couple waiting on the other side shook their heads in accidental unison. "You say that like it's a disease. I wanna help. If someone's being unfairly deported, what can I do? Neither of us knows the law or has the money to hire someone who does. I wanna be that someone, but affordable."

"Phew, for a minute there, I was worried you might make money. I was like, who are you and where's my sister?"

They continued down a narrow alleyway that smelled much too much like the butcher shop in it, but ended in the bright mirror of the Alster with its ships made blue-gray and miniature by distance.

"Tell me more about your new love interest. Other than how unimportant he is."

"I'd rather you reserve judgment until you meet him."

"He's coming?"

"You were right to hold two tickets." She dimpled one cheek, but her mouth was already moving on. "You mentioned a stalker?"

"Oh, it's not that bad." It felt wrong to say too much about July to someone who spent her time helping real victims. What did all her texts matter when people were being tortured, raped and killed? But that was false logic. Even Dr. Froheifer said so when he tried too hard to be good. One extreme was as bad as the other, but it was so hard to settle in between. He felt like a hockey puck getting slammed back and forth from egotism to crippling despair about humanity. But Franzi made helping sound easy, and she was a connection in the world, an anchor to ground him. He didn't have many, and tended to drift.

She checked that her loafers were on securely and sat down with her legs dangling over the water. He followed suit. The wind had a chill their grandmom would've attributed to the feasts of the Ice Saints or sheep-shearing season, but the air felt cleaner than it was, and the calling seagulls sounded like vacation.

"I'll put on the parental filter." She pantomimed pulling something over her mouth the way they did when something needed to stay between the two of them.

"There's this girl."

"A little girl? Teenager?"

"A few years younger than I am, I guess." He remembered July saying he only ever made guesses, and felt a fresh tremor of resentment.

"Pretty?"

"Average."

"Is she . . . ?"

"Let me explain," he said, and she did.

"Yikes, have you heard from her since?"

"The thing with Tanja was yesterday. I've been ignoring her texts."

"Why'd you—?"

They started when a bulldog moseyed over to nuzzle their empty cups until its owner whistled.

"Why'd I what?" Other than his inability to eliminate July from his life, he couldn't think of anything that was his fault.

"Why'd you make up such a specific girlfriend?"

"I got the name off this lost-cat poster and it sounded Japanese so I went with it. Then July asked why she never comes to shows so I said she's deaf."

She was struggling to keep a straight face. "I can see how that would happen. I name all my imaginary partners after other people's lost pets." She burst into that villainous but contagious laughter that didn't run in the family. It was a relief to join in, and he let her amusement carry him until he was tugging at his collar for air.

They gasped much longer than it was funny out of sheer inertia. Then she said, "Anything else I should know? Does she have a hook for a hand or purple eyes?"

He tried to gather the lies he'd scattered all over. "She was born in Berlin. Her mom's Japanese. Micha said she'd bleached her hair." He rested his hands on his knees and felt something warm and wet, lifted one to see a powdery white stain. "Great. A gull shat on me."

"It's good luck." She was laughing too hard to say much more but wiped his hand with some organic perfume and a crumpled napkin she promised was unused.

"Looks like I won't be wearing these to the show. Wanna stop by the hotel?"

"I have to get more flyers printed and prepare a certain somebody for the metaphysical experience of your acquaintance. But I'll be there early."

"With your boyfriend, right?" Great, he'd forgotten the guy's name.

"He's not my boyfriend. Don't forget you signed a non-disclosure agreement. Apropos, any romantic conquests that aren't made up?"

"Nope."

"Come on, Christian and I aren't that serious, but I told you. Not even a promising one-night stand?"

"Not even a bad one. Telling you that is more embarrassing than any secret I could be keeping."

"Well, you're not dead yet. See you like an hour before doors?"

"Great." He hoped July wouldn't get the same idea.

~~~

He knew he should look around Hamburg like a normal person, but he'd already been and was exhausted. He dropped off his pants at the hotel laundry and got in bed with the TV on low. Somewhere between infomercials, his phone woke him up.

Franzi in her usual phone persona, harried and out of breath. She wanted another guest pass.

"No problem; I'll be there to get you in. Is this a second boyfriend or a date for me?"

"You'll see." She hung up.

He rinsed the hotel glass with hot water and gargled. He felt groggy but knew he wouldn't fall asleep again. Micha and Tanja weren't in their room, so he changed into his rarely used workout clothes. Hopefully no one was in the gym. Didn't they all have somewhere to be and someone to be there with?

It was in the basement between the parking garage and the laundry where they were probably laughing at the shit on his jeans. There was the obligatory painful fluorescent lighting and blaring radio. He'd left his headphones upstairs and knew he'd never come back if he went to get them. Two unrealistically tan men in sleeveless shirts were lifting weights, veins looking like they were about to burst, and a wiry blonde in full marathon gear was on the treadmill. Of course, the room was lined with mirrors to eliminate any shred of privacy the sterile lighting had left.

He picked up a bottle of water from the counter, settled in one treadmill down from the blonde and ignored the glance she tossed him, not wanting to seem like an ogler. Which he felt like as he started walking and couldn't help seeing her in the mirror, her workout gear so form-fitting he could locate her clavicles, hipbones and the place where her thighs narrowed to a no doubt Brazilian-waxed concavity. Her arms were more muscular than his and as tan as the two weightlifters. He felt like some pale underground creature crawling up to the surface for the first time.

He moved up to a jog, panting out the far side of his mouth so she wouldn't see. Like she cared or was even his type. Just one more way to put himself down. Huffing and puffing and watching the ever-so-slight movement of her tight ass, being the slimy jerk with bags under his eyes and a filthy leer. He needed to think of other things.

The show later. No, bad idea. He moved away from the sensor so it wouldn't register the way his pulse jumped, and found himself returning to that ridiculous father-son montage. It was embarrassing, but also soothing. At least it made him feel like a loser instead of a bad person. Then Mei got mixed up in it and he zoned out, letting the scenes play between him and the reflection of his oafish steps, his jiggling flesh. Mei coming home from work to find Simon and Yosef making dinner, the family on a hike or watching some wholesome movie, Mei and Franzi best friends, his parents relieved, family vacations—without his parents, of course—and pictures to fill countless albums.

He slowed down to drink some water. The marathon woman was still going strong. One weightlifter had left, and the other had moved on to the rowing machine. An overweight woman with skin even paler than Simon's and painful-looking varicose veins was lifting the lightest weights. Good for her. He felt that they were in league against the superhuman athletes, but he must've smiled to himself because she looked over and scowled. He sped up and tried to return to his visions of blissful family life, but couldn't help remembering Franzi's question: whether he'd had any romantic conquests who weren't imaginary.

Why was it so easy to think about a relationship and family when the woman was made up and the kid someone he'd never meet and didn't have a common language with? And why did being alone forever seem so much more realistic?

He'd been joking when he asked whether Franzi was bringing him a date, and why? Because she wouldn't want to inflict him on anyone? She must think better of him than that. Hadn't he always tried to be a good brother? Wasn't she, in her own—healthier, more productive—way, as kooky as he was? She must think he didn't want to meet anyone. Other people were always striking up conversations, swiping through dating apps. Had his unwavering faith in ending up alone finally converted everyone around him? It was more a fear than a belief.

The best part of his Mei fantasy was the idea of a committed relationship with someone who'd already come to terms with his neuroses, so he didn't have to bend over backward pretending to be cool. Like that pop song from one of his teenage years, something about "she likes me for me."

Struggling to hide his panting, he lowered the speed, glancing over to see whether Iron Woman noticed. He'd never have a girlfriend like that. He didn't want to run marathons, although he'd totally cheer Mei on if she did. Mei might encourage him to keep in shape but wouldn't drag him out of bed for a five a.m. run. In his mind, Mei was all-accepting. And she didn't just accept him; she liked—loved—him the way he was.

He glugged water, spluttered and drank again. Drops of sweat drizzled at his feet. The only problem was that she wasn't real, and that was the biggest problem of all, the fear that the woman who could love him for who he was didn't exist, not in the form of a deaf Japanese-German woman with bleached hair, and not in any other, either.

But there was *someone* who liked him, even liked him too much. The only thing July couldn't accept about him was that he wasn't interested. Thinking about her usually left him somewhere between guilt and disgust, as if she reminded him of something he didn't like about himself. But you could also see the situation in a positive light. Even if she was unhinged, she adored him. Not the way other fans did, while he was lit by the glow of the stage. She analyzed his lyrics, spent every second she could near him and learned as much as she could about his personal life without ever finding a reason to despise him. There was something to be said for that.

She must be at least as lonely as he was. She never had anyone to bring to a concert, even though she wasn't ugly or crazy in a readily apparent way. Could he blame her for fixating? She must warm herself on the thought of him like he'd warmed himself with Mei. Of course, it was more complicated since he happened to be real, but maybe she wasn't totally nuts. It might've been the endorphins from this rare exercise making him feel euphoric and charitable, but he felt ready to exchange a couple words with her. If he managed to get across to her that they were never going to be together—he'd say he'd married Mei or realized he was gay—they could be friends. Or at least friendly acquaintances.

~~~

Back in his room, he messaged Micha and got in the shower. He was in one of those fragile moods where he felt happy but on the verge of tears. He told himself he was tired, overstimulated by the tour, enamored with the idea of being loved by someone other than July. The thought of his near miss, almost telling Franzi he'd adopt that kid, reminded him that he needed to get to the club early. And be likable and attentive with Christian, in case it got serious. He'd gotten a bad rap for being rude to her ex. Franzi had never apologized after she found out Dirk had cheated on her and, worse still, stolen donations she'd collected for a girls' school in rural India. Simon had the decency never to say he'd told her so.

By the time he got dressed, Micha had replied that they'd meet him at the hotel and order takeout from this great place they'd discovered. Simon always admired Micha's ability to eat, sleep and pursue women in a totally natural and uninhibited manner. Micha knew he needed to eat and didn't worry about looking like a pig. He never lay awake nights or felt like a lazy slob if he didn't leave his apartment until afternoon, and his attitude when single could be summed up as *Why not?* Simon wasn't jealous. It was only scientific curiosity, observing another species.

He wrote Franzi about dinner, and she replied, "Something veg for 3." He added himself to that figure and passed it on to Micha. He didn't want to look like some caveman gnawing a grisly bone if everyone else was a vegetarian.

Now what? He'd made the mistake of only packing *Dr. Faustus*, planning to finish it, but was too tired for paragraph-long sentences. If he walked to the club, he could leave sooner but might get lost and be late to meet Franzi and Christian. He tried not to wonder who else they were bringing. The effort of being likable for one stranger would be exhausting enough, and he was getting stage fright about making political statements. What if everyone could tell he didn't know what he was talking about?

He checked his phone again: nothing but notifications from their website. @JulyAllYear had shared links to their songs and tour list. Plus a zillion comments. He couldn't help reading a few. They seemed normal enough at first: praise for the new album, comparisons with earlier work and other artists. The creepy part was their frequency. Where did she find the time?

Worse still, one was addressed to him: "Love what you're working on, Simon.

Don't worry, your secret's safe with me. But for the rest of you . . ." Glowing compliments about the lyrics she'd snooped. He was having trouble feeling as flattered, as tolerant, as he had downstairs. The next comment called him a "classic misanthropic artist" and "tragicomic caricature of himself, Yorick forced to play Hamlet." No matter how far he scrolled, her silly username popped up over and over again.

His phone buzzed in his hands, and he felt a brief but profound terror that made him check all the corners of his room, the parking lot below and even the hallway. The timing was a coincidence, but the scare left a bad taste he couldn't get out of his mouth, a pounding of his heart it took too many breaths to slow.

July's text read: "If you see what I'm saying?"

He had no idea what the context was because he hadn't read the last million. He knew it was a bad idea to hit "Reply," but ignoring her hadn't worked, either.

"Sorry, had to get phone repaired. Really busy, no time to catch up."

Her response came impossibly quickly. "Don't worry, I'm not mad. Even if it's a lame excuse." Then: "Kidding!" And some stupid emojis. He didn't have the energy to read her other messages, but didn't delete them in case there was important information like a bomb threat. He switched on the TV and shrieked when someone knocked.

"Hello to you, too," Tanja said.

~~~

"They don't deliver," Micha explained as he drove, "but we'll drop you so you can meet Franzi."

"Thanks, make sure the coast is clear before you leave." He faked a laugh but knew they knew he meant it.

"Have you started keeping track of her insanity?" Tanja craned back from shotgun.

"It's mostly online or on my phone. I guess I shouldn't worry," he said more to himself than them. "If she's coming tonight, she would've said."

"Did you read all her messages?" Micha asked.

Simon didn't answer right away. As long as he didn't say it, he didn't have to think it. He hadn't wanted to get sucked into her texts, but that had been a big mistake in terms of reconnaissance. It was like a spider in the room: You had to keep an eye on it or it might suddenly crawl down the neck of your shirt. The difference being that you could smash a spider. "There were too many."

"So, um, how's Franzi?"

Before he could reply, Tanja said: "Speak of the devil!"

His stomach leapt into his throat, suffocating him, but all he saw was his sister, another woman and a tall, dark-skinned guy. That's right; they'd been talking about Franzi, not July. He couldn't escape a certain disappointment, the unsatisfying relief of a child who fails to find the monster under the bed—not because there *is* no monster, but because it's hiding somewhere else.

"See you later, kiddo," Tanja said. Micha clapped him on the shoulder as he got out.

"See you." Why did he always sit in the back? The arrangement reminded him of his parents dropping him at playdates when he was little. What did it say that the vibes between a lesbian and a straight guy infatuated with someone else reminded him of their marriage?

"Our hero!" Franzi said. "The bouncer wouldn't let us in. Where are those two off to?" Breathless rambling was her version of Simon's nervous silence.

"Picking up dinner." He flashed his ID at the bouncer, who could've used his paunch for sumo wrestling if things got ugly, and smiled over his shoulder at the strangers. "I'm Simon." He offered the guy his hand first. He was taller than Simon, muscular in a way that made him look healthy instead of like a gym rat, and had a warm smile that crinkled the corners of his eyes when Simon said, "You must be Christian." He bit his tongue to keep from adding "I've heard so much about you" because Franzi would've killed him.

The fact that Christian had come prepared to like him was a relief. Simon didn't trust the kind of scumbag who didn't care about making a good impression. Like himself. He wanted Franzi to date someone like this: polite, friendly, dress shirt and slacks that made him look employed or at least employable, since he was probably a student. Then again, getting off to a good start was scary, because things could only get worse.

He turned to the woman as they came into the unlit entryway, the ticket desk abandoned, posters of past acts peeling from the walls like sunburnt skin. "Simon," he said again.

"Sophie." She was Asian, with longish hair and diagonal bangs that exposed one eyebrow, and looked like she was barely holding in a laugh.

"Nice to meet you. Any friends of Franzi's are friends of mine." Before he could decide whether that sounded slimy, she burst out laughing.

"Actually, we just met," Franzi said as they continued into the empty concert hall where an overweight emo boy was unloading crates of Club Mate. "Can we get a drink? We had to run here."

"Sure." Was Sophie a fan they'd run into? He went over to the bar, where the boy froze in awe like Simon was a saint he'd been praying would appear to him. "I'm with the band."

"No shit," he stammered, and Simon felt gooey and touched even though this was a pimply eighteen-year-old with black eyeliner, not a waif Franzi wanted him to care about. "I love your work."

"Wow, I had no idea anyone knew us up here. Could we get a couple drinks before we set up?" The old approach-and-run-away, like a wary animal coming just close enough to snatch food from an outstretched hand. Grab the praise, but flee before you connect.

"Sure. Man, I've only been here a couple months and I was *so* excited when I saw you were coming. Your lyrics really speak to me." Something in Simon's face must've told him he was getting too close because he added "What'll it be?" in the same breath.

Simon called the others over to order, then asked for a coke. There was something to be said for being a role model, and Franzi would be happy he wasn't drinking.

The others took their drinks and settled on the edge of the stage while Simon fished out a twenty.

"No way, it's on the house."

"Sure, thanks, it's a tip." He was buying his way away from the bar, and the kid knew it. Or it was a normal, polite thing to do.

"Thanks. Hey, can I ask you something? Just one thing?" The boy's desperation was especially cringey since it felt so familiar. He wished he could give him some advice without hurting his feelings: *Fake it better. Don't wear your loser heart on your sleeve.*

"Sure."

"Were you cool in school? Like, with friends and parties? Or . . . girls?"

"No way." Simon didn't have to think about that. "I was a huge loser."

"But he turned out okay, right?" He hadn't heard Franzi approaching, but she smiled at the kid, who looked like he might cry with joy, and took Simon by the arm. "Mei needs you."

"Catch you later." Simon let Franzi guide him to the stage. "Mei?"

"Yep." She sat by Christian, leaving space next to Sophie, who was embarrassingly pretty in her polka-dotted dress, swinging her bare legs above the ballet flats she'd kicked off.

"Here's the best part." Sophie swept back her hair to reveal a hearing aid on one delicate, double-pierced ear. If Franzi wasn't so obviously behind this, Simon would've thought he was losing it.

"You're probably wondering where they drummed up a deaf Japanese woman on such short notice. I'm actually three-quarters Vietnamese and no quarters Japanese and I stole my grandpa's extra hearing aid."

"Franzi and I were getting some flyers printed," Christian said. "She told me about your problem." He nodded to Simon, who knew he'd eventually be sick with embarrassment about the number of near-strangers who knew he had a fake girlfriend. "Then we see Sophie behind the counter and think, maybe with a little imagination?"

"While we waited for our printouts," Franzi continued, "I asked if she wanted a free ticket. Voila: I give you Mei."

"Wow. I guess if July turns up, I'm safe." If she didn't, it would all be for naught. Would he have to find a new "girlfriend" every night until July saw her?

"We've got you covered either way." Franzi took out her phone. "Smile!"

Sophie leaned her head against his shoulder and pulled his arm around her waist. He tried to look natural as Franzi snapped a dozen pictures.

"I'll post some on your site. No one's there as often as your stalker. And if she does turn up, so much the better."

Sophie laughed. "I'll be like, back off, bitch."

Simon noticed he still had his arm around her and removed it under the guise of looking at his phone. Her slender legs still dangled below the stage, but she'd stopped swinging them. He'd usually have found the swallow tattoo on her ankle trite, but couldn't stop looking at the minute and perfect prettiness of its split tail, her skin glowing in the low light. He could still feel the warmth of her, the soft curve of her waist through the thin vintage fabric . . . Was it wrong that he was attracted to his fake girlfriend?

"So, darling." She stroked the back of his hand. "Tell me about us."

He went through everything he could remember telling July, and that she was supposed to have been blonde at some point. "Thanks to them." He jerked his head at Micha and Tanja, who were coming over, arms full of paper bags. "If you make anything else up, tell me so she can't trap us, okay?"

"Deal." She shook his hand and held it. But he reminded himself that he didn't see his sister that often and should get to know this guy who might become or already be an important part of her life instead of flirting with this cute extra in whatever was showing later.

"So, how'd you guys meet?" he asked Christian when Franzi got up to help with the takeout.

"At the refugee center. I've been there a couple years now. Franzi's really dedicated."

He was a refugee? Was he Middle Eastern or Black? There were lots of refugees from where was it, Eritrea? Ethiopia? Simon considered saying something about his flawless German but didn't want to sound condescending. "So, um, where're you from?"

"Germany." Christian's smile vanished. "I *volunteer* at the center, like your sister."

He felt himself blushing, but the stage lights were off so hopefully no one could tell. The last thing he wanted was to be one of those jerks who insist on knowing where people who don't look ethnically German are *really* from. He didn't have any Black friends he could bring to his defense like racists always did, but that wasn't his fault. In a good week, he saw two or three Black people. Although that might've been a reflection on how often he left his apartment. Soledad wasn't white, but she wasn't really Black, either. Did she count? He remembered a Turkish friend from school he'd thought was an American Indian until they were about twelve, and was glad he'd never asked her. "Sure, I mean, did you grow up in Hamburg? You have the accent."

"Sorry, yeah. I must sound like I have a huge chip on my shoulder. I get asked all the time where in *Africa* I'm from. One of my grandfathers was an American GI. Everyone thinks I wanna tell them about my African heritage even though it's been centuries since anyone I'm related to set foot on that continent. The best I could do is show them a bunch of old junk my mom has. Like, sorry, no drums or spear or whatever, but can I interest you in some big-band records and whatever the U.S. Army issued its occupation forces and never bothered to collect? My biggest interaction with that heritage was my grandma having a meltdown because she caught me playing dress-up with his old uniform and service pistol. Oh and two trips to Disney World. So, you know, Africa."

"People are stupid. It's like, our grandparents were from somewhere in Poland, but I have *no* idea about that. What, are we gonna ask everybody to pull out a family tree?"

"Tell me about it," Sophie said. "I was born in Germany. My parents were born in Germany. How far back do you have to go?"

"And what are 'Germans' supposed to look like, anyway?" Simon asked, feeling the warmth recede from his face as he regained sure footing in the conversation. "Back then, it was all like Prussians or Bavarians or something; nobody was *German*."

"What they really mean is white. You know I get employees at the center thinking I'm a refugee? It's like, I've been seeing you for *years*. I should start mixing them up with refugees from the Balkans."

"That must be so frustrating." Simon felt annoyed on behalf of Sophie and Christian, but mostly relieved that he'd managed to position himself on the right side of that annoyance.

"What?" Tanja asked, but continued without waiting for an answer, "Carnivores, your food's onstage. That's just you and me, Micha, now that Simon's gone over to the dark side."

"Are you a vegetarian?" Sophie asked.

"Just a wannabe."

"I'm actually a big meat-eater, but Franzi didn't know. What about Mei?"

"Up to you."

"I'm Tanja, by the way, and this is Micha." Tanja waved her chopsticks at Christian and Sophie and pointed to Micha, who already had his mouth full.

"Christian."

"Mei."

"Come again?"

"Hasn't he mentioned me?"

"You crazy kids."

Simon struggled to transport the very fluid curry and not very sticky rice into his mouth with chopsticks until he spotted some plastic spoons, and listened to Franzi retelling the story of "Mei." He felt the way he had with their opener last fall before July freaked him out again. Surrounded by friends.

After they finished eating, Christian arranged the flyers in a prominent position while Micha unpacked the merchandise and Franzi drilled Simon: "Focus on ISIS. That's in the news a lot so they'll pay attention. More people get killed by Assad, but that's too complicated for now. Remind them that Germany needs at least five hundred thousand non-EU immigrants a year to sustain social security. More than sixty million people are fleeing violence and persecution this year. You know, stuff people can quote later."

She went through a few more points and he repeated them back to her, watching Sophie out of the corner of his eye. Was she like he'd pictured?

"Very good," Franzi said. "Three gold stars. Now we'll let you get ready."

She walked away, but Sophie came over. "Looks like you're helping save the world."

He didn't know her well enough to tell whether she was being sarcastic. "That's all Franzi." Usually, he would've accepted the undeserved praise, knowing full well he was a lazy schlub who never thought about anyone else, here or on the other side of the planet, but he wasn't just trying to score. Although that was definitely also something he was interested in. Was she someone he could have a relationship with? The charade of it, his silly thoughts about Mei, made it seem more possible than it had since Nadine.

"It's sweet that you're helping her. I can't say I'm much of a social activist."

"I know what you mean."

"When two bad people meet." She laughed and combed her fingers through the long end of her bangs. He wanted to brush them behind her ear and kiss her to a crescendoing soundtrack.

"It's like it was meant to be." He didn't even have to say it ironically; it was impossible to say sincerely. Everything meaningful had already been felt, said and turned into a joke.

"Good luck." She kissed him on the cheek and walked away, her feet already in motion as her lips brushed his skin. He hurried backstage, not wanting to tip the delicate metaphysical balance that had allowed that to happen.

Setting his amp, he tried to think some sense into himself. She was fun and pretty, but he couldn't just fit her into his daydreams like some missing puzzle piece he'd found under a sofa cushion.

"Come on." Tanja nudged him. "What's it like to fall for someone you've been in a relationship with this long?"

"She kissed him," Micha said. "I saw it."

"What?! We better start shopping for wedding presents."

Much as her teasing could get to him, he didn't mind it now. It was silly, but also nice, like getting teased in school about the girl you actually liked.

"Only on the cheek. She's cute, right?"

"Yeah," Tanja said. "Aside from being good for the part, she could be good for you."

His stomach gave a slight lurch, weighed down by the meal he'd only eaten to fit in. He'd been so focused on Sophie and whether she could be his real-life Mei that he'd lost sight of why she was there.

"The stalker's gonna shit herself," Micha said. "Don't forget Mei used to be blonde."

"I won't." July was a hair on his tongue he couldn't get rid of. Illogical as it was, he felt like she was the one keeping his relationship with Sophie from being real. Calling his bluff. His sense of well-being seeped out like warmth through an open window. Then again, she hadn't shown up early. Maybe she couldn't make it or had a new obsession. You could always hope.

"Look." Tanja was more perceptive than Micha. "Let's forget about her. Did you know we sold out the club? We get a good cause into the mix thanks to Franzi, and, unless I'm way off, Sophie's into you. Everything's great, right?"

"Amen," Micha said.

"Amen," Simon repeated, because it was easier that way. She was right, of course. He had a knack for seeing the worst in things.

"If July does come," Micha said, "you don't have to be alone with her."

"Not if Mei has anything to say about it," Tanja said, "and I'm sure she will."

He felt like he had in school whenever a teacher announced that he'd gotten the highest grade: soaking up their approval but ashamed to show it, afraid the whole class knew how badly he wanted it. He was ashamed of needing Sophie to protect him from July, but flattered that she found him worth protecting.

~~~

They came out and played a track from *Georg's Friend* without waiting for the applause to die down—and there was plenty, so that was one more good thing—before he started his spiel. "I wanna welcome all of you, and also some people who probably couldn't make it out, the thousands of refugees in Hamburg and nationwide." It was a weak segue, but he had them; they applauded for a second at "refugees" and then subsided into rapt silence as he went through Franzi's soundbites. When he finished, the applause was deafening. Good to know your fans weren't neo-Nazis.

He was feeling so good he didn't realize 'til their set was almost over that he hadn't had a drink all evening, just that coke and the water he'd been swilling onstage. So that was another layer in the glow on and around him. But when they came back out for their encore, he felt a fleck of darkness. He could sense

July in the tightly packed audience, thinking she owned who he was and what he was about. That he was putting it on, a phony who'd never said a political or humanitarian word in his life. Because he hadn't, and if anybody knew it, she did. Well, fuck her. He had a life outside the band, even if she didn't. But he felt insincere and shabby, careful not to let his cheap mask fall off in front of everyone.

When he spotted July in the front row, he was surprised to see her frowning, arms crossed. Was she really judging him, or had she seen Sophie and put two and two together? She was tarnishing his glow for all she was worth, and the black hole of her presence forced him to give her a flinching smile. But then, a couple people down, he saw Mei. As Micha got the beat started for the first couple strophes that didn't need his tired voice, he knelt and leaned forward to kiss Mei's forehead. Or Sophie's; either way. He could feel July's darkness taking on thundercloud proportions, swelling like a storm about to burst, but it didn't matter, because Mei pulled him down to kiss him on the mouth, and he was so full of goodness, it didn't matter if it was real.

~~~

After the set he wanted to vanish, not even take the few steps offstage but dissolve into particles that would reassemble somewhere else. Somewhere Mei was and July wasn't. But, unplugging his guitar, he remembered he wasn't quite done.

He picked up the mic, and the audience cheered, anticipating an unheard-of third encore. Unheard-of for him, anyway, because why bother. He cleared his throat. "Maybe you're wondering what you can do to help? I know a lot of us feel like hey, people need help, but what can I do?" Dead silence. He felt sincere but sounded it less than ever. At least no one was laughing. That was all it would take now, one snigger, one shouted joke, and they'd all be hooting at his pathetic attempt to be real. He took a deep breath so he wouldn't talk too fast like he did when he was nervous. "While you're checking out our fantastic new album—" Now there was a friendly chuckle, but that was okay; they were on his side—"you can grab one of the fliers my lovely sister Franzi brought, whether you wanna donate money or time, or just be better informed."

He heard Franzi cheer, and then the audience picked it up. He should've thought of being a good person before—they loved it. Of course, it wasn't a costume you could put on every day.

Backstage, he felt endlessly thirsty and like his skull was a half-size too tight. He sat on an amp and chugged more water, putting off the moment when he'd have to face the crowd again. July was emitting hot dread like an oven that's turned off but could still burn you. He knew Mei would take care of her but had to see it to believe it. He hadn't looked at July since kissing Sophie. He tried to picture her expression. Angry or crushed? Defeated. Too late, he realized it was one of those thoughts it's best not to think.

Micha patted him on the back. "You were great."

Tanja, who'd gone into a corner to change into something less sweaty, called, "Yeah, what's Jack Nicholson say in that one movie? 'You make me wanna be a better man.'"

Simon laughed in case it was all a joke and he'd made a fool of himself, but she said, "No, really. I feel all warm and tingly inside. Although that might be the jumbo tequila our young fan poured me. Never mix tequila with curry. Too multicultural."

They meant it. Tanja could hardly ever stop teasing, but that didn't make her feelings less real. It was their band, too. They were glad to help. He wasn't the only one still figuring out how to be good.

"I'm heading out," Micha said. "You guys coming, or should I stream the vicious fight between July and Sophie? I can do live commentating."

"I'm gonna have a smoke," Tanja said. "Save me a front-row seat."

"Coming," Simon said.

~~~

Sophie was behind the table with Micha. Franzi and Christian stood nearby, engrossed in a discussion with some fans.

Sophie kissed him on the cheek and asked if he wanted a drink.

"Sure, thanks." He could smell her perfumed sweat—some expensive classic like Chanel—and the mint gum she was chewing. She pulled her hair into a ponytail that exposed her hearing aid and headed to the bar.

Dazed, he scribbled his name on the record Micha handed him with the marker Micha put in his hand. The flash of a camera dazzled his eyes. He felt drunk even though he'd almost never played a show this sober. A voice to his left said, "She's *ravishing*."

July was standing too close for him to turn and look at her. Was this an admission of defeat, or a test?

"Isn't she? I'm gonna marry her someday." If she was testing him, he'd pass. If she wasn't, he was twisting the knife.

"I'm here with someone, too," he thought he heard her say. "Or . . . I was."

"What's that?" Was that why she'd looked so grim? If someone had ditched her, they must've done it pretty early on. She didn't answer, and he stepped back to get a better look. She was staring straight ahead, face blank, like someone waiting for a train. He wanted to turn and talk to someone else, but Micha was rummaging through boxes, Tanja was chain-smoking or picking up a girl or being abducted by aliens—in any case, not here—and Franzi and Christian were busy raising awareness. Other fans were keeping their distance like July had pissed on him and they couldn't enter her territory. It was hard to believe she'd come with anyone.

"What brings you to Hamburg?"

"Mostly the show. It's pretty close."

He wished she'd lie. Preserve her dignity. She could say something about that invisible date of hers. Like he was one to talk. "Yeah. We drove up last night."

She nodded but didn't say anything. Was she swallowing back tears, analyzing how best to stalk him from here on out, or bored? He found her impossible to read, and not in an interesting way. She was like a newspaper in a foreign alphabet—something you'd glance at and set aside, knowing you couldn't get anything out of it. He wondered whether everyone felt this way around her and that was why she was always alone. He felt her sadness and tried to fight it. Feeling bad for her was one step away from feeling responsible. It wasn't his fault she'd come all this way.

"You played a good show." It sounded like an accusation. He noticed her new hairstyle for the first time—stern, straight bangs across her forehead, a failed attempt at a hip look like Sophie's—but didn't want her to know he had.

"I'd better . . ." He was saved from having to say what by something so cold it burned. There was Mei, handing him the apple spritzer she'd pressed against the back of his neck.

"Hi." She stuck out her hand. "You're June, right? You come to a lot of shows."

"It's July. I've never seen you."

"You must've been looking somewhere else." Before things could get even more awkward, she added, "When you can't hear the music, you look around more."

July made a fluttering gesture with her hands.

"That's okay. I can read lips, and anyway I've got this." She tapped the hearing aid, and Simon held his breath, wondering whether July would turn out to be an expert in that technology. "I don't wanna leave Simon out."

"Yeah. Nobody likes to be left out." Was she convinced? Even if she wasn't, there was no point in calling them out. The chemistry between him and Mei—*Sophie*, he reminded himself—was obvious. July had to know she didn't stand a chance. "Are you coming on the whole tour?"

Simon would've liked Sophie to say yes, to play out that fantasy for a little while, but she laughed and said, "I could ask you the same thing."

"The next couple stops, maybe," Simon said, imagining Sophie rushing home to pack, leaving with him in the morning. Dozing in the back of the van, head on his shoulder. Taking snapshots on the road. Something to look back on later. *Having* a later. "It depends on your work." He forced himself to snap out of it. He was turning into July, letting his imaginary life overshadow his real one. Because she must imagine all kinds of things about him or why would she bother? The band was good but not *that* good. His guitar lines weren't all they should be. People talked about "minimalism," but he just hadn't been able to play fast and sing at the same time when they started out, and it was too late to change styles now. The point being, they weren't earth-shattering.

"What do you do again?" July was going along with it now, facing Sophie and clearly forming the words with her lips, which were coated in gloss so pale it made her look ill. She must try so hard.

He wanted to signal that he couldn't remember, but Sophie was ten steps ahead of him.

"Top secret." She winked. "I'm about to start something new but I don't wanna jinx it."

"'Never praise the day before evening,' isn't that what they say?" July's voice sounded raw, like she'd been shouting or crying.

"Well, well." Tanja stuck her head into the group, startling Simon more than the others, who must've seen her coming. The club was too smoky for him to have smelled her approach. "Look who's leaving all the work to poor old Micha."

"Not like you've been helping." Simon was happy to let her pull him over to the table, where some tall skinny guy in an unseasonable black turtleneck wanted to talk them into bringing out cassette tapes.

"It's a unique quality of sound we sacrificed far too eagerly."

Simon was only half listening, wondering when July would disappear, feeling a little bad for lying, justifying it to himself. "What about eight-tracks?" He'd never had any, and the guy was too young to have been around for them but of course had a real, sincere opinion about eight-track audio and believed Simon did, too. Maybe he should've, being a musician and an object of interest to hipsters, but he didn't and was glad when the guy transitioned to a series of obscure bands Simon "absolutely had to know about" before melting into the crowd.

"We should set him up with July," Micha said. "I know soulmates when I see them."

Simon laughed and glanced at where she'd been, but Sophie was alone. The crowd had thinned enough for him to see July at the bar, deep in conversation with the emo bartender. The coke, apple juice and million bottles of water were weighing on his bladder, so he figured he'd take the opportunity to visit the men's room.

He expected July to pounce the second he came out, but she was still at the bar and had even picked someone up. He couldn't imagine her striking up a conversation with anyone not linked to him, but that was only his arrogance. She had needs like everyone else, and he sure wasn't satisfying them.

Disappointingly, she wasn't talking to the turtlenecked audio aficionado but some balding guy in a leather jacket. Maybe too old for her, maybe none of Simon's business. He hurried back before she could see him. If she met someone, she might be too busy for him.

"Jealous?" Tanja asked.

"Terribly." He looked back to see the guy kissing July.

"When two desperate people meet," Micha said. "I was wrong about her soulmate."

"So much the better," Sophie said. "She really needs to get laid."

Simon laughed and pushed away the feeling he had watching the guy, who had a chunky build and was even taller than Christian, run his hands down a suddenly fragile-looking July's back. It was there and gone before he really had time to feel it.

"Should we hang out near the hotel?" Micha asked. "I don't wanna drink and drive." Simon saw, and saw that Sophie saw, that Micha was trying to help him.

"Lemme ask Franzi. Hey, Franzi." He was embarrassed to realize he'd interrupted an intimate moment with Christian, and told himself that was the same thing he'd felt about July a moment before, embarrassed to see her outside the usual context.

"I heard everything," Franzi said. "We'll fit in the van if we leave the stalker."

"Deal," Sophie said before Simon could.

~~~

Franzi suggested they buy some beer to drink in the hotel "like the bums we are." They went for the room Micha and Tanja were sharing because it was bigger. Franzi texted Simon: "You're welcome!"

He knew he should be grateful but, cute as Sophie was, it was all starting to seem like a lot of bother. He'd given her the wrong idea, set the bar too high with some uncharacteristic flash of charm, and wasn't feeling up for the follow-through. All he wanted was to lie back and not be likable. To ask Franzi why he couldn't get his shit together, and have her answer instead of trying to make him feel better.

Tanja flipped through muted TV channels in sync with some aggressively sexual Joan Jett album she'd put on. Micha, brushing his teeth at the foot of her bed, said something no one understood. Franzi was on Christian's lap in the desk chair. She whispered in his ear, and he looked over at Simon. Simon lay on Micha's bed trying not to think about how hotels never wash the outer covers and hating his sister for probably saying he was having a dry spell. Sophie opened two beers on the side of the bathtub and sat down next to him. Maybe Franzi had only whispered some sweet nothing. Maybe they weren't all sorry for him.

"We're going to Amsterdam tomorrow," he said.

"I wish I could come but I have class," Franzi said.

He couldn't tell if she meant it or was setting up what happened next: Sophie lying back, her beer upright on her stomach like his, staring at the same mottled ceiling and saying, "Me, too. So jealous."

He craned upward to drink without choking, and heard Tanja say what he should've: "You're welcome to come if you don't mind sitting with Simon. He's a total pain on road trips."

"Am not." But he'd rather let the invitation fizzle out unanswered than have Sophie know how much he wanted her there. "Remember our trip to

Amsterdam, Franzi?" Franzi always said they'd had a terrible time, but she'd been too young to remember and must've gotten that from their mom. It was a safe topic, free of surprises.

"How could I forget? Mom and Dad fought the whole time. All Dad could talk about was how it was so expensive and the canals are a breeding ground for mosquitos. But Simon loved this boat we went on. I've been hearing about it for over twenty years."

"It was great. They gave me a sailor hat." He felt safe and drowsy, like a kid being carried up to bed. "I guess you can't get away from class, either?" he heard himself ask Sophie, even though he'd decided not to.

She poked him in the ribs. "I don't have class. Did you mix me up with Mei?"

He pushed away the squirmy memory of a similar conversation with July. "I can't remember." Mei was a dream already fading, and Sophie too much a stranger to take her place. It was a lonely way to start a night together, if they even made it that far. Had he expected too much or was it just harder with everyone here to watch him fail?

"I told what's-her-face Mei had a top-secret new job."

"July." He thought about her kissing that guy, and why? Because she'd thought it would matter to him? "Don't be jealous, Mei." He sat up with a rush of dizziness, and everyone laughed too late, like they weren't sure he was joking.

"Of that sad sack? Yeah right."

"The main thing," Christian said, "is that you got her off your back."

"All thanks to my brilliant inspiration," Franzi said. "And Sophie, but I recruited her."

"*We* did," Christian corrected her.

"You said it was a bad idea because the stalker would sense it."

"But you talked me into it."

"Okay, okay," Micha said. Simon had forgotten him, assumed he'd fallen asleep next to Tanja, who was halfheartedly drumming on the bedspread to the beat of the music. "Some of us have to drive tomorrow. Let's take the party next door."

Tanja said she was tired, and Franzi stuck around just long enough for a hug. Sophie was holding a case of beer, so he felt okay asking her in for last call.

"Sure. I've got tomorrow off."

"Lucky you."

~~~

"I really do like your music," she said after a longish silence in which they sat on the edge of his bed, drank warm beer and—at least he—felt wistful for all the things this was not.

"Thanks. I really like you." He leaned in to kiss her laughing mouth, feel the soft heft of her breasts against his chest, unzip her dress, fumble with the hooks of her bra and not, absolutely not, under any circumstances, think about

Mei. If only he were drunk so he'd have an excuse if things didn't go well. He avoided her eyes as he felt around the pocket of his duffle bag for a condom, as if this might have been a misunderstanding and she didn't want him after all.

"Pretend I'm Mei." She slipped out of her panties.

"You are." He pulled her onto him and everything was good, was now and Mei and Sophie and wanting and having her.

Afterward he held her in a spoon and felt his guts bursting with happiness, safe in the knowledge that he didn't have to say anything. She'd think he was asleep. He faked a snore that must've become real, because he woke to the first light through the curtains he'd forgotten to close, and there she was, breathing softly through her open mouth.

The excitement he felt was more than getting hard looking at her perfect body and thinking about having been under and in her. He felt a soaring happiness he would've called love if he'd known her better. Or at all. He wanted to hold her so tight neither of them could breathe, make love more intimately, shower with her, drape the bathrobe over her shoulders and bring her breakfast in bed. But he let her sleep because the sun was only half up and she growled when he kissed her cheek.

He slept again and dreamt he was married and lived in the jungle gym his spoiled cousins from the suburbs had when he was a kid, and then woke in terror because he heard something slithering up the slide. The bed was empty.

The realization was like the harrowing moment before the first big drop on a rollercoaster, when the cart hovers there to make sure you get what's about to happen. Then he felt the warmth of the hollow in the covers, heard the shower. Only when he knew how wonderfully okay everything was could he admit how sad—more than that, some gutting, primal feeling he had no word for—he would've been to find her gone. But the feeling was too ridiculous even for him, so he rearranged his face to look tired, indifferent.

"Hope you left me a towel." He smelled like old sweat and semen, but was scared she'd leave while he was in the shower.

"Good morning to you, too." She knocked on the miniature coffeemaker next to the room service menu. "Will you be less grumpy if I try to operate this?"

"I'm not grumpy." He'd never been good at mornings. "Let me shower and I'll take you to breakfast."

"You don't have to." She seemed to mean it.

"As a favor to me."

"Be quick. I'm starving."

~~~

She didn't know anything nearby, so he took her to Fair Weather. He texted Franzi to see if she could join them but was relieved when she didn't reply. Chummy as they'd all been the night before, things felt precarious now. In retrospect, it had been obvious that Sophie was interested, but now he felt like he had something to lose. How many of his random hookups had turned into more? No matter how he racked his brains while pretending to read the menu, he couldn't think of one he'd seen again.

When the waitress came, he ordered scrambled eggs and coffee.

"Again?" she asked with a smirk. Thought she was calling him out for taking a different woman to breakfast every morning.

"Franzi showed me this place." Sophie didn't look like she cared, but he felt bad enough about himself without getting blamed for stuff he hadn't done. He was as promiscuous as he could manage, but didn't have the calculating double-agent or serial-killer mentality to conceal an affair. Or a partner to cheat on.

"It must be nice to have a sister," Sophie said, maybe also for the waitress's benefit. "Do you have bacon?"

"Um, we have soy sausage. This is a vegetarian café."

"That's what I meant. And eggs and some rolls. And a latte. *Real* milk, please."

"You're such a brat," he said when they were alone again.

"I know, but you like it."

"True." It was a good sign that she was still flirting. Breakfast was a good sign, too. She could've just ordered coffee. Wasn't it good that she felt comfortable enough to eat? Unless he was the only one who felt awkward eating in front of strangers. At least ones he wasn't so busy pretending to know. "So, what's your story?"

"My story?"

"Like your life story." It was a lazy excuse for conversation, but he didn't know where else to start. He felt exposed, like one of those blind moles thrust into the light of day. The feeling was so familiar it was almost an old friend.

"Um, I grew up in the suburbs and went to college here. I'm like 'really' a writer but I work at a copy shop. I'm an only child in case you can't tell."

"What do you write?" That old struggle again. His interest was sincere, but sounded like an act. He'd recited the lines so often they came out scripted.

"Experimental. Hard to explain."

Just as if he'd been faking interest, he said, "I'd love to read something of yours."

"Yeah, sure. You have to say that or you'd look like a dick."

"I do anyway, so why bother?"

"Touché."

"So I look like a dick?"

"Look, it's private. I'm trying to get something published, but it's different if someone I know reads it. Because then you'll think you know me. If I show you a story about a girl who wants to be an astronaut, you'll be all, oh, Sophie wants to be an astronaut. If it's a story about a guy who's terrified of commitment, you'll think that's me, or at least my ex."

"I don't think you should become an astronaut."

"I'd be good at it," she said as their breakfast arrived. "I have a great sense of direction."

"Guten Appetit! What was it in Peter Pan again, turn left and straight on 'til morning?"

She laughed, so that was alright. "So." She put on a serious face. "What about you?"

"My story?" Even as he told her a version of it, he regretted the need to make himself sound cooler. But he couldn't remember the last time he'd felt this relaxed in broad daylight with a woman who might like him. Other than July, because he didn't want her to like him. Then again, he didn't feel relaxed around her, either. "This is nice. I don't do this a lot."

"Eat breakfast?"

"With a pretty, smart woman I enjoy talking to."

"Thanks."

They shared an uncomfortable laugh because he'd said a big thing and she'd said something so small. Instead of backpedaling like he usually would've, he let the mood carry him. "I wish you really were my girlfriend."

"If wishes were horses," she said in English, but neither of them could remember the rest of the saying.

"You sure scared off my stalker. I haven't heard from her in at least twelve hours." There, now he'd turned wishing she was his girlfriend into using her to ward off July, and reminded her that other women—disturbed as they might be—were interested.

"I'm very intimidating." She glanced at her phone. "Besides, it was a good cause, and I know how much you love those."

Was she flirting or making fun of him? It seemed safer to keep talking about July. "At least she didn't make a scene. I never know what to expect with her." The words came out feeling true, but when he thought about it, he couldn't remember her ever making one.

"Lucky for her. I love drama, but I hate a scene I'm not making."

"I bet." He already knew she'd say no when he said, "It would be cool if you came with us." Backpedal, be facetious. "I might need your protection again."

She laughed, and he wanted to say, *no, really*, but he'd only regret that or turn it into a joke. His defenses were so good even he couldn't get past them.

"Look, I had a nice time, and you're cute, talented and a weirdo, which I'm into, but you don't know me. You've come up with this whole love story, but what do you actually know about me?"

"You write experimental fiction."

"Maybe I made that up."

"You definitely work at a copy shop. Franzi and Christian saw you."

"That's not the point."

The point was the same as ever: rejection, inadequacy, things never quite working out. Him fucking up in some subtle way he might understand later, but could never avoid at the time. "I guess I wanna get to know you." There he was guessing again, and it sounded like another line. There was nothing left to say, nothing that hadn't already been said in some cheap romantic comedy they ran at odd hours, or the cheaper, sadder comedy of his love life. Was he scaring her off by sounding insincere, or by being too sincerely into her?

He tried to cover both scenarios. "I'm meeting Franzi, so you still have time to change your mind." He asked for her number on a non-bleached, FSC-certified napkin, such a cliché it was almost original. Nothing he'd copied from July.

"I'll give it to you, but . . ." Her pout would've been cute if it weren't so frustrating. Another riddle he was too dumb to crack. What had he done wrong? He no longer cared whether she came with them, even preferred that she didn't. He wanted to be alone and not try to do anything right.

"But?" he asked for the sake of form.

"Never mind. I'm not coming, but write me sometime."

Instead of asking again like he knew he should, he got the check.

~~~

Franzi sounded sleepy and said they'd come to his hotel. Because she was part of a "we" now, like everyone else managed to be, at least part of the time. But he was getting along okay. He tried to recall the warmth of doing good, but it was all wrapped up in Sophie now, and he felt that droning pressure in his head that only crying could relieve.

Tanja was waiting for the elevator, but he said he was sick and hurried past.

"Call me if you need anything!" she yelled through the closing doors, and something about a pharmacy.

Someone had cleaned the room, eliminated the smell of bodies. His laundered pants were on the bed, the bird shit gone, and maybe the luck, too. He packed and searched the sheets and parts of the room she hadn't even been in for a trace of Sophie. When he was too young to know it was about suicide, he'd read O. Henry's "The Furnished Room" over and over, fascinated by all the things years of tenants had left behind. But everything was sterile here; if she'd forgotten anything, it had been removed.

Sophie was right about him wanting her to play a certain role, but there was more to it than that. He slumped onto the desk chair so heavily it crashed into the radiator, and told himself everything was fine. In through the mouth and out through the nose. It wasn't just her looks. She was an artist like he was, although he'd never say that aloud. Besides, wasn't there something to be said for chemistry? Why not keep seeing someone you felt attracted to?

With great effort, he got up, triple-checked that he hadn't forgotten anything, and took his bag downstairs. After checking out, he collapsed into an overstuffed chair. The pressure in his head would fade. He felt people looking and wished he'd shaved or at least combed his hair, but he hadn't wanted to make Sophie wait. Dr. F said to imagine people were looking at him because they found him interesting or attractive, but he wasn't there yet.

He got out his phone: emails from their site and from his mom reminding him and Franzi to take pictures. He would, with or without Christian, but he knew what Franzi would prefer. He liked to think his parents wouldn't be weird about Christian, but knew his dad would. Then again, Franzi had been this secretive about almost everyone she'd dated. Maybe she was as scared as he was of getting caught in something she couldn't live up to and couldn't find her way back out of.

His phone vibrated. Was Franzi bailing? The timing was tight, but he'd be happy to see her even for half an hour. He unlocked his screen and saw a perfectly framed photo of him and Sophie. It took him a second to realize Sophie couldn't have sent it and scroll down to July's caption: "Such a cute couple! Thought you and Mei might want this."

Something was happening in the core of him, past all his muscles and guts. What did he feel? Sad about Sophie? Guilty about lying? Sorry for July? He didn't see the next line right away: "See you in Amsterdam. Hope Mei will be there!"

How could she? Unless she suspected Mei was a sham. If he were July, he'd think that was worse. Knowing he didn't want her even though he was available. Or did she think it was a joke they shared, a battle of wits where she'd catch him out and win a relationship with him?

Maybe she didn't care as much as he thought. Seeing her kiss that guy, he'd assumed she was trying to make him jealous or using someone else to stop a gaping wound, the way he often had. But it didn't have to be like that. Maybe she'd used him as a pickup line, bragged about knowing the singer. He hoped so, and that she wasn't struggling to put on a brave face. If she were, why come see him again?

He wrote, "Thanks, I like that picture," then replaced "I" with "we." After a nauseous wave of guilt, he deleted everything and wrote, "Thanks, great picture."

Someone touched his shoulder and he dropped his phone on his lap.

"Whoa there," Franzi said. "Sorry to interrupt Candy Crush."

"Good to see you again." Christian shook his hand.

"Or were you texting a giiiiiiiirl?" Franzi asked.

"Wanna take a walk? I'll leave my stuff at reception."

~~~

"I'm assuming you slept with her?" Franzi said.

Christian pretended to consider a shop window, which was nice, not because Simon minded talking about sex in front of someone he didn't know very well, but because it helped him avoid thinking about that someone sleeping with his sister.

"Yeah." The word was so small it got lost in his throat. "We got breakfast at that place you showed me."

"Sounds promising."

"Great story about how you met, too," Christian rejoined the conversation. Simon couldn't decide whether he liked or resented his tact. Did it mean Franzi had told Christian how awkward and neurotic he was? Or was that an awkward, neurotic thing to think?

"I asked her to come with us." They stopped walking, even though it was clear that nothing had come of it. Otherwise, he would've said she was coming, not that he'd asked. "It was the usual thing." Like there was anything usual about this situation. "I said I wanted to get to know her, and she said I didn't know her well enough."

"Be persistent," Christian said. "Show her you're really interested, so she knows it's worth her while." He put his arm around Franzi's waist, and they shared an inside-joke smile that left Simon out in the cold. So Franzi hadn't wanted to commit. Or Christian had seen through Simon to the schmuck who didn't call the next day or ever.

"I know it's tough," Franzi said, "but what've you got to lose? If she's not interested and you call, nothing will happen, same as if you don't. But if she is . . ."

"Yeah, thanks." He wanted to change the subject without actually changing it. They were passing a scrawny stretch of park with a couple benches and a view of the Inner Alster. "Mom wants a picture of us. This is probably the best backdrop we're gonna get, right?"

"I'll take it," Christian said before Franzi could say whether she wanted him in it.

She stood on her toes to put an arm around Simon's shoulders.

"Smile!" Christian took some pictures on Simon's phone and some on his, which made this look even less casual. Good for Franzi. Nobody was perfect, but the fact that they'd met doing charity work was a good sign, and Christian made the kind of solid impression Simon never could.

"I'll take one of you two." Simon ignored the warning look in Franzi's eyes.

Her face softened as Christian put his arm around her and broke into a laugh when he leaned into a dramatic Hollywood kiss as Simon snapped a dozen pictures. They smiled so naturally, like people with something to be happy about anytime and anywhere. He smiled back but felt outside of them again, a voyeur taking pictures of happy strangers.

"Let me know when I can send these to the press."

"Never. When're you setting off?"

"I'll get you guys a coffee before we head back." He gestured at a generic-looking coffee shop across the street, where people in suits were reading papers or talking on Bluetooths.

"I wish we had more time," Franzi said when he came out with three lattes.

"You guys have to come visit. I'm thinking of getting a bigger place." He hadn't been until he pictured welcoming them into his little hovel. Franzi had already seen it, but she was family.

"We'd love that," Christian said. "We can catch a Hertha game."

"Definitely," Simon agreed, though he never watched soccer. "If you guys can stand more than twenty-four hours of me." It came out like an accusation, even though he was the one who had to go. But he hated leaving people he cared about. At the same time, so much had happened, it was hard to believe he'd only been there a day.

"We could come between semesters," Christian said.

He couldn't tell whether Franzi was sulking about the pictures, sad he was leaving or tired of him. "It was great to see you," he said, and was rewarded with half a smile. "Now help a poor lost tourist find his hotel."

~~~

Tanja was smoking out front and hugged everybody like she hadn't seen them in years. She was family, too, Simon thought with a surge of fondness. She and Micha were like siblings you saw too often to appreciate, but it helped not to be leaving on his own.

"Micha's getting the van. He's gonna drive first while I nap, so don't make any noise." Tanja pantomimed looking past everyone. "Where's Sophie?"

"Who knows," Simon said.

"Oh?"

"I'll tell you after your nap."

~~~

The first half of the drive was dull because Micha had his headphones on so Tanja could sleep. Simon couldn't find a comfortable position. He hated to think of going onstage without any break in consciousness, but his eyelids burned when he closed them, and he was excruciatingly bored, as if he'd already thought all the thoughts he could ever have.

He checked his phone, but there was only a smiley from July. She was down to a normal level of contact, but he didn't feel as happy as he should've. He was too distracted by the message that wasn't there. Feelings were stupid bastards sometimes. Sophie didn't even have his number yet, but it still felt like a punch in the guts not to hear from her. Maybe the feeling was preemptive, experimenting with the silence to come. But they got stuck in traffic near the Dutch border, so he fished out that stupid napkin.

He entered her number under "Mei" as a private joke with himself and wrote, "Hey." Looking out at the noise barrier and all the drivers and passengers staring grimly ahead, he added, "Wish you were here. Anyway, now you have my number." He deleted that and wrote, "Make any interesting copies today?" but that sounded condescending, so he switched to: "How about sending me something to read?" It didn't matter what he wrote if she wasn't interested. And if she lost interest because he said the wrong thing, well, he was bound to say the wrong thing sooner or later, so it never would've worked anyway.

He turned off his phone and lay down. Relieved that he could no longer check for a reply, he managed to doze for a while.

~~~

When Simon came out of the bathroom after carefully avoiding contact with fixtures, faucets and door handles, Micha had finished filling up the tank and Tanja was outside the convenience store with a tray of coffees. Something seemed off about her until he realized she didn't have a cigarette in her hand or mouth.

"Thanks," he said when she handed him a cup. "So you heard?"

"What?"

"Smoking's bad for you."

"I'm cutting back. I figured, if that loser Simon can do it . . ."

"Good point."

"Speaking of you . . ."

"Yeah?"

"Or should we wait for Micha so you don't have to tell everything twice?"

"Makes sense." There was a heavy feeling on his shoulders that could've been exhaustion or dread. What was there to tell? He took out his phone to check the time—that was his excuse—and remembered that it was off. As long as he didn't turn it back on, the possibility of a text from Sophie existed. Schrödinger's SMS.

"Franzi seems happy." Tanja changing the subject to spare his feelings only made him feel worse. "I put the gas on my card," she said as Micha came over. "Here."

"Thanks." He stuffed the receipt in his wallet where he was keeping a haphazard record of their expenses. "So, last night . . . ?" He nudged Simon.

"I'll tell you in the car." It was fine if they laughed, as long as they didn't pity him. Maybe everything had gone well, and he needed to relax. How would he feel if some random hookup said she wished he was her boyfriend? He would've bailed, too. Not that she'd bailed; she just hadn't wanted to leave town with someone she barely knew.

He made a deal with fate that, if he could keep from checking his messages until after he told Tanja and Micha, there'd be one from Sophie.

~~~

"Start as soon as I'm on the highway." Tanja maneuvered the van through the narrow lane between two rows of trailer trucks.

"There's not much to tell," he said once she'd merged into traffic and the needle of the speedometer was moving steadily to the right. She was a good driver, but they had to get on her case in speed-limit zones. "We slept together, we ate breakfast." He cleared his throat, took a sip of coffee to fill the break in his voice. "I said I wished we really were together, like in reference to her pretending to be Mei, and asked her to come with us. She said I didn't know her and I said I wanted to. I texted her."

"And?" Tanja made big eyes in the rearview mirror.

"And what?"

"I think what our esteemed colleague wants to know," Micha said, "is whether she replied."

"My phone's off."

The two of them burst out laughing as if on cue.

"What?"

"Wow," Micha said. "You're so into her you turned off your phone. What if she's been calling for hours?"

"Trust me, she hasn't."

"If I wanted to be a dick," Tanja said, "I'd say something about karma. All the girls you never called. Was it more like 'I'm not looking for anything serious' or 'I need to focus on my career at Copies 'r' Us'?"

"You *did* just say that," Micha reminded her. "And you *are* being a dick."

Simon's laugh came out as a sigh.

"She did seem into you," Tanja said. "Sorry. You know I'm as bad as you are."

"Worse," Micha said, and Simon felt left out, like she'd confided in him. "Anyway, what'd she say?"

He wished he hadn't mentioned the text, but then they would've thought he wasn't making an effort. What if she said something embarrassing like the sex had sucked? He held down the button until his phone vibrated back to life.

Two messages in two conversations. The first was from Franzi, and he felt bad for being disappointed. "So great to see you! Keep me updated and don't tell parents about C. Or else ;)"

He wrote, "You too! Don't worry, I won't," filled with the sinking knowledge that there was only one message left, one chance in the lottery.

It was from July. "Hey, my friend's going to this cool party in Amsterdam tonight. Wanna come? Let me know or see how tired you are. Looking forward to you guys!"

That was it. Had he overlooked something? Accidentally marked a message as read? Nope. But he'd asked Sophie to send him her writing, and she probably didn't have any on her phone. He'd have to wait 'til she got home from work. Didn't she have today off, though?

He opened July's text again. She'd written "you guys." Did she mean the band, or him and Mei? She seemed insecure for once, offering him an out. All part of her slowly but surely getting the message. It remained to be seen whether this friend would be a little more tangible than he'd been the night before. Unless she had a whole coterie of made-up admirers.

"Well?" Tanja asked.

"Nothing. Just texting Franzi."

~~~

After passing dozens of colorful canal-side houses with peaked roofs, they reached a bigger road and the soulless high-rise they were staying in.

"Scenic," Simon said.

"As long as there's Wi-Fi and a tub, who cares?" Tanja said. "And we get our own rooms." It was a conference hotel whose compact rooms only had single beds, so the label wasn't making them share.

"True." Vegging out in the tub did sound good.

"Who's up for touring the red-light district and getting stoned?" Micha asked.

"I feel like my head's gonna explode."

"Withdrawal will do that to you," Simon said.

"Good point." Even though Micha hated when people smoked in his van, Tanja had a cigarette lit before her feet hit the floor of the parking garage. "Looks like I'm even more of a loser than Simon."

~~~

Simon went through half the antibacterial wipes he'd bought in the lobby, then rinsed the tub before filling it. He put his music on shuffle and turned up the volume.

One foot in the water to get used to the temperature, he reread July's message. Replying didn't make him any more likely to hear from Sophie, but he knew July would write back. When she did, there'd be a couple sweet seconds where he could believe someone else had. Against all logic, making sure he got *a* text made it seem more likely that he'd get the one he wanted. He set the phone down within reach.

Lying back and pouring sweat, he felt his curls expand like some alien life form and had a sudden urge to shave them off, run his hand over a scalp as clean as sterilized metal. But going bald was one of his big fears, so why do it on purpose? He ducked his head and listened to the noisy silence underwater, wet sounds like the gurgling of some massive stomach, the drip-drip of the tap whose rhythm alternated between soothing and maddening. He sank deeper, closed his eyes and let water cover his face. This was what he'd wanted from sleep, a warm refuge to bury himself in. But he'd woken from his doze in the car even more disheartened.

What could he write without giving July the wrong idea? Something to karmically trick the universe into granting him a message from Sophie, stability and something like how he imagined adulthood for other people. He lifted his head and breathed. The thought of karma reminded him of what Tanja had said. It wasn't entirely true—plenty of women hadn't called *him*—but he couldn't deny that he'd hurt a couple.

July would reply to anything, so there was no need to get her hopes up. Why even stay in touch when he'd finally found an excuse she'd accept?

The answer was more obvious than he liked to admit. He was feeling shitty about Sophie and wanted attention from anybody, even July. Or especially July, who was guaranteed to think he was amazing.

He tried to picture her life. Did she live alone? Were the walls of her apartment bare, or plastered with pictures of Hare vs. Hedgehog? Maybe she had a shrine. He ducked his head to clear that disturbing image.

The point was she'd admitted defeat. Otherwise, she'd never have kissed that guy in front of him or said how great he and Mei were together. He could afford to be generous, reply, go to her party. At least, he could justify it that way, even if he saw through his own tricks and knew he only wanted to use her to feel less used.

"Sophie couldn't make it. We're all pretty tired but I'll ask about the party." He added the obligatory smiley. Sending an emojiless message was like having a neutral expression while everyone else went around with big zombie grins plastered over their faces.

She noticed before he did.

"Sophie?"

"Stupid autocorrect! *SHE. Mei." He wouldn't have answered so quickly, but he wanted to fix his mistake before she had time to think about it.

"Too bad. Wanna get dinner? My friend's working late so I'm on my own, too."

How could anyone text that fast? And why did she have a friend here or in Hamburg when she barely knew a soul in Berlin? She was an enigma, but not one he cared to solve. He'd wait five or ten minutes. Not long enough to offend her, but enough to slow things down. He drained the tub and wondered whether he'd be able to sleep if he got off and went straight to bed. He reached down to fondle himself, but his phone was like a person in the room watching.

He set an alarm and left his phone by the bed. Then he closed the bathroom door, dropped a dollop of complimentary lotion into his palm and got down to business. The lotion smelled like lemon, which had the pleasant if not sexy association of cleaning products. He pictured Sophie's soft, wet warmth, hard nipples and little belly pressing against his, her biting kisses. Just as he was getting hard, he heard his phone vibrating, July interrupting the image of Sophie like an emergency broadcast.

With great effort, he summoned up Sophie's mischievous smile, the feel of her skin. His breathing sped up, everything felt good and simple, and he was about to come when his phone went off again, the thought of July popped up like an ad, and things fizzled out in a few sad drops. He stepped back into the tub to rinse off. Even when July wasn't there, she managed to insinuate herself. But once he'd texted her that he was taking a nap, he felt a profound relief, and drifted off to cozy thoughts of all the things he didn't like about her.

His first thought when the alarm went off was how great it was that he'd slept. He felt empty, clean, like he'd been reset. Then he remembered that intrusive thought of July. He'd considered eating dinner with her to be charitable, donating time to make her happy. Now he felt grossed out.

He brushed his teeth, washed his face and checked his phone. Tanja said Micha was stoned and did he want to get dinner or a prostitute from one of those shop windows (just kidding)? Micha said, "Check this out!" and sent a selfie of him stuffing his face with space cake. July said okay. Sophie said nothing at all.

Even though he knew it was ridiculous, he wondered while getting dressed whether Sophie had somehow missed his message. What if she'd accidentally deleted it? He was inches away from calling her, so he called Tanja instead.

"It's fucking beautiful here!" she said. "I'll meet you downstairs."

He texted July that he was eating with Tanja. Then, because he felt invisible in the elevator, he called Sophie and hung up.

Walking across the lobby, he took pride in his brilliant inspiration. When she called back, he'd pretend he'd butt-dialed her. Oops, how are you, anyway? But by the time he spotted Tanja, he knew he'd made a mistake. He'd wasted his one call and had no way of knowing whether she'd noticed it. Besides, it wasn't realistic to call by mistake and hang up after one ring. If he tried again, the missed calls would start to pile up. He should've stayed on to reinforce the impression of an accident. Although it would've been creepy if she'd just heard him breathing.

"Hey." Tanja took his arm to steer him past a crowd of British men in neon bachelor-party t-shirts outside the hotel bar. One of these shallow, hearty young men, rowdy even before they were drunk, had found someone willing to spend her life with him. And Simon couldn't even get a text message.

Tanja led him along one of the canals, snapping pictures and raving about everything. They stopped to watch a move in progress across the water. A crane was lifting a piano to the top of a townhouse whose windows were open to receive it.

"I could totally live here."

"Yeah, I guess." What was she so chipper about? "Did you meet the woman of your dreams, too?" he asked as they continued walking.

"There's more to life than that. For some of us."

He could tell from the hard sound of her voice that he'd hurt her feelings, and wished he hadn't said anything. What a mean thing to wonder. Like people didn't have the right to be happy. "Sorry, I'm a douchebag." That got her smiling again. "I'm wrapped up in my stupid drama. It is nice here. Clean."

~~~

The club was in a former brick dairy with some glass add-ons. It was bigger than most places they played, but their opener was local. Besides, the further you traveled, the more tickets you had to sell.

"Fuck it, I'm faint with hunger and all I've heard from Micha is a stupid selfie," Tanja said once they'd taken a picture out front. "Let's find a restaurant, send him the coordinates, and it's his problem."

"Maybe he's full from that cake. Or tired of us."

"Who can blame him?"

She was in a great mood again the second they sat down at a sidewalk table nearby. They ordered beer, fries and croquettes whose contents they couldn't decipher.

"How's pining?" she asked after the fries and beer arrived, and he was about to say he felt okay when he saw her eyes go wide like a cobra had just reared up behind his chair.

"*There* you are," July said as if they'd had plans. She pulled up a chair.

"We only just ordered," Tanja said, and Simon kicked her under the table for apologizing, even though he had to bite his tongue not to.

"My friend loves this place," July said. "Best fries in the neighborhood." She grabbed one from their plate and slipped it into her mouth in an attempt at seductiveness that made her look like she might need the Heimlich maneuver any minute now.

"Is he Dutch?" he asked for the same reason she kept asking about Mei. Except that he didn't care whether she was lying. Or shouldn't.

She chewed for an unreasonable amount of time. "Yeah, but he's between here and Germany. How was your trip?" She turned to Tanja. "Simon said you were tired."

"Did he?" Her eyebrows rose.

"Yeah. What a shame Mei couldn't make it."

Tanja kicked Simon under the table, and he wanted to tell her it wasn't how it looked. July was only piecing together scraps of information he'd thrown her. He tried to stomp on her foot, but it was July who winced.

"Hey!"

"Sorry, I thought you were the table leg."

"Typical Simon," she said to Tanja, who laughed in the fakest way possible. "What's Mei's deal, anyway?"

Thank goodness for Tanja, who said, "I think he'd rather not talk about it."

"Did you have a fight? I'm sure it's no big deal." She tousled his hair, which might've been nice with someone else on the other end of the hand. Did she really think *she* could make him feel better? It just went to show she didn't actually give a shit about his feelings, but was always looking for her angle. How she could worm her way in with a touch here, some relationship advice there, and never the least shyness or restraint, no acknowledgment that they weren't close. It was like being followed by a private eye who didn't mind bending the law to chase down a lead. So far, she'd only skipped merrily over the boundaries of what was socially acceptable, but give her time.

"I really don't wanna talk about it."

"That bad, huh?"

He had one of his rare bursts of energetic anger, not the sullen resentment that often slumbered within him, but the burning urge to knock over their table. Then a waiter brought their croquettes and took July's order, and the moment passed.

"How about *your* love life?" Tanja asked. "I saw that make-out session."

"I'm just single and looking around." But she wasn't; she was staring so fixedly he couldn't eat. "I haven't been in a relationship since . . ." To Simon's relief, she trailed off instead of referring to her obsession with him.

"Anyway, the drive wasn't bad since Micha and I split it. Speaking of which . . ." Luckily, even someone as bizarre as July had to look at the person talking. As Tanja wondered aloud where Micha was and what he was on, Simon took the opportunity to wolf down his food until July turned back to him.

"I always thought you were the wild one, Siiimon." There it was again, that possessive way she said his name. Like a pet name only she used.

"I lead a quiet life."

"That's what they sent you to Springtime for? Your quiet life?"

He opened his mouth, then froze. How'd she know the name? He took a shallow breath. There was nothing uncanny about it. Rehab was a real experience he'd had in the physical world, even if it felt like it had taken place on another planet, outside of time. He couldn't remember mentioning the name in any interviews, but he had enough acquaintances she could've scoured for information. Tanja looked more shocked by his reaction than July's jibe, so he hurried to say, "That was just to get a possession charge dropped. And a lot has changed since then."

"I know." She knew or thought she knew everything. "A lot can change in a couple years. Sure has for me."

He wished he could take pleasure in someone calling their band life-changing, but it was only July.

"Simon's the marrying kind and looking to settle down," Tanja said. This time he aimed carefully before kicking her. "Mei just needs time to figure things out."

He couldn't tell whether she was saying that to console him or to keep July from getting her hopes up. Either one was a nice gesture, and he regretted kicking her. July was making yet another attempt to look like she got a lot of action by talking about the guy who'd driven her here or some past affair; he'd lost track. Even nodding was wearing him out. All he could think about was how much he'd rather eat alone with Tanja, or if there was a burst of smoke and July turned into Micha or pretty much anyone else. How could he have forgotten how stressful she was? It took him a second to notice she'd stopped talking.

"So when'd you break up?" Tanja asked her.

"A couple years ago, but he's a very emotional guy. He didn't wanna lose touch forever."

Struggling to imagine how anyone could pass up the opportunity to lose touch with July forever, Simon left Tanja to take the brunt of the small talk, first about Tanja's past gigs and then about July's copywriting work.

"Did you study that?"

"No, but I took a course. The Employment Agency was really eager to help me set up a business."

"Cool," he managed to say. A dazzling conversationalist as ever.

"What were you doing before that?" Tanja took over again.

"Oh." July turned to Simon, laughed and clapped him on the arm. "Not much of anything, right?" Like he had any idea.

Tanja asked for the check, and they all set out for the club. "Amsterdam's beautiful, isn't it?"

"Totally." Simon was grateful to her for this harmless topic and for her presence beside him, a buffer between him and July. Whatever he was so afraid of her doing, she couldn't do it now.

"I know," July said. "I used to think about moving up here, but it didn't pan out. Just another one of my escapist fantasies."

At the club, she made herself scarce by her standards, waiting outside for her friend, who did seem to exist since Simon later saw a white guy with dreadlocks put his arm around her, the two of them standing further from the stage than she ever did alone. She didn't even stop by the merch table after the show.

~~~

He hoped the party would feel like an afterparty since it was near the club. That people would come gush about the show or ask for autographs—all the things that usually embarrassed him, but might give him a boost tonight. July got there first and texted him the address. Since she'd never left a concert that fast on her own, it did seem like she was with that guy, but, July being July, Simon had trouble believing it was kosher. Was she passing off a random stranger as a friend? He couldn't see the point.

When they got there, he hesitated, trying to ready himself for human interaction until Tanja asked, "Are we planning to spend the whole night in the doorway?"

"It *is* a nice doorway." Micha had been loopy all evening, but at least it hadn't affected his rhythm.

The party was in a high-ceilinged building that could've been a gutted office or apartment block. The walls were shedding paint and there were piles of plaster in the corners. The colorful lights they'd seen from outside indicated that the crowd filled the whole place, but Simon was chary of using the dilapidated staircase. Some weird remix of a crooning singer from the twenties was playing. Judging by the people slumped on the few pieces of furniture, there was a good supply of drugs on site. He felt bored thinking about the effort of conversation, embarrassed that everyone would speak better English than he did.

Could he slip out? Tanja was at the bar, maybe a former reception desk, holding up her thumb and two fingers, so he'd have to stay for a drink. Micha was talking to some hipsters, but Simon had missed the moment to join the conversation, and the two steps it would take were too many. Was this social anxiety or apathy?

"House special," Tanja shouted in his ear, handing him a paper cup filled with eerie neon-green liquid.

"What's in it?"

She shrugged and slapped Micha on the back 'til he turned and took one of the cups.

Simon banished all thoughts of grimy hands making the drink and took a sip. It was sickly sweet with a high-proof aftertaste that burned his throat. "Did they have beer?" he asked, but Tanja had joined Micha and the hipsters. One was bald, and one had shaggy hair, but both had dramatic mustaches—a handlebar that made the bald one look like a villain who tied distressed damsels to railroad tracks, and a thick dictator mustache on the other. Simon put his arm around Tanja to draw himself in.

The villainous hipster was saying something about Nietzsche in broken German. He lifted the edge of his t-shirt to show them a Sanskrit tattoo.

"He can't remember what it says," the shaggy one said.

"Hey, let's get tattoos," Micha said.

"I already have twenty-two," Tanja reminded him, which shouldn't have been necessary since she was wearing a sleeveless shirt.

"But as a *band*." Micha was so touched he had tears in his eyes.

"Good idea," Simon said, although not only the needle but also the entire studio would have to come in a hermetically sealed pouch for him to be interested. The main thing was joining in. That way, after he sneaked out, the others would know he'd been there. He was annoyed with himself for being in such a bad mood. He would've had a great time showing Sophie off or making fun of other partygoers with her, and it seemed so pointless that she wasn't there. No, what was pointless was having met her at all, briefly entertaining the idea that it could work. Not just with her but the whole relationship thing. It was a drug like success. A taste was great, but it didn't last, and you needed it again and again to even sometimes feel satisfied. He'd been happy when they signed with Poor Dog, happy about every good review, but it didn't stick, and neither did some little shred of affection. He felt hollow, or like a tiny person trapped within the resounding emptiness of himself. If he banged on his chest, it would echo. "Does the Tin Man get a heart in the end?"

The shaggy hipster he'd interrupted glared at him.

"No." July's voice echoed and filled the room like the Great and Powerful Oz, then came into focus next to him. "Just a heart-shaped watch. Tick tock." She knocked on her chest, and he wondered whether she was hollow, too, and whether she knew he was. She handed him a paper cup, and he dropped the empty one he'd been holding.

"Thanks." The drink was a thin, blood-in-water red this time, but tasted the same. He would've preferred any other potable liquid, but it was easier not to leave the security of the group.

She drew him closer. "How about one of these?" As if performing a magic trick, she opened her hand to reveal two small pink pills.

"No thanks. I'm not into that kind of thing."

"Right. Just getting a charge dropped, wasn't it?" She sighed. "I should've known you never had it that bad. I mean, you're *you*." He wasn't sure what she was getting at. Maybe she'd already sampled a couple pills herself. "I don't have a problem, either. These are totally harmless and herbal."

"Sure. Coke comes from a plant, too. And cyanide and stuff."

"Cyanide doesn't come from a plant. But suit yourself. I thought it was your kind of thing." She tucked the pills into the condom pocket of her jeans.

"You thought cyanide was my kind of thing?"

She threw back her head and laughed like she'd probably read she should in some guide to flirting. He saw a cluster of red marks like bruises forming on one side of her throat.

"Wild night?" He pointed.

She slapped his hand. "That's a birthmark."

Although he was almost certain she was lying, there was a margin of doubt. She usually wore her hair down. He looked for other marks to see whether he remembered them. There was a beauty mark on one side of her jaw, a pimple or scar next to her nose, freckles on her forearms and, just below the sleeve of her H vs. H t-shirt, a broad fleck that could've been a fresh bruise or a shadow. Maybe if he saw her in a different light.

"What're you looking at?"

Another one of those glorious moments when she was caught off-guard. "Nothing. Let's see if they have something other than the house special." The lights were brighter at the bar.

"Drowning your sorrows?" she asked while they waited in line.

"You could say that." Because she was on his side, even if he didn't want her there. She'd feel bad for him if he said things were bad, think he was great when he knew he was a failure, and sympathize with his problems, whether or not they existed. Too bad she *was* one of his problems. In that sense, she reminded him of someone else who was supposedly looking out for him but always just tagged along and got in the way: himself.

She ordered in Dutch and threw some money on the bar, handed him a beer. He'd been letting people buy him drinks this whole time. What an asshole.

"Thanks. Next round's on me." He thought of the Spanish waiter, the Dutch bartender, the sign language she'd whipped out. "How come you speak so many languages?"

"I only know a little of each, except Dutch. It's different when you have . . . a reason to learn. Like with you and Japanese."

"Hm."

"So spill, Siiimon."

Trying not to wince when she said his name, he searched for the bruises but couldn't remember which side they'd been on, and now a green searchlight was playing over her skin.

"Does Mei not wanna be Frau Kemper?"

"Cheers." He knocked his bottle against hers. "The thing is . . ." He wanted the relief of confiding without providing any real information. "I'm not sure she's as serious as I am."

Before she could apply the balm of pity to his vague and dishonest wounds, a shadow fell between them. Her dreadlocked friend put a hand on her lower back and asked whether they were having fun. There was something uneven about his features and he had the kind of pale eyes Simon found unnerving, but he seemed nice. Wouldn't you have to be, to voluntarily seek out July?

"Yeah, great party!" Was he imagining it, or was July tense? Stretching her mouth below unsmiling eyes? She must be mad at her friend for interrupting.

Dreadlocks didn't introduce himself, but he bought them a round of house special before moving on, so Simon knew he meant well. He finished his beer and nipped at the sugary punch. A woman down the bar told him she'd been at the concert, and July held his drink and didn't even look jealous while they took a picture together. By the time the woman had gone back to her friends, he was starting to feel how strong the punch was. He didn't trust the warmth he felt toward July. If there was one sure sign he wasn't in his right mind, that was it.

But he didn't pursue the thought, because he was having enough trouble keeping up. He kept trying to tell her about Sophie, then they'd be at the other end of the room, talking to strangers. A few more had been at his show, but he didn't care anymore. He was terribly thirsty even though he kept sipping the disgusting punch.

July offered to get him some water. That was a great idea and why hadn't he thought of it? He'd take it easy. Then she was yanking his arm out of the socket and telling him he couldn't sit here. A group of girls was laughing and calling something to him. He couldn't understand and thought he was losing his mind until he remembered they were speaking Dutch. July dragged him out to the courtyard where the cool air was heavy with cigarette smoke and an occasional skunky whiff of pot.

"As I was saying." He couldn't remember what he'd been saying.

"About Mei." She put an arm around him to help him stand. Good old July.

"She didn't write back." There was a gentle blurring of real and imagined, things he'd told her, things he wanted to be true and things that were, and it was good of her to understand. He leaned in to kiss her, caught her burning-hot cheek instead of her mouth and adjusted his aim.

She kissed him back for ages before putting her hands on his chest to push him away. "What're you *doing*?" A few faces turned toward them from behind clouds of smoke. "I can't do that to Mei, or you."

"You already have." He no longer felt like kissing her, standing next to her or even standing at all, but was pleased with this unbeatable argument.

"You're upset, right? You can tell me."

Then they were on damp cobblestones even though she hadn't let him sit down inside and that was somehow like her. "I want what everybody wants." His tongue felt like it was falling asleep. "A wife and kids and somebody to tell me it's okay."

"It is okay. Tell me what happened."

He put his leaden head on her shoulder and felt the curve of her breast below his chin. Every time she took a breath, he had to focus on not spilling his punch. What was this about? Sophie. "Says I don't know her."

"Do you feel like that's true?"

He took a sip that made his eyes water and dribbled on her shirt. "Won't let me. But I want to." He wasn't sure which woman he was talking about, but it was the type of thing you said before kissing someone, so he lifted his head and even landed close to her mouth, but this time she yelled "Stop it!" so loud the background of voices hushed. He could hear crickets chirping in time to the music, or was that tinnitus?

"But you want me to," he murmured, surprised and bewildered when she burst into tears. He'd opened a book to the wrong page, and nothing was like where he'd left off.

She was towering over him, so he stood up, too. He had to hold onto her arm, but he finished his drink with dignity. She was saying, "How can you if you love her?"

"Who?" She stared at him with fish-wide eyes, already done crying, so he tried to remember. "Won't let me."

"I know how you feel." He'd said the right thing because her arm was around his waist, warmer than the air, than the wet on his face. He was crying, too. Why? Was he happy about this warm person? Knew how he felt. About what? Thinking was a physical exertion that was getting harder and harder. Was he sad because she wouldn't kiss him? She dabbed his face with her jacket and said, "There, there."

With the last of his mental energy, he remembered: "We're not together." The way his tongue stumbled over the words made him wonder whether he was speaking a foreign language like everyone else.

"You broke up? When?"

He couldn't remember. He tried to kiss her again but she was holding her jacket to his face, so he kept crying because they'd broken up. She was asking questions or maybe that was the crickets again, just sound. Maybe he was asleep, asleep standing up like a horse. Maybe he was a horse. He laughed, and she said "there, there" again.

"Were never together," he remembered, still laughing even though nothing had been funny for ages. A sudden pain in his face knocked him off his feet and onto something sharp and cold. Lightning? No, she'd hit him. Why?

"Is that true?"

The warmth on the back of his leg was pleasant until he realized it was part of a larger hurt. He pulled a shard of slimy glass out of the leg of his jeans.

"Oh, you're bleeding! I'm sorry!"

He touched his face to see if he was bleeding but couldn't tell. He wanted to cool it off with his drink, but the cup was empty so he dropped it.

"Were you lying this whole time?"

A smoky shadow moved closer.

"I think." He hadn't been listening but didn't want to offend her.

"You *think*?! What the hell's the matter with you?"

"Dunno."

She slapped him again, but it didn't hurt as much. No, he'd put his head on the ground.

"Go to hell. I'm leaving."

"Wait!" He reached for her arm and got a leg.

"Ow, stop!" Now she was next to him.

He wasn't sure she could hear him. "Help."

"Yeah, I'm good enough for that. Will you get up, you asshole?"

"Taxi," he slurred.

"It's okay, he'll take us."

He was having trouble keeping his eyes open. There was some fuss about walking, but then he sat down somewhere warm. The van? When he called out, Micha didn't answer, so he wrenched his eyes open. Not the van. A man in a baseball cap was driving, a cup of punch in the pull-out holder between the seats; he'd vomit if he had any more. July's voice speaking gibberish; no, Dutch; then, "Go back to sleep, Siiimon."

~~~

He must've slept a long time, because the next thing he was aware of was lying in bed surrounded by glaring sunlight and a terrible smell. Someone—he, because he was covered in it—had vomited all over. He couldn't believe that much had fit in his stomach, but the stench made him think more might come out. There was a noise, too, a pounding coming from outside his head. He tried to get up, but the room was a shaken snow globe.

"Coming!" His throat felt like he'd eaten broken glass, and he remembered something about that, but the knocking continued, so he crawled to the door and pulled himself up by the knob. The blinding pain between his eyes made it hard to see Tanja.

"Holy shit, are you okay? It reeks in here!"

"I need . . ." It took a lot of energy to bring that thought to a close. ". . . help."

"I'll get Micha."

He sat in the shower with his clothes on and didn't undress until he'd gotten the vomit off. He traced the brown trickle of blood to the back of his left leg. That was it, the thing about glass. He felt the wound to make sure there was none left in it, hung his wet clothing over the shower rail and gargled hot water before struggling into clean clothes. The pain in his head was so glaring he couldn't keep his eyes open, but he found his sunglasses, and that helped.

He had to sit and rest a few times, but managed to wipe up most of the puke with towels and complimentary shampoo. He must've left the door open because Micha came in without knocking.

"Rough night, huh? Tanja's getting you some breakfast."

"Mm." He didn't think he could eat, now or ever again.

"Let's go to my room." Micha used his right arm to prop Simon up and his left hand to cover his mouth and nose.

~~~

Simon threw up one more time, but just in his mouth. Micha was a little worse for the wear, but Tanja looked like a good night's sleep.

"You disappeared last night," Micha said as Simon gargled with his mouthwash, wondering which of them he was talking to.

"I met a girl," Tanja said.

"That explains why I didn't see you. I saw *you*, though." Micha winked at Simon in the bathroom mirror.

"Come on," Tanja said. "We're already late."

"Time flies, huh?" Micha seemed to think Simon's condition was some kind of lark.

"The bags are downstairs," she said. "They let us stay because I said you were too sick to move. Try to look ill."

"Shouldn't be hard."

~~~

"Did you take something last night?" Tanja asked after he spent the first fifteen minutes of the drive dry-heaving out the window.

"Nope, just punch and beer."

"It was a fun party," Micha said, "but who knows what was in that house special. I mostly stuck to beer and pot; at least you know what you're getting. Although I was wigging out a bit. I could feel that old building closing in on me. So I went outside, and you know what I saw?"

"Leave him alone. Can't you see he's sick as a dog?"

Simon tried to think what Micha was talking about. The part of the night he couldn't remember seemed to consist of vomiting in his room. Had he taken a taxi? No, he'd been in the car with that guy and an angry woman who wasn't Tanja, telling him to sleep. Why angry? July, angry because he'd kissed her. No, something else. He focused on breathing and sipping water until he felt safe closing the window. He had most of the pieces but needed to put them together in the right order, and each one weighed a ton. He was pouring sweat. "What'd you see?"

"You at July's feet! I thought she'd offed you, but then you moved."

"And?" If he'd seen him kiss her, that would be the obvious thing to tease him about.

"Nothing. I went to get a snack. Was there more to the story?"

They'd find out sooner or later, if not from him, then from July. How many shows was she coming to? He looked for his phone and wallet, was relieved to find them in his bag. Good thinking, whoever put them there. Otherwise, his phone would've showered with him. So much for handing in his keycard; it was tucked into his wallet, envelope and all. Some cash was missing, but that could be from buying drinks. "Can you plug in my phone?"

Micha reached back for it. "Only if you tell us what happened."

"I kissed July. I was totally out of my head. I told her I made up Mei."

"Why'd you tell her?" Tanja asked. "Sort of defeats the purpose."

"So she wouldn't be mad? I don't know. That's when she hit me and I fell on that bottle." He patted the back of his leg, swaddled in toilet paper under his jeans.

"Why'd you kiss her?" Micha asked. "You must've been sooo wasted."

"It's like I didn't remember who she was."

"That party was bad news," Tanja said. "I wouldn't be surprised if somebody slipped you something."

"I wouldn't be surprised if *July* slipped him something. Think about it: She gets you alone in an unfamiliar place. You're having a polite drink, then, next thing you know, you're kissing a person you usually avoid at all costs, then you're violently ill. Sounds pretty suspicious to me."

Simon couldn't picture her doing that. Bizarre as July was, criminal activity would've been a dramatic development. Anyway, why drug him and then turn him down? It could've been a mind game, but why toy with somebody who could hardly stand? Another piece of the puzzle was weighing on him. When he turned it over, he saw two pills in July's hand.

"She wanted me to take these pills, but I didn't."

"Did you have any other symptoms?" Tanja asked. "Other than being totally fucked?"

He strained to force his thoughts into their proper places. "I was so thirsty. She said she'd get me some water." Had she? All he could remember was sticky punch.

"Were you all touchy-feely?" she asked.

"Yeah . . ." He remembered his head on her chest. But did he have to be drugged to long for human warmth?

"Fact is," Micha said, "you should find out. Say you don't wanna press charges but you need to tell the doctor."

His stomach lurched all over again at the thought of calling July, who now saw him for what he really was, all smoke and mirrors and imaginary girlfriends. "I don't . . ."

Tanja interrupted. "I'll call and say you're in the hospital. She'll panic. And you can still press charges. We'd back you up."

"Thanks." He felt like he'd entangled himself in an even more elaborate lie. Until he told her about Sophie, July hadn't had any more reason to be pissed than usual, and his consciousness was already flagging by then.

Tanja's eyes caught his in the rearview mirror. "You don't have to say, but did you have sex?"

"No." He remembered that period of darkness. "I don't think so."

"You don't think so?" She shifted into the exit lane.

"I passed out."

"So she might've taken advantage."

Micha snickered.

"The fuck are you laughing at?" she snapped. "You think sexual assault is funny?"

"No, I was . . . thinking about something else. Sorry."

"I wouldn't have been able to . . . but . . ." The thought was terrifying. Lying there, unable to move; July vindictive, enjoying having him in her power.

"Don't worry; I'll handle it." She turned down the service road. "Just unlock your phone."

His eyes automatically moved to the notifications once the screen came on, but there were no new messages, and what did he care? Sophie was a million miles in the past, separated from him by hours of bitterness and years of wasted hopes. Not to mention all the vomit. It was strange that July hadn't written, but that only confirmed their suspicions. Why text someone you've taken some bizarre revenge on? "I had my clothes on when I woke up," he remembered with relief as he was starting to feel the entomological after-touch of strange hands on his clammy, goosebump-covered skin.

"Good." Tanja pulled into a parking space. "Why don't you guys get some snacks while I call our little friend?"

Micha headed for the store, but Simon lingered to ask, "Your friend, the one with the stalker?"

She inhaled sharply. "Yeah?"

"Did the police charge him?"

"That was a really different situation. He was menacing from the start."

"So?"

"He broke in and killed her. Sorry I brought it up. I was just trying to tell you what to expect if you reported July."

"I'm sorry." He felt the need to say something about her dead friend, but also like she was right to offer him her regret. Not because she'd told him something upsetting, but because of what was waiting for him down the road. He could've taken July in a fair fight, but what if she drugged him again? She could've slit his throat without waking him.

"You coming?" Micha called from the doorway.

~~~

He forced himself not to think of anything except what food wouldn't turn his stomach. But he was constantly aware of Tanja outside on his phone, July waiting to pop up when he least expected it. The convenience store was blaring generic, self-congratulatory pop about clubbing. His head throbbed to the beat.

Micha caught him staring into space, and he grabbed a bag of pretzels.

"Listen." It was that tone Simon hated, the pre-pity tone. "I wanna apologize for laughing. It has nothing to do with masculinity. If you're drugged, even a baby can do something to you. I mean, not an actual baby, because they can't even hold up their own heads, but certainly a toddler, I think, or . . ."

"Thanks, Micha." Did he think he was making it any less uncomfortable? Aside from any issues Simon would've had about being a victim of sexual assault, he was ninety-nine-percent sure he wasn't. It felt wrong to accept Micha's sympathy, but if he insisted nothing had happened, they'd think he was putting on a stiff upper lip. It was his fake drug addiction all over again.

They thought they knew exactly why he was upset, but they were wrong. Not even he did. He stood outside, not having a cigarette because he didn't want to worry about dying even more often, but wanting one. He'd left Micha to pay, and Micha hadn't complained because the stalker was going to murder him, so everyone had to be nice.

Was that it? His vulnerability the night before? He wasn't sure he'd had anything except too much alcohol. But they could test for that. He'd see a doctor. He spoke a little French, or did they speak Flemish in Brussels? It would be alright. If she'd given him something really harmful, he'd be feeling worse and not minimally better.

When Micha came out, he reached to take one of the shopping bags, and the bottled water dragged him down like a weight tied to the string of a balloon. But Micha was a few steps ahead and didn't notice, so he straightened up and carried on.

He couldn't believe Tanja was still on his phone. Wasn't it supposed to seem urgent?

"I'll let him know." She hung up and handed it to him.

His most recent call wasn't from July. It was from Sophie.

~~~

"Let's talk about July first," Tanja said when they were back on the highway, Simon mechanically grinding pretzels between his molars, imagining the bland matter soaking up toxic green liquid in his stomach as he watched half-intelligible billboards go by: "Elke zondag open!" "Makkelijk en snel!"

"Yeah, let's." That was a known problem, not out of left field like the other call. He knew he'd be more upset, intrigued or anxious if his head weren't filled with the world's thickest molasses, but he could listen to Tanja now and feel something later.

"I couldn't reach her. Go figure: The object of her obsession calls for the first time ever and she doesn't answer? There's no way, unless she's feeling guilty or planning something else. I say we tell the police."

"The police?" he echoed the meaningless words. "I thought I'd see a doctor."

"If it makes you feel better, of course," Micha said with such hearty concern that he immediately lost interest.

"We can tell the Belgian police in case she turns up, then file a complaint back home."

"Okay, if you think . . ." He was overcome with lethargy and put the pretzels away. If he closed his eyes now, if they stopped talking, he'd still be too weary to sleep. The thought of all the calls, language barriers and paperwork made him feel like he was on another planet whose heavier atmosphere was crushing him inch by inch.

"Don't worry; I'll help," Tanja said.

"Me, too," said Micha.

"Thanks, let's just get there first." Again, he had the feeling that everyone was being nice because something terrible was about to happen to him. He tried to dismiss it as paranoia but couldn't get himself to believe his own rational arguments. How could he feel so sure July would kill him when he wasn't even sure she'd drugged him? Maybe because he was perpetually crying wolf, spinning a web of lies, and now trapped and waiting to be sucked dry.

He closed his eyes, slipped off his chest strap and lay down. The buckle from another seat was digging into his neck but he didn't care enough to move.

"Don't you wanna know about Sophie?" Tanja asked from a million miles away.

"No," he either thought or said. He remembered calling out from the back-seat of that other car. There he was again, hearing a woman's voice, July instead of Tanja. The guy in a cap. He yelled, but no one answered. He clambered into the front to find that the empty cap was propped on the headrest, and he was speeding into oncoming traffic. Instead of screaming or trying to wrench the wheel in another direction, he sat back and watched it come.

~~~

The piss test was negative, which the friendly doctor said didn't mean much. In his great English and almost unintelligible accent, he offered to do a blood test, which Simon felt too woozy for, or a hair test. Once Simon understood that drugs would show up in his hair for longer, he said he'd wait. The doctor gave him some charcoal tablets and wished him a pleasant stay in Brussels.

In the waiting room, Tanja looked up and Simon shrugged. "I'll get a hair test when we get home." There was something exhausting about the words *when we get home*. He'd never been in love with Berlin, but now he felt every inch of the distance, like he was floating in space. Like getting home wasn't all that certain. Then his visit to Franzi kicked in, and he felt guilty because so many people in the world could never go home. He resolved to help again, but the intention was less sincere than the guilt.

"I found the closest police station," Tanja was saying.

He sighed. "Let's wait and see if she turns up. We can tell the German police, though, right? She's been stalking me in Germany, right?" He caught himself needing affirmation after every sentence. Was it right, or was he blowing this out of all proportion? Maybe he was someone who'd always had a problem with moderation and had a few too many with a clingy fan. Was he trying to get back at her for not wanting him the one time in all of history he'd wanted her? Or was he falling back into the usual stagnating laziness that made it so much easier to agonize over hypochondriac fears than to see a doctor? Talking to the police would be a hassle.

"Sure," she said. "I'll call them."

He couldn't tell whether she was keeping something from him. She'd said on the way to the doctor that she told Sophie he was sick.

"That's it?" he'd asked.

"Pretty much."

That "pretty much" was bothering him now. The call had lasted too long.

They had to cross the Grand Place to get to their hotel, and she wanted to stop and take a picture of every gilded and molded facade, to know which trade had once had its headquarters there. He didn't know whether it was the travel or her conquest the night before putting her in such a good mood. He was feeling good himself in the euphoric aftermath of nausea, thrilled to keep down those pretzels and see straight. He let her enthusiasm carry him, shared her anger when tour groups wandered in front of her pictures or scaffolding covered an important landmark.

I stay in my room too much, he thought, but it was only an idle observation, not an impulse to change. Even though he was feeling better, locking himself in a room sounded great. At least he'd visited one more sight here than in Amsterdam.

~~~

Predictably, the police didn't just want to talk to Tanja, so she brought her phone into the room Simon was sharing with Micha. Repeating the address of their hotel in Amsterdam, he could tell the call would take ages and not get him anywhere. It was one of those awkward conversations where someone keeps asking questions but doesn't seem interested in the answers. Was she even recording them? The sense of futility kept his responses short, but then he'd worry about sounding cagey and go into unnecessary detail.

Tanja slipped him a note on hotel stationery: "Should we wait?"

He shook his head and made a blah-blah gesture as she and Micha left. "Sorry, what?"

The officer wanted to know if July had left anything behind or stolen anything.

"I'm not sure," he said for the millionth time.

"Would you like us to give her an official warning?"

"Please do." They'd already been through the fact that he didn't know her last name, and it couldn't be *that* hard to find someone named July. "I'll give you her number."

"You have her number?"

"She, uh, stole my phone and put it in." That sounded like something he should've mentioned. Or like an excuse he'd made up. "I was having coffee in Volkspark Friedrichshain, and she turned up. She did it while I was in the bathroom."

"You left your belongings where she had access to them?"

"We were having coffee. I didn't . . ."

"Yes?"

"I didn't take it seriously. I thought she was just annoying and I was doing her a favor."

"Doing her a favor," she repeated, as if reading from notes he wasn't sure existed.

"I know I sound like an asshole," he said before he could help himself. "But it's hard to tell where you draw the line with fans. I mean, lots of strangers take pictures of me or want autographs." Hopefully Tanja had explained about the band so it didn't sound like he had delusions of grandeur.

"I certainly don't think you're an asshole," she said in a dry bureaucratic tone that put everything in quotes. "What was that number?"

Afterward she thanked him and said, "We'll have a word with her."

"Thanks, I feel a lot better now," he lied.

~~~

He texted Franzi to ask when she could talk, thought about calling Sophie but didn't know what to say. The urgency of that situation had petered out in her silence. He might not feel that way if he heard from her, and maybe that was what he wanted to avoid.

He had the urge to write something about the creepiness of the night before, but that would practically be an invitation for July to keep stalking him, so he returned to that Poe image and the diseases where people back then would think you'd died and bury you alive. Under the working title "Fainting Sickness," he described the feeling of watching the preparations for his own autopsy from behind seemingly dead eyes. Half-spoken verses and then the hook, which he sketched out as "I am in your hands / I am under your hands / and you can cut me open / again and again." He messed around on his guitar until he'd put a skeleton together, starting with the chorus, then slowing it down and adding a few melodic excursions for the intro. Once he'd gotten that far, he got out his phone to research a better name, but got distracted by a nineteenth-century church where parishioners had passed out because of fumes rising from the burial plots the corrupt pastor was selling under the floor. Later someone had turned it into a dance hall. Now if that wasn't great material.

Then the impossible happened: He felt hungry. He headed back the way he and Tanja had come, thinking they'd speak English in that touristy area and he wouldn't get lost. But he did, and found himself in a crowded market selling everything from horsemeat to bathrobes. He bought a crepe and a latte, then made his way to the less smelly end, away from the fish and cheese, near the textiles and impostor perfumes. All the benches were taken so he sat on a bollard to eat and add: "Did you hear my prayers / Are you dancing with me / Are you in my lungs / or under my feet?" A more intimate creepiness. For the bridge, he took an incremental refrain he'd written at rehab, missing and hating Nadine, but never used: from "And I promise you this, baby, I'll put flowers at the foot / of your unmade bed" to ". . . I'll lay flowers at the foot / of your unmarked grave." It felt true, not only about his fear of being physically trapped, but also the trap of all love-hate relationships. Was there any other kind? He could've sworn he'd never thought about killing Nadine, but the lyrics suggested otherwise. There were things you preferred not to know about yourself.

He didn't have the distance to see whether it was any good, but at least he'd left his room. Tanja and Micha would see that he wasn't freaking out. He sent them a picture of the market so he'd look like a normal, fun person having a normal, fun time. By the time he finished eating, Micha had replied with the coordinates to a chocolatier, and he hurried there before the urge to return to his lair could get the upper hand.

His phone buzzed twice. Should he hope for two texts from Sophie, desperate to reach him? Or something incriminating from July? That thought made the food squirm in his stomach, so it probably wasn't what he wanted.

He had two messages from Franzi, one asking if he had time that evening, then another saying she was dumb for forgetting his show and could he call the next day? She'd be working but try to pick up.

"Cool, talk to you then." The foreign city underscored his loneliness in a way Berlin never did, and he tried to think of someone else to contact. If he called his parents from the tour, they'd think something terrible had happened. Sophie would take more concentration than he could muster with the sun broiling the back of his neck and all the sidewalk tables and tourists to squeeze past. Most numbers in his phone were outdated, people he'd lost touch with. He had Soledad's but only ever messaged her to trade shifts or share the occasional meme. He remembered being in the same situation with Micha, letting a random coworker see the depths of his despair, and decided to skip it. He stopped for fresh-squeezed juice to keep his hands full and convince himself he wasn't coming down with anything, and then he was there, Tanja insisting he try the "decadent" hot chocolate she and Micha were having at a sidewalk table, and everything a bit irrelevant. But they had a chair and menu for him, so he tried to smile and seem present.

Micha interrupted Tanja's meandering description of the EU district and some palace to say, "I know you've had a lot of crazy shit happen lately, and I wanted to say, it's chill if you're mixed up. I'd personally be way worse off."

"Thanks," he said over the resentment filling him up to the back of his throat. He was grateful when Tanja asked if he'd called Sophie and teased him about playing hard to get. It felt more natural.

"What do you think she wanted?"

"To say hi? It's on her since she called."

"Yeah, but I called first. And texted."

"Make like you're being a gentleman 'cause you slept with her. Women like that." Micha looked at Tanja. "Right?"

"I don't know about gentlemen; I'm all about the three-day rule."

Micha tried to find out more about Lara from the party, but Tanja was evasive. Simon had hot chocolate and a double espresso, feeling too warm but also more alive. He decided to call Sophie. It would be good to be nervous about that, take the heat off the show and July, who hadn't so much as posted on their site. The evidence was damning, but he didn't quite believe it. He'd never given two shits about her, so he couldn't figure out why he was so eager for her to be innocent. It was high time he focused on people who mattered, and let her disappear with the little dignity that remained her.

~~~

Sophie didn't answer, and that was a relief because he had no clue what to say, and the fear of the call going badly made her less appealing, like a funhouse mirror that turns even a beautiful face grotesque. He was well on his way to convincing himself he was better off without, or at least making that the official party line.

He didn't see July before, during or after the show, and that was less of a relief than it should've been. Because it meant he'd falsely accused her, or because he needed another hit of unconditional adoration to keep going? He told Micha he wasn't feeling well.

"Try again tomorrow." Micha turned off the overhead and switched on his reading light. "Sophie was probably at work."

Simon made his breathing slow and loud, let Micha think or pretend to think he was asleep.

~~~

He called Franzi from the van but couldn't say everything he wanted to because the others were there, probably wondering why he was calling his sister instead of the first viable love interest he'd had in ages.

Franzi was worried about him drinking too much. It didn't occur to her that he might've been drugged until he said so. "Wow." He could hear someone in the background and a staticky sound as she covered the receiver. "That's what you think?"

"I haven't heard from her since, which makes her look guilty. Right?"

"Yeah, or the police scared her off."

"Yeah." He didn't bother explaining that she'd stopped contacting him before he reported her; Franzi was on break, and he didn't want to waste time.

"I missed Sophie's call and haven't been able to reach her since." He tried to make it sound like a trivial aside, but the effort made it seem even more important.

"I hope you guys are cool, 'cause she let us use her discount. No, seriously, give her another call. What've you got to lose?"

A voice in the background interrupted. "Gotta run. I know where she works so I'll beat her up if she's mean."

"Franzi? I want you to help me do something good."

"Like what?"

"I'm not sure, I . . ."

"Great, the second you get back. Bye!"

What did he have to lose? It was one of those useful and useless catchalls that applied to every situation and therefore meant nothing. He tapped "Mei," but hit Cancel instead of Call. No need to rush. That was another brilliant piece of advice. He was coasting toward old age and death, but why hurry? What did he have to lose?

He texted Sophie to ask when she got off work. She replied that she had the day off, and he felt cold sweat between his fingers and on the back of his neck, that feeling of being watched, though Micha probably thought he was playing a game, and Tanja should've had her eyes on the road. It was less the feeling of being seen than of being seen through, by Sophie and the world at large. No matter what lengths his craving for approval drove him to, it was never enough. Behind the record deal and the fans, he was still the same old loser without a date to the school dance. The guy in the train you avoided eye contact with, the lone wolf heading home for the night while everyone else went out. No, more like a lone poodle.

He wanted to hand everyone he met a disclaimer saying he wasn't fun or interesting; they bore sole liability if he wasted their time. But he always ended up caving and letting someone think he was cool, and the mere thought of keeping up that charade wore him out. Still, no amount of agonizing prepares you to jump off a cliff, so he made his mind a blank and called Sophie. "Hey, how are you?"

She laughed. "I saw your sister's boyfriend. How can anybody need so many copies?"

"Don't complain; they're keeping you in business." He tried to think where they'd left off. "You never sent me anything. I've been bored out of my mind."

"That's why I called," she said, even though he had first. "What's your email address?"

Spelling it out, he wondered whether she'd really send something and what this was all about on her end, but had no time to catch hold of the thoughts as they scurried across his mind, leaving only faint tracks. He told her about the night of the party, skipping over the kissing and slapping, but she sounded so unsurprised he knew Tanja already had. "What've you been up to?"

"Do you like horror movies?"

"Yeah, but I haven't seen one in a while." He had a membership at the video store where Micha worked, but it had been a while since he rented a movie instead of flipping channels. Still, he loved horror movies for their cathartic nature, for the rare gift of fear that was optional, not his, could be turned off and would be defeated in a couple hours regardless.

"I saw this great one about a monster under the bed. Or sometimes in the closet. I had to sleep on the sofa because there's no room for a monster under it."

"I think I saw that one." That monster who'd shooed all his anxieties away for the length of the movie, only to join them later: Was it a sign? Be calm; try to flirt. "Too bad I'm away. Monsters never come out when I'm there. We have an unwritten agreement."

She laughed, and he thought, there are plenty of copy shops in Berlin. His heart leapt into his throat in case she knew what he was thinking, but she kept talking about movies. She preferred the gory ones and mentioned some torture-porn flics he'd never wanted to see. By the time she said she had to go, they'd been talking for twenty minutes and hardly said anything.

What was the harm in asking whether she was seeing anyone? "Sophie?" But he remembered that she was going to email him and the question might be easier in writing. "Don't forget that story."

"Sure." She hung up before either of them said bye.

~~~

After two more shows without a sign of July, Simon felt more relaxed. They had some time off in Paris, and Tanja was leading them on an endless hike up Montmartre. He hid his lack of breath behind a silly grin as they wound through a narrow street, past shops selling postcards, feather boas, and Eifel Towers from thimble-sized to wouldn't-fit-in-a-suitcase. His last trip to Paris had been right after his parents' divorce when his mom took him and Franzi to show their dad how great life was without him. He'd gotten lost in the Louvre and cried silently for what felt like hours, but when he found the others at the Mona Lisa, he pretended he'd only gone to the bathroom.

He stopped to take pictures on the stone steps leading to Sacre Coeur. It was warm but wouldn't have been too warm without the hike, and the sky had that brilliant blue they always Photoshop onto postcards. They'd arrived early that morning or late the night before, crashed for a couple hours in one room with French TV running, and woken at sunrise. Or been woken by Tanja, who insisted she knew her way around Saint-Germain-des-Prés. They must've trudged past the same moss-covered cemetery about five times before she let them use Google Maps. He'd had the most expensive cappuccino of his life at Café de Flore, but it was cool to think Hemingway had hung out there, which of course was what they were counting on him thinking.

Sitting outside the café like in that one Van Gogh painting, or panting at the doors of Sacre Coeur now, he felt what every other schmuck here felt, like he had some special understanding and appreciation, a connection to the city. That only an *artist* like himself... What nonsense. He'd forgotten most of the French he'd learned in school, and his aesthetic was all wrong for chansons and Second Empire architecture.

Then he felt the other thing every other idiot here was feeling, except the ones who'd been smart enough to bring a date. Looking down at the impossibly green lawn—why wasn't it trampled? Did they replace it once a week?—and fairytale buildings shrinking in the distance, he thought, if only I had someone to share this with.

He did, of course, and Micha soon had his arms around him and Tanja for a selfie, but it wasn't the same. Much as he knew the feeling was an illusion and having a date would only have distracted him, he was overcome by wistfulness that filled and lightened him like joy even as it pumped tears into the space behind his eyes. He wasn't longing for Sophie or any past love, but some perfect someone who'd understand without a word, or look at him and say, "I know."

"Okay, take three, because someone's eyes were closed *again*."

~~~

The Eiffel Tower was more exciting from below because the view from inside was through a metal grid. Safety first, though. Otherwise, Simon would've been too scared to go up. By the time they got back down, he was beat, but didn't want to say so. He'd be hearing about it forever, how they went to Paris and he stayed in the room. Or thinking it himself, which was worse.

Micha wanted a snack from the makeshift fair behind the tower, and Tanja said she'd buy Simon a drink if he let her take his picture on the double-decker merry-go-round. "For our next album cover."

"Sure." Look how fun he was. "But you come, too, so I don't look like a pedophile."

"I'll take it," Micha offered, tucking his paper cone of fries under one arm and wiping his greasy hands on his jeans.

Simon was glad to sit down, even on a blue horse with a plume on its head. His mount rose and fell to a kitschy waltz he was on the point of identifying when his phone rang.

A Berlin number. He had the sinking feeling he knew whose.

"Hello?" It was expensive to take calls abroad, but there was always the slim chance of good news. Sophie saying she'd moved to Berlin. Or something realistic. Tanja rolled her eyes from the unicorn on his left.

"Herr Kemper?" He didn't recognize the man's voice.

"Yes?"

"Berlin Police Department, Detective Weinert speaking. You filed a complaint last week?"

"Yes." He had to bite his tongue to keep from pouring forth all his justifications.

"We've been trying to reach Frau Tappet at the number you provided and her landline. We're looking into her employer, but—"

"She freelances."

"Oh?" The voice was like a raised eyebrow.

"She said so when she turned up near my apartment on a weekday. To explain why she wasn't at work." Why was he feeling defensive? Did they think he'd made it up?

"I see."

"She must know I reported her for what happened in Amsterdam."

"And what happened in Amsterdam?"

"I think she . . . someone slipped something in my drink." There, he hadn't said it was her. "I passed out and then got really sick."

"Where are you now?"

"On a carousel," he blurted out, then cleared his throat. "In Paris."

"And yesterday?"

"Amiens."

"Are you traveling alone?"

"No, my band's on tour." Everything was topsy-turvy. He gasped when Tanja took him by the arm. He hadn't noticed the ride was over.

He followed the others across a busy street while he told the absurd police officer what he'd been doing—sitting in the van and playing concerts—and yes, hundreds of fans could confirm it. Sounding arrogant was better than sounding guilty. Of what?

"So you last saw Frau Tappet when she drove you to your hotel, possibly after drugging you?"

Tanja and Micha ducked into a coffee shop that looked like every other chain but with better pastries and smaller cups.

He stumbled to the nearest table. "She wasn't driving. Some guy was. Tanja—my bassist—called the next day to find out what she put in my drink, but she didn't answer. That's why I figure she's lying low."

"We're considering the possibility that something's happened to her. When did you say you'd be back?"

"Next week." He couldn't swallow.

"Why don't we talk then? In the meantime, let me know if you hear from her."

"Sure," he croaked. "Bye."

"Who was that?" Tanja dropped a tray on the table, and a little coffee sloshed out of every cup. "Sophie's boyfriend?"

"The police."

"About July?"

How did they know? Then he remembered that there was another, expected reason for the police to call. "Yeah."

"Did they give her a stern talking-to?" Micha's jokey tone sounded phony.

Simon burned his tongue. "Apparently she might be . . . missing?"

"Missing how?" Tanja asked.

"They can't reach her."

She snorted. "Do they declare bank robbers missing? She's *hiding*. Or she's with that friend."

"Oh right, him. Should I call back?"

"Can't hurt," Tanja said as Micha said, "To be on the safe side."

Safe from what? The detective picked up almost as soon as he hit Call.

"It's Herr Kemper. We just spoke?" He moved the phone away to swallow hard.

"Yes?"

"I realized I didn't mention a friend July might be staying with in Amsterdam."

"Great, what's his name?"

"I don't know. He's about thirty-five, with dreadlocks. There's also the guy with short hair and a baseball cap who drove me home."

"I thought you blacked out in the car?"

"I was awake at first."

Tanja nodded encouragingly. Micha seemed to be holding his breath.

"This was after the party?"

"Yes."

"Two male friends, one with dreadlocks and one with short hair and a cap?"

"Yes." He regretted calling back. In the nineties, he would've blown into the receiver and hung up.

"Did you know she'd be at the party?"

"Sure." It was one of those times you could only keep digging. "She invited us before the show, at the show, after . . . She really wanted us to come."

"'Us' being your band?"

"Yes." He didn't elaborate. Every word was a trap.

"In other words, you not only knew she'd be there, but accepted her invitation?"

"Yes." This time he had to explain. "She's very persistent. We thought we'd stop by, you know?"

"Hm." Weinert didn't sound like he knew.

"Until that night, she was just clingy." Tanja was shaking her head, but shrugged when he looked over. "She'd post all over our website, text me all day, send mail to our label. Nothing frightening. Anyway, gotta go. Just thought it might help."

"Thanks. Don't forget to call when you're in Berlin."

He checked to make sure he'd hung up. "I wonder if something happened."

"Doubt it," Tanja said. "Anyway, I heard about this great jazz club in Montparnasse, you up for it?"

"Sounds great." He wanted more than ever to curl up and sleep, or at least not do anything. Not even think. But what was Dr. Froheifer always saying? Not to lose track. What was wrong? Nothing. He hadn't liked that officer's tone, but that could just be bad phone manners. Next time the police called, they'd say July had been staying with friends and thanks again for helping.

~~~

But a few days later and a couple hours from Barcelona, "Weinert Police" came up on Simon's phone.

"Hi there, Weinert again." He sounded like he had a cold, and Simon made a mental note to attribute any grouchiness to a stuffy nose. He hadn't heard from Sophie, their last venue hadn't sold out or even come close, and he was feeling pretty grouchy himself. But having the whole July thing cleared up would be a load off.

"So she turned up?"

"No." Weinert sneezed, and Simon resisted the irrational urge to sanitize his phone. "I wanted to let you know we've filed a missing-person report."

"Can't you trace her phone?" They always did that on TV, but maybe there was some privacy law.

"We did. It was by the side of the road in Amsterdam. Outside your hotel, in fact."

An image was forming in Simon's mind like a developing photo. His first thought was: That's why she didn't pick up.

"Herr Kemper?"

"Guys, turn down the radio," Simon called, even though the music wasn't loud. "I guess someone wanted to steal it?" He pictured a struggle, the phone falling to the ground as July wrenched herself free.

"People tend to keep things they steal."

"You think something happened to her?" The picture was still blurry, but clear enough to make out the form. Something on the ground, not a phone. A body. He couldn't breathe. Was that what it came down to? He pictured those handprint bruises on the throats of strangulation victims, and the image was oddly familiar. The song he'd been working on intruded on his thoughts like a dirty joke at a funeral, inappropriate and impossible to overhear: *I'll lay flowers at the foot / of your unmarked grave.*

Weinert inhaled and exhaled. Maybe he did breathing exercises, too. "We have to assume that."

The picture was filling his head, and it was hard to tell what he'd seen and what he was afraid to see. No one said anything after he hung up. He wished he were home. The tour felt irrelevant. Everything did. His entire infuriating acquaintance with July, Dr. F's empowering advice, everything anyone had said was irrelevant if she was rotting in a ditch somewhere. Beyond the horror of that thought, he felt something like guilt.

Micha turned up the radio.

~~~

Their hotel was near the beach, which was good, because "I wanna get some sun" sounded less depressing than "I'd rather stay in." Before Weinert's call, he'd been planning to send Soledad some kitschy Spanish postcard, but now anything frivolous felt like a sick joke.

After the others left for Sagrada Familia, he thought about only pretending to go out, but the preemptive shame of getting caught was too much, so he took a fifty and left his wallet in case he was robbed, then stopped in the shop downstairs for sunscreen, snacks and water. Best to get all human contact out of the way at once.

The beach was packed but since he was on his own, he managed to find a spot. It was hot but not as hot as he'd expected. He spread out his towel and undressed, hoping no one would notice he was in plaid boxers instead of trunks. Hoping no one would notice him at all.

He spread SPF50 over his ghostly skin and lay down on his stomach. The beach was a relaxing place. What you were supposed to picture when you felt anxious or wanted to fall asleep. Now would be the perfect time for a nap, but he'd never been great at sleeping around strangers, and someone might take his phone. And then the police would be all, *Stolen phone, huh? How convenient.* Like he was trying to avoid them. But why would he?

He felt his heart pause before the idea made it to his brain. He wasn't only feeling guilty because July had come to Amsterdam to see him. He was thinking what they must be. Her phone had been near his hotel. If he wanted her out of his life, why go to her party? Even worse, what if they *did* believe he'd wanted her out? Badly.

He thought about calling Tanja or Micha, but then they'd want to come look after him. He just needed to hear it was crazy. Everyone had seen him drugged. And then? He'd been alone with her and that guy. They could've been jumping on his bed while he puked, for all he knew. Or he could've been throttling her, for all anyone else knew.

It was too much. He was feeling the heat now, either sun or feverish awareness. He hadn't done anything. But that wasn't enough. He needed to be able to prove it. To himself or the police? He cupped a hand over his nose and mouth to feel himself breathing.

Franzi didn't pick up. Neither did Sophie, but that was for the best since a hysterical call about being a suspect might not improve his chances. He tried his mom but hung up after one ring. There was too much background information. He'd have to start with July stalking him and go from there, peppered with irrelevant questions.

Dr. Froheifer's receptionist said she was in session but would be out in ten minutes.

"Could you have her call me? It's an emergency. I mean . . ."—*emergency* sounded like he had a gun to his head—". . . it's important."

"Of course." Her chipper voice was like a pat on the head. After hanging up, he lay back and let time pass, the crash of each wave reminding him of that session winding down, help on its way to the phone.

The thought was so soothing he'd almost dozed off by the time Dr. F called.

"Simon." She sounded like when his mom had caught him cutting class as a kid, less exasperated by his offense than the hassle of dealing with it. "Aren't you on tour?"

"Yes, but can we talk?"

Her sigh into the receiver sounded like a wave breaking. "You know I don't do that. Unless this is some 'emergency'"—He pictured her ringed fingers tracing the word—"in which case I'd like you to talk to the police."

"I did." Not for the reason she thought, but at least he had her attention.

"Okay, what's going on?"

"You remember that girl who was stalking me? She came on my tour and I pretended this other woman was my girlfriend so she'd leave me alone." Dr. F always said there was no point in telling her anything unless he told her everything. "The stalker made my band go to this party, and I passed out and called the police in case she'd drugged me. But now she's missing, and I'm scared they think I'm involved. Even though I blacked out," he added in case the police had gotten permission to tap his phone. A little girl was watching him with wide eyes while her mother tried to turn her away. He hoped they didn't understand German.

"First, you need to calm down." He heard her finish chewing and swallow, and thought it was decent of her to talk him through this on her break, even if she'd written her doctoral thesis on symbolism and not symptoms. "Now filter out what you're *feeling*, and tell me what you're worried about."

The question seemed ridiculous, but it slowed things down. He waited a couple seconds so she'd think he was thinking about it, listened to his pulse slowing and waves breaking. "I'm worried she's been kidnapped or murdered."

"Go on."

"I'm scared they think I did it."

"Has anyone accused you of anything?"

"No, but they wanna talk when I'm back."

"Anything else?"

"Just the usual."

"We can deal with 'the usual' later. For now, the only way you can help is telling the police everything. Have you done that?"

"Yes." Why did he have that biley aftertaste of a lie? He hadn't told them every last detail, but not everything mattered. Unless he was a suspect.

"When you get back, they'll ask a few questions or have found her, okay?"

"Okay." He tried to convince himself talking to her had helped. He could see the logic of what she'd said, but felt sure she'd missed something crucial. "Thanks." There was nothing more embarrassing than clinging to a call.

"This is an unusual situation, and it's normal to feel upset."

Only after hanging up did he realize what he'd left unsaid. Dr. F was wrong about there being nothing more he could do. How much energy would the police put into this case, when her phone was the only sign anything had happened? You could drop a phone.

He closed his eyes, feeling the relief he'd sought. He wouldn't just tell them what he knew; he'd find out more. Look into people who'd gone to his shows. Did that balding guy seem suspicious? There were any number of angles to follow up. Back in Berlin, they'd practice, do the occasional show, earn money. Other than that, he'd have all the time in the world.

He remembered asking Franzi to help him do good. Was that what this was? He pictured himself finding July, receiving a medal. The mayor would speak, who was it now, not Wowi but that guy with glasses . . . In his pleasant doze, the July he rescued wasn't infuriating, but a frail shape convalescing—not dead—in the background while he said he'd just done what anyone would do.

He woke to hot sand on his face and wanted to shout at the prankster responsible, but it was only someone walking by in flipflops. He wrapped his phone and money in his t-shirt and hid them under his towel.

The water was cool but not cold enough to have to get used to. Strands of seaweed wound themselves around his legs like affectionate cats. More awake now, he wasn't sure how he'd track down July, but it still seemed possible. He saw himself crouching in the bushes outside the criminal's den, calling Weinert to whisper the address. He waded past a bulky raft and a girl clinging to her boyfriend's back like a koala, then swam toward the glittering whale-shaped building down the beach. He checked his distance from the shore at regular intervals, because people drowned like this all the time. Would his body wash up or be sucked out?

Something slimy clung to his wrist, but it was a plastic bag and not a jellyfish.

His arm jiggled when he shook it off. He didn't exercise enough. He was soft all over. But he felt healthy in the tepid seawater that flexed his muscles and hid his pitiful torso. Despite the seaweed, debris and other people, he felt clean, like the water was washing away more than sweat. He was alive, with things ahead of him. When he got home, he'd exercise, volunteer, find July.

He felt faint by the time he waddled to shore. The glittering building looked less like a whale close-up. He headed back on foot, enjoying the feel of the sun drying his skin, and even the emptiness in his stomach, in all of him.

Weaving around towels, umbrellas and children transporting pails of wet sand, he added another item to his list: seeing Sophie. It would be different once he had his shit together. He wouldn't be broken, and she wouldn't be scared of having to fix him. Had that been his problem before? Or his unwillingness to undergo repair.

He went an extra hundred meters before realizing he'd passed his towel. All his stuff was still there; only the mother and daughter were gone. Micha had sent a selfie with his head blocking some altarpiece. Sophie had texted: "Check your emails for once."

He'd forgotten about her story. July had been so much more present. He hoped Sophie didn't think wanting to read it had been bullshit. His first instinct was to say his phone hadn't been working, but nobody would believe that—July hadn't—and it would be a blight on his newfound cleanliness. If he went back now, he could read it before replying. And then sift through July's messages. What was white noise, and what was a clue.

~~~

Maybe it was all the sun, but he didn't know where to start. He put off looking at Sophie's story to take a shower, then opened the file on his laptop but put off reading it to turn on his favorite mix of soothingly depressing songs while looking through July's messages. There were so many words and so little meaning it made his head swim, so he googled her instead.

Her website looked tasteful but like she'd made it herself. She offered copy-writing and editing from an address in Prenzlauer Berg. He got out the notebook she'd once snooped through and wrote "What I Know About July" on the back cover, at the opposite end from his lyrics.

What *did* he know? She'd brought him to his hotel the night she disappeared, and her evenings before that had revolved around his shows. Maybe other fans had seen something. Or maybe one of them was involved. He struggled through an English email to the club in Amsterdam requesting a list of attendees, explaining the urgent situation and his band's terrible concern for a missing fan, offering to sign a data protection agreement. What was the point of being a tiny bit famous if you couldn't call in a favor? He wrote the club in Hamburg to the same effect. What about the one in Berlin? But that was only July's usual environment; she'd been to dozens of Berlin shows without vanishing, so there probably wasn't much to find out there.

He returned to her messages, but found little to write down except when she stopped sending them. She'd said more in person, but had he listened?

What about those pills? She must've had some touristy idea about Amsterdam. Or wanted to impress him, thinking that was his scene. What else? The balding guy, the hickeys that might've been bruises, the supposed friend and ex-affair.

What was he doing, playing detective with a serious case like this? But the admonition was only at the surface; underneath, he felt sure he was getting somewhere, or would soon. He returned to Sophie's story. It was a little wordy and he wasn't sure what made it experimental but would never have admitted that. This woman tries to convince her fiancé she's a cannibal to get out of marrying him, but becomes increasingly unsure she's making it up. By the end, the cannibal marries her understanding, open-minded fiancé.

He texted Sophie: "Wanted to discuss your story." So what if he'd called about July? The story was pretty good. Not amazing, but better than we-slept-together-so-I-have-to-pretend. Right? At least it wasn't boring. He tried to imagine what he'd think if the author were some gnarled, unsexy male: not his favorite, but fine. He felt relieved and then guilty. He hadn't expected it to be good.

Nadine wasn't a prodigy, but she did have real talent. He'd loved her for not knowing it. There must be something pathological about being attracted to insecurity. How would he have felt if Sophie's story were awful? Would he have thought, good, she's a hack like me? No, because on a level he was even more ashamed of, he believed he was very talented and profound. He would've thought: another superficial fake, like everyone *but* me.

Instead of calling her, he dialed the number in his notebook. No one picked up, and then there was July's recorded voice trying to sound professional. Or sounding professional, but not to him.

Franzi was online so he sent her an update, adding that he'd been at the beach so it wouldn't sound like he was freaking out.

"She's unstable and took off?" she wrote. "Also, what would your motive be?"

"True." Wanting to be left alone? Or wanting the wrong things from her at the wrong time. "I wanna volunteer when I get back."

"What did you have in mind?"

Did he really want to, or only to congratulate himself on wanting to? It was probably hard to find anything that didn't require human contact. "Something like what you do."

Sophie was calling. He raved about her story and mentioned July like an afterthought.

"So you're a suspect?"

"They have some questions."

"Did you do it?"

"There's no 'it.'"

"It's just a matter of time before a body turns up."

Did she have to sound so eager? She'd met July but wasn't thinking of her as a real person. Or she was incredibly callous. He pushed aside that inconvenient thought. Maybe she was trying to comfort him in some weird way.

"I wish you'd come on tour with us . . . I could've let you talk to the police for me. We'd both be in jail by now." Same old, same old: approach and recede. Like it was all just a joke to him, too. He wasn't as desperate about her as he'd been, which was a relief but also a loss. He'd felt more for her than anyone since Nadine.

"Yeah, I really missed out."

Three

He called the police as soon as Micha dropped him off. Nobody guilty would do that. Unless they thought it would make them look innocent. The phone rang for ages, so he hung up and showered. Traveling made him feel dirty.

He called again.

"Herr Kemper, thanks for getting in touch. Get back alright?" Weinert didn't wait for an answer. "Mind stopping by?"

"Sure."

Weinert gave him an address in Prenzlauer Berg, so it must be based on where July lived. Or had lived. He took the tram, notebook in his pocket. He could add anything he found out. And go by July's afterward. Ring and see what happened. Check for suspicious characters lurking there. Other than himself. He was sweating more than the stuffy tram called for, and had to remind himself that this wasn't where he cracked the case. It was something to get out of the way, like seeing the dentist. He'd stroll in, a helpful citizen, annoyed about the stalking but hoping nothing bad had happened.

The station wasn't that different from a dentist's office. He came through glass doors with a camera above them—okay, that was different, unless the dentist had a lot of disgruntled patients—to a receptionist's desk, where he waited in line until a blond guy about Franzi's age took down his name. Like a dental hygienist, he handled preliminaries like scraping off plaque, or in this case sending Simon to get his fingerprints scanned: "If you don't mind? Just so they can rule you out." Actually, it was more like a job interview than getting your teeth checked. The false importance of the people you dealt with, uncertainty about the questions you'd be asked, hurrying there and then having to wait in some hallway, maintaining your composure because you never knew who was watching.

To distract himself, he went over his to-do list. Unpack, buy groceries, call both of his parents, psych himself up to ask Sophie out or whatever you did when you lived in different cities and had already slept together. Clean his apartment and start looking for a bigger one. He got involved in calculating how much space he could afford and reminded himself that it was only for visitors, nothing he needed for, say, a girlfriend.

That thought felt so grim that he was happy to see Weinert. Remembering how contagious he'd sounded on the phone, Simon was relieved when the slight man with an unkempt beard greeted him in a clear, phlegm-free voice. It made it easier to shake the detective's hand, though Simon was always waiting for the next opportunity to wash his own.

"Sorry about the wait. Right this way."

Simon followed him into a small room with a desk that looked like a regular office and didn't even have any two-way mirrors. He felt a pang of disappointment at yet another experience that was less exciting, less real than in the movies. Then he remembered that it *was* real and he wanted out as soon as possible.

"Have a seat." Weinert sat down at the desk, which featured a kitten-of-the-day calendar Simon hoped was meant ironically, a picture of his family—wife with artsy glasses, two androgynous toddlers and a bulldog—a monitor and tons of papers. "Mind if I record this? My hand cramps up when I take notes."

"No problem." Not only was he innocent, but he'd had years of singing to get over hating the sound of his voice. Although Weinert probably wasn't going to play it back to him.

The first questions sounded like small talk—where he lived, worked, etc. When Weinert asked how he and July had met, Simon felt like she'd dragged him to some dinner party and left him alone with the host.

"She always comes to our shows." How much should he say? He mentioned her posts and messages, the time she'd stolen his phone and the evening at the tapas place, making it sound like she'd tagged along.

"Would you describe her as a friend?"

"No."

"Do you think she considers you a friend?"

"I don't see how she could. She contacts me a lot, but I usually ignore it."

"Why?"

He hesitated, struggling to find the words for something so obvious. Maybe Weinert would also ask why he was subject to gravity. "She makes me uncomfortable. She's never threatened me, but she's clingy and possessive even though I barely know her."

"It sounds like you've known her for a while."

Even now, she was insinuating herself. Getting on record as his friend. "I have no control over who comes to our concerts. It's like if some customer at Café Astral thought we were friends because I made their coffee."

"Hm." Weinert looked down at his desk, even though he wasn't taking notes. Did he have a list to keep him on the right line of questioning? That reminded

Simon that he needed to stay on track, too. He wasn't here to prove July was stalking him, just that he hadn't had motive or opportunity. For what?

"She calmed down once she met this woman I'm seeing in Hamburg. She even picked up some guy in the club."

"Did you meet him?"

That's right: Let's consider other suspects. "No, but we saw them kissing. Balding guy in a leather jacket."

"Who's 'we'?"

"Me, my sister and her boyfriend, the band, the woman I mentioned."

"Would you recognize him?"

"Maybe." Was that guy really a suspect? July had been alive and well after.

"You saw her again in Amsterdam? Socially?"

"Tanja and I were eating, and she turned up."

"Did you think that was odd?"

He shrugged. "It was near the club. She could've been passing by."

"Or?"

"Or she could've checked all the restaurants near the club. But it was probably a coincidence."

"Like in the park? Was the party a coincidence, too?"

"No, she invited us. I didn't want to go, but Micha and Tanja did."

"The other members of your band?"

"Yes."

"What happened when you got there?"

"Tanja got us drinks and we were talking to these guys with ironic mustaches."

"Ironic mustaches?"

"You know, hipsters." In light of Weinert's beard and flannel shirt, he felt uncomfortable, as if forced to repeat a racial slur in front of a minority. "Then July came and gave me some punch. It was the same as before but a different color."

"What color?"

"One was green, and the other was red." Like blood. But it hadn't tasted metallic, just sickly sweet. The evening was clear enough at that point, like a movie he'd watched a few times without paying too much attention. When had the screen started to go dark? "She offered me these pink pills. Said she thought they were my thing."

"Any reason she'd think that?"

If he thought he was onto something, he was dead wrong. "I used to take drugs sometimes. Some of our songs mention that. And there's an old post on our website from when I got out of rehab."

"Is Frau Tappet a recreational drug user?"

"That was the first time I saw her with anything. Anyway, I noticed these marks on her throat. I thought it was a hickey, but she said it was a birthmark.

I guess you could look at some old pictures and see?" Weinert didn't answer, so he continued. "I also thought I saw a bruise on her arm, but the lighting was too weird to tell. We saw her friend with dreadlocks at the bar. I was feeling woozy and tried to sit down, but July dragged me outside to ask about the woman I'm seeing." He'd brought Sophie up, desperate for a shoulder to cry on, no matter whose, but only July knew that. "We kissed. Things were hazy. I fell on a bottle."

"Did she kiss you or did you kiss her?"

"I'm not sure." What was this, a slumber party?

"Then you fell? Did you lose consciousness?"

"Not then. I think she pushed me." It was important to be somewhat vague in case he messed up, but not so vague that they wouldn't believe any evidence he supplied. *Pushed* made her sound violent, whereas *slapped* would sound like he'd deserved it. He had, but not in any way that mattered.

"Was there an altercation?"

"What?" Could you call July hitting somebody who was barely lucid an altercation?

"Did you have a fight?"

He took a deep breath. What did it matter if some random stranger thought he didn't know what "altercation" meant? "She was angry because of the woman I'm seeing." He was aware of repeating that phrase too often, like he had something to prove.

"Were you ever romantically involved with Frau Tappet before?"

"I was never romantically involved with her!" Too emphatic.

"But you kissed her."

It didn't seem like a question, but he answered anyway. "Probably because I got drugged and didn't know what I was doing."

"She already knew you were seeing someone. Why get upset right then?"

There it was. He could've gotten away with all kinds of lies, but the one most embarrassing thing had to come up. He tried to think of a spin to put on it, but didn't want to seem like he was stalling. The best he could do was, "I'd said I was in a relationship, but I'd only just met Sophie."

"In other words, you told her you were with someone before you were?"

"My friends thought that would get her off my back. Then July saw Sophie and assumed she was my girlfriend. She was mad when she found out the truth."

"After you kissed."

"I think so."

"How did the fight continue?"

"It didn't. I asked her to call a cab, but she told me someone would give us a ride."

"The man in the cap?"

"Yes."

"Did you get a look at his face?"

"No."

"You're sure it was a man? Not a short-haired woman?"

"Yeah, I must've heard his voice."

"What language was he speaking?"

Trying to remember was like pushing against a wall with his bare hands. "I don't know. July was speaking Dutch."

"You're sure it was Frau Tappet?"

"Yeah, I asked about Micha and she said to go to sleep."

"Did Frau Tappet get out at your hotel?"

"I don't know. The next thing I remember is waking up covered in vomit."

"Have you heard from her since?"

"No."

Weinert asked for all their tour stops, but Simon could tell they were winding down. Nothing like playing in front of audiences, sharing hotel rooms and getting drugged to give you great alibis. The only time he'd been conscious and no one could account for him was on the beach, and by then, July had been missing too long for it to matter.

"Thanks again." Weinert offered Simon his hand. Simon saw a flash of tattoo under the cuff of his shirt, and wondered whether it was a generic tribal or something hipper. Before he could shake Weinert's hand, Weinert withdrew it.

"You don't have your phone on you, do you? Would you mind if we took a look? Frau Tappet's messages might seem trivial, but there's a chance we could find something."

He didn't have time to think how incriminating, let alone humiliating, the messages might be. "For how long? I don't have a landline." Better to put it that way and not say they needed a warrant or whatever. As with the fingerprints, saying no would make him look guilty.

"Two hours? We'll download what we need."

Simon stood hesitating like a departing guest wondering where he left his coat. "You'll only look at stuff from July, right? Some things are . . . personal." Weinert probably thought he had dungeon porn or something, not just shame about his sparse personal life.

"Herr Kemper, we're not Stasi spies. We have no interest in anything that doesn't pertain to this case."

Simon wanted to say something to limit this invasion of his privacy but, reaching into his pocket, he felt the spiral of his notebook: "What I Know About July" and "unmarked grave" in a single volume, along with her home address. He shoved it down as far as it would go, thrust his phone into Weinert's hands and told him the pin.

"See you in two hours!" He walked as fast as he could without running, but the back and armpits of his shirt were drenched in sweat by the time he got outside, with another damp spot under his pocket, as if something in it were giving off heat.

~~~

It wasn't until he was en route to July's apartment that he noticed the nuance in Weinert's words. Not that they'd only look at her texts, but that they'd only look at what was relevant. If Simon was a suspect, that could be anything.

He had a childish urge to run back, shout, "You tricked me!" and snatch his phone, but it was like July reading his lyrics: best not to think about. Or like how Dr. F was only supposed to consider how stuff affected his psyche, not judge him.

July's place was close enough to the main drag of Prenzlauer Allee to be loud and less chichi, but it couldn't be cheap. Copywriting must pay okay. It was a beige prewar with sunflower moldings and retrofitted balconies that didn't do it justice. According to the doorbells, her apartment was on the street side. He held down the buzzer. Nothing. Most of her neighbors were probably at work, much as he was hoping one would walk by and happen to mention some juicy clue. He looked around for suspicious cars or passersby, but saw only the usual: parents with strollers, teenagers sauntering between parks and convenience stores, luxury sedans, car-sharing Smarts, an East German Trabant someone must've bought at a hundred times the original value. Tappet was the only name on the bell. For all he knew, she was up there now, peering out the window and laughing.

~~~

He went home to finish unpacking by dumping the contents of his bag on the floor. Shaking out the lint and sand, he noticed it was heavier on one side. There was a bulge in the inner pocket where he kept condoms and a fifty for emergencies. He unzipped it and took out a robin's-egg-blue wallet with two heart-shaped buttons.

That's not mine, was his first ridiculous thought. Someone must've forgotten it in his hotel room, and the maid had put it in so it wouldn't get lost. It was too cutesy for Tanja. Franzi didn't buy leather. Sophie? Odd that no one had mentioned it if it had been there since Hamburg.

Then he undid the buttons and saw the ID in its plastic sheath, knew what he'd tried not to know since he found it. It hadn't been there since Hamburg, just since Amsterdam. There was July's face, thinner, unsmiling, without bangs. The picture reminded him of someone, but he couldn't say who. There were her debit, credit and library cards; license, movie theater membership and surprisingly thick stack of large bills.

July's in trouble, he thought. No, I am.

His first instinct was to pry up a floorboard and hide it like a telltale heart, but if anyone found it, he'd look guilty as sin. What if he dropped it near her apartment? Or the police station? His fingerprints must be all over it. Even if he wiped it off, they could do something with DNA. What would an innocent person do? Well, whatever he'd do, since he was innocent.

July hadn't been in his room in Hamburg. He hadn't brought his bag to the party or either show, so she must've been in his room in Amsterdam, either when he wasn't there or the night she'd disappeared, in which case, shit.

He made coffee and wondered who could talk him through this, other than a defense attorney. Franzi was family and had to stand by him. She'd cut him off over that supposed addiction, but that had only been tough love. He was the victim here, if not of July, at least of very odd circumstances. He spent ages looking for his phone before he remembered where it was, then opened Skype on his laptop. Franzi didn't pick up but wrote saying she was at work. "Check out this link. OK to sign you up?"

Must be some charitable initiative. Here I am suspected of murder, and she thinks I'm trying to do good. Then again, volunteering would look good in court. The thought was so ridiculous it reassured him. It was all a big mix-up. How often had he been sure he had an incurable disease, only to have the benign symptoms that had freaked him out disappear on their own?

"Sure, let's talk later." He considered saying more but didn't want her to worry.

Micha didn't pick up. Couldn't tear himself away from Mina after being separated for the tour. Tanja did, even if she sounded like he'd woken her up.

"I'm worried about July," he said before she could get mad.

"Come on. She's a weird girl, off doing weird things."

"I found her wallet."

"Her what?"

"Her wallet."

Tanja yawned, but sounded awake now. "You sure it's hers?"

"Her ID's in it."

"Where'd you find it?"

"It was in my bag." Don't get defensive.

She went through the same steps he had, came to the same conclusion that July could only have put it there while he was unconscious or out.

"What now? They'll think . . ."

"Shh. Let me think. I'd be happy to say I found it, but if we get caught, it'll look worse. Don't freak out. You didn't do anything?"

"Of course not."

"Even when you were drugged?"

"I was unconscious and sick to my stomach. You saw me in the morning; picture me the night before."

"Sorry, I just wanna make sure we cover everything. Tell the police. One, that makes you look less guilty, and two, it's a clue."

"At first I thought of a maid putting it there, but I was so sick they didn't clean until we left, remember?" He took a sip of coffee and narrowly avoided burning his tongue. He needed to buy milk. Strange having such an ordinary thought at a time like this. He heard her swallow and imagined her doing the same thing, sitting around with a cup of black coffee, wondering what the hell was going on.

"She could've wanted you to contact her. You know, like on *Seinfeld* where people forget things at other people's apartments so they have an excuse to come back?"

He didn't, but he got her point. "She's hoping I'll get in touch, then drops off the face of the Earth?" He played the scenes in his head, but the frames didn't line up.

"Good point. Luckily, I have an alternate theory. She's trying to *Gone Girl* you."

"To what me?"

"Wow, I thought you read. It was only a fucking international bestseller and in theaters all last fall . . . She's framing you, get it?"

"I guess." He wouldn't put it past July. His only objection to the theory was how eager he was to believe it.

"I'll come with you."

"You don't have to." The offer made him so happy he could've cried. But she didn't need to know that.

"Gimme half an hour."

~~~

Tanja asked to see the wallet, but only looked at the ID. "That's her."

No shit, Simon wanted to say, but he was even more at a loss than she was. He still hadn't figured out who July looked like in that picture. "Should we head over?"

She nodded. "You don't remember anything between the car and the next morning?"

"Not even whether I got out or they carried me. You really think she's setting me up?"

"It's farfetched, but less farfetched than other things." She put a hand on his shoulder. "Let's not pretend I didn't ask myself whether you did something to her. But I've met tougher Girl Scouts."

"Thanks."

"I'd testify to that." They laughed, but he felt something cold and hard in the pit of his stomach. Was she teasing, or really saying she'd testify on his behalf? Of course she would. She, Micha and Franzi would, and the few other people in his life who mattered. Only one person in his life hadn't mattered to him, and she was gone.

~~~

At the station, he got his phone back in a little baggy and signed a receipt.

"You're good to go," the clerk said, and how tempting that was. He could walk out and no one but Tanja would know. But then it would end like all those thrillers: He'd decide he couldn't trust her and had to kill her, too. Too?

"Is Detective Weinert here?"

"No, can I take a message?"

"Is there another officer we can talk to?" Tanja asked.

The clerk's face fell. He must hate when people thought he wasn't a real cop because he sat at the front desk. "Which case is this about? We have a *lot* of cases."

Simon knew all about feeling, about being, less than. It was better to think of how he and the clerk had that in common than of what separated them: One was here for work, and one to hand over the missing person's property he just happened to have.

"I think the number's on the receipt?" he said.

The clerk entered it on his computer and raised his eyebrows. "Oh, I see ..." Simon was sure it was only a dull administrative record, but who knew. There could be a column labeled "Suspects" with his picture. "You were just here."

"Yep."

"If it's important, I'll try his private number."

"It is," Tanja said.

"If you say so." He made a theatrical gesture of finding the number on his screen with one finger, then dialed. When Weinert picked up, he swiveled his chair away, like that would keep them from hearing.

"Wanna get coffee after this?" Tanja asked.

"Sure." Simon felt pulled back to Earth from some far corner of outer space, but his gravity was a little off. He'd go back to July's another time. He caught himself thinking there was no hurry, and that was bad because if she was alive, trapped somewhere, of course they had to hurry. He forced himself to smile and say, "I hope Soledad's working. Barbara won't give me the employee discount anymore."

"Not him," the receptionist was saying. "Kemper." So he wasn't the only suspect. "... didn't seem to want to say, but—"

"Excuse me!" Tanja shouted.

"Just a second." The clerk perched the phone between his chin and shoulder and swiveled around. "Yes?"

"We're happy to say," she said loud enough for Weinert to hear. "You never asked."

"Well?"

"It seems to be the missing person's wallet."

"It seems to be the missing person's wallet," he repeated into the phone, a little pink in the face. He hung up. "He's on his way."

"We found this while we were unpacking." Tanja handed Weinert the wallet when he arrived out of breath and still out of uniform, his flannel shirt now unbuttoned to reveal a t-shirt from some band Simon was too uninformed to know. "Cool shirt," she added.

"Thanks. You must be Herr Kemper's . . . ?"

"Bassist. Or he's my guitarist."

Weinert laughed. Simon felt like some fatal condition he'd been keeping secret had turned out to be curable. Then Weinert straightened out his face and asked, "Do you have time to make a statement, Frau . . . ?

"Stift. Sure. Simon, be a doll and get me a latte."

"You see how they treat me?" It was easier than he'd thought to smile, not run out screaming. Instead he strolled into the nearest café, ordered and locked himself in the bathroom to splash cold water on his face and wonder what she was saying. Was she trying to make it sound like it could've been in her luggage? It could've, but hadn't. He'd shared a room with her or Micha enough nights for their things to get mixed up—he wouldn't be surprised to discover some XL Looney Tunes boxers in his laundry later—but he'd had his own room the night July disappeared.

Someone rattled the knob and his hair stood on end. "Be right out!" He dried his face, grabbed the lattes and left. Tanja was probably waiting outside. How much could she have to say? Then again, she'd been at the party and knew July. Weinert didn't know she was into women and might think it was a jealousy thing. Or he might know and still think it was jealousy, her being into July. The possibilities were endless, and they weren't. Only one thing had happened, there was only one place July was, and one person who'd get convicted.

Tanja wasn't waiting outside. After getting cooked by the sun through the glass awning, he went in and saw she wasn't there, either. Was she explaining her framing theory?

"They're still back there?" he asked the clerk.

"Yep."

"Think it'll be a while?"

"I really couldn't say."

"Hot out." Or he was bathed in nervous sweat. Thank goodness he had a strong deodorant. Police could probably smell fear, like dogs.

"Guess so."

"You want this?" He held up Tanja's latte. "It'll get cold if she's not done soon. It's not poisoned, I promise."

The clerk laughed and took it. "Yeah, why bother? I'm not important."

Simon smiled. Until recently, that had been his attitude, too. But now that someone had gone to the trouble of stalking, drugging and maybe framing him, he couldn't be so sure. "There's nothing more annoying than calling and not getting through, or those robots who never understand what you're saying. People who answer the phone keep the world going."

"Keep the world going? I like that. Thanks."

"How's working here?" He was feeling unusually chatty, either because his heart rate had tripled when he found the wallet and never slowed back down, or because he needed an ally until Tanja got back. This guy knew what it was like to be a loser. Then again, he was young, clean and employed, with a brightish future ahead of him. Depending on what you thought of police work.

"Good. I see a lot of interesting characters. Once I finish training, I start on the force."

"That sounds exciting." Simon hadn't seen any characters more interesting than Tanja come in. Maybe it was a slow day.

"What do you do?"

"I'm in a band."

"I mean, I heard, but really?"

"I sometimes work at a café, too."

"Have I heard of your band?"

"You tell me. Hare vs. Hedgehog?"

"I'll have to check it out."

Hearing Tanja's voice, Simon finished his coffee and threw away the cup.

"Tag." She swiped at him. "You're it."

"Do you have another minute, Herr Kemper?" Weinert wanted to know.

"Wanna meet after?" Simon asked Tanja.

"I'll head over to Astral."

"Sure," Simon said to Weinert. "If it's quick."

She clapped him on the back. "See ya later, alligator."

He couldn't remember what rhymed with crocodile.

~~~

Simon felt less nervous now, as if it were all just a matter of practice. As if he didn't look much guiltier. Having Tanja there had helped. Look at me, a normal guy with normal friends.

"We had a look at your record. You were in court-ordered rehab."

"I made some bad choices." Spoken like a politician. He was clean, and they could take all the tests in the world, in fact please do. They might see what July had put in his drink. Still, he was glad he'd mentioned rehab before so it wouldn't seem like he'd been hiding it.

"Did you know Frau Tappet through the drug scene?"

"I don't think she does drugs."

"But she offered you some?"

"Lots of people try stuff out in Amsterdam. Like Micha…" He'd said enough. Micha wouldn't be in trouble, but it could reflect poorly on them. "Maybe she felt like she had to because she was there."

"Did you take anything?"

"Not unless you count someone drugging me." He was the victim here. Well, July was the real victim, but he was *a* victim.

"You know Frau Tappet was also sentenced to rehab?"

"No way."

"Why not?"

"I can't picture it."

"Picture this: While I was talking to your colleague, Officer Peters found this." He held up a small plastic baggy of colorful pills. "She said it was tucked under the money. Unlike the rest of the wallet, it didn't have any fingerprints from you or Frau Stift." He pointed to a pink pill. "Is this what she offered you?"

"Maybe." He remembered the fact of their being pink more than any clear visual. He couldn't imagine July being involved in a drug scene, or any scene at all, other than the local indie scene. And she wasn't really involved in that; she was just there. But some primitive, self-preserving part of his brain was rejoicing even before he formed the conscious thought: She was involved with criminals. He was off the hook.

"Would you mind if we took a sample of your hair?"

"Sure, saves me a trip to the doctor." Everything was good again. Well, not good, but safe; they'd put him back in the right category, stricken him from the suspect list.

"I also have a few questions about this wallet."

"Fire away." Under his thin facade of cheer, he felt gutted again.

"How'd you come to have Frau Tappet's wallet?"

"When I got home, I dumped out everything in my bag. I noticed this bulge in a pocket where I only ever put … small things. That's where it was."

"Do you have any idea how it got there?"

"I don't know when, why or how July put it there. She was never in my room, unless while I was passed out or somewhere else."

"Who else had access to your bag?"

"Sometimes I shared a room with Micha or Tanja. The cleaning staff, I guess. Some people were in my room in Hamburg—no, they were in the other room, so only Sophie was—but I would've noticed it then."

"What makes you so sure?"

"That's where I keep condoms." He hated himself for blushing. His sex life was so beside the point.

"Did you get out a condom on any other occasion since then?"

"No. That is, uh, not from my travel bag." Was this really someone he needed to save face in front of?

"In other words, the wallet could only have gotten into that pocket after you had sex the night before you last saw Frau Tappet?"

"I guess."

"What time was that?"

With his luck, Weinert's next question would be how long it had lasted. "Around two in the morning." It didn't help his case, but as a gesture of good-will, he added, "She must've put it there in Amsterdam if someone let her in, or while I was passed out."

"Or anyone could've anytime between two in the morning the night you were in Hamburg and today."

"True." It was tactful not to mention the other possibility, that he'd had it all along.

"Where did you say you went to rehab?"

"I didn't. In southern Brandenburg. Springtime Healthy Living." Its chipper English name was the only foreign language he'd encountered out there in the boonies.

"Sounds nice." Before Simon could correct him, he added, "That was in 2011?"

Simon nodded, thinking back to another lifetime that had started with reclusive crying fits, ceded into apathy and ultimately taken on a peaceful, reflective quality. It hadn't been that bad, to the extent that he'd managed to choke down the bland food and fundamentalist Christianity, elude the other sad sacks sentenced or diagnosed to join him. The longtime unemployed from the meth-addled countryside, petty criminals and grim older patients like his roommate were a distasteful blur he tried to wipe from his mind.

"Looks like you were classmates. Can you remember anything about her at rehab?"

"You've got something mixed up. There was no one . . . like her." He almost said "attractive," not that he found her attractive, but he would've back then. Her or any okay-looking woman. He and Nadine had still been involved, but that was in another world outside Springtime. Nadine had only ever meant to visit, never actually turned up.

More importantly, there was no way he'd forget someone as invasive as July. He was still struggling to reconcile her cloying self-satisfaction with a drug problem, and now Weinert was seeing connections that weren't there.

"Think hard."

The reality of Springtime felt tenuous, like a dream he'd had as a child and never told anyone about. The women lived in a separate cabin. How many had there been? That veiny old heroin addict whose voice had always sounded like laryngitis. The skeletal girl who should've been at school instead of Springtime—a memento mori to cure you of wanting to take anything stronger than aspirin. Then Tammy, of course, the heavyset ringleader of those abrasive middle-aged women with high-waisted pants and pockmarked, leathery skin. The thin one with chronic nosebleeds was Sally or Sandy, and the one with spiky hair and no front teeth had left before he did. Anyway, they were too old. So was Frau Obern, who ran the place with her husband, and the heavyset Polish nurse who handled withdrawal patients.

He shook his head. "She wasn't there."

Weinert handed him a picture, and Simon felt his stomach hit his throat like on the plunging drop of a rollercoaster. Seeing those hollow eyes, the busted lips in that haggard face, he understood who the picture on July's ID had reminded him of. Did she look as damaged now, wherever she was, as she had back then?

"But she was just a kid." He thought back to that day in the park, July flattered that he thought she was still in school, and knew he was wrong.

"No, she was already an adult. It's the emaciation that makes her look so young here." He paused, waiting for a reaction that didn't come. "Her name was Julia Barer back then."

"She changed her name?"

"She got divorced."

"She was *married*?"

"You do recognize her?"

"I didn't realize that was her."

"Her husband was a small-time dealer. Terrible what people do to themselves with drugs."

Simon nodded, annoyed that Weinert felt like he had to say that, but too busy reassembling his concepts to care. That July was a Julia came as something of a surprise since she'd made such a big deal of her unique name. But an ex-addict with an ex-husband? "We never talked. She was in bad shape."

"How bad was your condition? Could she have recognized you after?"

"I was okay." What did this mean? Was she even really a fan? Something cold and slimy roped its way down his spine and landed heavily in his gut. "I got rid of my beard later, but she still could've recognized me." Could've and had. Hadn't she said at that first show that she liked him better without? And like an idiot he'd thought she was talking about some old picture of him.

Weinert handed Simon a business card. "Let me know if you remember anyone who visited her, friends she made."

"Of course."

"Just stop by the lab at the end of the hall to give your sample."

"Sure." He left in a daze, forgetting to shake Weinert's hand or greet the technician who chopped off a lock of his hair down to the scalp. Oh well, he couldn't see the top of his own head anyway. Still, he mussed his hair a bit to cover the spot.

~~~

He took notes on the tram, but his heart wasn't in it. July's damaged face was projected over the whole surface of his mind. No matter how far his thoughts wandered, someone kept turning the dial that much further, expanding the image to cover everything.

He felt so stupid. It had been right in front of him all along—*she* had. Asking whether she'd gained too much weight, not because she was fishing for compliments but because she'd been so thin when he last saw her. Of course she hadn't been to any of his tiny solo shows before the band—when she talked about seeing him play on his own, she'd meant at Springtime. And how many times had he been annoyed at her insensitivity? He remembered standing outside the tapas restaurant with her, trying to make her understand how grim rehab had felt by telling her about that poor girl—herself. She must've thought he was teasing.

Why hadn't she ever said anything? But she had, more than once, even calling the facility by name. That was the exception, though. Most of the time, she'd stuck to what he told her at their first meeting, or what he'd thought was their first: that he didn't like to talk about rehab. What had she said that night? *I feel you. Keep looking ahead.* He'd taken every reference to their shared past as some generic expression of sympathy or encouragement, or worse still some attempt at an in with him.

As if she'd needed one. He felt like the people in Dürrenmatt's *The Visit* when they find out their town is impoverished by design rather than chance, that nothing was ever up to them. It couldn't be a coincidence, could it? She'd found him. But why?

~~~

"Simon's here!" Soledad shouted when he came in. "Now the place's full of celebs." She pointed to Tanja sitting at the small table next to the milk jugs that was always available. He felt the floor move beneath him, felt every customer in the place watching him, even the ones who didn't turn to look.

"You okay?"

"Tired. How's business?" He nodded at the teenage boy busing the tables, whose name he could never remember. Other than Soledad, the staff here was such a shifting cast of characters, a new face every other week. He called everyone "you." What did it matter? What did anything matter.

"Busy. The woman Barbara replaced you with is pregnant, but I'm not supposed to tell."

"Oh man. How's school?" He felt like a spy, poorly equipped with snippets of information about Simon Kemper's life and sent to impersonate him. Somehow, he was getting away with it.

She told him school was great, then said, "I'll make you a hot chocolate. You're sad about that woman."

"What?" He was a cage at the zoo, and everyone could look in and poke at what was inside.

"You'll get over whoever-she-is soon and meet someone new. I should know!" So she thought he was suffering from unrequited love. She'd spent at least five shifts detailing different breakups to him, but always laughed when he reassured her that she'd find someone better, "or at least a *different* loser." She was smart, vibrant and of course gorgeous in her haphazard way, though he'd started training himself not to notice from the first day they worked together. He was at his grayest then, and the thought of getting involved with anyone after Nadine had made him feel like vomiting the way he had in Amsterdam. Or more like that was the reaction he'd inspire in a woman. "You have to cheer up even when someone tears apart your heart." Soledad pantomimed the tearing. A couple customers had gathered at the register, but it wasn't the kind of place where people were in a hurry.

"Thanks. *Tienes razón.*" She'd taught him that, the first thing you need to be able to say to a woman: *You're right.* Other than please and thank you, that was all the Spanish he could retain.

"Sorry," Tanja said when he sat down. Her dishes were empty, but his brain wasn't working well enough to know how long she'd been waiting. "I said you were having girl trouble. People can tell when something's the matter, but they'll believe anything you say about love."

"Yeah." He tried to remember the kind of thing Simon would've said. "How's what's-her-name?"

"You look terrible. Don't try to be a good listener."

Either he hadn't been convincing, or she didn't want to talk about it. But she didn't know what he knew. He got out his notebook.

"Are you insane?"

"What?"

"'What I Know About July'? What the hell is this?"

"My notes."

"Okay, this is just my outside perspective, but if you're a suspect, you don't sit around reading your notes about the victim in public."

His stomach dropped like a wet sandbag. "No one said I was. How else can I solve the case?" Shit. He should've said something about helping the police.

"First of all, we're doing this." She tore off the cardboard cover, folded it up and tossed it in the trash. "You're not Emil, boy detective. This is a person we wanted nothing to do with and, regrettable and scary as this is, we aren't responsible. Whatever quest you think you're on, stop."

"I just wanna make sure I don't forget anything important." His face was scorched by shame, but there was that comforting "we" again. *We* didn't want her around, but it's not *our* fault.

"Special delivery!" Simon started as Soledad set down his drink. "It's me, silly." She patted him on the back and left.

"You barely knew her," Tanja said.

"Know her," he corrected her even before he remembered why it was important. "Turns out I've known her longer than I thought." That got her attention long enough for him to explain. In the back of his mind, he was replaying all the times he'd hated July's inappropriate laughter, all the jokes she must've thought he understood. No wonder she'd never told him about her past: She thought he knew. And before that? Drugs and an ex-husband, maybe a few more things she'd rather forget. He remembered her usual refrain in group therapy about getting out, out, out, and wondered for the first time whether she'd meant out of rehab, or wherever she'd been before.

"She never looked familiar?"

"Not until I saw the old picture on her ID, and even then I didn't realize." He still couldn't get his head around it. All the times he'd resented her for acting like she knew him, like she'd known him before he was famous: she had.

Tanja asked the same question he couldn't answer for himself: "What's it mean?"

"Is it a coincidence?"

She fidgeted with her dishes, stacked the cup on the plate. "Is that possible?"

He shrugged. It was too much of a headache for now. "What did you talk about with Weinert?"

"Whether we went in each other's rooms, the interaction between Sophie and July, whether you were aggressive . . ."

"What?"

"You know, whether you—or any of us—ever got aggressive."

"No, about Sophie."

"Don't worry; I said she laughed it off. But I know, right? What a way to start a relationship."

"Tell me about it." Sophie would never do anything to July, but had he involved her in something dangerous? Then again, no one even knew Sophie's last name. Franzi only knew where she worked. Then he felt even worse, because shouldn't he worry about his sister first and foremost? Not that she seemed too concerned, judging by the few messages they'd exchanged.

"I told him you'd harm neither a fly nor a stalker and you were just too polite to tell her to fuck off. Right?"

"Sure." He sipped his neglected hot chocolate, lukewarm now, most of the cocoa settled on the bottom. Why was she asking? She was supposed to tell the truth, not what made him look good. There should've been enough overlap between the two.

"What else?"

She followed a couple coming through the door with her eyes. "That's about it."

He stirred his drink with her spoon only because he knew she hadn't used it, then finished it in one go. "Wanna head out?"

"I should get home. You, too. It's been a long day."

He walked her to the stop but didn't wait for her tram.

She caught him by the arm. "They'll have to find her ex-husband. It's always the ex, isn't it?"

"Unless there's someone more recent."

"Try to think about something else!" she called as he walked away.

~~~

Something else. Keep busy, don't dwell on it. He walked around the same block until he must've looked crazy, then turned off into a grocery store. Hard to believe it was only early evening. The day seemed endless, all those minutes like the mouths of baby birds, squawking to be filled. He couldn't focus and spent ages trying to figure out what he felt like eating.

At home, he got his mom on the phone while he ate a prewashed salad and bread he tore from the loaf.

"Honey, I'm so proud. Franzi told me your concert was great and you're seeing a nice woman. Things are really coming together, aren't they?"

"Thanks, Mom." Just like Franzi to ban any mention of Christian and then blab about Sophie.

"Did they mind you taking off from work?"

"I quit." He held the receiver away from his mouth to chew.

"Are you sure you'll be okay? You remember the ant and the grasshopper, don't you?"

"Where the grasshopper's a shiftless musician who starves to death? Thanks."

"I just want to make sure you'll be okay. I know I haven't been able to give you as much . . ." She gulped.

He wasn't up for teary recriminations. "I'm earning money with my music, and Barbara said I can have my job back anytime." More like Soledad said he could have a free drink whenever Barbara wasn't there. Same difference.

"I knew you'd figure things out. You were such a smart boy. Now tell me more about this Sophie." Franzi was merciless. Now that his mom knew Sophie's name, it would be no use replacing her with a different woman if things didn't work out.

"Um, she's pretty. She's a writer, but she also works in a . . . *business services center*." He said the words in English so she'd be too impressed to ask questions.

"The problem is, she lives in Hamburg, but she's planning on moving to Berlin."
If only that were the problem. If only that were true.

"How long have you been seeing each other?"

He wondered what Franzi had said. "It's pretty recent, but it's a good fit."
As with Mei, lying filled him with a weird happiness, like it made things true.
What stories had July told herself about their shared past and what lay ahead?
The thought of her was as invasive as she'd been in person, but he forced himself
to focus on the call.

"That's great," his mom was saying. "If you're off the market as long as I was . . ."

"The main thing is that you're happy now." He wished her all the happiness
in the world, even if he only wanted to hear so much about it. Ever since his dad
had started talking about his great sex life when Simon was about sixteen, he'd
had a clammy fear of getting trapped in that kind of conversation. He didn't
have to worry as much with his mom, who referred to sex as "*you* know."

"I just wish your sister would meet somebody."

Tit for tat. "I don't know whether they're together, but I noticed her spending
a lot of time with this one friend. Great guy."

"I'm glad *someone* tells me things." Her sulkiness was a pitch for more
information.

"I guess she's waiting 'til they're official. You know how it is; everything's
always up in the air."

"Don't I know it. Sorry for saying this, because I don't want to criticize all of
you, but plenty of men are only looking for *you* know as fast as they can get it."

That was as far as he wanted to go in that direction. "Yeah, lots of people
don't wanna commit."

"Lucky Sophie isn't like that."

"Yeah. But it's been stressful because this fan who was obsessed with our band
disappeared, so the police have been questioning us. It looks like her ex-husband
might be involved or it's drug-related." He'd mention being a suspect next time.
Hopefully it would be a moot point by then.

"I don't like to hear about you getting mixed up in that kind of thing."

Leave it to her to home in on the word *drug*. "I'm not mixed up in anything.
I hope she's okay."

"Of course I do, too. Terrible what happens nowadays. You know the baker's
son, not the big bakery but the one at the grocery store, died of an overdose?"

He didn't know the baker or his son. "That's awful." He hated these cautionary
tales, but how many times had he seen her since getting "well"? Bad impressions
were the most lasting. "How's work?"

"Same old, same old. Good thing I signed that post-nup, right?" She was a
receptionist and nurse's aide at an old-folk's home, and always joked that she was
in it for the discount later. The part about her unfavorable divorce settlement

was even less funny. He always felt, but never said, that it would've been worth investing in legal counsel.

"Hindsight's twenty-twenty. Anyway, gotta go. I promised Sophie I'd call." How many white lies were you allowed in a day? "Think you'll make it to Berlin soon?" That was the last thing he needed, but he wanted to end the call on a happy note for her.

"We were just talking about it."

"Keep me posted. Have a good evening." Knowing they were coming was exhausting enough. He didn't have the energy for exact dates.

"You, too. Stay out of trouble."

~~~

He rinsed out the tub and turned on the hot water. Sweat it all out. His skin went red when he stepped in, his blood the mercury in some primitive thermometer. He held his notes about July above the water, but he'd already read and reread everything. What if Tanja was right, and he shouldn't get any more involved than he already was?

But he'd *been* there. Just hours, minutes, kilometers or meters away from whatever had happened. And he'd known her so long. She must've had a reason to make a beeline for him as soon as she got out. All he'd seen in her at rehab was a not-too-near miss, a stranger's tragic fate he was relieved not to share. What had she seen in him and been so desperate to keep seeing after?

He sloshed out of the tub to answer his phone. It was David about an invitation to play a charity concert. "No pay, but you're allowed to sell merch if a percentage goes to the charity. It's a great marketing op." To call David their manager was a stretch. He was one of five to ten at the whole label, depending on whether you counted interns.

"Sounds good." He felt ridiculous standing there naked and dripping, but it would be more embarrassing if David heard him get back in the tub.

"Micha said your number-one fan's AWOL?"

"Yeah."

"Crazy stuff. I'm sure they'll find her, though."

"Yeah." Who wasn't sure they'd find her, dead or alive? His throat closed. That happened, too, didn't it—that they never found a body? How would it feel to think about this years from now and still not know?

"Probably off doing something wild. Kids today, right?" David was at most ten years older than Simon, but talked about their fans like he was their grandfather. "You'd know. By the by, I gave your email address to this music blog. Pretty popular. Can you fit in an interview?"

"Sure."

Back in the tub, he wondered where to go from here. Obsessed as July was, she had a whole history outside the band, and even outside of Springtime. Like that ex-husband. He could look him up, hope he was listed, not dangerous or crazy. Although not being dangerous or crazy wouldn't make him the best suspect.

His phone was buzzing again, but he couldn't be bothered. This wasn't the kind of day where it would be Sophie. Just in case, he checked the missed call after getting dressed, but it was an unknown number. He was ready to veg out in front of a detective movie he'd missed the beginning of, when he got a text from Franzi.

"You home?"

"Yep." A smiley to make it less depressing. Not like there was anywhere he'd rather be.

"Make up a bed, please! You're expecting company."

Her line was busy when he called. What was she doing here? Did "company" mean just her, or Christian, too? Sophie? But Sophie would've contacted him herself, and Franzi wouldn't expect them to sleep in separate beds.

He tore open the boxes his air mattress and bedding had come in. He hadn't expected to need them so soon. He'd wanted to find a bigger apartment before he had guests. The airbed took up about ninety percent of the floor space in the kitchen-slash-living room, but it was better to give Franzi some privacy, even if she came alone.

He made up the bed, folded his one threadbare extra towel on top. It was almost eleven. What a time to drop in.

This time he got ahold of her. "I'm so glad you're home," she said. "Apparently it's a real shit show."

"What is?"

"The reception center in Berlin. Hundreds of people arriving exhausted, nowhere to go. Anna said it's pouring rain, too. But you're not getting a brand-new arrival. I think he speaks German. Or English."

He squinted into the darkness outside. Sure enough, it was raining. He'd mistaken the steady rattle for something caught in the plumbing. "You're not in Berlin?"

"Were you asleep? You're so out of it. Anna called me because I put myself as a backup contact when I signed you up to host."

"Host?"

"You *said* to sign you up."

"Oh, shit." He could've killed himself for not taking two seconds to open a link.

"What?"

His doorbell rang, and he buzzed open the front door. "I didn't realize it would be so soon."

"Lucky you! Call if you need anything."

The doorbell rang again, and he opened to a blonde woman in a poncho and her early forties, behind her a thin Middle Eastern man about Simon's age, his t-shirt soaked through and his slight beard dripping. For a second, Simon stood there like in those dreams where you can't move or speak, then he managed to say, "Hi, I'm Simon."

"Anna, and this is Farid. Thank God you're home. Farid's group home was overfilled, he got a voucher for a hostel, but the hostels don't want any more refugees. You speak English, right?" Barely awaiting his nod, she continued, "I hate to rush off, but you have no idea what it's like. Thanks so much." She was three steps down before Simon and Farid shook hands.

Farid followed him in and left his backpack by the door.

"Can I get you something to drink?"

Farid pointed to himself. "Not good German. Syria."

"Tea?" Simon asked in English.

"Thank you, thank you."

Simon wasn't sure if he was referring to the apartment or the tea, but he showed Farid his bathroom and the mattress, trying not to worry about how his place looked. He's just happy to get in out of the rain, he reminded himself, and put on the kettle while Farid got cleaned up. His mind was heavy and blank, and he had to force himself to grasp what was going on. Franzi had suggested taking in a refugee. He'd been too busy obsessing about July to pay attention. Now Farid was here. For how long? He'd ask Franzi. If he asked Farid, it would sound like he wanted to get rid of him. Which he did, of course, but he didn't want him to know that.

He felt the cringing discomfort he remembered from sharing an apartment or crashing with friends: that sense of never doing the appropriate thing, the constant risk of getting caught being odd. Even with that old man at Springtime who'd cried and wet himself in his sleep, Simon had felt ashamed and out of place, not knowing how to be when someone else was looking. He reminded himself of the usual: It's not all about you. Wanting to help others was a lot easier, a lot more comfortable, than actually doing it. At least the language barrier was a blessing in disguise. No pressure to say the right thing.

Next to the mattress, he left a cup of tea and the granola bars he'd bought for when he was too lazy to cook. He set the other cup on his nightstand. Take a deep breath. Whether you're cool is the last thing this guy cares about. He's just happy nobody's bombing him. Now that the surprise was wearing off, he thought how naive his ideas always were. Everyone knew it was mostly men who fled Syria by land, but he'd still been picturing his big volunteering moment as what, smiling fondly as some vaguely foreign-looking kid scribbled in a coloring book? He hadn't expected someone his own age.

He heard the bathroom door open, got his extra set of keys and went out to where Farid was sitting on the mattress in clothes that weren't much cleaner, but at least looked dryer than what he'd arrived in. He handed him the keys and tried to explain in English which was which: "This here, this down there."

Farid thanked him again.

"I go to sleep now. Help yourself to everything." He waved his hands around the apartment and made a thumbs-up.

"Yes, nice house," Farid agreed. "Good night."

"Good night." He closed his door and turned on his reading light. It felt weird having someone here. Before Sophie, the last person he'd spent the night with was nail-biting Ilse who'd rushed him out the next morning, and they'd been at her place. He'd never had a normal guest here. Franzi had been to Berlin since he moved in, but slept in a hostel. That still hurt. At least she'd come over later, realized she could've stayed here. Otherwise, she wouldn't have asked him to host anyone.

Was it weird to give Farid the keys? What difference did it make? He was already here. He felt bad for worrying, but not too bad to move his amp in front of the door as quietly as he could. The door had its own lock, but he'd be embarrassed if Farid heard him use it. He hoped it was July's disappearance making him anxious and not racism he'd unwittingly inherited from his dad, who was personally affronted if anyone spoke a language he didn't, and only knew German.

He got in bed and opened *Dr. Faustus.* His mom was just the opposite, one of those people whose attempts at cultural sensitivity were almost as cringey as prejudice. She referred to headscarves as "those stylish accessories Turkish ladies wear" and Black people as "a tad darker than we are," and seemed to picture "abroad" as the bazaar in Disney's *Aladdin.* Still, her heart was in the right place, and it was lucky she'd gotten custody. He didn't hate his dad; he just . . .

You could say one thing for this situation: It sure was taking his mind off of July.

~~~

He woke feeling that something was different, then remembered what was, and struggled to psych himself up for human interaction. He lifted the amp to avoid a scraping sound, but when he came out, the room was empty.

Farid had left a note on a square of toilet paper: "Hallo Siman, I wait at Social. Auf Wiedersehen, Danke."

He'd be waiting all day at the Office for Health and Social Affairs if Anna was right about the number of people arriving. Simon made up for the selfish relief of that thought by laying out some clean clothes for him and texting Franzi about what he'd need.

"Internet access! Is it going okay?"

He tore a page from his July notebook and wrote down his Wi-Fi password and phone number. "Sure."

She sent him a list of supplies she must've had ready, but didn't reply when he accused her of telling their mom about Sophie, and maybe it wasn't that big a deal.

He skimmed his emails on the off chance of a new post from @JulyAllYear, saying she was fine and asking if anyone had seen her phone or wallet. But the only notifications from their site were replies to the post about refugees, which he didn't bother reading. Both clubs had responded to his requests: The one in Amsterdam wrote that it wasn't technically allowed but they understood the extreme situation and would do their best; they'd already gotten in touch with the booking service. The one in Hamburg wrote with rambling concern and well wishes for his missing fan, and a data protection agreement for him to sign before they proceeded. He thanked both of them and sent a digital signature. He hadn't thought to tell Weinert about the requests, but, unless he found something out, there wasn't much to tell.

The blogger had emailed him, but he didn't feel like replying, so he forwarded it to Micha and Tanja with a question mark and got ready to go out. It was important to keep busy.

~~~

He stopped for coffee and a croissant he soon converted to crumbs all over his clothes and the tram. He had nothing to read, but that was just as well. He needed to remember.

He got up to give his seat to a frail old lady with an infinitesimal Yorkie, but a potbellied man in paint-flecked blue overalls snatched it before opening a bottle of beer with his lighter. Simon thought about saying something but knew he never would. It wasn't worth taking off his headphones to hear the comeback.

So the first time he'd seen July. The first time after rehab, anyway. She was still two different people to him. At the merch table, she'd said, "Simon, right?" Now that he thought about it, she'd known that even before the show. Had she introduced herself as July or Julia? She'd looked young, thin but not unhealthy.

The potbellied man stepped on Simon's foot getting out, but apologized when he said "ow" loud enough for the whole car to hear. The old lady got a seat, and the Yorkie rested its head on one of her orthopedic beige shoes. Of course, July's face had healed by the time he saw her again. That busted lip had been a real eye-catcher, one of those features you spend so much energy not looking at you barely see the person underneath. He'd never thought about how she got it. It had seemed like the natural result of a bad scene.

A crowd of tourists got on and forced him into the joint between the cars, where the ground moved beneath his feet. He could still feel the vibrations as the flow of passengers washed him out at Alexanderplatz, and it took him a second to realize they were coming from his pocket.

"Did you see my message?" Micha asked as soon as he picked up.

"No, why?"

"Mina and I wanna go away for a couple days."

"Sounds nice." Weaving through all the panhandlers, tourists and disaffected teenagers between him and Galeria Kaufhof, he wondered what Micha wanted. He sounded like he was asking for a favor.

"What with me having been away, she thought, I mean, I thought I need to step up and show how committed I am. Spend some quality time."

"Sure." Simon stopped to watch a bulldog skateboard back and forth with unimaginable levels of apathy on its fat, jowled face, but didn't want to look like some gaping yokel, so he continued through the glass doors of the department store, past the suited guards and the clinical smell of the cosmetics department.

"So could we do the interview today? I know you're busy, but I'd call the guy."

Him, busy? Micha definitely needed a favor. "Sure, can we meet near Alexanderplatz?"

"Sure. Tanja already said today's fine."

"Great." He got off the escalator in the books section and grabbed a pocket-sized German-Arabic dictionary from the bestsellers table.

"See, we don't have *that* much money. You know how it is at the video store."

"You need to borrow some?" There was no reason for Micha to feel weird about it. Simon had crashed at his place long enough. Carrying the dictionary away from his body to avoid being taken for a shoplifter, he moved on to stationery.

"No, what I mean is, I was thinking maybe we could stay at your dad's lake house."

Simon sighed. It wasn't a lot to ask. He just needed a minute to cope with the dread it entailed.

"If you think he'd be chill about it."

"I'll call him."

"You know, it feels great to take a leap of faith and commit. It's freeing."

"I'm sure it is." He was ready to hang up and take a leap to the cash register.

~~~

Instead of calling, he wrote his dad to ask whether a friend could use the house. As an afterthought, he added "Hey, how are you?" before hitting Send. He'd never stayed there himself and only mentioned it to say what a dick his dad could be, paying the bare minimum when they were growing up, then expecting them to be grateful when he said they could use his vacation home.

He paid and went to the men's department. He could've gotten clothes cheaper somewhere else, but didn't want to make twenty stops or seem stingy. In front of who? Was Franzi going to come accuse him of dressing his guest in cheap clothing? Obviously, Farid had other worries. Okay, so he was also doing it for himself. It was healthier than other things he could've indulged in. He bought shirts, pants, socks and underwear, adding a heavy sweater because, warm as it was now, most of the year wasn't t-shirt weather. Hopefully, Farid would be living somewhere else before he needed it. He bought a travel bag, put everything in it and headed across the square, where the bulldog had been replaced by the grating tones of a bagpipe. When his phone rang in the drugstore, he overcame the urge to let it go to voicemail.

"Simon, my boy," his dad boomed in his usual falsely hearty tone. "That's a fine thing, not hearing from you in months and then 'can my friend come stay'!" Or maybe it was real heartiness. He could never tell whether his dad was so used to being insincere he couldn't stop, or if he was just that sure of himself. Dr. Froheifer had told him to channel his happy memory, which wasn't a memory at all but a waterlogged picture of them playing soccer he'd found when he was helping his mom replace her old fridge. He was four or five, and they did look happy.

"I figured you'd be at work."

"I am. But when you're as successful as I am, you can take a call."

"Sure." His dad had been a business consultant for a while now, but Simon still had trouble understanding why people would pay to talk to him. He'd pay not to. He fought the usual sense of himself as some cringing Kafka roach afraid of being stomped. It wasn't like his dad had hit them or anything. He was just so . . . present.

"What's so important you couldn't check in with your old man?"

If he paid his dues, Micha could use the house and he'd be off the hook for a while. The other trick he was supposed to use was imagining how he'd feel if his dad died when they were on bad terms, but that made him too panicky. "We were touring Europe and . . ." Don't mention July. Or, worse still, Sophie. "I have a friend visiting." Anything but his love life. He couldn't stomach any gross just-us-boys remarks right now.

"Another one of your layabout musicians?"

Simon had never had any layabout musicians other than himself staying in his apartment. He didn't know what Farid did, but knew what would sound best to his dad. "No, Farid's an engineer."

"Farid? That some Turk?"

Why hadn't he made up a German name? On the other hand, he wasn't going to feel bad about doing something he wished he wasn't, but knew was right. "He's from Syria."

"What are you, running an ISIS exchange program?"

"He's a refugee."

"I knew we had one nutty do-gooder in the family, but now you've caught it. You know I hate to refuse you anything." Except help paying for music lessons and college, Simon didn't say, because that had been directed at his mom, not him. His dad had always made good money at VW, but only climbed really high after his second marriage, leaving in time to avoid the tricky emissions questions scientists were starting to ask. Withholding money had been about power rather than greed. "I'm not racist, but I don't want some Al Qaeda mooch in a house I bought with my hard-earned money."

There was no point trying to talk sense into him, or there was and it would've been the right thing to do, but he just wanted his dad to let Micha use the house so he could hang up.

"I'm asking whether *Micha* can stay there. My drummer, from Leipzig?"

"Oh, that's fine." He explained where the spare key was and what rules Micha needed to follow before returning to cringey remarks Simon hoped no one would overhear. He got desperate enough for a new topic to mention Sophie, who was branded an unstable groupie.

"How's Cindi?"

"Sassy as ever. Put on a little weight, though."

That was enough. He hung up in the middle of a sentence, ignored his dad's call, called back and hung up, then texted that he had no reception "in this damn tunnel." For the thousandth or millionth time, he assured himself that his dad must've been different when he was conceived. Even if she'd been young, his mother must've had higher standards. Then again, maybe his dad loved him and was genuinely worried about him being murdered by terrorists or crazed groupies. The latter wasn't that unrealistic. Groupie, not groupies. But the thought seemed in poor taste now.

He and Micha called each other at the same time, then he let Micha's call come through in the mile-long line where three giggling teens kept pulling the cord to summon more cashiers, even though all the registers were open.

"Telepathy, man. We're meeting in half an hour. That pretentious café behind the tracks."

"My dad says it's okay. He also says my roommate's in ISIS *and* Al Qaeda, and Sophie's a crazy groupie."

"What roommate? Listen—"

The line was speeding up. "Okay, see you."

~~~

Simon was there first, of course, because that was what he'd wanted to avoid. It was like a blind date, trying to look like you were looking for someone without making eye contact with anyone. He should've googled the guy. Or brought *Dr. Faustus*, although that might look like he wanted to be seen reading it.

The safest option was getting in line. Nobody could fault you for that. The only question was whether to get black coffee to look tough, or a flat white to look hip.

"Simon!" A lanky man with black-framed glasses, sparse blond hair and a t-shirt in Brittany stripes tapped his arm. "I'm Jan."

"Great to meet you!" Everyone loves enthusiasm. "The others will be here soon. What can I get you?" Was he that concerned about some blog? No, he just wanted Jan and everybody else to like him.

"You've got your shopping; let me."

"Oh, it's not mine, I mean . . . Thanks." He was already making a fool of himself. There was no need to be ashamed of shopping bags. "A latte would be great." He would've gotten a snack but didn't want to look like he was taking advantage of someone else paying.

The only table left was surrounded by a sprawling leather sofa and a square ottoman. Simon sat down at one arm of the sofa, careful not to let his face slip out of a neutral smile. Did knowing you were pathetic make you less pathetic?

Tanja must not have worried about looking like a mooch, because when she joined him on the sofa, she had a monumental slice of chocolate cake and a huge glass of bright green iced tea with slices of pineapple sticking out.

"Try a bite? I got another fork because of my extra-infectious germs, but I licked it."

"Thanks." He took a bite. Asking her not to make him sound neurotic might backfire. "How are you?"

"Good. I had to clean up our site a little." He pictured her struggling with the settings at her ancient desktop, its fans whirring with exertion. Like he knew anything about technology. "Now that July's not filling up the comments, some far-right troll posted this poorly spelled rant below that refugee thing of Franzi's. I signed up for the gym, too; can you tell?" She flexed her arm in the sleeve of a loose black sweater. "I haven't gone yet, but I think my lungs can bear it soon. Think how much I haven't smoked lately."

"I heard the tobacco industry wants a bailout. What'd the troll say?"

"The usual about how we're naive do-gooders playing into the Islamists' hands."

"Oh, I saw that." Jan handed Simon a latte and sat down on the ottoman with his own cold brew and tonic. "We get those, too. These weirdos search for anything pro-refugee. To those right-wing Pegida nuts, I'm part of the 'lying press' anyway, so who cares?" He had the kind of laid-back manner that put Simon at ease and was impossible for him to imitate. He made a mental note—July's disappearance: neo-Nazis?—before dismissing it as absurd.

Micha came in huffing and puffing with a story about getting the van inspected, then hurried to the counter.

"Micha's in love," Tanja said. "It makes him a little dumber."

"I thought we'd start with your development as a band, but our readers do always want to know more about the people behind the music."

Simon's phone vibrated. Should he check whether it was an emergency? But there was no emergency where he'd be able to help. He preferred to believe it was

Sophie and he could tell her about this later. Because yeah, getting interviewed sounded a lot cooler than anything else he'd done lately.

" . . . Simon's stripped-down, cerebral sound, which we flesh out," Tanja was saying as Micha slipped onto the sofa with his head down like a kid sneaking into class after the bell. "I wasn't involved in the first album, but that balance between human frailty and a sudden affirming beat is built into our style. That helped me decide to join."

She was a professional in a way Simon would never be. He hadn't even gone to her first meeting with Poor Dog, which was probably a good thing. She looked the part today, all in black, ungelled hair hanging like a Beatle's, thoughtful pose with her chin on one fist.

"Did it feel risky to replace two different bassists?" Jan was sipping his drink and recording instead of taking notes. Like Weinert.

"I was at a difficult point in my life," she said as Simon prayed they wouldn't go into why Tom and Nadine had left. It wasn't all his fault. It couldn't always be. "A crossroads. The album really spoke to me with its hope-against-hope brightness. The choruses like that depressing thought you can't get out of your head, then each verse moving forward. I wasn't listening to much indie back then, but I was sold right away." Whether or not that was true, it was nice to hear. She didn't go into detail about her "crossroads," but that didn't mean she'd made it up. Noisy waters could also run deep.

"Did you worry about establishing your place in the band?"

"I thought, hell, I'll give it a try." Slipping out of her role. Simon couldn't help but smile. "Then I realized I could really contribute."

To Jan, but also because it was something he didn't say often enough, might never have said, Simon added, "At first, it was like, we need a bassist, let's get a bassist, and we found these talented musicians." In case Nadine or Tom read this. "But Tanja really took charge. We've rewritten songs around the bassline because it was so powerful." Only two, but who was counting?

Micha put his hand in front of a mouthful of sandwich. "Totally."

"Thanks." She was blushing. Simon's face was hot, too. Only Micha was unconcerned, counting on them to steer this in the right direction. Good man. Wanted Simon to take a leap and be happy, wouldn't be embarrassed if thousands of people read about him talking with his mouth full. Simon felt lucky to be in a band with exactly these people.

"Without Micha, there wouldn't be a band. I played with Andreas Odem a while, but Micha was the one who convinced me we could start our own band after I left that one."

"Was that around when your drug problem started?"

Hats off for Jan's first pointed question. But there were only right answers, as long as he didn't do the honest thing and deny it. He was a musician, not running for chancellor. "Yeah. I lost sight of who I wanted to be, and I'm lucky my family and friends were ready to be part of my life again after. You couldn't pay me to take drugs now. It's the hard-earned happiness that counts, not some cheap fix that makes things feel better while making everything worse." He was overdoing it. Most people reading this took MDMA in clubs every weekend or had subscriptions for organic pot. He sounded like one of those speakers they brought into your health class. He needed more of the penitential sinner à la Johnny Cash. "I can't undo the pain I caused. All I can do is try to live a good life now." That was the right note, and sort of true.

After discussing their first album, they moved on to *Georg's Friend in St. Petersburg*. Micha had finished eating so he took over while Simon picked at Tanja's cake, drank his coffee, and felt that sense of well-being that usually only comes after an averted crisis.

"You mentioned that troll on your site. How'd you decide to speak out in favor of refugees?"

"My sister does a lot of volunteering, and she asked us to."

"There shouldn't be any question about whether to help people fleeing from war and terror but, unfortunately, it needs to be said." Tanja was back in her thoughtful pose after slurping her drink down to the ice.

"Are you involved in any other charitable projects?"

The silence felt long enough for Simon to mumble, "A Syrian guy's staying in my living room." Saying that felt like bragging about something he'd never meant to sign up for. Then Tanja mentioned the benefit concert, and he wished he'd kept his mouth shut.

Jan said he'd link to it, then turned to Simon. "You're hosting a refugee?"

Tanja maintained an unsurprised silence, but Micha said, "Oh, *that's* why your dad—"

No matter what, he had to prevent Micha from repeating what his dad had said. "Yep, my sister arranged it."

"I admire that." Jan must've noticed his embarrassment. "Micha, I hear you're in love." He winked at Tanja. "How has the band's success affected your relationship?"

"Since we met at a show, I wouldn't be in this relationship otherwise. For me, it's all about going the extra mile. We're not the youngest people in the world, so you have to know what's important."

"Could that level of commitment ever cause you to quit?"

"Even big bands don't tour all the time. But if it came down to it, I know what I'd choose."

News to me, Simon thought. Micha was really playing up the commitment thing, when the fact was that he always had some girlfriend. But maybe this was *the* girlfriend.

"Simon?"

"Sorry, what?"

"Whether you have any trouble maintaining relationships between touring and working odd hours," Tanja summarized.

"No, not because of that. That is . . ." Great, now it sounded like he had trouble with relationships in general. It was bad enough that it was true without him blabbing about it to some hipster blog. "The relationship has to be at a certain point before you can commit."

"You've been characterized as a womanizer. How do you see your attitude toward women?"

What, had they interviewed Dr. F? No, this had Nadine written all over it. He'd seen, but not read, an interview with her band by the same blog. "I'd never wanna see myself that way. I hope Tanja would back me up in saying I really respect women." The old "I have lots of female friends" card. "I'm just insecure and have trouble believing someone would want a relationship with me."

"Was it like that with former bassist Nadine Amsel, now of The Apathy Collective?"

"Insecurity was a factor, along with putting my life back together after rehab." His heart sank thinking about what would come up now that he'd mentioned rehab again, then he remembered that Jan couldn't know about July having been at Springtime.

"You have a reputation for taking home a different fan at every show."

Definitely Nadine, since July wasn't around to say so. "I'm not good at meeting women, so any 'one-night stand'"—Make it sound like there's nothing more abhorrent—"was initiated by the other person. But my therapist helped me realize none of those women was looking for a relationship, so I avoided any romantic involvement for about a year." Sure, that was on purpose.

"And now?"

Sophie couldn't call him on this without admitting she'd googled him and read the interview. "I met a writer."

Tanja gave his shoulder a squeeze, her grip a little too hard. "I don't think there's much more to say about that."

Then a few safe topics like where they'd grown up. Talking about his struggling single mother would help counteract any supposed womanizing. They had to be done soon. He could tell by his stomach—clenched to hold in the growling—that a lot of time had passed. He should've gotten his own cake.

"Okay, last thing before pictures." Jan rummaged in his upcycled rice sack. Nobody had mentioned pictures. Then again, Simon never looked much better than now. Jan produced the last thing he would've expected: a tabloid with a title story about criminal foreigners. He opened it to a page reading "Berlin Woman

Missing," and Simon was surprised to recognize July. It must've been a recent picture because she had a healthy weight and those new bangs.

"I came across this while researching you. Apparently, she'd gone to your show. She's also the number-one poster on your website. You know her?"

Anybody but me.

"Slightly," Tanja said. "She comes to a lot of shows."

Having gotten ahold of himself, Simon added, "We've been trying to help, but it's hard given how little we know her." Was that a lie? Well, how little they knew *about* her. Not even enough to fill a pocket-sized notebook. "Anyone who knows anything should contact the police."

"Judging by her posts, it almost seems like she was stalking you. Did you feel threatened?"

Tanja again, before Simon could say anything inappropriate: "No, she knew we only have a limited amount of time for each fan."

"I'll certainly remind readers to share any information they have. This sofa's perfect. We can do some serious pictures and some silly ones."

~~~

They let Jan leave first.

"That went okay," Simon said. "Right?"

"We were golden," Tanja said.

"The July part was out of left field," said honest Micha.

"I didn't expect it to be in the papers." He was so self-obsessed he'd only thought of how it affected him. His guilt, his fear of being a suspect, his heroic quest. When she might have loved ones trying to get the word out however they could. Even in a low-brow, high-circulation tabloid. Then again, the tabloid could've found out on its own. They tended to latch onto local crime stories. Or was that his inability to imagine anyone worrying about July?

"We came across as concerned," Tanja said. "How about some fresh air? My ass is glued to this sofa."

"You really killed it," Micha said. "We didn't say anything nearly as good."

"I knew you wouldn't. That's why I prepared all those sophisticated insights."

They passed the neighborhood's unique blend of erotic shops, vintage clothing and Scandinavian furnishings, then the theater making its usual painful effort to be provocative by flying flags that read "Eat Shit" and "We Hate You." Simon was half listening to the others, half listening to the formless dread within him. Was it Nietzsche who said guilt was fear of punishment? He didn't seriously think he'd serve time because of July, or that anyone would openly call him a failure. But he'd never know for sure whether everyone thought he was guilty and pathetic. He told himself he was only hungry and some questions had caught him off-guard. It was easy to forget there were no secrets in the internet age. Not as long as your ex was giving interviews.

"I felt weird about Nadine."

"Are you sure you're over her?" Tanja asked.

"It's been ages," Micha said. "How long were you even together?"

"About as long as you and Mina, I guess." He regretted the words, which brought them to a halt below the red flags of the leftist party headquarters, as soon as he'd said them. "I'm over her."

"Is this because you're jealous?" Micha said as Tanja asked, "You're sure?"

"How about you both lay off?"

"Okay, I'm sorry," Micha said in that filler way people who aren't at all sorry use to catch their breath before the next onslaught. "But I feel like, why can't you be happy for me? Why's it about how we haven't been together long enough, or like, oh, that's big dumb Micha and his feelings aren't as, um, *smart* as my feelings, because I'm Simon the genius who—"

"Guys, let's not ruin a good—"

But they ignored Tanja.

"Oh, that's rich. Like *I'm* the one going on about my smart feelings. I'm *begging* for another lecture about leaps of faith. What I really need—"

"What you need is to grow the fuck—"

"Guess I've been wasting my time at therapy when I know such a brilliant— Ow! Why'd you hit me and not him?"

Tanja elbowed Micha in the gut to even things out. "Both of you shut up. I'm not in the mood for reality-TV bullshit. Wanna get dinner?"

"Mina's waiting for me. You know, the trip." Micha blushed, maybe remembering where they were staying.

Simon bit his tongue, because it wasn't worth it. Later, Micha would somehow turn out to have been in the right. "I'm sorry." Try to sound sincere, despite the sarcastic age we live in, our inability to turn off the irony. "You're right. I'd like to settle down, too, so it's hard for me to be as happy for you as I'd like to." Was it wrong that he was thinking about how much effort it would take to replace Micha? It was always wrong if you had to ask.

"Thanks, man. I appreciate you having the guts to admit it. I know you're stressed, and I'm sorry I lashed out. You're like a little brother to me, you know?"

"Thanks for looking out for me." With a big brother like this, no wonder he was a loser.

~~~

"That was heartwarming," Tanja said when Micha was out of earshot. "Thanks for not being an aggressive ass for *too* long. Although next time go ahead and skip it."

"Thanks for hitting us, I guess. No one's waiting for me, so . . ."

"I know this great falafel place. We'll just have to kill someone to get a seat."

"To answer your question, I'm over her, but not over having been such a fuckup, and probably still being one."

It felt good to say that, but also good not to talk about it at dinner, where Tanja said that Lara of brief Amsterdam fame probably wasn't coming to Berlin. "Micha's gotten pretty preachy," she added, "but he's right that we're not getting any younger."

"Sure." He was still bummed, but having something in his stomach put a buffer between him and his roiling mess of anxieties. The buzz of background chatter and Arabic synth pop helped fill any dangerous gaps in his mind where unwanted thoughts might slip in.

"Anyway, call Sophie. If that doesn't work out, keep looking. You hear a lot of bullshit about finding someone when you're not looking, but have you ever found anything you weren't looking for? Anything good, I mean. Yeah, we're leaving," she snapped at the people hovering behind their stools.

"I will." He remembered that missed call, but didn't look at his phone. He could feel it emitting a sad little hope, the kind you don't want to verify because that would reveal it for the hopelessness it is.

"Don't let it get to you," she said outside.

"What?"

"Any of it. You getting the train?"

"I'll walk." Because he remembered that someone *was* home waiting for him, and like the antisocial creep he was, he didn't feel like hanging out with his guest.

~~~

The missed call was from his mom, with one voicemail where she thought he'd picked up and another saying when she and Reinhardt were coming. He called back but only let it ring once, knowing the phone would be too deep in her purse for her to hear, but wanting her to feel like she had a dutiful son. He texted: "Can't wait!"

Farid wasn't home, but Simon could never really enjoy solitude unless he knew it wouldn't be interrupted. Funny how you could feel lonely and crave being alone at the same time. He took the price tags off his purchases and left them by the mattress.

He was brushing his teeth when he heard the door open, so he finished up and came out. You knew it was the right thing when it was the last thing you felt like doing. "Hey, how are you?"

"Okay." Farid shrugged. "I wait, wait, wait."

"You'll have your appointment soon." Probably not, but what were you supposed to say? "Some things for you," he said in English.

Farid looked in the bag and shook his head.

"Doch." Simon didn't think English had a special word for insisting in the face of disagreement.

Farid moved his hands back and forth, sweeping things off some invisible surface. "Danke, but not good buy things for me."

Doch, Simon thought, it is good. How to get around the language barrier and explain that Farid was helping him feel better? Anything he was doing for him, he was also doing for himself. How could he express that in any language without making Farid feel used or condescended to? He settled for: "Use if you need. If not, give back later."

"Okay, danke," In slow, measured German, Farid said, "When Germany have war, you come with me in Syria."

Their laugh was sheepish.

"You speak good German. Are you taking a class?"

"No, three month here, then can have class. But I do this." On his phone, he pulled up a video of a man writing German and Arabic words on a whiteboard. "Man, woman, girl, boy, hungry, thirsty, tired, Germany, Syria."

Then came that conscience Simon had on backward that so often gave him a creeping sense of guilt at the thought of doing something good. "I'll help you learn."

"Thanks, good speak German, but today tired."

"Of course." In English, he said, "We make a different time. Good night."

"Good night."

Simon closed the door to his stuffy room and opened a window. He could hear Farid getting ready for bed and cars driving by. His head was full of more than he could think at once. But inside him there was a bright and peaceful silence like snowflakes under a streetlight, falling softly onto those that came before. Maybe there was good in him, after all.

He woke when he heard the door close, and then a few hazy dreams later to his phone.

"I didn't wake you, did I?" Weinert asked.

"No. Yeah."

"Is it a good time?"

He got the feeling it would have to be.

Four

In the tram, he read his emails to avoid thinking. Franzi said she and Christian might come to the benefit concert. David loved how the interview had come out. Simon was surprised that it already had, but then it wasn't like they'd had to print it. Some software or intern must've converted it to text. He needed five whole minutes to get himself to open Sophie's email. It was blank. He was about to send a question mark when he saw the attachment.

The file name was a string of numbers, but when he opened it, the title read: "The Stalker." Was it a cruel joke? A coincidence? He wrote: "Looking forward to reading this after the police station."

She replied: "Heavy."

He wanted to take advantage of her communicative mood, but didn't know what to say. Luckily she'd already written: "What's the latest on the case? FAS-CINATED by this July stuff." Then, "Sorry for being pushy. Call me after?" And a meaningless winky face to put everything in quotes.

"Will do." There was comfort in knowing there was an after. When he was sick, unhappy or dreading something, he always felt like nothing existed outside the present, that he'd always be sick, miserable, afraid. If there was a hell, maybe it was that, except without the tiny rational part of his mind telling him it would be over soon. He needed to think of it as a dentist's visit again. Doctors were scary because they could diagnose terrible diseases, but dentists couldn't come up with much more than an expensive root canal. Weinert would ask questions, not throw him in jail. This was a democracy with due process and the rest.

He considered reading the story, but didn't want it in his head while he talked to Weinert. It was like Sophie had slipped him some top-secret intel that could be tortured out of him. Sort of.

He was almost there, the same stop he would've gotten out at for July's apartment. He hadn't been back. Busy or losing interest? Maybe Tanja's reality check was sinking in.

~~~

Seeing the same receptionist was reassuring, like a familiar face at a party where you didn't expect to know anyone.

"How's the music biz?" he asked after calling Weinert.

"Great, we just—"

But Weinert was already there. Either the case had gotten more important or it was a slow time for crime-solving. Walking down the corridor with its pamphlets and memo boards, Simon thought again how differently he'd pictured a police station. Where were the flashy pimps, the fistfights breaking out?

"Sorry to wake you." Weinert offered him a belated handshake. "We're in here today." He led Simon into a room with a table, two plastic chairs, an opaque window and a blinking red light in one corner of the ceiling, already recording. Had July gotten more missing or had he gotten more suspicious? At least he didn't have his notes on him. He tried not to read into it, reminding himself that, in the movies, the police came to your home. Wasn't it a good sign that they weren't interested in catching him in some act? He brushed off his chair and sat down opposite Weinert.

"Any progress?" It felt like small talk again, asking about someone's family or hobby.

"We were thinking she might just have taken off. But the phone, wallet and lack of bank activity looked bad. Now we've heard from our colleagues in Amsterdam."

"Oh?"

"They found a body. Been in the canal for days."

"A body?" he repeated with the glaring stupidity of shock. The words barely managed to slip past the bulky nausea filling his throat and creeping into the back of his mouth.

"We're not a-hundred-percent sure." There were dark rings under Weinert's eyes like someone had woken him up even earlier. "But it looks like we've got a murder on our hands."

Blood was pounding in Simon's ears so loud he could hardly hear. "She's . . . ?"

"Are you alright? Need something to drink?" Weinert gestured to the glasses and pitcher on the table, bubbles already forming in the stagnant water.

"That's okay." Who knew if they washed the cups between suspects? He ran the icy back of his hand over his burning forehead. Deep breath. Everything's okay, even if it isn't. You're alive, even if she's not.

"Do you have any travel plans, Herr Kemper?" Weinert asked, as if it really were all just small talk.

"I might go to Hamburg sometime, but nothing definite." Blood was redistributing itself painfully, as if his head and limbs had fallen asleep in an awkward position.

"I'd like to ask you not to go anywhere for now. As a favor to me."

"Why?" But he was already a step further, already the criminal they thought he was: If they had anything on me, he wouldn't be asking for favors.

"You're an important witness. We'd also like to speak to your drummer, of course, but you may have been one of the last people to see the victim alive."

"Micha's away for a couple days. Am I a suspect?"

"We can't rule anybody out. But the other reason I asked you to come in is because we got your test back. The hair segments indicate a single dose of GHB around mid-June. You can pick up the exact results on your way out." Weinert poured himself a glass of water, but didn't drink from it. "Now, people do take it recreationally, but not usually such a high dose." So he really had been drugged. "Of course, the analysis isn't as precise as we'd like it to be. We can't say exactly when you consumed it."

"I wouldn't have been able to play the show if I'd taken it beforehand." But if mid-June was the best they could do, he could've killed her, hidden the body and then roofied himself for an alibi. If he'd thought of that, so had they. But the main thing was knowing he hadn't done anything. Did he?

"We have witnesses saying you were incoherent at the party. I'm inclined to believe you."

"Thanks, I guess."

"I don't think you killed anyone, so you can be honest with me."

"I am." Remember that you were too sick to murder her, even if . . . what?

"We also have statements saying you and the victim had a loud fight, and you repeatedly tried to kiss the victim, who slapped you. Sound familiar?"

"Didn't we already talk about this?" He hated the easy blush he felt spilling over his face like a warm liquid. Like the blood it was.

"You didn't mention aggressively coming on to her."

"I wasn't sure exactly what happened, or what's relevant."

"Everything's relevant. From now on."

He was a lot quieter, but Weinert suddenly reminded Simon of when his dad used to get mad at him or Franzi. Usually about some minor thing, but he'd never let up until they'd admitted their guilt while their mom stood off to one side like a footnote nobody reads, moving her mouth in weak protest they couldn't hear over the shouting.

"Okay. We had drinks with her friend with the dreadlocks. I was talking about the woman July thought was my girlfriend. I was a little woozy and tried to sit on the floor, but she pulled me outside. I kissed her. She didn't want me to because of my girlfriend, and I said I made that up. She slapped me. I fell and cut my leg. She was gonna leave me there, but I held onto her leg like a kid, you know, because I was on the ground? I was having trouble thinking. I wanted a cab, but she knew someone who'd drive us. In the car, she was speaking Dutch. When I asked about Micha, she told me to go to sleep." And that was the last time I'll ever hear her voice. A hard, hot hand clutched his heart, held it back a few beats. He hadn't even liked her, but he'd . . . what? Known her?

"Who gave you your last drink?"

"I'm not sure." All the cups of punch were one nauseating blur.

"Who drove?"

"The man."

"He was wearing a cap?"

"Yes."

"What'd the cap look like?"

It seemed like a stupid question in light of all the bigger questions. "Maybe black. It was dark."

"But there was enough light for you to recognize the victim?"

"I guess I recognized her voice." Even if a later transcript would seem to show some doubt, he'd known it was her the way you know someone in a dream: that innate, primal sense of identity. How? His brain felt impotent, or flaccid after spewing out its contents. He was having trouble stirring it again. And this was the case he'd planned to solve. "She has—had this way of saying my name. She'd draw out the first syllable, 'Siii.' Like when someone's teasing you?" He could almost hear it now, like that creak of a floorboard in a room you know should be empty. "Besides, she and Tanja were the only women there who knew me, and Tanja left with this girl."

"Romantically?"

"Yeah." So she hadn't mentioned Lara. That was the thing about the truth: It only worked if everybody stuck to it.

"Was there any overlap between people at your concert and the party?"

"Some, I guess."

"Did you say your name onstage?"

"Sure."

"So some people knew who you were?"

"Yeah, but like I said . . ."

"You felt sure it was her."

"She said we'd get a ride with her friend, then I'm in a car with a guy and a woman exactly like her."

"I don't like to assume anything." Weinert sounded as worn out as Simon felt, probably from hard work rather than emotional vertigo. "I'd like you to look at some pictures." He pushed a manila envelope over his desk. "Tell me who was at the party."

"Sure." An envelope, how retro. But Weinert probably had the pictures saved under "Murder Suspects" and "Decoy Photos" on his computer.

Simon shook his head at some Black men with dreadlocks. He'd neglected to mention that both guys were white. There was one with a crew cut he couldn't place but found vaguely familiar; a freckled, smiling woman and a serious-looking South Asian one who might've been in the group laughing at him. At least he was sure about the mustachioed hipsters. Then came a guy with a ruddy complexion, light blue eyes and a nose that looked like it had been broken.

"I can't . . ." But he could. He covered the edges of the face and its short curls. "It's an old picture, isn't it? I'm pretty sure this is July's friend with the dreadlocks."

"How sure is pretty sure?"

"If I saw him, I'd think, where do I know that guy from? Don't you have a more recent picture?"

"This was what they had on record."

"On record?"

"Let's get through the rest."

He identified the bartender, then was startled to recognize a picture of H vs. H. He felt like he'd run into himself on a crowded street corner.

Weinert hurried to turn to the next picture.

"It's okay; I get it."

"We'd usually have asked, but it was online."

"Sure." Then thuggish and athletic types in baseball caps at various angles. He couldn't identify any of them. He fidgeted in his seat, which was slowly gluing itself to his skin through his clothes.

"Are you in a hurry?"

"No, it's okay." There was no hurry anymore, no rush to question suspicious lurkers or ex-husbands. No hurry and no point, because you couldn't undo a body. But they still had to find the killer. Why? The usual clichés about bringing him—or her?—to justice, preventing more killings. No, not clichés, well-worn truths. And there must be people who'd miss July.

"Tell me about the car."

"I don't remember what kind."

"How big was it?"

"Normal."

"What color?"

"I don't remember."

"You said you could see the back of the man's head. No headrests?"

"Doch. I couldn't see the back of July's head. He must've been taller." He tried to picture how a person's head looked in the driver's seat. Had the driver been a giant? "Or there was a headrest on her side and not his."

"What about the interior?"

"Dark."

"Leather or fabric?"

It had been warm in the car, but he hadn't stuck to the seat like he was sticking to this chair. "I think fabric."

"You made a couple calls to the victim's cell phone the day you left Amsterdam."

"That was Tanja calling to ask what she drugged me with, but no one picked up."

"And the calls to Frau Tappet's landline? Was that also someone else?"

"No. I wanted to see if she'd come home in the meantime." He felt ashamed, caught out, but, at the end of the day, having called made him look less like he'd dumped her body the week before. Hopefully. "Are we done?"

"For now. You remember what we said about traveling?"

"I won't."

"Thanks. Sorry for the inconvenience."

Simon shook his hand and headed out to the reception desk, where the clerk handed him an envelope with his name on it.

"Thanks. Wait." He hurried back, no longer sure which of the identical doors they'd been talking behind. "Detective Weinert!" Heads poked out, and the clerk jogged over to point out the right room. What was worth making a fool of himself? Nothing. Exactly that. The nothing between the two front seats, the empty space below that last cup of punch.

He burst in without knocking. "There was no center console in the front of the car!" It sounded a little anticlimactic once he'd said it aloud.

~~~

Out in the light of midday, he savored the dry heat, his evaporating sweat the only source of humidity. He hadn't cracked the case, but might've helped, for what it was worth now. Had the gearshift been on the steering column or the wheel? Or somewhere else entirely? He didn't know much about cars, but if the Netherlands were anything like Germany, that would narrow things down.

He opened his test results, but there were only a few lines of abbreviations and numbers with a lot of decimal places, plus a website he could visit for more information. He crumpled them up to throw away, then pocketed them instead. This was a murder case now. He wasn't about to toss good evidence.

On his way to the tram, he remembered the call he was supposed to make, and his sweat went cold. The body changed everything. Sophie's interest in July had always been a little macabre; now it seemed sick, even if she couldn't know. He might not have the highest moral standards, but he wasn't going to use July's death. Or was he just chicken?

~~~

Walking home from his stop, his legs were ten times their usual weight and his back ached with every step. He tried to remember July and not think about her at the same time. What had she seen in him at Springtime, while he tried not to look at her? Someone recovering? But she'd recovered, too. And after? Everything was a shapeless blur of hurt. He had the selfish wish never to have known her, or at least not to know she was dead. If he hadn't gotten involved, he would've assumed she'd lost interest. But it would've been worse to find out some other way, her death in the paper like a stranger's. He went home and got in bed, telling Farid he wasn't feeling well, and no thanks, he didn't want any tea.

He didn't want to totally blow off Sophie, so he wrote, "It's been a rough day, call you tomorrow." He felt weak enough to add "Come to Berlin so we can talk" before turning off his phone to keep from waiting for her reply. Instead, he opened her story on his laptop.

"He just couldn't get rid of her," the first sentence read, and he felt a tight shudder of guilt. If he hadn't found out she was missing—and now dead—he would've been glad July was gone. But this story wasn't about him. Even if Sophie thought it was. She didn't know him well enough. He was too upset to tell whether it was any good. It started like with July and even included them going out for tapas—he'd told Sophie about that?—but instead of disappearing, the character, creatively called Jessi, gets a boyfriend and forgets "Sebastian." Missing the attention, he starts calling the number she gave him ages ago, turning up outside her place. When the police drag him away at the end, he shouts that they've got it all wrong; he's the victim and she's the stalker.

It seemed as true as what had happened, an equally valid alternative. The best thing would be to believe it for a while, put some distance between himself and the knowledge. His notes, useless now, were still on his nightstand, but he set his laptop on top of them. When he had the energy, he'd tear out the lyrics and throw the rest away. He lay down and closed his eyes, but July was all he could think about. Not her exactly, but the fact of her death, and all the meaningless questions surrounding it.

He tried to force the void inside him into the shape of her. He'd known her a long time. Had they ever had a real conversation in rehab? She'd seemed so absent, with her indistinct mumbles and eyes that skimmed the surface of yours without stopping. She must've been introduced like everybody else. Frau Obern would've made them all stand up and say, "Welcome, Julia!" He still remembered the unreal cringe of his own arrival. What else? Like other patients, she'd sometimes lurked nearby when he was out playing his guitar as far from the cabins as they were allowed. Was she there the time stout, boorish Tammy had caught him blubbering over his chords? Someone else—July or anyone less glaring than Tammy—had been watching when she called, "Play me a song, crybaby!" and grinned with black-lined teeth. Was that all there was, July a shadow behind some unpleasant acquaintance?

He must've said the usual things: excuse me, good morning. Hers had been one of the clammy or scaly hands holding his when they said grace. In group therapy, he'd parroted the others—saying things had been hard and gotten out of control; he'd made bad choices—while she mumbled about getting away and no one asked from who or what. Whatever it had been, she was out for good now. Or had something caught up with her? He seemed to remember her watching him leave Springtime on his last day, but he was only pasting her face over someone else's. The memory was even less convincing because he saw her the way she looked in the picture, and her lips would've healed by then. He'd thought a faint echo of that broken girl would be with him always, a symbol of what he didn't want. But she'd been right there in the flesh all along, and he hadn't known until she wasn't.

He recalled her eager face in front rows, her confidence elbowing past bouncers. How flustered she'd gotten when he said he had a girlfriend. That and the time she'd called him an asshole were the most he'd ever felt for her. A twinge of something, not real feelings but *something*, like when he'd sensed her wanting him to be jealous. And the coziness he'd felt—despite and not because of her—on two evenings in her company: at the tapas restaurant and then the concert where he met Sophie. AKA the night before July's murder.

Remembering that was a jarring pain that left him dizzy, like catching your skull on the corner of a cabinet: blunt shock, then a pointed throb that wouldn't go away. Later, it would be a convex bruise he could run his fingers over, press on to feel a little something, until even that wasn't there anymore.

He didn't realize he was crying until he felt the wet rasp of the pillowcase against his cheek, then he bit down on it and sobbed until his physical discomfort was enough to black out everything else. He lay and listened to his churning stomach, seasick with anguish and unsure who he was crying for.

~~~

He woke with a feeling of excitement that turned to dread, then flopped back and forth between the two like a landed fish. He'd remembered that clue about the car, but it no longer mattered. He came to a rest on dry, hard, but stable dread. However long he'd known her, July was dead.

He decided to call Sophie after all, try for some pity instead of morbid fascination. He let it ring for ages, hung up on her voicemail.

He knew he'd be more or less okay—probably less—if he made it through the day. He couldn't tell which was worse: being alone or having to tell someone what was wrong.

Farid was probably waiting in some Kafkaesque government office, anyway.

Washing his puffy face, he tried to feel alive. Farid was from a warzone. He probably knew people who were dead. Could they talk about it if he spoke better German or Simon spoke Arabic? Or would it be insensitive to talk about the death of someone he'd never liked, without knowing how many loved ones Farid might've lost? He checked again for word from Sophie and wondered whether Farid had a girlfriend, whether people dated in Syria or had arranged marriages like in some clichéd movie his mom would watch to hone her cultural sensitivity.

It felt frivolous and irrelevant in the face of death, but he couldn't help wondering why—given his good quality of life, lack of grievous deal-breakers and residence in a country where pretty much anything went—he couldn't get his shit together.

He could, though. Sophie was the one flaking out. She and the world around him. He hadn't asked July to be obsessed with him. Or wash up in some canal. Who'd found her? A commuter biking to work or a tourist looking down to consult a map? No, better stick to the other subject.

What was Sophie's deal? He'd gone out on more than one limb, and they kept snapping under his weight. Telling her he wished she was his girlfriend. Inviting her on tour and to Berlin.

Why contact him if she wasn't interested? Maybe she was, but not enough. He remembered Tanja saying there wasn't much to say about his love life, and knew she was right. At least she'd stopped him from raving about Sophie in the interview.

He played his guitar a while to put off leaving the apartment, and was just putting it away when Farid came in. Some wishes did come true: Hadn't he wanted company? Only the important things never magically sorted themselves out.

"How'd it go?"

"Okay. I have to give address. Is okay here?"

"Sure." On the plus side, Farid's chances of having his building burned down by neo-Nazis were lower here than in group housing. And, much as Simon had dreaded having someone in his apartment, there were times when it helped. Like now. He signed the form Farid handed him. "Wanna get coffee? Speak German?"

"Yes, thank you very." Farid poured himself a glass of water, drank it in one gulp, then poured and drank another. Simon felt noble and selfish and glad to have something, anything to take his mind off of July.

~~~

"Germany good," Farid said as they crossed Volkspark's dry grass scorched by barbecues, past amateur tightrope walkers, the volleyball net where an errant serve narrowly missed Simon's head, and a group of bachelorettes in colorful wigs spraying obscene graffiti on the climbing rocks.

"Yes," Simon agreed, though he'd never thought much of or about Germany. "Berlin's the best." Did refugees get to pick where they lived?

"Yes, Berlin's the best." Farid was the right age to be any old friend of Simon's—if he'd had more friends—enjoying a summer day off from work. Not a care in the world, that was how they must look.

"What did—what do you do?" Please say engineer or doctor.

"What?"

"Your job? I'm a musician." He pantomimed playing a guitar.

"Programmer," Farid said in English, then repeated the German word Simon told him.

"That's good. Lots of jobs." Was he giving him false hope? Franzi had said getting a work permit could take ages. "But first you have to learn German."

"Learn German, get job. And family in Germany."

Simon didn't ask whether he was planning to bring one over, or find one here.

~~~

Soledad was bored and happy to see them.

"You're always here," Simon said. "Don't you ever go home?"

"You're never awake to see when I'm not here." He didn't correct her. "Maria left early. She's starting to show but Barbara's clueless. Last week she complimented her on her 'vibrant aura.'"

Simon introduced Farid and she said, "It's all on the house for you guys." She made the same sweeping gesture Farid had when Simon gave him the clothes, which reminded him to feel guiltily flattered that Farid was wearing them.

Simon ordered a latte and talked Farid into a late lunch because he had a grandmotherly fear of him not eating enough. Hard to tell if he was a scrawny computer nerd or malnourished. Ditto his goatee—was that a look or a lack of opportunities for shaving? Soledad brought their order while Simon conjugated "haben" and "sein" in Farid's notebook and said examples aloud: "I *am* German, you *are* Syrian, we *are* in a café. This *is* a table. I *have* a latte, you *have* an espresso, we *have* coffee." July *is* dead, his mind insisted, but he pushed the thought away.

He watched Farid take notes in an intricate script. "Arabic's a hard language."

Farid shook his head. "German's hard, Arabic's . . ."

"Easy. For you." That brought them to opposites, and then they had another coffee and did modal verbs until Farid said, "Enough," and put a hand in front of his forehead to indicate that his head either hurt or couldn't hold any more German for now.

"Okay." Simon knew how he felt. Despite the coffee, his own head felt heavy from the effort of making himself understood. Being a good person was draining. If only it could empty him all the way.

"Never knew you were such a good teacher." Soledad patted him on the shoulder before leaving with their dishes.

"You woman?" Farid asked.

Simon shook his head. "Just a friend." He drew three smiling stick figures in triangular skirts to explain female friend, and then a heart around a girlfriend in a skirt and a boyfriend in pants. A little heteronormative, but it got the point across.

Farid nodded and showed Simon the background on his phone, a woman with black-lined doe eyes and streaked hair in a flowered scarf. "My girlfriend, now wife before go. Syria, but less danger part. For now."

Simon had never had less idea what to say. "Is she coming to Germany?"

"Not safe to do like me. Walk long, bad men, not can swim good when boat . . ." He raised one hand and dropped it rapidly. "She come with . . ." He spread his arms like wings.

"Plane?"

Farid nodded. "I make visa, ask for bring wife. But long wait."

"I'm sure it'll be okay," Simon lied. "She'll be here soon."

"I want very." Farid hid his face in his hands. "I want to live life, like others. Wife, children, work, house."

Simon was still at a loss for words. "Me, too." For both of them. All things being equal, Farid would already have managed all that.

On their way out, Simon asked if Soledad wanted to get dinner with them soon. She'd had to learn German herself and might have some useful tips, which would take the pressure off of him. And dinner in a group wasn't a date. It would be nice to see her outside of Astral, but why complicate one of his few bright spots? Things had gotten weird enough as it was.

"Sure. You owe me for all the coffee."

Farid wanted to hang out in the park, so Simon went ahead to therapy.

~~~

As always, he dawdled to keep from being early, then had to rush. One of the two underfed receptionists who might or might not be related was on the phone and nodded toward the open door.

"Long time no see," Dr. Froheifer said.

He took his time closing the door so he could catch his breath. Like the police, therapy hadn't lived up to the movies. He never lay on a couch, and they only sometimes talked about his mom. First, it had been addiction and his "sense" of faking it, then self-loathing and from there they'd stalled out at insecurity and problems with relationships. But he felt okay most of the time when he didn't have a corpse to deal with, so something had to be working.

"Let's talk about why you called."

"Yeah, so, July. That fan I mentioned?" He was hesitant to use the word "stalker" after reading Sophie's story. He couldn't remember what he'd already said, so he summed it up: "It turns out she knew me from rehab, even though I didn't recognize her. I was worried about being a suspect but I was drugged that night. I wanted to help, but now they found a body, and . . ." He couldn't seem to clear his throat, and stood up to fill a paper cup at the water cooler.

"You feel like it's 'your fault'?" Dr. F liked to cut to the chase. She didn't seem as interested in his past with July as Weinert was.

He had his voice back by the time he sat down. "She was there because of me. I couldn't help them find her. And now she's dead." He had to remind himself that none of that was the same as murder. The difference seemed petty at this point.

"I'm very sorry you have to go through this. But bear in mind, you don't know why she was murdered. Was she 'in the wrong place at the wrong time'? Murdered for reasons that have nothing to do with you? If she was killed right after you saw her, nothing you remembered could have made a difference. If anyone's to blame, other than the murderer, it's whoever drugged you. And they may well be the same person."

"I guess I didn't think of it like that." She didn't like him to be quiet too long. She wanted to hear what he was thinking, she said, not what he thought she wanted to hear. What if he hadn't had time to think? But there was no shortage of things he needed someone else to sort out for him. "Then there's Sophie, who I . . . got involved with on tour, but she only wants to talk about the case. I don't wanna use July to keep her interested."

"Do you feel like it takes a murder for a woman to be interested in you?"

"Not usually." For the sake of clarity, he recapped the whole Sophie-Mei story.

"Let me first say there's some growth here. It sounds like the first time since we started meeting that you've approached a relationship. However, your progress was surrounded by juvenile actions. Why the elaborate lie rather than what we discussed?"

"I panicked."

"You planned this whole setup in a moment of 'panic'?" The silver frames of her rings caught the light as she put his general state of being in quotes.

"No, Franzi brought this woman, and it just happened."

"You seem to feel like a lot of things 'just happen.' Are there any parts of your life you do feel in control of?"

"I'm helping a refugee learn German." He left out how that had just happened, even though you weren't supposed to lie to your therapist. Like with the police.

"That's wonderful. You're making real leaps and bounds under difficult circumstances."

He loved and hated the warm glow of praise. It was a bright spotlight in a world of darkness, but he couldn't bear the attention it drew to him. Or maybe it was others knowing how badly he craved their attention, their approval, that he couldn't bear. Was this what he'd come for? To hear how well he was doing, when he felt like his life was falling apart?

Toward the end, they talked about his mother after all, but only as a foil: rehashing his well-meaning mom and guilt about not liking his dad.

"Let's pick up there next time."

"Sure." He found himself wondering whether there'd be a next time, with the same dread he'd felt on his way to the police station. Did anything come after now?

~~~

He called Sophie, hung up, and called Soledad. Café Astral was a lot closer than Hamburg. "How about dinner?"

"What, now?" He heard the whine of a vacuum turning off, so she must be closing up. He didn't think she was the type who raced home and started cleaning.

"If you're free." Already, he felt like pretending to remember he had other plans. But this wasn't romantic. Did that make it any better? If she said no, it wasn't "you're not my type," but "I don't wanna hang out even without having to sleep with you." Like how he'd felt about . . . No, don't think about her.

"Just warning you, I'm all sweaty from work."

"That's okay; I'm all sweaty from therapy." Laugh like it's a joke. "Meet at Astral?"

"Great, see you!"

Cutting through the park, he called Farid, but it just rang. Maybe he was talking to his wife. Anyway, it would be nice to have someone's undivided, non-diagnostic attention long enough to come to terms with that body a few hours from here, in a fridge or getting autopsied as he strolled past where he and the body had once had coffee. Now that the shock had worn off, there was nothing to buffer him from the blunt fact of it. He almost missed worrying about being a suspect. At least that had kept him from worrying about July. But that was before they found her.

Soledad was outside, compressing her frizzy hair into a bun. She smelled like coffee and disinfectant.

"Long time no see." That echo of Dr. Froheifer seemed like an inside joke with his brain, the kind of senseless repetition that happens in dreams. "Where's Farid?"

"I couldn't reach him. I think he's had enough German for today. How was work?"

As they walked, she told a few anecdotes he'd usually have laughed at, but his mind kept bouncing off the surface of her words. He had to tell her so she wouldn't think he was being rude. And because he had to tell someone. Now. If he waited until they sat down next to tables of eavesdroppers looking for a diversion from their own sparse conversations, he'd choke up.

"Sorry, but I need to tell you something."

The lights were green, but they stopped in front of the rusted colossus of an old East German gym. He looked at the traffic, the graffiti on the orange building, his shoes and the pale blue sky past the top of her head. "I'm not having relationship problems. You remember that creepy fan?" For all her clinginess, July had only come to the café twice. Once, right after he'd started, Barbara in all her linen and patchouli had been there to say Herr Kemper was *very* busy, and once he'd spotted her in time to hide and have Soledad say he'd quit. "She disappeared in Amsterdam. I'm one of the last people who saw her alive."

"Tell me everything. We can walk slow."

There was so much to tell that they did a few zigzags before stumbling into a kitschy Indian restaurant with silk umbrellas on the ceiling and twenty-four happy hours a day. He'd told her the facts. They could cover coping mechanisms over dinner.

"Are you okay? You can't be," she said in one breath, and shouted to a passing waiter, who brought two neon-colored cocktails overflowing with pineapple and paper umbrellas.

"I don't understand why it happened. I could just as easily have stayed in, or left early or stuck with Micha. Or July could've stayed home."

"Let's order, though. I don't wanna interrupt this crisis with some aloo gobi, you know?"

He let her order. He'd been too distracted to realize he was ravenous, and was still too distracted to care what he ate.

"Her being at rehab with me, stalking me, disappearing on my tour . . . It seems like there has to be a reason."

"You mean an actual connection, or like God wants you to solve the mystery?"

He looked closely to see if she was joking. The sickly blue of her cocktail was reflected in the sheen on her face after a long day. She seemed to mean it.

"Neither. Both. I don't know about, like, *God*. But like it's something I'm supposed to do?"

"If you hadn't filed a complaint, it would've taken them longer to notice."

"True."

She gave him her 1920s pout. "So there's really—"

"One second." He hurried out to take Weinert's call.

". . . want to apologize," Weinert was saying.

"What?" In his rush to get somewhere quieter, he'd missed the beginning.

"You were upset when we talked. I shouldn't have said anything about that body. It was a false lead. There's a dental match with a local prostitute."

The words drifted through his head like bubbles, empty, bright, vanishing when he tried to grasp them: upset, dental, prostitute. "So that means she's . . .?

"Not Julia Tappet."

Why couldn't Weinert tell he was asking about July, not some random Dutch prostitute? Although that was heartless, since she was a person, too, and just as dead as, no, much more dead than July. "So that means July's alive?"

"I'm sure you've heard how many missing persons turn up alive."

"Um."

"The numbers aren't great. I'm being honest since you're not family or a close friend."

"Thanks."

"If you remember anything . . ."

"Actually," he said before he could decide whether the question was brilliant or insane, "what was her ex-husband's name? Since I didn't know she was married, I could've met him without realizing."

"Thomas Barer. Ring any bells?"

"No, sorry, but I'll ask the band."

Their food had arrived, and Soledad was sipping her drink with half-closed eyes, watching some daydreamy point between the edge of the table and the golden Ganesh across the room. Her eyes snapped open when he sat down.

"The body wasn't hers."

"Guten Appetit." She took a bite and covered her mouth. "Great. I'll help you find her."

"Guten Appetit. How?"

"Well, um, what were you planning to do?"

"I found out her ex-husband's name."

"Okay, let's start with him."

He couldn't tell if she was joking. "How?"

She considered. "We'll find him and call or stop by. It's better in person because it's easier to tell if someone's lying."

"Wait." He choked on a piece of paneer and cleared his throat. What had seemed logical, even inevitable, when he was the one doing it seemed preposterous when she suggested it. "What if she's there with her mouth taped shut?"

"That would be great. Then we'd know where she is."

~~~

Soledad's room was less cluttered than he'd imagined, but not tidy enough to make him feel bad, with clothing folded on a small gray sofa that might once have been blue, and a dozen books open on her bed, nightstand, desk and floor. He was almost never in another person's apartment unless he slept over and, when he did, he didn't spend much time looking around. Nadine's was the last apartment he'd taken a close look at, and he'd been staying there. Staying, not living.

And what was he doing here? Other than telling himself they couldn't possibly be serious. They found two Thomas Barers in Berlin. One was a doctor. In the picture on his practice's website, he looked to be somewhere between seventy and eighty. The other owned an auto repair shop and looked just young enough to have conceivably been married to July. The registered address for his website was a residential building.

Soledad brought Simon a cup of chai that smelled like a Christmas market minus the farm animals, and sat down at the other end of the sofa, the laundry between them like a vigilant chaperone. Since he categorically refused to impersonate a police officer, she was designing business cards.

"How's this?" She turned her laptop toward him. The cards were white with a black magnifying glass. The back read: "We find answers." On the front was "A. Müller, Private Investigators" and a phone number.

"We can both use them since it's only an initial. I put my number because I don't have my name on the voicemail."

"Brilliant. Except when did you last hear of a private detective outside a film noir?"

"I googled it and there are tons. Some list Missing Person Services."

"Our specialty." He wanted to say how ridiculous this was, but then they'd have to stop. Bizarrely, he hadn't felt this good in a while. "Let's try this again. He asks who we're working for."

"A concerned party who wishes to remain anonymous."

"And when he shoots us?"

"Why's he shoot us?"

He sighed. "You know, when we see her bound and gagged."

"Come on, Simon; think. You have your ex-wife wrapped in duct tape. What's the last thing you wanna do?"

"Um?"

"Attract attention! Before you say what if he has a silencer, we'll tell him we were *sent* to talk to him, so he knows someone knows where we are."

"Ingenious." It was a ridiculous plan they'd never go through with. It just might take him a while to figure out why.

"It would be great if we had a toy gun. You tuck it into your belt and it's like, I'm a tough detective who doesn't have to show my gun, but we both know it's there."

"Then there's a shootout and I take out my water pistol?"

"Don't be so negative. Wanna interview her neighbors instead?"

"Isn't it a little late?" He hadn't looked at the time, but her roommate Lea had already gone to bed.

"This is when people are home! Neighbors or ex-husband?"

"I guess criminals are more likely to expect visitors at night."

"Good call." She pulled a box out from under her bed and started rifling through it. "I never get rid of old props or costumes; you never know when they'll come in handy." She tossed him a pair of fake glasses and a scarf. "Here. And put it on so it covers your mouth but not all the way. Too bad there's no time for you to grow a beard."

"Yeah, too bad." July had recognized him without, but that didn't mean her ex-husband would. Barer wouldn't be home, wouldn't let them in, or they'd be killed. Nothing to worry about. Better use the bathroom, though, in case they got held hostage without a toilet.

When he came back, she was wearing glasses, a beret à la Patty Hearst, and no pants. She was struggling to tear off a strip of duct tape while pressing a small device against the curve of her thigh below red lace panties, which he looked away from but couldn't unsee.

"I got it." He handed her a piece of tape, trying not to look like he was trying not to look. "What's that?"

"Audio recorder. I use it for sound effects."

"You're not serious."

She hopped into a pair of pants loose enough to conceal it. "A camera would be better, but mine's too big and I can't check one out of the university this late. I'll wear sneakers, right? In case we need to run? I haven't actually done this before."

~~~

"We're making a movie," Soledad explained as he paid for the business cards at a 24-hour copy shop. The heavyset cashier with hennaed hair and the scent of a crowded smoker's lounge nodded like she gave a shit and turned up the Schlager station she had on. Maybe Sophie could have her job.

"So, good cop, bad cop? Or seedy underworld?" Soledad asked in the U-Bahn station. He'd always appreciated her vibrancy, but never spent enough time with her to realize she was insane. He wasn't backing out now, though.

"Uh, you decide."

"Okay, seedy underworld. Because he can relate. It's this just-between-us thing where we know we're all involved in illegal activities. Oh, if you're thirsty, get a drink here, not at his place."

"I think I learned that lesson."

~~~

They had to stop again so she could look away while he peed against a construction fence. He didn't want to have to use Barer's bathroom. Or have his bladder empty itself when he was killed. What if Soledad survived and forever remembered their last moment together as him wetting his pants?

The building looked like all the others on the street: nineteenth-century molding in disrepair, graffiti up to head height, crumbling balconies that should've been condemned.

"Let me do most of the talking, okay?" She held down the buzzer.

"Gladly."

~~~

A fortysomething who looked like he'd had a rough time of it stuck his head out into the stairwell. On his website, he had longish hair and a warm smile. In person, he had a crew cut, cheeks that hung like he'd bought them a size too big, and a scratch along his jaw that could've come from shaving with a knife. Or from a fingernail? But he stood a head taller than Simon and might still have been handsome in certain lights. He looked so familiar that Simon wondered whether he'd seen him before or was only remembering the picture online. Or one from Weinert's folder? When Barer stepped into the hallway, they saw his threadbare undershirt, sweatpants and socks with holes in the toes. Not the Bond villain Simon had imagined, but appearances could be deceiving.

"May we come in?" Soledad handed him a card.

"Barer." He offered them his hand.

"Müller." They followed him in.

The hallway was lined with empty bottles and lit by a single dangling bulb. "Admiring my Russian chandelier?"

"Very much." Simon didn't have to decide whether to smile because Soledad's scarf covered most of his mouth.

"Let's talk in here." He led them through a frosted-glass door to a carpeted room where Simon could feel the cinder-block flooring through his shoes. Must be an extension behind the old facade. He and Soledad sat down on a beige leather sofa opposite a TV playing some action movie. When Barer switched it off, the sudden silence echoed like a shot.

Simon noticed a few pictures on the far wall, but he was taking cues from Soledad, so he didn't get up to look.

"Want a beer?" Barer was hovering like a nervous host.

"Sure," Soledad said to Simon's surprise. "You gotta see how Herr Müller opens a bottle." But when Barer returned with three beers, she said, "Sorry, just a joke at my colleague's expense. We'll need an opener."

Simon admired her resourcefulness. A couple centimeters away, he was sure he could feel her pulse. But maybe that was just his, banging away hard and fast enough for two.

Barer handed Soledad the opener and flopped down on a threadbare armchair. "What can I do for you?"

She opened the bottles. "You don't know?"

Barer took a long drink of beer while Simon sipped his and watched him for telltale signs like beads of sweat or darting eyes. "You're looking for Julia?" He'd switched to the informal you, and Simon worried because they hadn't agreed on first names, but then there was no need to use names at all. At least they had the right guy.

"Someone wants to talk to her," Soledad said. "But he can't reach her."

Barer sighed and drummed on the arms of his chair. "Is it that . . .? Er, I mean, does she, uh . . . owe somebody else money?"

"We aren't at liberty to . . ."

"If you're having trouble collecting a debt," Soledad said before Simon could decide whether to finish his sentence, "we do work in that field. I could throw some numbers at you."

"I'm all ears. Just out of curiosity."

She took a deep breath. "Twelve percent above ten-thousand, seven-five above fifty, and we do a flat fee for small sums. They're not worth it unless it's personal.

Is it a personal matter, or are we talking a percentage? If the cases overlap, we might round down."

"A . . . percentage."

"I don't blame you for hesitating. Why pay when you can just ask nicely?"

Barer gave an unexpectedly hearty laugh, and Simon saw how he'd clean up good. "That's what I thought, like the sucker I am. But you know how a girl like that can get you right around her finger."

"Haven't had the pleasure, but we've seen pictures, of course."

"Funny, I feel like I've seen you somewhere." He was looking at Simon, who could only hope July had never brought him to an H vs. H show.

Simon sucked in his cheeks, willing his face to change. "I meet a lot of people."

"Tell us about Julia," Soledad suggested.

"I check in with her now and again. About my money," he added with another belly laugh. Simon caught the dull glint of gold in his molars. "I, uh, lent it to her after the divorce. She said I owed her for messing up her life. It wasn't like that, you know."

"What was it like?" Soledad still had an accent, but it was unidentifiable, buried under a layer of Russian spy.

"We met at a club. Bright girl with no life experience. She was taking anything anybody was handing out, and her friends left without her. I'm a good guy, so I offer to drive her home. She says she doesn't live in Berlin, can she stay with me. What could I say?"

"What *did* you say?" she asked, and Simon felt like he'd been drifting off behind the wheel. Now that the adrenaline was fading, he was just tired and worried they'd fuck this up worse than it already was.

Barer was settling into his story, though. There were a lot of lonely people out there. "I said okay. Drove her back out to the suburbs the next day, let her out at a corner like she asked me to. That's when I figured she still lived with her parents."

"How old were you?" Simon asked. Did it matter? Just because he'd been too old for her then didn't mean he'd kidnapped her now. But it was hard to picture her even younger than she'd looked at rehab and getting involved with this guy.

"Late thirties. Didn't look it, though." He slapped his thigh like he'd made a great joke. "Business was good, I had a nice car. A couple girls, but nothing serious. You get older and you want something solid. Julia came every weekend, told her parents she was with a girlfriend. Then she graduated and stopped going back, started doing a little sales work for me. She's good at approaching people. She didn't ask to move in, but she never left." That sounded like July. "I got drunk and sentimental and asked her to marry me, and we took the next train to Denmark. The paperwork goes so fast up there, we were married by the weekend. We had a great time before things went south."

"When did you notice she was taking drugs?" Soledad asked.

"She'd been stealing cash, but I didn't mind about small amounts. We were married. But it got to be more, and she got really thin. Said it was a diet, but I'm not stupid. Her lips were all blistered up. And not from anything I was carrying."

"Is that when you started hitting her?" Simon asked, trying to keep all accusation out of his voice. This was about finding her, no value judgments here.

"She didn't get those bruises from me. We tussled a bit when I tied her up, but I'd never hit a woman." He nodded to Soledad. "I'm a gentleman." Another flash of gold as he chuckled.

"Tied her up?" Soledad glanced at Simon. Was this where he'd pull July out of the cupboard?

"To get her clean. But she got out. We had a hell of a shouting match when she got back. Neighbors called the cops. I said we'd had an argument, meanwhile she's all loopy saying, 'Morning, officers,' and saluting. I said she was drunk."

"Did they buy that?" Soledad asked.

"They were just happy I wasn't beating her."

"How'd she end up in rehab?" Simon asked.

"I had a delivery to make, but I decided to follow her. I couldn't tell if the guy she was meeting was a boyfriend or dealer. Aggressive son-of-a-bitch. All I did was ask a few questions, and he jumped me out of nowhere like a fucking animal. She got in the middle of it. All of us were screaming our heads off so the cops turned up. She was high as a kite, and I had too much on me. I sat a few months before parole, and she got rehab. I don't know what happened to the guy. Right before I got out, she said there was someone else." His eyes were moist, but that could've been tipsiness. "Probably that jerk. The divorce went fast because she pled hardship.

"It was a real wakeup call. I could always fix cars, and they had this business program for when you get out. Good money, my garage. I couldn't say no when she asked for a loan. Said she wanted to start a business, too." He took a swig of beer. "Then she disappears. Not like now, I mean. Just avoiding me. Then I'm making my usual dunning call, and she says, sorry can't, she's in Amsterdam. I say what a coincidence, me, too."

"When was that?" Simon had a pretty good idea.

"Mid-June? She says she can pay back some of my money and wants to meet at this concert, but it was sold out. Then she says meet at this party. When I finally find her, she's with this guy who's falling-down drunk. I ask if he's the new boyfriend, and she says he's her cousin. Like I buy that. Guy's so wasted she has to go through his pockets to see where he's staying. We drive him to his hotel, prop him up between us and haul him into bed, come back down. Then she says she forgot the money upstairs, wait here. The police came about some party, and I'm not supposed to leave town, so I went out to the car. I called to let her know, but she didn't pick up. I dozed off, called again. Nothing. I went back the next day and asked about that room, but they wouldn't give me the guy's name."

"What's he look like?" Soledad asked before Simon could signal not to.

"I didn't get much of a look because he was bent double."

"Was it the same man you saw the day you were arrested?" Simon asked before Barer had time to think too hard.

"I don't think so. This guy was pale, and that guy had a blotchy red face and light eyes. I couldn't say what color eyes this guy had, but nothing that jumped out at you."

He still felt safer changing the subject. "Do you speak Dutch?"

"No, we always speak English when I'm in Amsterdam."

"Who's we?"

"Nothing to do with Julia."

"Then we don't care," Soledad said. "Anything else about the guy she was meeting when you were arrested?"

"Yeah, kind of a weird nose. Julia sure picked a winner. Be right back."

Soledad shook off Simon's weak attempt to restrain her as soon as Barer was in the bathroom. He could hear her dashing through the apartment, opening and closing doors. What, did she think July was hiding behind one of them? What was Barer supposed to think? If Simon could hear her, so could he.

Soledad settled back on the sofa seconds before he returned. "Sorry, could I use your bathroom?"

"Oh, is that what you were looking for? There's only one, first door on your left."

"Thanks." Soledad stepped out into the hall.

Barer looked at Simon far longer than he was comfortable with. "Your partner's really something."

"Isn't she. Do you know what Julia's plans were?"

"Uh, looks like they were pissing off with my money."

"Well, if you need our help getting it back, leave a message." He shook Barer's hand and Soledad, slipping back into the room, did the same.

"We'll be in touch," she said.

"I hope so." Barer gave her a rakish wink her expression didn't register.

~~~

A taxi pulled up as they came out. Simon got in because nothing could surprise him now. Soledad gave the driver an address while he sat in the back like a child, counting on the responsible adult to make decisions. Not that this adult seemed very responsible.

He leaned back and closed his eyes, remembering another boat ride his family had taken a couple years after their trip to Amsterdam, this time in Athens. His mom had wanted the ferry, but his dad had made them take a Flying Dolphin because it was faster, and she and Franzi had gotten seasick from the bouncing. They'd all gone out for some air, but there wasn't any deck, just a noisy half-covered engine room where his parents had put their mouths to each other's ears to continue fighting. Even as he held onto the railing to keep his balance, feeling the ground shudder out from under him, he'd known something important and maybe dangerous was happening outside his understanding. He had the same sense of urgency now, blunted by the same detachment.

Groggy with fatigue, he saw fairy rings of lantern light and yellow-lit windows passing in familiar and unfamiliar streets, the glowing orb and needle of the TV tower getting bigger and then smaller again, and the dark front of the car, where he could just make out the gearstick in the middle, and higher up the very top of the cabbie's head and some of Soledad's curls on one side. That was how it looked when both seats had headrests. But he knew whose car he'd been in.

They got out in a cobblestoned side street, dark except for a convenience store and the low-lit windows of a bar. Soledad paid for the cab. After it pulled away, she said, "Ahhhhhh!" and waved her arms above her head.

"Um, everything okay?"

In response, she took his limp, cold hands in hers and wrenched him around in circles until dizziness took over and he was laughing, too, without knowing why.

"I can't *believe* we went through with that!" she said. "You're crazy."

"I'm crazy? You made me!"

"Buy me a drink, and let's talk about what to do next."

"Here?"

She dropped his hands as they went in, and he felt embarrassed for holding hers so long. Then again, why worry about being socially acceptable on a night like this?

"This is my favorite bar." She led him to an antique writing desk in the corner furthest from the windows and other customers. The instrumental music playing sounded like a 1970s horror soundtrack, and the only light came from a candle melting into a bottle so covered with wax drippings it looked like a tower of the Sagrada Familia, at least judging by Micha's pictures. He thought of saying so, but he'd feel stupid if she was from Barcelona. No, she spoke Spanish, not Catalan. Madrid? He was a jerk and couldn't remember. In the fantastical *Alice in Wonderland* painting on the wall beside them, anthropomorphic rabbits and walking houses seemed to move every time a draft made the candlelight flicker. Tonight, it wouldn't have surprised him if they did.

"I live around the corner," she said as a lanky, unsmiling waitress in clothes as old as the furnishings dropped a menu and left. "Well, a couple corners."

"So we're back in Neukölln?" After all they'd found out, he caught himself thinking of irrelevant things, like whether she meant the same thing a woman in a bar usually did when she said she lived nearby. Of course not. It was just her favorite bar.

"I had the cab drop us here in the unlikely event we were followed," she said as if she knew what he was thinking. "And because I wanna get a drink and debrief. I used a taxi app in Barer's bathroom. Don't worry; I left the door open so the recorder wouldn't miss anything."

He wondered whether it was still running. The thought made him self-conscious. "Who would follow us? He wasn't exactly . . ."

"What you expected?"

"I thought he'd be more sinister. And glamorous. He's my first real criminal."

She laughed, not in a flirty way but like that embarrassing guffawer the whole movie theater can hear. If she'd had a drink, it might've come out her nose like Tanja's always did. "I wonder whether his first private detectives lived up to his expectations."

"If so, they must've been pretty low." Since she'd taken off her disguise, he took off his glasses and scarf and handed them to her. "He must be pretty lonely to tell us so much."

"Do you think? I'll have a mojito," she said to the waitress, who'd sauntered over.

"Me, too," Simon said to get rid of her. "What do you mean?"

"Maybe the whole lonely-drunk thing's an act. Like about him always being so nice to July. Why'd she leave him, then?"

"I don't know; people break up. Why lie?"

"Why tell us?"

"Good point. The part about Amsterdam lines up with what I remember, though."

"What if somebody he knew drove?"

"Shit, we should've checked his car."

She shrugged and said, "Let the police handle that," as the waitress set down their drinks on promotional coasters for a local theater.

"Couldn't we have said that about the whole thing?"

"Sure, but I thought doing something would make you feel better. Less helpless." She reached over and patted the top of his head, two hard pats, like he was a big dog. "It's not like this is what I usually do for fun, either, but I *do* have a lot of great props, and it doesn't hurt that I've spent like a year of my life watching old detective movies. Anyway." She lifted her glass. "To our agency. And our cut of that debt. The real money's in breaking legs."

"To us and A. Müller." He knocked his glass against hers, and two sprigs of mint fell tangled on the table. "The one thing that didn't line up was him saying he doesn't speak Dutch. July was speaking it in the car."

"You're sure?"

"Yep."

"Okay, we can gather more information, tell the police, or both."

"What do you think?" With their risky caper safely in the past, he felt so drowsy he would've thought Barer had slipped him something after all if they hadn't been so careful.

"We should tell the police."

"And then?" He felt a little more awake, a little less comfortable, at the thought of having to explain how he got the information. And why.

"What, is it illegal to pretend to be a private detective?"

He laughed, on his guard not to let any more kooky ideas seduce him. "Probably."

She shrugged. "I foreigner, not know. No, I'd say you told me about July and I was trying to help."

"You'd do that?" He only just managed to bite the words "for me" off the end of his sentence and keep them squirming in his mouth. This was one of those crazy situations like a shipwreck or zombie outbreak where really unlikely people got together because of the crazy shit going on. Were they that unlikely? Besides, who said they were getting together? What would Dr. F say about a crush on his only straight female friend? She's not the boss of me, he thought in a surge of childish rebellion, but he was more worried about his conscience than his counselor. There was still the matter of Sophie. And July. And all kinds of other matters, or things the matter.

"Sure, what's the worst that could happen?"

"I don't know."

"See? If I go to jail, I'll make a fascinating documentary. My big breakthrough."

"That's a load off."

"Do you ever think about what you'd do in jail?"

"Try not to get raped or hazed, I guess. Suck up to get out sooner."

Her laugh was softer now. "I mean to pass the time. You know Malcom X copied a whole dictionary by hand?"

"Wow. I guess I'd do a lot of reading, write some songs. Like in rehab."

"Did you like it there?"

"Of course not. Sometimes a little. When I got to be alone. But there was always this fake big-happy-family thing. I had to share my room with this fat old guy who was always in his underwear. The kind who would've balanced a bottle on his gut if we'd been allowed to have beer. Luckily, he left after a couple months."

"Sometimes I think it would be cool, like *The Magic Mountain* without the tuberculosis. Being in this closed-off little world in the mountains, breathing fresh air and forgetting about everyday life."

He ignored the impulse to make some overly specific reference so she'd know he'd really read it. "I was in East Germany, not Davos."

"You'll have to tell me about it sometime. Unless it's too personal?"

He sipped his drink but left the last few centimeters because he wasn't sure how long they'd stay. The bar wasn't very full, which could mean it was early, late, or unpopular. He felt like they'd been at Barer's for ages.

"I don't mind talking about it another time." Why did her interest in him feel less morbid than Sophie's—on the rare occasions Sophie *showed* interest? Was it the absence of a corpse, or was he right in feeling like Soledad cared about more than gory details? Dr. F had asked if he thought he needed a murder to get women interested. But Soledad hadn't known he had a murder mystery up his sleeve. Assuming it was still murder. "Enough about me." His tone put it all in quotes, because was that really his best line? "What's new? You seeing anyone?" No, wait, that would end up flirty or disappointing, even though she always used to tell him about her dates at work. "What film are you working on?"

"I don't think I'm seeing anyone."

He was just going to nurse his drink and not pry or feel anything. Because he *was* seeing someone. Then it hit him: Of course he'd talk himself into a crush right now. He was scared Sophie would reject him, so he was inventing feelings for someone else as a safety net. And he'd always felt so comfortable around Soledad.

". . . everybody wants to film a plastic bag or something," she was saying. "But nobody wants to watch a bag for two hours. People want stories."

"What's the main conflict?" He hoped she hadn't already said.

"Thematically, you could say it's about people trying to trust each other. But I'd really rather you watch it when it's done. Everything sounds so trite when you try to summarize it."

"I'd like to see it." That, at least, was true.

"You can do a cameo. Think how it would up my street cred."

"I can't act."

"Not even as a detective? I could work one into the plot."

"If I were good at playing detective, we'd know more. Use one of our songs if you wanna namedrop."

"For real? That would be amazing. Everyone in my class always mixes some shitty techno soundtrack. But come on, that was only our first witness." She yawned into her hand, and he felt the contagious pull on his jaw, but inhaled through his nose instead.

"What do you think happened?"

"My best guess is someone from her past. I think we can rule out her being in Herr Barer's cellar because the neighbors would notice. Anyway, cellar doors are always just splintery wood. She'd get out."

"Good point." Now he did yawn, one of those deep but unsatisfying ones that never quite comes to a close. It left his eyelashes and the tip of his nose damp. He noticed her glass was empty and hurried to catch up.

"You can sleep on my sofa if you want."

He stalled by waving to the waitress. "Thanks, I'm really tired." His first instinct had been to say, "I don't think that's a good idea," but that would imply that a.) she was offering for sexual reasons and b.) he wasn't interested in those reasons.

<center>~~~</center>

He was asleep before he thought about it, which never happened when he slept away from home, let alone with another person in the room, but he woke feeling like he'd spent the night in an accordion case.

Soledad, who hadn't taken off anything but the audio recorder the night before, wasn't in her bed. He stretched, sniffed under his arms, winced and hoped he could sneak into the bathroom unnoticed. Her last date had used the spare toothbrush she'd thought she had, and his mouth tasted like a used garbage bag.

"I'm making breakfast," she called as he creaked down the hall. "Lea just left so the bathroom's free."

"Great, thanks." He shuffled in, pissed out the cocktail he'd been too tired to process before bed, washed his hands and face. There was an unopened pack of toothbrushes on the sink. That was so nice of her. On the other hand, she seemed to go through a lot. Maybe this was routine restocking. He shouldn't be ungrateful, though. Even if the tiny sofa had given him a real going-over, she'd done a lot for him.

He took out a toothbrush, rinsed off any residue of production chemicals and found her toothpaste tube in a crumpled curl. Guess buying toothbrushes didn't remind her. Well, waste not want not. His mom used to make them cut open the tube and fish out the paste with their toothbrushes, which he'd always found unsanitary. Who knew what Franzi had put in her mouth at elementary school?

Despite the cricks in his neck and his curious inability to bend over without shooting pains, he felt great. Like things were, if not good, at least on their way there. It had been hard to believe the police were getting anywhere, but now that he'd seen what it was like on the investigating end, he figured they were probably further along than he'd thought. And there was something to be said for doing something crazy. He felt alive.

Soledad had scrambled eggs, milk and an espresso pot on the stove. Hers was the typical Berlin kitchen, an afterthought two people could hardly stand next to each other in, with an untreated wooden floor that was never and would never be clean, a David Bowie poster with one corner coming untaped, and a postage-stamp-sized table by the window whose sill housed sacks of flour and lentils, an orange crate full of spices.

"Thanks for the toothbrush. Can I help?"

"Just get out of the way." She shooed him onto one of two uncomfortable chairs. "Look." She handed him her phone.

She had a local tabloid open, and he thought she wanted to show him some funny typo or nonevent hyped to fill extra space until he recognized the nineties glass overhang of the police station. It took him a second to recognize the figure in front of it.

"Singer Implicated in Fan's Disappearance." No: "Singer Implicated in Fan's Disappearance?" That question mark was probably to protect them from the lawsuit he'd never in a million years have the energy to wage.

"Shit, how'd they come up with this?"

"Go ahead and read it."

It was a short piece. They didn't have much information but must've liked the headline. Other than facts stolen from their rival's original article about July, this one made much of him being "questioned multiple times" and having "known the victim well." At least there was no reference to Springtime.

"You want my opinion?" The toast popped out on a shelf uncomfortably close to his head as she set the frying pan down on a magazine. "Someone tipped them off. See how there's no photo credit?"

"You really are a detective." It was like he'd taken a nasty spill and needed to figure out where he was injured. To his surprise, he felt fine. "Who'd do that?"

"Do you have any enemies?"

"What am I, in third grade?"

"Does your band have any . . . what's the opposite of fans?"

"We're not big enough. Maybe next album."

"Can you get the toast? Careful, sometimes it sparks. My other ideas were an ex or the husband of a married woman you slept with."

"I don't have any ex-girlfriends recent enough to be that mad. The only woman I slept with lately was Sophie, and she's not married."

"Are you sure?"

"I guess she could be, but why hide it?"

She moved out of the range in which he could turn his stiff neck, then reappeared with two lattes.

"Guten Appetit. You're probably right. The alternative is that the person who abducted July or . . . whatever is trying to divert attention."

"So it's someone I know?"

"Someone who knows you."

"If I were as smart as you, I'd know who it was."

She laughed. "Think it over."

He took her suggestion literally, and they ate in silence. The coffee was great, the salty eggs on buttered toast exactly what he needed, and thinking was the last thing he felt like doing. Everything was a dead end. He wanted to be out taking action. The paper wouldn't want to tell him where they'd gotten the story. But if someone else asked?

"I have an idea." He called Weinert.

"Herr Kemper?"

"There's an article about July with a picture of me."

"You want to file a complaint?"

"It might be a lead." No, too boy-detective. "There's no photo credit."

"So?"

"I just . . . Could you ask who took it?"

He sighed. "Alright. Feel free to call anytime you actually know something, okay? We're very thorough. If you've thought of it, the professionals will, too."

Maybe that jibe made him feel like he had something to prove; maybe he should've finished his coffee before calling. "When I spoke to Herr Barer, he said he drove me and July to my hotel. But I guess you knew that."

"So you do know him?"

"I stopped by to . . . see if I recognized him. I mentioned July and he asked me in."

"Interesting."

He remembered A. Müller and his heart sank. Soledad was grimacing and making throat-slitting gestures. "The thing is, I used a false name in case he was dangerous, so I'd prefer if you didn't mention me."

She gave him a thumbs-up.

"Did you take notes?"

"We—I recorded it." He ignored Soledad's facepalm.

"Are you at home?"

"I'm at a friend's."

"Mind if I stop by?"

He put his hand over the receiver, but she was already nodding.

~~~

"You know that's fraud, right?" Weinert said. "I'm assuming you're not actually working for this agency."

Soledad had made more coffee and brought her yoga ball so they could all sit. She rolled forward to pause the recorder. "It's not allowed? Sorry, I'll call Herr Barer and explain."

Weinert reached as if to stop her, then said, "Let's hear it first."

They listened in silence, Simon a little embarrassed and a little proud of their handiwork.

"I'll tell you what, I'll overlook it for now, and you tell me if he calls." Weinert pocketed the recorder. "You'll get this back later."

"Okay."

"But don't do anything else like this."

He was looking at Simon, but she said, "It was my idea. I convinced him July was tied up in Herr Barer's apartment."

"Don't get any more ideas. Or if you do, run them by me."

"I did think it might be one of Simon's enemies setting him up, but he's not convinced."

~~~

They had a fit of giggles after Weinert left, like kids who've gotten off with a minor talking-to after some big prank.

"This is probably the weirdest twenty-four hours of my life," she said.

"But in a good way, right?"

They laughed until they both had tears in their eyes. But a moment later, he felt like he'd stayed too long. Too long to go home and have a normal day, but also too long to keep sitting here drinking coffee, even if that was all he felt like doing. She was still wobbling back and forth on her big yellow ball, and that made it all a little surreal.

She checked the time. "Should we case her apartment?"

"I have to call Sophie," he said in the world's lamest excuse, then, "but we can go after," like he needed to make up for it. Was it worth showering without clean underwear? He could turn his inside out. "I'm gonna take a quick shower."

"Let me know how it goes."

"The shower?"

"The call, stupid." She clenched her thumbs in her fists to wish him luck.

~~~

It was a nice day, cozy on the sunny side of the street, cool in the shadows. He decided to get calling his mom out of the way. No, to be honest, he decided to call her so he'd be gone the length of a call whether or not Sophie answered.

"Simon, how are you? Franzi sent me the nicest article about your band. I've been showing everybody."

"Great, Mom. How's everything going?"

Her back hurt, his dad had made a snide remark through Franzi, work was work. "Franzi's coming. I hope she's bringing her new beau. She didn't sound too happy when I mentioned him. As if her own mother . . ."

"Oh, you know Franzi." Franzi probably had to say that all the time: Oh, you know Simon. About different things. Having circled the block twice, he continued on, out of range of the knobby old woman watching from behind the gnomes and geraniums on her balcony. He came to a small green—although it was more yellowish-brown—with a few rotting benches and a dirt path he followed through sparse shrubbery while his mom listed things she wanted to do in Berlin someday. There was no way they'd have tea at Sanssouci Palace this time around, but what was the harm? Or was he dragging it out to put off his next call?

"Do I get to meet Sophie?"

"She might not be here."

"Doesn't she come on weekends?"

"I don't work normal hours, so we visit during the week." Funny how magnetic a lie was, pulling so many little flakes of untruth after it.

"Don't you want us to meet?"

"The thing is, we're having a difficult phase."

"You're not getting cold feet?"

"It's hard to explain." He remembered how serious he'd made it sound the last time, and how upset he needed to sound now. Maybe he could act in Soledad's film, after all. Everything he said was a line. Although that didn't mean his performance was convincing, just that his repertoire included not only Private I, but also Good Son.

"Tell her I say hi, anyway. She's not married, is she? I hope I raised you—"

"Of course not." Funny how that was the second time someone asked. Lies weren't the only things that traveled in packs. "Gotta go, love you!"

"You, too. Take care."

Faced with the prospect of calling Sophie, he discovered a sudden, urgent need to check the news, the weather, his emails. The clubs had sent the lists, one sometime around his corpse-related meltdown the day before, and the other only minutes ago. He forwarded them to Soledad, even though that made it clear he wasn't actually making a call, and then he was all out of excuses not to.

Sophie picked up after eight rings during which he pictured her toying with her phone like a cat with its prey. Sometimes you could tell people were there.

"If it isn't the jailbird. Is this your one call?"

"Very funny." Witty banter wasn't his strong suit, but he pulled himself together. "When are you bringing the cake with a screwdriver in it?" It was his millionth loop around the little park, so he stopped at a crumbling bench below flaking trellises that looked elegant only from afar. The ground beneath the bench was littered with sunflower seed shells someone had spat out. He realized when he sat down that it had rained, but the damage was done, so he stayed put.

"I'm not a good baker. How about tunneling out with a spoon from the dining hall?"

He laughed and thought about how Soledad had said she'd take the fall for him. That had been banter, too. Then again, she had taken the blame in front of Weinert. That was the difference between friends and new love interests, though. No loyalty here. Yet. "At least come and sob into the receiver on the other side of the glass." How long did they have to keep this up before they talked about something real? "Your story was good, but sort of creepy."

"Why 'but'? Everything good is sort of creepy."

"It wasn't great timing. They found a body in Amsterdam."

"That's impossible."

That was the opposite of how he'd reacted, seeing it as the inevitable outcome of years of dread. But everyone handled shock differently. "I was gutted, but it wasn't her after all."

"Were you freaking out about getting blamed?"

"Mostly I was sad she was dead and felt like it was my fault."

"Why?"

"She was there for my concert."

"Isn't that a little self-centered? Trying to co-opt a murder that potentially has nothing to do with you?"

He couldn't tell whether she was kidding. "That's me in a nutshell. All ego." He couldn't tell whether he was, either. "How are you?"

"Same as ever."

"Up for a change of scenery?"

"Why don't you come here?"

"I'm not supposed to leave town."

"Oh man, you *are* a suspect. I'd hate to miss the chase scene where they swoop up on you on the highway."

"It would certainly give you something to write about." That came out snider than he'd intended. "So you'll come?"

"We'll see." He heard a door open and close. "Talk to you later."

"Bye." She'd already hung up. Could you miss someone who'd never been part of your life? He noticed she hadn't asked how he was, and felt a petty little hurt. What would he tell his mom? She'd adored Nadine. No use introducing some supposed girlfriend she'd be asking about for the next year. He thought of that door in the background and dismissed the ridiculous thought that Sophie could actually be married.

He had a voicemail he figured would be his mom again, but it was Weinert saying the photo was sent anonymously using a contact form. The IT department was on it.

He hurried back to tell Soledad the news.

~~~

Her bedroom door was open a crack and dramatic organ-grinder music was playing. She was on her stomach watching Murnau's *Faust* with a cup of tea precariously balanced on the mattress. Because she knows I like silent films? was his first inane thought. Then he remembered she hadn't been there that night an eternity ago when he worried about sounding pretentious for liking *Nosferatu*. She wasn't July; not everything she did was about him. As it turned out, not even everything July had done had been about him.

"There you are!" She got up too fast, and he caught her tea just before it hit the keyboard. But she missed the heroic gesture. After pausing the movie, she opened a spreadsheet. "Did you look at those lists yet? I combined them and marked the people who were at both concerts so we don't contact them twice."

But he wasn't looking at the highlighted names. "That's impossible."

"What?"

But it was very possible. She didn't know him well enough for it to be a prank. Toward the bottom, tucked away like a colorful Easter egg among everyday objects, was "Nadine Amsel." How could he not have noticed?

"My ex-girlfriend was in Amsterdam. You know, my ex-bassist." It was less weird when you looked at it that way: Nadine seeing what her old band was up to. Why hadn't Micha said anything? He must not have noticed.

"Technically she might not have been. This is just who bought tickets online."

"Even if she was, I'm not sure we're on speaking terms." She'd dropped a lot of his stuff out her window when he left, and it was only luck—his, not hers—that his last bottle of beer exploded on the sidewalk instead of his skull. The violence of her anger always came as a surprise, erupting out of her spacy placidity. But it had been more than two years. He felt agitated in a way that had nothing to do with the matter at hand. That reminded him that there *was* a matter at hand, though, so he filed the bulging folder of flattery, anxiety, guilt and nostalgia away for later. "Let's see those overlaps. July, of course. I've never heard of these other people. Her friend must've bought his tickets separately, since she only bought hers. Now what?"

"Do we contact them?"

"Why don't we tell Weinert?" Simon remembered what he'd meant to tell her before Nadine's name in 10-point font had blown his mind clear. "The picture was sent anonymously."

"Totally a clue! Telling him the names will save us some legwork, eh, Herr Müller?"

"Then we can stop by July's." The last part slipped out of its own accord. He'd been thinking this whole time about having stayed too long, and here he was suggesting another shared activity. Which was also selfish. Like she didn't have her own life.

"Sure, we just can't be ages, I've got this screening."

"Cool, what of?" Perfect, a built-in cutoff point.

"A friend made this film. You can come if you want."

"Sounds great." He watched the moment in which he could say "but . . ." pass before his eyes, vanish in the distance. But that was alright. Sooner or later it would be nighttime. Sleeping over once was a tipsy lark; spending two nights in a row together was tantamount to marriage. Besides, he was already uncomfortable about yesterday's underwear and whether she knew he'd used her apricot-scented face cream because he was afraid a day without moisturizer would permanently wrinkle him.

"Do you mind calling Weinert in the kitchen? I have something to finish up here." She handed him a piece of paper she'd scrawled the names on and gently pushed him out.

Weinert heard him out and then said, "Why does going to both shows make them suspects?"

It was a question they'd failed to discuss. It had seemed obvious, but now he saw that the two nights being significant for him had created the illusion of a connection. "Someone gave July a ride from Hamburg to Amsterdam, supposedly some old fling? At the very least, these people were around before she disappeared." And something else, something he couldn't put into words. The sense that something had happened between those two nights, changed things.

"Sure, sure. Would you mind emailing me the lists? They both wanted a warrant when *we* asked, and it's taking ages. They seemed to think we were using the situation to get our hands on people's personal information. With some ulterior motive, of course."

"Sure." He had the sinking feeling of not being taken seriously. "You'll check them out, won't you?"

"Herr Kemper, we're all trained, experienced officers. At the end of the day—just a minute." There was a muffled, staticky sound, and the line went dead.

He forwarded the lists without calling back. But not because he was sulking.

~~~

Soledad pressed all the buzzers until the door opened. They made their way upstairs, checking the names on the doorbells until they saw that July's was the one with the police seal across the door. Was that a hairline tear or an actual hair stuck to it? He resisted the urge to check: fingerprints, DNA, returning to the scene of the crime.

"Damn, I forgot my picklock."

He wasn't sure she was joking until she gave him a dig in the ribs and rang the doorbell across the way.

They could hear more than one child shrieking. A pale woman with bags under her eyes and a wailing baby on her hip answered, looking like she might cry, too.

"Annika Müller." Soledad flashed her card. "We wanted to ask about July Tappet."

"Who?" She craned her head out to elude the squalling.

"Your neighbor." He pointed to July's door.

"I already told you everything." She must think they were the police. "She's quiet. I think she works odd hours."

"Does she get a lot of visitors?" Soledad asked.

"I never heard anyone." A loud wail cut through the scene like a flash of lightning, making them all wince. "Listen, I . . ."

"We understand. Thanks," Soledad said.

"Now what?"

"Work our way down? Lower-down neighbors see more people."

No one answered at the apartment below the hassled mother. Below July's, a twentysomething they'd woken up told them he'd never spoken to July but thought she sometimes had a guy over. That seemed promising, but he responded to all of Soledad's eager questions with yawns, shrugs and noncommittal answers. No, he hadn't seen him, yawn, couldn't make out what they'd said, couldn't name a time the guy had been there or say whether it was always the same guy.

"Try to think," she urged him.

"Um."

Simon handed him a card. "Let us know if you remember anything."

One story below, a faint voice called, "Coming!"

Simon held his breath until a withered old woman with a slight hunchback opened the door.

"Are you from Caritas? I called, you know. My neighbor's doing my shopping."

"We're not from a charity," Simon said. "You know Frau Tappet?"

"Of course, July's my angel. Are you friends of hers? She's on vacation. I'm sorry you've missed her. Do come in and have some coffee."

"That's very nice of you." Soledad put the business card back in her purse, and they stepped inside. "Please let me make it. We don't want to be any trouble."

"I couldn't possibly."

"She makes great coffee. I'm Simon by the way; this is Soledad."

"Edeltraut. If you absolutely insist, the kitchen's that way."

Soledad abandoned him, and he followed Edeltraut's slow progress into the living room. He was sure he wouldn't be comfortable using her first name, but then July apparently had.

The room was small, tidy, and full of lace, from the curtains to the trim on the flowered sofa and the stiff-backed chair he sat down in. Antique shelves of even older books extended from floor to ceiling. It looked like nothing had been renovated in decades. She'd probably lived here so long it was rent-controlled. Even if July's apartment had the same modest floorplan, she must've been doing pretty well with her toothpaste ads to be able to afford her own place in this neighborhood. He took a deep breath he hoped would come out as the right thing to say, but luckily Edeltraut took over.

"July's so lovely. Since she moved in, the charity service hardly ever has to come. She's always doing my shopping and taking me to appointments. I'm so spoiled it's hard when she's away. The lady across the hall only helps me for money. Did July ask you to check on me?"

"Frau . . . that is, Edeltraut." He cleared his throat. "July isn't on vacation. She's missing." He caught himself speaking slowly, and hot shame spilled over his face. There was no reason to assume she was senile because she thought July was on vacation. It was a normal thing to think if you hadn't seen your neighbor lately.

"Oh dear, did something happen while she was away?"

He hesitated. "Did she say she was going on vacation?"

Soledad came in with a French press and a Delftware tea set on a tarnished tray. She poured the coffee and handed Edeltraut a cup.

"Thank you." She turned back to Simon. "Of course, she always tells me beforehand."

"When was that?" Could it be that simple? There was no proof July wasn't on vacation.

"Let me see." She picked up a planner from the coffee table, licked one trembling finger to page through it.

The thought of July's wallet and phone brought him back down to Earth. Funny way to go on vacation. Had she brought luggage to Amsterdam? He hadn't known where she was staying. With that friend? Was he the same person as that ex-affair she'd mentioned? She'd been so present, and he'd done all he could not to see or hear her. But anything was possible. What if she'd come back, stopped by Edeltraut's and left town again, unaware of the investigation? Or at least preferring to ignore the police tape until she got back. She might've thought her apartment had been broken into.

"Here it is, June sixteenth. She wasn't sure for how long." Edeltraut didn't seem upset, maybe because she thought they'd misunderstood. "She loves to travel, especially for her music shows."

Soledad gave Simon a look he couldn't read. "I'm sorry to say this is serious. The police are looking for her."

"Ach, jemine!" Edeltraut set down her cup too fast and coffee spilled onto the saucer. Please don't die or go into shock, Simon thought as Soledad wiped it up.

"Do you know any other friends of hers?"

"Let me think. There's the nice Spanish boy; do you know him?" She looked at Soledad, who shook her head. "A certain low-brow character helped her move in. Later she said, 'Edeltraut, can you believe we used to be married?' I got married young, too, God rest my Willibald's soul, but the two of them! I always say when a man lets himself go . . ."

Afraid this might turn into a longer excursion, Simon asked, "Anyone else?"

"Oh, her cousin."

"What's he like?" Soledad asked.

"Just between us," Edeltraut chuckled, "good looks don't always run in the family. But he's a kind fellow, quite devoted. If they weren't related, I'd think he was in love with her."

"Do they have the same last name?" Simon asked.

"I didn't think to ask. He has an unusual first name. I'm afraid I'm not much help. You should see how long the crossword takes me." She shrugged her frail shoulders. "Oh, yes—"

The doorbell rang twice in quick succession. He told himself over and over as he heard the door open, shoes being kicked off and footsteps that it wasn't, couldn't be, July back from a casual vacation.

It wasn't. A dumpy woman in her fifties dropped two shopping bags on the floor. "You could've said you had visitors coming, Frau Weiden. Just 'cause I'm outta work—"

"She wasn't expecting us," Soledad said. "We stopped by to ask about July."

Simon wanted to tell them to shut up so he could rewind a couple seconds to where Edeltraut had remembered the cousin's name, but now she was all shrugs and apologetic smiles. Hadn't Barer mentioned a cousin, too? But that had been July lying about who Simon was. Maybe this wasn't a real cousin, either.

"You the cops?"

"Simon and Soledad are friends of July's," Edeltraut explained in the same over-articulated tone Simon had taken with her at first. "Did you know she's missing, Frau Heimstett?"

"Of course. The cops were here."

"Oh dear, I suppose I was at the doctor's office."

"Look, you can't just let strangers in. There's all kinds of people here now. Terrorists, burglars. You should see the people that come in and out of this building."

"If you say so." Edeltraut gave Simon and Soledad a conspiratorial smile. "Would you like some coffee?"

"Got anything stronger?" Frau Heimstett plopped down on the sofa, nearly knocking over Edeltraut, who laughed like she was joking.

"I'll grab those." Soledad took the groceries into the kitchen while Simon poured another cup. He could smell Frau Heimstett's high-proof sweat when he handed it to her.

"I don't mean her kind." Frau Heimstett cocked her head toward the kitchen. "But they let anybody in nowadays. We'll all be speaking Arabic and following those Shania laws soon. You wait and see if there's not some foreigner behind what happened to July. I saw this Oriental in the building just now"—Simon continued to bite his tongue—"and asked real nice what she's doing here. She says, 'None of your business.' Last week, these Arabs . . ."

"Sounds like you really keep an eye on things." Soledad took her seat in the narrow space left on the sofa. "You're just the person to ask. You wouldn't happen to know any of July's friends, would you?"

"It's like you say, I'm sort of the unofficial superintendent. Let's see . . ."

He was sure Soledad had miscalculated. The way this woman smelled, she must start drinking before breakfast.

"I told them about that cousin and the Spanish fellow," Edeltraut said helpfully.

"Yeah, that's what I was gonna say. And that older guy . . . not a real social butterfly, your July." She smirked at Edeltraut like this was something they'd talked about, reminding Simon of a jealous child angling to put her sibling in a bad light.

"Better to have a few good friends than a lot of superficial ones."

He noticed Soledad checking the time and remembered the screening they had to get to. Before the two neighbors could start bickering, he asked, "Do you remember her cousin's name, Frau Heimstett?"

"*I* do!" Edeltraut raised a lilac-veined fist in triumph, as if she'd solved the last clue in the crossword. "She called him Janssi."

This could be big, but also seemed like the most they could expect out of today's visit. And they'd always have an in if they needed to come back, now that they were supposedly July's friends.

Soledad looked relieved when he said, "We'd better be going. Thanks for the coffee."

~~~

He had a sinking feeling when Soledad gave him an address near his place. It was up to him whether to invite her over later, but sometimes you moved on autopilot with dreamlike jump-cuts from one scene to the next. What Dr. F would call skirting responsibility.

He said he needed to stop by his apartment, because he couldn't bring himself to go in yesterday's clothes. That and the irrational feeling that going home would reset everything, clear his head like a night of blank sleep.

"There you are," Farid greeted him. Simon felt bad for not having said he'd be away, but he hadn't known. Anyway, Farid must've been happy to have some space. Simon sure would be.

"Hello, your name again?" Farid asked Soledad.

She spelled it. "Spanish for when you're alone."

"Good name. Mine is for . . ." He started to look it up on his phone.

"Tell him about the movie." Simon went to the bathroom. It was suddenly important that she invite Farid. He couldn't tell whether that was because he felt bad for not spending more time with someone who barely knew anyone, or because he wanted to put a buffer between himself and her. He didn't reflect on why that was important, because every question dragged smaller, more troublesome ones after it like cans behind a car.

He felt better after a shower with only those thoughts that land like shaken dice in your brain. What was the difference between rabbits and hares? Chee-tahs and leopards?

His heart came up hard against his tonsils—his last spaced-out thought was: How come people have tonsils?—when he bumped into Soledad in his bedroom.

She handed him his phone. "Tanja called. I invited her."

"Great, thanks."

Her eyes flitted down to where his hands were clenched over his phone and the towel not quite flat around his waist. She laughed and went into the kitchen. He listened to her speaking pidgin German with Farid and wondered what she'd been laughing at. It wasn't much of an erection, more an acknowledgment of her presence and his being undressed. She probably hadn't noticed. He'd had the phone in front of it. Anyway, why had she picked up? What if it had been Sophie?

On the other hand, it could've been something important about July. If it had been Sophie, Soledad wouldn't have picked up. Although it was nice in a nasty way to think about. Would Sophie have been jealous? Demanded to know who it was? No, but she might've asked later. He liked the idea the same way he'd liked when Nadine, dangling by the last thread holding them together, said how jealous she'd be of "all those heroin-chic girls" at Springtime. That reminded him of how much more he'd learned about July, and he made a hasty entry in his spiral notebook, glad he hadn't thrown it away after all.

"Hurry up!" Farid called through the door. His careful enunciation indicated that Soledad had just taught him the phrase. "You're too slow." They were laughing.

~~~

"Tanja's meeting us there," Soledad said as they walked over. "There'll be food."

"Cool." He hoped that was an FYI and not a response to the growl he was using all his stomach muscles to suppress.

When they arrived, she vanished into a swarm of students and film buffs whose names were flung at Simon faster than he could catch them. The cuisine was Turkish-goes-hipster, so he ordered a beet-and-manioc pide and craft beer.

Something minimalist was playing over the general chatter, and he had to lean in to hear Farid. It was hard to make conversation with a near-stranger in elementary German while watching someone move around a crowded room, so he kept stopping to look. More than once, he caught sight of Soledad next to the tall guy with a ponytail who'd held their table for them. Someone important like the director. Or just important to her. She'd said she wasn't seeing anyone. She didn't *think* she was. What did that mean?

"Sorry, what?" He'd missed Farid's remark again, watching the two of them pose for a picture in front of the projection screen.

"Is it taste good, you beer?"

"Oh yeah, it's good. How about your beer?" He emphasized the "your." Actively correcting mistakes brought the conversation to a standstill.

"Interesting." They'd ordered at random, and Simon had ended up with a local pilsner while Farid had gotten ale brewed with cacao beans. "Who's he?" Farid pantomimed putting his hair in a ponytail.

Simon shrugged. "A friend?"

Farid took a moment to remember yesterday's lesson. "A friend or boyfriend?"

Simon laughed. Vocabulary was so much easier to explain than real life. "Your guess is as good as mine."

"What?"

"I think a friend." He was glad to see Tanja in the doorway, one hand to her forehead as if the room were lit by bright sunlight instead of antique lamps. He waved. "My friend from my band."

Tanja introduced herself, then the lights got even lower as Soledad pulled up a chair.

~~~

To say Simon didn't understand the film would be an understatement, or maybe an overstatement. He hated it. It was the visual equivalent of radio static. Did he not know enough to appreciate it? It started off with the camera on the dashboard of a car, like they were going somewhere. Then endless stray images: keys, a growling dog, pine trees, a construction site, feet walking, and on, and on, and on. Once he realized there was never going to be a context, he let his mind wander. But his thoughts were like frantic animals locked up too long, and scurried all over. Could he save July? Bad things happening everywhere. What about Farid's wife? How would xenophobic Germany handle all these new people? Talk to Franzi about it. Had she seen Sophie? Should call Sophie. Why? Or why *should*? She was ruining it for him. Playing or actually hard to get? Something odd about her. He was distracted by a familiar figure on-screen, Soledad on the edge of a bed, brushing her wild hair.

Her long flannel pajamas didn't exactly scream sex, but he had a forceful sense of intimacy that made him certain her involvement with the director went beyond professional. It was her total lack of self-consciousness, as if the person behind the camera were always in a bedroom with her.

The thought of being that close to someone, feeling that secure, made his throat close up in a way that went beyond his resentment of PDA or endless social-media documentation of How Happy We Are. Viscerally, albeit not literally, he was dying to feel that way. Then he watched tires spinning, paint drying, rain. His mind went dull and his eyes were hot. He picked up his glass, but it was empty. Tanja was squinting and screwing up her forehead as if trying to make out distant writing. Farid glanced at his phone. Soledad's expression was an attentive blank, but one corner of her mouth sprang up on his behalf.

He turned back to the screen. The final scene, the director painting his nails in a last-ditch effort to be provocative, lasted from the first stroke until every nail was dry.

After the applause, Soledad and Tanja got in line for the bathroom.

"I don't please this film," Farid whispered.

"I didn't like it, either. Maybe we don't understand it?"

"He wants we think that." Farid cocked his head at the ponytailed director, who was accepting congratulations from all sides.

"It was too long. Should we take a beer with us?"

"Yes, please. This time no chocolate."

Simon ordered and then got out his phone for the dictionary app, but immediately forgot what he'd meant to look up. He had two missed calls and a text from Sophie: "In Berlin answer your phone loser." Charming. Well, it did make him smile.

"One second." Her phone rang forever. It had been over an hour. She was in a club or bed by now, hers or someone else's. Why hadn't she said she was coming? And why wasn't he happier? He was tired and unprepared. "The woman I like. She's not always in Berlin, but she is now."

"Difficult." Farid patted his shoulder.

Simon forced himself not to compare their situations, because that would make it impossible to have a conversation that wasn't drenched in pity and guilt. If Farid's wife were there, they wouldn't spend every second thinking about the sorry state of the world, either. Still, Simon was impressed with how much attention Farid gave his trivial problems. He must be the less self-centered type, like Franzi.

"Woman nice like Soledad?"

"One second." He called again to avoid answering.

"Woman call Simon, now he call her," Farid told Tanja as they went outside, Soledad trailing behind to hug friends of hers who no longer mattered to Simon, or shouldn't have.

Tanja didn't offer her opinion until Farid and Soledad were engrossed in a discussion of the film. Judging by their snickers, Soledad shared the general opinion, despite her cameo.

"Soledad's too good for you," Tanja said. "Which isn't necessarily a deal-breaker. Sophie . . ."

"She is, too, right?"

"She's something else." He wasn't sure how she meant that. "But by all means." She pantomimed letting him go ahead. "But don't . . ."

"I'm not leading Soledad on. We just get along well." Was it a mistake to admit he knew what she meant?

"Well." Her tone indicated the exact opposite of her words. "You know best."

~~~

When Tanja and Soledad were in the U-Bahn, Farid was in the kitchen, and Simon was in bed trying not to wait for a call, he remembered worrying about how to make sure Soledad didn't stay over. Had they dodged a bullet? Alone and wide awake, he'd rather have been hit. She could've lain there radiating security like a nightlight. But it would've meant something. And once it meant something, Sophie calling would be a problem. He reminded himself that Soledad's wild curls would've tickled his face, his stomach would've made embarrassing gurgling noises, and she would've fallen asleep on his arm and cut off his circulation. It was better this way. He fell asleep not quite convinced but glad to have made an official decision.

Five

He woke to neighbors drilling in the wall. No, his phone, making the books and stagnating glasses of water on his nightstand tremble. News about July?

"I'll let you take me to breakfast even though you ignored me."

"Morning. I was at a movie." At least he felt happier at the prospect of seeing Sophie than he had the night before. He'd been caught off-guard; that was all.

"With a girl?"

"Two."

"I slept in Prenzlauer Berg. Come meet me?"

She didn't say where, let alone with whom. Did it matter? He'd have to see her to find out. And he was starving. He remembered thinking about Soledad hearing his stomach gurgle, and felt himself blush as if Sophie could read his thoughts. As if she cared. "Sure."

"I'm near Eberswalder Strasse."

"Okay, I'll head over." Right by July's place. It was crazy how close Sophie had been to him and Soledad yesterday. They could've walked right by her. Or maybe she'd gotten in late. Planned on staying with him. And then? Gone home with a plan B?

"Meet me at the tram. I don't wanna get lost."

He was being paranoid. She'd stayed in a hotel. Wouldn't she be having breakfast with her plan B otherwise? Unless it was a random hookup. Which would at least mean she was single. Right?

Farid was asleep, so he crept into the bathroom to get ready. Because he was considerate, not because he was worried some guy he'd known for a couple days was judging him for leading someone on. Nobody had said that except Tanja. It would be arrogant to assume Soledad had feelings for him. Other than pity.

~~~

The air had a tense feel to it like it might storm. He could've made the tram if he'd run, but his legs had the molasses quality of nightmare chase scenes. He slowed down so the passengers couldn't enjoy watching him miss it. He kept turning up the music on his headphones, but it remained a textureless gruel of sounds, the lyrics meaningless.

It started to drizzle, and he had to back further and further into the little glass shelter to make room for five elderly people to fight over seats and viciously side-eye the woman smoking over her plastic-hooded baby carriage. He felt blank, as if the anxiety he should've felt had been removed in a few neat surgical strokes, and he was still anesthetized. But someone reimplanted it as he got on the tram, and he wondered why he hadn't spent the wait coming up with witty ripostes and subtle ways to find out if Sophie was available.

The tram smelled like a wet dog, and there was a suspicious puddle out of all proportion to how much it had rained. Why was she here? He could just as easily have been out of town. Then again, she knew he wasn't supposed to travel. He was so busy thinking about her he didn't see her at the stop until someone socked him in the arm. Luckily, he recognized her before hitting back.

"Hey, you." She kissed him on the cheek.

"This way." He took her arm to guide her through the crowd, and they walked a few blocks like a couple out of some past century, along the noisy whirr of Danziger Strasse and into the intimacy of Kollwitzstrasse with its cobblestones, double-parked cars and canopy of birches. He asked how she'd gotten here (by car) and how the trip had gone (okay). She'd gotten in late yesterday afternoon, but it felt pushy to ask why she hadn't called sooner.

It had stopped drizzling by the time they picked a café, but he didn't trust the weather enough to sit outside. After all the hype about seeing her again, he'd hate having to rush away from clammy seats and rain watering down their coffee.

"So what're you doing here?" he asked after they'd ordered: muesli he felt too nervous to eat, and some plate with a million things added and replaced for her. He hoped the waitress had followed it better than he had.

"This and that. Having brunch with you."

When he laughed, the tension in his jaw made him feel like the Tin Man. He had a sense of déjà vu, but couldn't pin down when he'd thought that before. Asking if she was going out of her way to be mysterious might sound possessive. "Visiting friends?"

"No. Yeah. You know?"

"Sure." He didn't know anything. "You in a hotel?"

"I had something for last night. But I was hoping . . ." He felt her ankle trace the inside of his leg. So she could be direct when she wanted to.

"You're more than welcome." He wasn't thrilled, but would be. His happiness just needed to percolate through the thick filter of surprise. Aptly, their coffees arrived.

He must've sounded less ecstatic than she expected because she said, "Don't worry; I won't start slipping notes in your pockets or reading your lyrics."

He choked on his coffee and couldn't breathe even when he stopped coughing, remembering the cold sweat of that day in the park when everything in him longed to run but couldn't because July had reached in and grabbed him by the guts, gotten ahold of his lyrics. Of all their infuriating interactions, those few seconds of her gloating voice reading his song aloud had probably been the one where he most wished her dead—or himself. But the moment had passed before the feeling could sink in. He'd gotten his notebook back and escaped, nobody but July the wiser. Or so he'd thought.

He cleared his throat. "How do you know about that?"

"You okay there?" Sophie slapped him on the back, even though he'd clearly stopped choking. "How do I know about what? I figured you must hate people looking at what you're working on. I'm a writer, so I know."

"Oh, of course. Sorry." He drank some coffee to smooth his raw throat. "For a second there, I thought you were referring to the time July did that."

She shrugged. "Maybe you told me about it? It sounds vaguely familiar now that you mention it."

"I shouldn't tell you things like that. It'll only give you ideas." He tried to steer them back to the flirty tone they'd had before he choked on her words. He must've told her. It was too much of a coincidence that she'd mentioned both the note and the lyrics. He talked too much about July and would put Sophie off if he wasn't careful. Or did he just *think* too much about July, reading her into an unrelated comment? After all, July hadn't invented slipping someone a note.

"Believe me, I have enough ideas on my own."

What did that mean? Nothing. He'd opened the Pandora's box of July, and now he was overthinking everything. Sophie wanting to sleep over was great, something he could look forward to without agonizing. Or should be able to. Maybe he felt weird because he hadn't mentioned Farid. "It'll be a little cozy. This guy's staying in my living room." Lucky they'd already slept together so it didn't sound like a lame excuse to get her in his bed. "He's, um, a refugee."

"Oh." She wrinkled her nose. "Tell me if it's too much trouble."

"Not at all. He's barely home."

"Okay, cool."

He wasn't trying to get credit for his selflessness, but her response wasn't what he'd expected. Then again, it was Mei, not the woman who played her, who'd been so eager to adopt Yosef. "Don't you have any luggage?"

"It was sort of spontaneous."

He had a lot more questions but didn't want to interrogate her. Their breakfast arrived, his with an elaborate fruit topping like a lounge singer's hat; hers with three kinds of meat, a sunny-side-up egg, toast with the crusts cut off, half white and half whole wheat, and a slab of pineapple with a side of ketchup.

She dunked a bite of egg in the ketchup. "Like *When Harry Met Sally*."

"I must've missed that part."

"You think I'm horrible for not ordering from the menu?"

"No way." He thought she was cute enough to get away with it. But he wanted to clear up one thing before she lulled him into a false sense of security with her throaty laugh, sparkling eyes and knees pressed against his.

"I know this is a weird question, but can you not be weird about it?"

"I'll try."

"Are you married?"

"What?" A cloud of crumbs burst out of her mouth. "Do I *look* married?"

"What's a married person look like? So, no, right?"

"Totally. Now do I get the explanation?" She leaned back against the gold-painted wall and, looking at her parted lips, he thought she had the same elegant sensuality as the Klimt reproduction above her.

"No boyfriend, either?"

"I'm having a promising second date." She winked but everything had a thin layer of irony over it, so it was only a nod to how someone else might wink. "Why?"

"My mom and, um . . . coworker said you might be."

"You told your mom about me? I hope you said something nice, like, 'Hi, Mom, I had the most incredible one-night stand.' Am I close?"

He'd walked right into that one. He never would've mentioned his mom if he hadn't been worrying about what to call Soledad, and why should he? "Franzi told her." At least he had an excuse. "And then I didn't want to disappoint her."

"Honestly? Why don't you try dating for real instead of making up girlfriends?"

That hurt, and like any good blow, took a second to recover from. "I am trying."

"So when do I meet your mom? She must be getting impatient about grandkids."

"She's actually coming tomorrow."

"If you'd known I was gonna be here, I'd think you did that on purpose."

"Please, I never *ask* my mom to come."

"She's that bad?"

"No, she's great; it's just . . ." What? The exhausting responsibility for another person's happiness? He'd felt that way when his family came rushing to save him, and he hadn't had the guts to insist that he wasn't an addict, just sad. It had been easier to keep wallowing and let other people make the decisions.

"Parents, right?" she said after he'd been quiet too long. "Wanna go shopping?"

"Sure. There're some nice boutiques around here."

"I was thinking like, full-on, heinous trip to the mall. I don't need boutiques; I need enough socks and underwear for this visit."

"I'm in." Asking how much she'd need would be too obvious.

~~~

It was fun at first, waiting outside the fitting room and imagining her beautiful body inside, then seeing her cute poses as she modeled each item—including the toothbrush—but, after a while, the entertainment value wore off. By the time he'd paid for and schlepped a dress, shirts, jeans, cosmetics and kilos of lingerie, he was out of compliments and relieved to hear she had some other errands to run. He knew he should offer to go with her, but his spirits were flagging. It wasn't worth getting cranky and saying the wrong thing. After escorting her to her car, he stopped at an ATM and had to check his balance twice to believe it. It couldn't be that low just from today. The problem was on the incoming end. He'd been stupid to think their last album would keep selling like it had the first month.

There was nothing he had more of a knee-jerk reaction against than stinginess, but as he collapsed onto a seat in the tram, he allowed himself a little resentment that she'd let or made him pay for everything. It had started with a lace-collared dress he thought looked just like her. He'd insisted on buying that. At the drugstore, he hadn't minded buying a toothbrush for a guest, even if ten other items came with it. Everywhere else, he'd expected her to stay at the register with her purchases, but she'd stepped aside until he got out his wallet. He only wasn't letting himself feel used because of how insulting that would be to her. She must think musicians earned a lot. Dr. F would have a field day: You think a woman could only be interested in you for money?

He was so caught up in trying to justify his feelings and her behavior that it took him a second to notice Farid peering out from behind the bathroom door.

"Everything alright?"

Farid said, "Police!" as if that explained everything.

"What?" Maybe an ambulance had driven by and triggered some traumatic memory.

"Door makes ring, I think is friend of yours. I . . ." He pantomimed pressing the buzzer. "Man not have clothes like police, say things I not understand and 'Police, open up!' I don't." Farid took Simon by the arm. "I *not* do wrong. I go always to Social Office. I make not problem for be in Germany."

Weinert must've gotten mad because he thought Simon was there but not letting him in. "Don't worry." Despite Farid's anxiety, Simon couldn't help but be impressed with how much he could express in German. He felt a twinge of pride, even if more of it came from YouTube than his tutoring. "I know the police officer. No problem for you."

Farid took a deep, ragged breath. "I'm sorry, I think wrong."

"It's okay. I'll make us some tea." Simon was hungry but didn't want to eat until Sophie got there.

They sat in the two chairs pressed against the wall to accommodate the mattress, and set their tea on the sill behind them. He patted Farid on the shoulder, which was a lot for him.

"You know the woman I like? She's coming here."

"Live here?"

"Just . . ." She had underwear for at least a week. "A couple days."

"Now girlfriend?"

"I hope."

"Hope?"

"I want it to be that. Hope."

"Ah. I hope my wife also . . ." Farid swallowed audibly and reached for his tea even though it was too hot to drink.

"Can I do anything to help?"

"I can't bring until visa and no . . ." He consulted his phone. "No German embassy in Syria. Must in different country."

"I'll ask my sister. She'll help."

"You're good."

Simon opened his mouth and found he was close to tears. "Thanks." It wasn't worth scaling the language barrier to explain why he wasn't.

"I go before woman here?"

"No, I want your opinion."

"Not understand."

"Opinion is . . . what you think."

"Okay, if you want I go, say."

"Thanks, you're good, too." He mumbled something about getting ready and went to his room. Was it weird that he didn't feel like seeing her alone? But that reminded him of their shopping spree, so instead of pondering the question, he messaged Soledad about getting some shifts at Café Astral.

"I'll see what I can do. Hope it's going well with Sophie!!"

If that wasn't a sign they were just friends, he didn't know what was. He took a deep breath, feeling empty enough for the air to rush through him like a wind tunnel. Judgey as she'd been the night before, he wished Tanja were here to talk him through this, or maybe Franzi since she'd gotten him into this mess. He lay back on his bed. Not that it was a mess. He'd forgotten how to be happy. He closed his eyes and made a list of things to be thankful for, skipping the part about not having to flee from a brutal civil war because he felt guilty thinking it. Sophie was beautiful, smart, fun. Even if she couldn't admit it, she must've come to see him.

He drifted off and then he was cleaning his room, the furniture so light he could lift it with one hand. He felt invincible. Everything shone. He was expecting a woman. But when he lifted his bed, there was a pile of bones underneath. He screamed a choking, silent scream, and suddenly the bed was so heavy he dropped it with a thud that shattered the windows. When he bent to sweep up the glass, he saw that his floor was covered with bloody handprints. The woman was knocking. He tried to pull the blanket over the blood, but it was caught on something. The knocking got louder, so he pulled harder, and a pale, bloated arm came off with the blanket, the fingers in a death grip on the edge.

He heard his own scream as he shot up and saw Farid looking in with wide eyes.

"Everything okay? Police here."

"Fine, thanks, I'm coming."

Weinert's shirt was unbuttoned over a t-shirt from a band Simon was pretty sure had once opened for them, but not sure enough to say so. He was sitting in one of the chairs, a cup of coffee on the sill. Simon nodded his gratitude to Farid. It must've taken a while to wake him.

Farid nodded back. "I go." So much for getting his opinion on Sophie.

"Sorry," Weinert said after he left. "I probably gave him a scare with all that shouting and knocking earlier. I got a little worried something might've happened to you."

"I should've told him you might come by. He's sort of nervous."

"That's a fine thing you're doing."

"Thanks." He felt again how insufficient and almost always wrong that word was. "It's no big deal." There was still coffee in the pot, so he poured himself some and sat in the other chair. He had a sudden flashback to that fleshy white arm, and for a split second thought he might vomit. Then the feeling passed. "Any new developments?"

He couldn't shake the sense of guilt. He had nothing particular to feel bad about, but the arbitrary dream logic still applied, where you were charged with crimes you never remembered committing. If there really was a skeleton under his bed? Nonsense. He was just dreading Sophie bursting in and . . . what?

"When we asked Herr Barer about his supposed trip to Amsterdam," Weinert was saying, "he said he never left Berlin and was just stringing along some very dubious detectives who barged into his apartment. Oh, and he said one of them looked awfully familiar. In case you need any extra incentive not to dress up as Sherlock Holmes."

"But he knew so much." He'd forgotten to put milk in his coffee, but didn't want to get up. His armpits were soaked, and his hands felt clammy. Was this all a pretext for Weinert to get a look inside his apartment?

Weinert used his thumb and index finger to smooth his beard. The gesture seemed studied, like he'd practiced in front of a mirror. Simon wondered how long he'd been a cop and whether this case was a big deal for him, like the first time you see people in the audience singing along. "He drives a convertible with a red leather interior and a gold center console, so unless your memory deceives you, that wasn't the car. Besides, it was getting repaired. There's footage of it in the garage."

"It's his garage." Like Weinert didn't know. "What if he messed with the camera?"

"We already thought of that and plenty of other things that don't concern you, whether or not he really was in Amsterdam that night. I want to talk about something else."

Bloody handprints, bones under his bed. "What?" He cleared his throat to cover a pubescent crack in his voice.

"I've been thinking about what your friend said. Do you have any enemies?"

He tried to laugh. "Who has enemies as an adult?" What he meant was: everyone. I am surrounded by the disapproval and loathing of others. Deep breath.

"The person who sent the paper that picture wasn't after money or fame. Now that we're almost certain who it was, it's hard to rule out a personal motive."

"Who was it?" He thought back to Tanja saying July had faked her disappearance. If she had, she'd want to make sure the story got out. But it couldn't have been her. Not only was she probably rotting in some canal they just hadn't dredged yet, but if they'd found out it was her, they would've called off the search.

Weinert sighed. "I'd rather not say until we've spoken with this person. The point is: What if it's not about Frau Tappet? What if it's about you?"

That dream finger pointing, singling him out in the middle of a crowd, guilty even now that he was no longer a suspect. "What do you mean?"

"You're too involved not to be involved." Weinert must've realized how that sounded, because he went red, starting in a swath that bridged his cheeks and nose. "I'm not saying you . . . What I mean is, you've known her so long, been seen with her; she's all over your website. People know there's a connection. What if someone did something to her to hurt you? Either thinking you were close, or hoping you'd be blamed?"

"Who would do that?"

"That's what I'm asking. I've read about you causing people to leave your band, alienating friends or partners . . ."

"Thanks."

"Sorry. It's only a theory. Would you think about it and come by later? I've got a couple hours off and then I'm on late shift." He took a long pull of coffee like someone trying to finish up and leave.

"I'm not that important. It doesn't seem—just a minute." He held down the buzzer.

"Your roommate?"

"No, my . . . the woman I'm seeing."

"The one you mentioned?"

"Yeah."

"I don't want to interrupt." But he remained standing as Simon let Sophie in, wet hair clinging to her from some storm he'd missed entirely. If they were alone, he might've had the courage to take her in his arms and dry her face on his chest. Or he'd still just have handed her a dishtowel.

"Weinert." He offered her his hand. "You're Frau . . . ?"

"Müller."

Simon clenched his teeth to keep from laughing. Then he realized she wasn't in on that. "He's from the police." He dreaded an outlandish reaction but wanted to get it over with.

"Oh." All the blood went out of her face, and it took her a second to close her mouth. Then she rearranged it into a distracted smile. "I'm gonna hop in the shower."

Why had she gone so pale? People got nervous around the police. Her teasing had been all talk. Now it was real for her. Maybe that would make other things real, too.

~~~

"Wanna get something to eat and swing by the station?" he asked when she came out in one of his t-shirts with her hair wrapped in his towel.

"You sure know how to show a girl a good time. What'll they book me for?"

"Aiding and abetting."

Did her smile look pained? "Whom?"

~~~

"I was just here," she said when they got off the tram.

"I know. We'll get around more in the next few days." Was that subtle enough?

"I'll be too busy looking at baby pictures with your mom and complaining about our menfolk."

"Menfolk's a topic you'll wanna steer clear of with her." Much as he dreaded some rant about his dad, a warm glow spread from his gut like mulled wine when he thought about introducing Sophie to his mom.

"I can't blame her."

~~~

While they waited in line, Simon mumbled about his mom's visit and tried not to look nervous. The clerk had long, dark hair and would've been pretty if she ever cracked a smile.

"Is Detective Weinert here?" he asked when it was his turn. "My name's Kemper." He could hear phones ringing, and the station seemed more crowded than usual. Must be more of an evening destination.

"He's on his way." She spoke out of one side of her mouth. "There's a great ice cream shop around the corner." She gave a gulping laugh, and he saw that one of her front teeth was broken off diagonally, leaving a dark triangle in her smile.

"Thanks." He hoped she hadn't noticed him looking. "Will he be long?"

She shrugged.

He turned to Sophie. "Do you . . . ?"

"I'm down for ice cream."

"Go left 'til the inflatable sundae."

~~~

"Imagine we were murderers," Sophie said. "What if we came to turn ourselves in, and she sent us for ice cream?"

"It could be a setup and they'll ambush us there." He felt like he'd gotten a day off from school, even though they'd have to go back. At least she'd waited until they were outside to make that remark.

"Like so they don't get the station dirty? Listen, I . . ."

But he wasn't listening; he was looking. As they neared the end of the line that all but obscured the inflatable sundae, he knew with dead certainty that the short-haired blonde ahead of them had been the supposed love of his life. He'd thought he'd seen Nadine so many times, but now, when he least expected her, he recognized the cursive W of hair at the nape of her neck, the sunburnt tattoo of an octopus on her left shoulder, and the peculiar fluttery way she had of moving her hand when she smoked. Was there any way out of this?

"What a line," he muttered. "Should we go somewhere else?"

"What?"

"Wanna go somewhere else?"

"No way, she said this one's good. And everywhere will be crowded. We're on our last days of summer, so everybody's gotta stuff themselves with ice cream."

"You're right." It was safer to talk in a normal voice and pretend not to see her. It had been a long time and she'd chopped off one of her defining features. Despite the shame roiling like lava in the pit of his stomach, what could she really say? He'd neglected her and flirted with women he didn't have the energy to sleep with, they'd broken up a few times, she'd pitied his fake addiction and let him move in, then they'd broken up again. She'd done all the smashing and most of the shouting. But even after all this time, he felt like she had access to the slimy, unworthy core of him, could reach in and drag it out for all to see.

"Am I a pig if I get three? How many are you getting?"

"I have to see the flavors." Sound normal. Pretend the stage notes read: carefree and debonair. "But you're definitely not a pig. Sometimes there are three great flavors, and you can't choose just one."

"Like with women," said that soft, surprisingly deep voice. If Nadine weren't clearly there by herself, he'd never have thought she was talking to him. But when she turned, she was smiling. "How've you been?"

"Nadine!" He hoped his surprise sounded genuine. "I didn't recognize you without—"

"My youthful good looks?"

"Your hair. This is, um, Sophie."

"Hi, 'um Sophie.'"

"Enchantée." Their handshake was like two dogs circling each other, when you're not sure whether they want to play or rip each other's throats out.

They inched forward as a family came out with easily twenty scoops.

"So, what're you, like, his girlfriend?" Nadine took a long drag, then dropped her cigarette and stomped it longer than necessary. But it was nothing personal. She'd always been bad at this kind of thing. "Sorry, I mean . . . ?"

"Not yet," Sophie said.

"Good luck. No, really." Looking past Sophie, she said, "I read your interview. Thanks for being . . . How shall I say . . . tactful?"

"I've always had a lot of respect for you." Respect, fear, shameful need, what difference did it make now?

She laughed once, that harsh exhalation when you disagree but can't be bothered to argue. "Likewise." She was fiddling with the belt loops of her loose cutoffs. He realized she didn't know what to do with her hands, was feeling at least a fraction of his discomfort. He was even at an advantage, having Sophie here. Although she'd outed him as not her boyfriend, so that might be another tally in the womanizing column. Even if it felt more like Sophie was—was that a word?—manizing him.

"You live around here?" he asked to keep them talking.

"No, I'm still up in Wedding. You?"

"I live in Hamburg," Sophie volunteered.

"I'm in Friedrichshain now. We're here to see the police. Remember our stalker?" It felt funny, but also good, to make July their fan and not just his. That was how it had seemed at first, though there hadn't been much overlap between Nadine and July.

"I heard; she disappeared, right?"

"Or was brutally murdered," Sophie put in.

"She was following us on tour. That's why they think we might be able to help."

"Of course. Well." Nadine swallowed loudly. "I better make up my mind. About the flavors." She craned through the mass of customers ahead of her.

"Your ex?" Sophie mouthed.

He nodded.

He'd thought Nadine was taking the opportunity to bow out, but when he and Sophie squeezed past the line with their ice cream, he saw her lingering at the curb.

"Let's talk sometime," she said. "Clear the air."

"I'd like that." The air being clear. Not the process of getting there.

"Give my regards to the long arm of the law." Her eyes flicked back and forth between him and Sophie in that slightly manic way that always made him nervous and came to the fore when she smoked too much. She shuffled down the block.

"You attract the crazy types, don't you?"

"I don't know." Somehow, that hurt. Nadine was eccentric, said the wrong thing if she said anything, but she wasn't crazy. He felt like he was cheating both Sophie and Nadine by failing to convey her innate specialness, that magical air she sometimes had, as if caught up in telling a fairytale—entranced and entrancing. The way her motions could be graceful instead of frenetic, and her dear, secret smile just for herself when she played a show or sat on the edge of her bed to read him weird personals ads she'd found. He dismissed the memory of Soledad on the edge of that other bed, inured to the camera. It didn't matter about her now, or Nadine, either. He'd have plenty of time to explain if Sophie worked out. Lines from T.S. Eliot flitted through his brain but didn't catch, something about ices and crisis. Apt. "What's that say about you?" Maybe that was all she wanted to hear.

"A lot." They were nearing the station, so they turned into a side street.

"I hope it doesn't take a crazy person to want to be with me." His words felt very far away. But there'd be time for everything later, once they found July.

They circled the dusty square around the old stone water tower, then trekked to the top to finish their melting ice cream. Someone had planted a few sad grapevines, and the grass was up to their ankles. There were too many picnickers for it to really be romantic, they'd missed sunset and the view was only a higher-up version of the street, but he put his arm around her. Then let go to slap a mosquito on his elbow. The bright flash of blood reminded him of his dream, but the horror had faded. He threw away his cup and that sandpapery napkin they always gave you at ice cream stands.

"I have to think about my enemies. That's what he wants to know." It was hard to think of enemies and talk at the same time, so the conversation petered out. Nadine was his only ex who'd been seriously upset, and look how friendly she was just now. He'd annoyed some old friends when he was between apartments, but they were more likely to keep avoiding him than plot an elaborate revenge. In a flash of paranoia, he remembered his fight with Micha, even though that was after July disappeared. A lot of resentment there. He ruled out Tanja; she was too practical about the band. She'd probably help him hush it up if he had done something. Who else? His disdain for his dad's wife was too great for him to actually hate her, and the feeling was mutual. Cindi didn't care enough to know the name of his band, let alone abduct a fan.

That was as far as he'd gotten by the time they reached the station. He rolled his eyes about having to wait again, but Sophie wasn't looking. For an instant, she was a stranger in line; irrelevant, self-contained. He remembered his stupid question, and wondered how stupid it was. If there were another man in her life, how would he feel about Simon? Not good. He could've been at the show. Simon would never have noticed. He hadn't even noticed Nadine. How could he have forgotten to ask her about that? They could discuss it during the air-clearing. If she ever got in touch.

"Sorry, what?" He hadn't realized it was their turn.

"Weinert's on his way," Sophie repeated.

"Detective Harken would be happy to see you in the meantime." Simon was about to follow the clerk when she turned to Sophie, who opened her mouth but didn't say anything. "She has a few questions."

Weinert arrived a moment later, out of breath and with a coffee stain on his t-shirt. He was carrying the culprit with two hands, one on the sleeve, the other holding down the lid.

"Perfect timing. Sophie's talking to your colleague."

"You haven't seen Frau Amsel, have you?"

"What are you, a mind-reader? We just saw her at the ice cream shop."

"She wasn't here?"

"Better ask her." He gestured to the woman returning to the desk. "I'm guessing she recommended us the same ice cream."

"Did you end up going?" she asked.

"Was a Nadine Amsel here?"

"Sure, five, ten minutes before him. Said she'd be right back."

"That's fantastic. You know, you work for the police, not that ice cream shop."

"I think she left because of me," Simon cut in.

"Well, you're here, anyway. I'll be ready for you in a minute." To the clerk, he said, "Call Frau Amsel again."

"Sure. You've got a little something there." She pointed to the immense coffee stain.

"Thanks." He wiped ineffectually with one hand.

"The couple who owns the ice cream shop drove me to the hospital when I had my bike accident," she said after Weinert left. "And nobody likes waiting here."

"Sure." Since he decided not to ask if that was how she'd chipped her tooth, the conversation died out. He was surprised how alone he felt with Sophie just down the hall.

~~~

"I couldn't come up with much."

Weinert crossed his arms over the stain on his t-shirt. Simon could make out the legs of some woodland creature tattooed on one.

"I thought of Nadine, of course, but she was normal just now. As normal as ever."

"What's that mean?"

"Nothing. I've known her so long, but Sophie thought she was . . ."

"Unstable?"

"I was the more unstable one. She meditated and had this Zen feel, you know? She just . . . couldn't handle certain situations." He recalled the potted cactus that, thanks to his instinctive dodge, had only grazed his cheek when she hurled it at him. And it was her cactus. That was before she calmed down enough to start dropping his stuff out the window. And why, because he'd flirted with some rando at a show? Mentioned moving out? It hadn't taken much.

"How do you think she's handling things now?"

"Before tonight, I hadn't seen her in ages." Okay, so she'd been unstable. Hadn't he been worse? Volatile and spoiling for a fight, or distant, hiding in whatever room he could to starve the relationship and think about Nothing, not as a numbing Mannian expanse like the sea, but as a towering dread, a diabolical Mephisto opening its cloak to cast a shadow over everything. But how much of Nadine's jealousy, her constant disappointment, had been his fault? He'd blamed himself and let her blame him. But when he thought back, she seemed no more solid than a dandelion seed, soft and pale and settling lightly on him, but never all there. "She seems fine now."

"You know why we're interested?"

"If you're thinking she kidnapped July, she could've done it sooner. July was around back when she was in the band."

"Revenge is a dish best served cold. No, I see your point. The reason I'm interested is that she sent that picture to the paper."

"That's ridiculous."

"We traced the IP address."

"She's got a strange sense of humor." Why did he feel the need to defend her? Because Sophie had called her crazy, or because she'd put up with so much? Then again, he'd put up with plenty from her, and he hadn't rehashed it all in interviews like she had.

"That's what I'm wondering, whether it was a joke—I don't see the punch-line—or revenge. Or the third possibility, which is the most interesting."

"She's guilty and trying to frame me?"

"Do you think it's within the realm of possibility?"

"Yes, but not likely."

"She was at your show in Amsterdam."

"I didn't see her at the party."

"It was a big party, wasn't it?"

"I guess." The party had been blurry even before his consciousness was on the wane. Darkness and colorful lights, faces and noise. There could've been ten Nadines there. Or was it crazy to consider her a suspect? Him trying to feel less guilty about failing as a partner: It wasn't his fault; she was unhinged. A kidnapper. Or worse. Something hard and heavy moved in his guts. He couldn't imagine Nadine holding July prisoner. Nadine's flashes of temper were as brief as they were terrible. She didn't have the stamina. But . . . Well, she probably wasn't strong enough to kill anyone.

He wasn't much help. He hadn't seen Nadine in Amsterdam, and Weinert said she'd been on tour afterward. They talked about her character again, but the more possible her guilt seemed, the more Simon had to deny it.

"Are we almost done?" he asked at last. "I don't know how long Sophie's in town for."

"Of course, but let's hear your other enemies."

Every name on his short list was a stretch. Weinert might as well have asked him to come up with some close friends.

~~~

Sophie was talking to the receptionist when he came out, but looked bored and tired, slumped forward in her chair.

"Let's go home," he said. "We've got a big day tomorrow."

"Mm."

On the tram, resting his head against the window with hers on his shoulder, he said, "Nadine sent that picture." He wondered why she didn't respond until he realized it was Soledad who found that article. They were too different to mix up unless you were thinking of the role in your life instead of the person filling it.

After he explained, she snorted with laughter. "Sounds guilty to me." She patted his arm, raising her fingertips above her palm like someone who's never had a pet handling a friend's dog. She took a quick, shallow breath like she was about to say something, then didn't.

"Let's not talk about it tomorrow. I don't want my mom to worry."

"Mm."

"What'd they ask?"

"Uh, not much. They can tell I'm not involved."

~~~

He slept heavily after the brief high of sex, feeling wanted after all and able to forget himself for a safe little window of time. If he dreamt anything, he forgot it.

He heard the shower when he woke up. They'd have breakfast, not expend too much energy until his mom arrived. He was wondering whether they'd be able to get a table at the café in the park when she came in and said, "Morning," without looking at him.

"I'll shower and we can get something to eat."

"Mm."

When he came back, she'd packed and was looking around for lost items.

"I thought we'd—"

Her loud intake of breath cut him off as if she'd spoken. She looked out toward the front door. "Something's come up."

"Oh." He took a deep breath, struggling to maintain control. Not be pathetic or snide. "I thought you wanted to meet my mom."

"Sorry, I . . ."

He waited long enough for her to give any number of explanations, but all she said was, "No news about July?"

"Nope. But we should eat before you go." Maybe this was a mood, that instinct to run when you saw someone getting close. He needed to buy time.

"There's a bakery near where I parked."

Farid had his headphones on and was mouthing German words from his video. He looked up as Sophie walked by with her overstuffed shopping bag. Behind her back, Simon shrugged and grimaced to say things weren't going as planned. Farid made the same gestures in reverse order to say he didn't know why.

Breakfast was quick and weighed down by the pressure of pretending not to care. For him, anyway. She clearly didn't, or she'd at least have made an excuse. But when he walked her to her car, she kissed him and said, "Don't worry so much about July; I just have this feeling she's fine. And come see me sometime."

He watched her drive away.

~~~

He found her toothbrush in the bathroom and tried to make that a good sign. Then again, she had another one at home. And probably another man. Was that ridiculous? Maybe the police had freaked her out or he hadn't been good in bed. Maybe something really had come up, or she was afraid of meeting his mom. She could've said so, though.

He had the distorted, funhouse-mirror version of everything he'd wanted: Instead of Mei, their adopted son Yosef and July keeping her distance, he had a not-girlfriend who'd pretended to be Mei, an adult he didn't know how to help living in his kitchen, and July so far gone she might never have existed.

He needed to talk to someone who might understand, aside from the language part. "You busy?" he asked as soon as Farid took off his headphones.

~~~

Soledad was coping with a long line, so they took the last table next to the napkin dispensers. Simon brought her the dishes she hadn't had time to bus, and she gave him a smile so fleeting she was taking an order before he could return it. It was always like that on overcast days; people set out optimistically, then decided a cloudburst was imminent and rushed into the café.

"My mom and her boyfriend are coming later," he told Farid.

"Nice, happy for you." Farid patted his shoulder, and Simon thought how uptight Germans were about physical contact, and especially how uptight he was. It was better not to ask where Farid's parents were. "Sad she not see Sophie?"

"A little. You know . . ." He didn't know how to say it, and vocabulary wasn't the issue. "I thought she wanted to go out with me. Now I don't know. She's smart, funny and sexy, but there's something a little off sometimes."

"What?"

"Something . . . not right." Like how she hadn't even pretended to be cool with Farid being there. Or his mom. Or how she never asked how he was, just wanted juicy facts about the case. So what, she was a little self-centered? That practically made them soulmates.

"Ask her girlfriend, yes or no? My wife says when first see me, I want this, not this. Then we know."

"Yeah, that would be good." That was what he needed, someone to tell him what was what. Except he was too afraid of the answer to ask. "What if she doesn't like me?"

"When she doesn't like, she doesn't like also with not ask. Is that right?"

Simon reassembled the sentence for him. "Yeah, but now I can at least hope she does."

"At least?"

"That means I have that, even if I have nothing else."

"Not good have wrong hope."

"You're right." The rain had started, and the café looked like evening. "What should I say?" He didn't usually talk this much about his insecurities outside therapy, but he had the excuse that they were practicing German.

"Maybe, I want . . ." He looked something up on his phone, and Simon felt the usual silly awe that everything was in Arabic. " . . . relationship. Please say if not want."

"But at the beginning, I made like . . . I mean, I didn't know what I was looking for, so I was like . . ."

"Slow."

"Before, I said I don't want a relationship."

"Say, new thing: I want a relationship. Do you want?"

"Easy, right?"

Farid patted him again. "Easy me say to you."

"Yeah."

"Different woman is your girlfriend when not Sophie."

Simon laughed. "Then why am I single?"

Farid shrugged, laughing, too. "You not do what you need?"

"Hey, you can't just sit here and not order anything!" Soledad said in a deep voice that made them both jump. Simon lunged back to grab her, but she wriggled out of reach, and then he was glad he'd missed. Like dogs chasing cars, that was what his mom always said about men going after women: If they ever catch one, they don't know what to do with it.

"I'll have a cappuccino and a job."

"Broke again?" She turned to Farid.

"Coffee, please."

"Sure." To Simon she said, "Maria's a maternity-leave time bomb."

"I was hoping to start sooner."

"Don't worry; Barbara can't refuse me anything. What if I quit and she had to stop meditating over healing crystals and run this place?"

"Not understand."

"The owner's a little strange," Simon said.

"Where's Sophie?" Soledad asked when she came back with their drinks. The first crack of thunder chopped off Sophie's name, but he'd known the question was coming.

"She went back." Funny how thunder always seemed like an anomaly in the city, like weather was reserved for the countryside. Funny how little he felt about Sophie being gone, when you left out the big picture of his love life and what to tell his mom.

"Did something happen? You don't have to tell me, but I'm a detective so I'll find out either way."

"She spent the night in an undisclosed location. We had breakfast, I bought her half the mall, we had dinner, talked to the police, ran into Nadine—holy shit, I haven't told you about Nadine!"

"One thing at a time. Unless you ran into Nadine carrying July's body over her shoulder, I wanna hear about Sophie first."

"Okay, we saw Nadine and that was awkward, we went to the police, then back to my place and um . . ." He was glad Farid couldn't follow what he was saying. It was bad enough that she could.

"Was it good?"

"Um, for me."

"I'm sure it was for her, too." She patted him on the shoulder like everyone kept doing lately. He must seem like he needed encouragement. Then she noticed the growing line. "Shit! Call me later?"

She was gone before he could use his mom as an excuse.

"Soledad nice."

"Let's work on sentence structure."

~~~

Afterward, Farid headed home, and Simon went straight to Hauptbahnhof. It had stopped raining, but the sky was metallic, and the glassed-in expanse of the train station with the enormous robot horse sculpture looked dystopian. Inside, just past the information desk, was a board of missing-person notices. He averted his eyes like they were a crowd July might've emerged from back when he was avoiding and not looking for her. He wondered if that lost cat, Mei's namesake, had ever turned up.

He picked up a bouquet at the florist and rushed to the platform only to find that there was a delay. When the train rolled in, he had the rare good luck of being near the right exit, snagging his visitors before they could get lost.

His mom seemed younger and older than she really was. She had the same delicate build as ever, but could never commit to dyeing her hair or letting it go gray, so the silvery streaks in her dark, shoulder-length curls started at the roots and came to an abrupt stop at her ears. She looked like she'd been taking fashion advice from the residents of the home where she worked, wearing high-waisted beige pants and a frumpy pinkish sweater too close to the color of her skin. She had few wrinkles, but pronounced reverse dimples around her mouth, as if from years of uninterrupted frowning. She was smiling now, though, and going on about how nice of him to pick them up, book them a hotel, show them around . . .

Reinhardt freed a hand from the array of suitcases to shake Simon's. He was tall, neither fat nor thin, and had more hair under his nose than on his head. He taught math or something, and reminded Simon of all the generically dorky teachers he'd had growing up: never anyone's favorite, but nothing specific to make fun of. Franzi thought he was boring, and so did Simon, but mostly he thought Reinhardt contributed to their mom's material and psychological well-being.

"I'm dying to see what you've done with your place," his mom said. "When you moved in, you didn't have a stick of furniture."

Not much had changed there. "Let's get to your hotel first. You can come over tomorrow."

~~~

They got soaked walking from the subway. His mom and Reinhardt wanted to change, so Simon waited downstairs and called Soledad after all.

"Hey, I'm drenched; are you?" she shouted over the pounding rain.

"Are you outside? You're crazy!"

"I'm in a bus shelter. It always ends quickly when it rains this hard."

"That sounds like a metaphor."

"For what?"

He would've said something about passion if he were trying to pick her up or even a little drunk, but instead he asked, "What do I tell my mom about Sophie?"

"She had an emergency at work. She's sorry to miss their visit. Imply that she's switching jobs so your mom won't worry about her stressful career."

"You're incredible." One of those thoughts you wished you hadn't said aloud. "No wonder your detective agency's so successful."

"*Our* agency. I'd offer to fill in, but look how much trouble fake girlfriends have gotten you in so far."

"It's tempting, but I see your point." Too tempting. Because Sophie was right, and he liked pretending more than the real thing? "You'll never guess who sent that picture."

"Nadine?"

"Okay, you guessed." He got her up to date on the case.

"Ay ay ay. Have fun anyway! I don't wanna keep you. I'll help you agonize later. I'm great at agonizing."

"Me, too, but I always like a second opinion."

"Oh, I almost forgot! Barbara said I should tell her which shifts I need you for because her head's too far up her ass. No, she didn't actually say that part."

"What would I do without you?" Another thing you shouldn't say aloud. "Bye!" He nearly jumped out of his skin when he felt a hand on his shoulder and turned to see his mom. Reinhardt was absorbed in some pamphlet from reception.

"I could tell from the look on your face you were talking to your girlfriend. Will Sophie be joining us?"

Soledad's advice worked like a charm. His mom tore Sophie's high-profile job a new one, Reinhardt tutted sympathetically, and Simon managed to insert a few comments about not being sure where the relationship was headed, which didn't prompt any reaction now, but might spare his mom undue disappointment later. He realized he was already preparing himself for the same disappointment. It was a bad sign that Sophie had left without an explanation, but then she hadn't had one for turning up, either. Had she meant it when she asked him to visit, or was that some last vestige of politeness? He made a generic comment to imply he was listening to Reinhardt's dusty anecdote about misbehaving students, or was it faculty members? Soledad was right. He still had a lot of agonizing to do.

~~~

Simon didn't notice until the next morning how spotless the apartment was, not just clean but asserting its cleanliness in a way it hadn't since he moved in. The kitchen sink shone, the bathroom fixtures sparkled, and even the trim at the bottom of the wall was free of dust. Farid was nowhere in sight, but he'd pushed his mattress against the wall and filled a glass with dandelions, purple henbit and buttercups he must've picked in the park. The window was open, and the apartment smelled like fresh air and that lavender cleaning solution Simon used so rarely the bottle itself needed dusting. Only his bedroom didn't pass muster, but they wouldn't go in there.

His mom and Reinhardt had insisted they could find their way over. Simon had suggested they come before breakfast because that would limit the amount of time they stood around awkwardly, wondering why he didn't have enough chairs for them to sit, or a girlfriend to sit there with them.

Why stop there? He shuffled into the shower, scrubbed the usual suspects for BO, and got dressed. His mom would settle for a girlfriend, but why not a wife and kids? He was old enough to have them. Plenty of his old classmates did. At least Franzi would have a career his mom could brag about and cute kids. Plus a Nobel Prize or something.

But his mom liked to brag about him, too. She printed all the reviews Franzi emailed her because he was too embarrassed to, and kept them in an album or on the fridge to be washed out by spills but treasured nonetheless.

Farid's key in the lock woke him from his reverie. They should be here by now. He texted his mom, but she was probably looking at a map on the smartphone he and Franzi had gotten her. She couldn't multitask yet.

Simon came into the kitchen. "Thanks for cleaning. That was really nice of you."

"No problem. Mom is sad not to see Sophie?"

"No, she thinks she will later."

"And you think?"

"Just a second." He buzzed open the door.

~~~

"Really nice place," Reinhardt said the moment they came in. Maybe the smell of cleaning products did it for him.

"And so tidy," his mom added. "You must be Fa . . . ?"

"Farid," Simon helped her.

Farid took her hand and bowed his head slightly. "So happy to meet mom of Simon. Simon's a very good friend." He shook Reinhardt's hand and said, "Happy to meet you," maybe because it was too hard to say he was happy to meet his friend's mom's boyfriend.

"Nice to meet you, too," Reinhardt said. "Welcome to Germany. We need motivated young people like you."

Simon wasn't sure Farid had understood, but Farid smiled and thanked Reinhardt, then retreated to a corner of the kitchen while Simon took his visitors on the brief tour his apartment permitted.

"Great floorplan," Reinhardt said.

"Such a nice young man," his mom whispered before asking, "Will you be joining us for breakfast?"

"No, thank you, I eat before and now study."

"You speak very good German," she said. "Have you been here long?"

"Two month, but my wife and I learn since we know leave Syria."

"Is she here, too?"

"No."

There was a long silence. "I'll pray for the two of you."

"What's pray?"

Simon pressed his hands together and looked up, and Farid thanked his mom. When Simon was younger, he'd almost died of embarrassment when she said things like that, but now he felt a surge of tenderness. She was a nice person.

~~~

They trusted the sky enough to take a table in the park, and Simon was startled to realize it was the same one he'd shared with July. That didn't feel very long ago, but she seemed an eternity away, like some friend from daycare remembered only from his mom's anecdotes.

The subject of Farid was a welcome distraction while they ate.

"How terrible to have to leave his wife behind."

"I read in the paper," Reinhardt said with the same bland earnestness he said everything, "that the men take the dangerous route on foot and in those little boats so their relatives can fly over when they get their papers."

"Why don't they all fly? Is it the cost?"

"No, Mom, smugglers are more expensive than plane tickets. The airlines won't take them because they'd have to pay for the return flight if the EU won't let them in." His shallow expertise, borrowed from Franzi, was deep enough for now.

"It's a terrible world," she said, but, being specific by nature, added, "You know, Reinhardt and I are moving in together, and we'll have a lot of things double. Farid and his wife might need some of them. Dishes, lamps, the sofa . . ."

"You guy are moving in together?" Simon said with his mouth full. "Wow, um, congratulations." Funny to hear about it this way. Was it not a big deal for them, or had she been waiting to tell him in person? "Does Franzi know?"

"Oh, Simon, at our age . . ." Her cheeks were flushed, and he had one of those occasional glimpses of how she'd looked before all the years and worries.

"It'll be more convenient," Reinhardt said.

"We'll have more money for traveling and so on."

He felt a pang of guilt for all the years of laughing at her penuriousness, and sympathy for the hopes and yearnings she must've kept locked in a drawer labeled "traveling and so on." Then again, the only time *he* left the city, let alone the country, was for work.

"We've talked about marriage, too." Reinhardt put a hand on his mom's. She smiled, looked down and then back at Simon, a crevice deepening among the fine lines on her forehead.

"I wanted to hear what you and Franzi think." Her fingers tearing off pieces of her croissant seemed more like a nervous tic than a way of eating. "I know you were both a little upset when your dad remarried."

A little upset was their default attitude toward their dad. When he married Cindi, they'd considered severing the last thin threads of contact, but their mom had talked them out of it in her practical way: "He's the only father you've got."

"This is nothing like that. I'm so excited!" Because "I'm happy for you" never came out of his mouth sincere.

"See?" Reinhardt turned to her.

"Here's to you." Simon raised his cup and the others did the same.

"And to that lady friend you're so mysterious about," his mom added.

"If only I were the one being mysterious."

~~~

They spent a few hours doing tourism lite, the kind for visitors who've already seen the postcard monuments: Simon's nearest flea market, where his mom "could just see" everything in their new place but only bought a small ceramic swan; the Botanical Garden, where the train ride was longer than their visit because it started pouring after they left the greenhouses; and Café Astral.

Soledad was wiping down the counter, dancing to the radio like a housewife in some old commercial for cleaning products. She looked happy, but not surprised, to see them. Simon could hear Maria or one of the teenagers slamming the mop around the kitchen. It was late for coffee, so Soledad had time to chat while she made their drinks.

He thought she'd come to their table since there was no line, but she continued cleaning. Not that he was looking.

"She's sweet," his mom said. "Have you known her long?"

"We've worked together for a while."

"It's a nice café," Reinhardt put in.

Soledad messaged him: "Didn't want to intrude."

He replied: "Please do." It would be rude not to. And being rude would mean admitting to what was bothering him. For all Tanja's talk, Farid's hints and the little smile his mom thought she was hiding, he wasn't getting the right talk, hints and smile from *her*. She was happy to see him because she was bored. She wasn't worried about being disheveled from work, or anxious about meeting his parents. That was a relief, wasn't it? One less thing to feel guilty about.

Soledad sat down and asked a million questions after he told her their news: how they'd decorate the new place, where they'd get married, what they'd do for a honeymoon. He admired her ability to show so much interest in strangers. His mom was having the time of her life. Must be nice to have it be about her for once, he thought with a fresh twinge of guilt, but Reinhardt probably showered—or at least sprinkled—her with safe, moderate affection.

"You know a lot about the subject," his mom said. "Are you married? Or engaged?"

"No, but a girl can dream."

"Better to be single than marry the wrong guy. I should know."

"But now you met the right one." Soledad patted his mom's hand and smiled at Reinhardt. Simon felt a little extraneous like he often did at family events, his or other people's. Nadine had likened his attempts at small talk to those impromptu presenters they throw onstage when the performers are late, looking at their watches as they ramble on, then drifting away with great gray relief when the real act arrives. That was what she called things she didn't like: "gray." His conversation was gray, his passion for her was gray, his feelings were stunted and gray. It had been like learning after all the years that there was a word for what he hated about himself.

Everyone was looking at him. "Sorry, what?"

"Whether you wanna get married." Soledad looked up as a customer came in, but a woman with stringy blonde hair and a round belly under her apron came out to take the order.

"Sure." He tried to sound casual, like he'd never thought about marrying his imaginary girlfriend. He remembered a Weezer song he'd listened to as a kid: "We were good as married in my mind / but married in my mind's no good." His English hadn't been good enough to get that it was about falling for a lesbian. Not quite the problem he was having with Sophie, but close enough. He didn't have to know why she was so lukewarm to see that married in his mind wasn't panning out. But say something normal. "If I met the right person. Commitment's more important than a wedding, but who doesn't love a party?" There, that had started off gray, but then he'd presented himself as a person who loved parties, like all the other colorful people out there. Then again, Sophie thought Nadine was crazy. Was crazy better than gray?

"Yeah," Soledad agreed. "It has to be a hell of a party, though."

"'If,' Simon? Are things that bad with Sophie?" his mom asked.

"Uh, just not there yet, and not sure we will be."

Reinhardt said, "I'm going to tell you something my dad told me." Simon was touched but too self-conscious to admit it, so he pretended they were acting in some TV movie. "If it's not there, it's not there. If someone isn't serious about you, or you're not serious about her, sticking around is a waste of everybody's time."

"Well now, that's a little harsh." His mom was cranky that the fluffy wedding talk was being squashed. "He's got plenty of time to figure that out."

"Never too soon to make the right decision." Reinhardt was divorced, too, but you'd think he'd never had a moment's doubt in his life.

~~~

Reinhardt had to grade some exams the next day, so Simon took his mom for a walk along the canal. She took the opportunity to bring up what she must've thought he wouldn't want Reinhardt to hear.

"You're sure you've got enough to get by?" she asked while they were pelting mixed nuts at the swans because you weren't supposed to give them bread.

"Of course. Anyway, I'm starting at the café again."

"It must be nice to have a friend to work with."

"Yeah." His hand grasped the emptiness inside the bag, and he shook out the crumbs.

"It's almost a shame you can't meet some nice girl here." She was a bird-in-the-hand person: He hadn't produced his supposed girlfriend, so she was looking for the nearest eligible female.

"Yeah." He crumpled up the bag but there was no trashcan, so he stuffed it in his pocket as they continued across Admiralbrücke, where normal, non-fraught young people were listening to an only slightly fraught young man play guitar; smoking, nodding along and delaying cars that wanted to cross the bridge. "I saw Nadine."

"I didn't realize you kept in touch."

"We don't." Passing all the people sunning themselves on the burnt and bristling lawn, he felt like the only person on the planet who had to tell his mother things like this. "Remember how that fan disappeared? The police wanna question Nadine because she tried to make it look like I was involved. She even sent this tabloid a picture of me."

"That doesn't sound like Nadine."

Of course it didn't, because Nadine never made a scene when other people were looking. That would make it too hard to play the victim. "She was in Amsterdam the night the girl disappeared."

"Do they have any leads?"

"They think it might be someone like Nadine." He stopped short of mentioning enemies. She could decide for herself what "like Nadine" meant.

"I can't imagine . . . although . . ." He doubted she had any real reason to suspect Nadine. The "although" probably signified that any suspect was more likely than her son. "What was it like seeing her?"

"Sophie was there, so it was a little weird. But she was friendly. I think the newspaper thing was some kind of joke."

"A pretty tasteless one! I suppose I didn't know her as well as I thought, but we had a lot going on back then. You're not involved in anything . . . illegal, are you?"

"Don't be ridiculous."

"I don't think I am, considering your history. I know you weren't able to have the same kind of childhood your friends did, but . . ." The usual catch in her throat. She seemed to see him having done drugs as her personal failing, directly traceable to a deprived childhood.

"Mom, to be honest?" He stopped before the café boat he'd planned to take her to, because he didn't want anyone to overhear, and because he wanted her to really listen. "I was never addicted." Strange how July had believed him right away. Or not strange at all, because she'd been there to see him.

"But, Simon . . ."

"I was having trouble getting my life together and too depressed to deal with it. I only ever took drugs a couple times to try and handle how bad I felt. And I let you all think I was addicted because I wanted to feel like you cared." Great, now he was dripping tears and snot all over the place. She plunged one hand into the depths of her purse, running the other over his unruly hair like she always had when he cried.

"Oh, Simon." The cool touch of her hand was as soothing as ever, except now he had to duck to accommodate it. "Whatever the problem was, we wanted to be there for you. All that matters is that you're okay now. Are you okay?"

"I'm okay," he said once she produced a tissue he could hide his face behind. "I never told Nadine. We only got back together because she felt like she had to look after me."

"A smart, handsome, talented young man like you surely doesn't believe that." She handed him another tissue. "I'm sorry I wasn't astute enough to notice. I was very unhappy myself." The catch was in her throat again, as if they were tossing it back and forth, but at least she had the tissues handy.

"Are you okay?"

She smiled through the inertia of continuing tears. "Better than okay. I have two wonderful children and a kind, devoted man in my life. What more could I ask for?"

He let the question remain rhetorical. "Mom?"

"Yes?"

"Sometimes I don't like Dad."

"You don't have to like him, just love him."

That took him from tears to laughter, but he still had to ask: "Is it ever difficult for you that Franzi's so much more successful and well-adjusted than I am?"

"It might be, if I knew what you were talking about."

He took a deep breath and tried to see his life as she did: He was young, in a band she believed to be wildly successful, and seeing someone. Had his own place in the city. "Just a joke between me and Franzi. Should we get coffee here?"

~~~

He spent the first couple days after his mom left tutoring Farid, taking over shifts so Soledad could finish an assignment, and losing his appetite listening to Maria puke in the employee restroom. Sometimes Farid studied at Astral. Simon was hardly ever alone and didn't even mind. Wanting people around was an unusual feeling he didn't know what to do with.

Franzi finally called as he was walking home from work about a week later. He filled her in on Sophie.

"I'm sorry I brought her. Christian was saying she's fun, but also . . . a little mean?"

"Really?"

"Oh, just something he heard her say to July. I don't like when people who are doing well shit on people who aren't, you know?"

"I'm sure it was a joke."

"Sure. Come visit again. I'll find you someone better."

"I don't want someone better; I want . . ." He wasn't sure how to finish his sentence.

"Her. But how long do you wanna get strung along? No offense, but there's definitely some stringing going on."

"I think she's just generally noncommittal."

"You're really selling me on this. At least Mom didn't have the chance to fall for her."

"She's finally seen the dark side of Nadine. Did you know she's moving in with Reinhardt?"

"Yawn, Reinhardt. As long as she's happy."

"They're gonna get married. She seemed really happy when she and Soledad were talking about weddings."

"Who?"

"This woman I work with."

"As long as she's happy," she said again. "She's earned it, right?"

"Haven't we all."

"You know, Christian thinks we're not official enough. Like he's asking when we're gonna meet each other's parents."

"When are you?"

"Can you imagine what a nightmare Dad will be?"

"Mom says we don't have to like him, just love him."

"That sounds like her."

"If it makes you feel better, introducing literally anyone to him would be a nightmare. I was so uncomfortable telling him about Farid."

"A *literal* nightmare, right?" She laughed. "By the way, I hate to say it, but there's not much you can do to help Farid's wife. He doesn't have his visa yet, right?"

"No."

"She can't come until then. I'm assuming they've made an appointment in Lebanon."

"Lebanon?" Another country he couldn't have found on a map.

"It's the closest German embassy that's still open. Or they might try somewhere she can fly without a visa."

"He's a really nice guy. I just . . ."

"You're doing all you can. Don't underestimate how important language is."

"We've been practicing."

"That's great." He could hear the distance that always came into her voice when she was running out of time, an echo like she was slowly drifting away. "I know you wanna be a good person, and you are, Simple Simon. But there's only so much you can do. I have to tell myself that all the time. Like with July. Where's all the obsessing gotten you?"

"Well…" He remembered what Soledad had said about making him feel less helpless. Their amateur sleuthing felt therapeutic, but also real, like they were approaching the truth. Circling around it on a mountain road, closer at every turn. "Soledad thinks it will make me feel better."

He heard her talking to someone, probably saying, *hang on, I just need to handle my neurotic big brother.* "It's great that you feel better. Don't worry so much."

Why did her last words stand out after he hung up? They were a standard formula. Then he remembered Sophie saying she had the feeling July was okay. But he wasn't a big believer in intuition. Almost everything he ever really felt like doing was wrong. Like right now he wanted to call Soledad, interrupt her evening with her study group or that ponytailed director who filmed her in bedrooms, and tell her everything, even though almost nothing had changed. And that was exactly what he shouldn't do, something selfish to comfort him at someone else's expense. He had no idea what she needed, but it wasn't him.

He was too restless to go home, so he continued along the park, making unnecessary detours and thinking about what he'd say if he did call her. He had a Bob Dylan song he couldn't remember all the words to stuck in his head: "It ain't me you're lookin' for." His dad had hated all the foreign music he'd listened to growing up, even the classics. He was too old to rebel now, but the music you listened to as a kid stayed with you. He wished he could still feel a happiness as pure as singing along with Johnny Cash or Die Toten Hosen as a teenager. At what age did everything go flat and complicated? No relationship had ever made him as happy as his crush in third grade, where there was only the pleasure of chasing Sisi Boeller on the playground, without all the guilt and crushing fear.

To keep from doing anything he'd regret, he messaged Tanja. "I'm a bad person."

"You, too?! Come watch a movie? Birds of a feather, etc."

There was nothing else he felt like doing, so he grabbed a falafel and ate it on the bus to Moabit, ignoring dirty looks from law-abiding citizens who knew he knew you weren't supposed to eat on public transit, especially if you hadn't said to hold the onions.

Tanja had Netflix up and craft beer on the table. Looked like a good evening, once they got her lecture out of the way.

"Micha gets back tonight. You should hang with him, make sure everything's cool."

"Good idea." Don't be offended that Micha didn't tell you. Tanja probably messaged him. He sat down on the overstuffed sofa and spread a crumpled blanket over his legs, even though he wasn't cold. Tanja's apartment was a chaotic mess of pictures, souvenirs, and records in and out of their cases, but it was cozy. She usually shared it with one or two foreign exchange students, but they must've been between semesters because all the shoes in the front hallway were hers.

"I have a confession to make." She sat down and belched like this wasn't her first beer. "But it sounds like you do, too. Wanna go first?"

"Nah, I need a break from being judged." No one ever gave her shit about womanizing. Maybe it was supposed to be okay since she was a woman, but that seemed like a double standard. Still, he doubted she was about to tell him she'd been a cad to Lara. Something nasty Micha had said about him? No, that was paranoid. And self-centered.

She opened a beer for him and took a deep breath. "I saw July in the hotel that night. Outside your room."

"What?"

"She must've woken me up trying to get in. I came out and yelled at her. It was fucking creepy."

"Then what?"

"Nothing. She ran off, and I went back to sleep. I was gonna tell you but when I saw you the next day I figured we had bigger problems and that would only freak you out."

"You didn't think she was there with me?"

"Was she?"

"Not as far as I know."

"It looked like she was trying to break in. I'm pretty sure I would've woken up if she came back. You know I'm a light sleeper. The cops breaking up that bachelor party woke me up, and that was all the way downstairs."

"What about Lara? Did she hear anything?"

Tanja sighed. "No, she wasn't there."

"What do you mean?"

"I mean I exaggerated a little. She didn't sleep over. Sure, we talked about her coming to Berlin at first, but only like the bullshit you say when you're picking someone up. We hooked up at the party and, I don't know, it was so fucking depressing I left early. I knew even getting her number it wouldn't go anywhere, but I wanted to be part of the happily-in-love club for a minute. Can you blame me?"

"Of course not." He was too fixated on her first reveal for her second one to register. "Barer said July left her money in my room and then went back for it. I guess if she'd made it back in, I wouldn't have found her wallet later. If he was telling the truth about not seeing her after that, then you were one of the last to see her alive. I mean, non-missing. Have you told the police?"

"Slow down. Who's Barer?"

"Her ex-husband. Soledad and I looked him up. He told us he was there that night." He felt overwhelmed and wished Soledad were here to help absorb this information. No one else knew as much, except the culprit and maybe the police. "So did you tell Weinert?"

"I said I thought I saw her in the lobby but wasn't sure."

"Why?"

"Same reason I chased her off. I don't wanna go all Micha on you and say you're my little brother—if I had a brother, the genetic odds are against him being anything like you—but I wanted to protect you." She swallowed hard, but he wasn't up for delving into the psychology of her friend having been murdered by a stalker.

"By lying to the police?"

She rolled her eyes. "I didn't lie so much as leave out a bit. Come on, Simon. Think. I see July and think a.) July's a real creeper and b.) this lines up with what Simon said. The police hear that and think, bingo, the victim was outside Simon's room."

"I still think you should tell Weinert." It felt strange that whatever had happened while he was unconscious hadn't just involved him, July and some shadowy culprit, but whoever else was around that night, including Tanja. She'd been around hours before that, though. "Remember how July turned up while we were eating? And she was talking about some ex?"

"Sure, why?"

"Do you remember what she said?"

"Look, Simon, I know you think you can crack this case, but don't try to drag me into it."

"Humor me."

"Fine, whatever. They broke up but stayed friends or something, I don't know. You were there."

"Anything else?"

"You mean like did she name names? No, all I took from it was: 'Other guys love me and Simon should, too.'"

"Right." For a fleeting instant, he'd believed he could go back and find out what he'd missed, make up for not having paid attention the first time around. But Tanja didn't know any more than he did. "Thanks anyway."

"So what's your dirty little secret? It can't be much worse than mine."

"Actually, it's not. Just that you might be right about Soledad. The only thing I'm sure of is, whatever's going on between us, I'm fucking it up."

"Shit, I can't believe I told you all that. When you texted, I thought it was about July."

"Like what? I hid her body in the minibar?" He was sleepy, pissed at her for giving him another complication to think about.

"No, something harmless you couldn't tell the police. Like what I said."

"I don't know how harmless that is." For an instant, the glimmer of an idea lit his mind. Tanja thought July had gone too far. Had to be stopped. Not just for his sake—her career was all wrapped up in him, and then there was her dead friend. Had she lied about Lara to have an alibi? But the idea of Tanja murdering July for being outside his room was too ridiculous even to crack a tasteless joke about.

"Now I feel bad. I'll tell Weinert I was embarrassed 'cause I lied about Lara. I wouldn't even have told you, except I'm tipsy and thought you'd confess something and we'd be quits."

"Were you drinking here?" He didn't like himself in the role of concerned friend, but drinking alone wasn't like Tanja.

"Nah, I had to go to this baby shower and the mom kept pouring everybody shots. My advice? Soledad's a catch. Finish up with Sophie before you ask her out. Or whatever you kids do nowadays." She finished her beer, laid her head back and yawned.

"You don't think it's going anywhere with Sophie?"

"I figured it must not be if you're scrounging around for a new crush."

"I wasn't scrounging. We just . . . started hanging out."

"Just like that?"

Maybe he did need to take more responsibility. "Okay, I asked her to dinner. Then we impersonated detectives."

"You need a new hobby. But anyway, you did initiate it."

"I guess." He wanted to resent her, but now her second confession was sinking in. She'd faked a connection because she couldn't find a real one. Dear, tough Tanja.

"Fuck it. Let's watch a braindead comedy and regroup tomorrow."

~~~

He nodded off on the couch, but woke refreshed and happy, like he had something to look forward to. The feeling disappeared when Tanja brought him a coffee and said, "Micha gave Nadine your new number."

"Nadine?" A word he'd looked up recently but couldn't remember the meaning of.

"He said he thought you only changed it because of July, so you wouldn't mind. *I* would've asked first."

"What's she want?"

"Who knows? I gotta run if I wanna see the cops before work. Pull the door shut behind you."

"Thanks." He finished the coffee and decided to go home and shower. No use looking like a bum when he saw Nadine. She'd already texted: "Wanna talk?"

He didn't reply until he was dressed and as ready as he could be. "Sure, when should I come by?" Inviting himself over might've sounded forward if they hadn't been so completely out of touch. There was no one he was less likely to hook up with. He'd thought that about July, too, but in her case, the repulsion hadn't been mutual. Let Nadine suspect an ulterior motive if she wanted. All he wanted was to make sure she didn't have July hidden anywhere.

"Whatever, now."

He stopped for more coffee and a roll to settle his stomach before whatever agonizing revisiting of the past the otherwise pleasant, sunny day had in store. He texted Sophie for moral support. At best, she'd be snarky; at worst, she'd think he was trying to make her jealous. No, at worst she wouldn't answer.

Since she decided to go with the worst-case scenario, he sent a group message to Tanja and Micha. Tanja said: "I'm seeing a lot of songwriting material here." Micha said: "Sorry, didn't want her to get mad. Call cops if you're not done soon?"

~~~

"After all this time," Nadine said instead of hello.

"It's only been a couple days."

Some melancholy folk singer was drowning out any background noise, but he got the feeling Nadine was home alone. She shooed him into the kitchen and went to turn down the music. He sat down in one of the wicker chairs at her lawn table without being asked. The furniture was new, at least to him, but she still had the same ironic cuckoo clock and mismatched ornamental teacups in that splintery china cabinet.

"Want something to drink?" she asked, hovering behind his chair.

"Water, please."

"I made coffee."

"Okay, I'll have a little." He didn't want to get shaky this early in the day, or offend her this early in the visit. "Place looks good," he said while she poured him a brimful cup.

"Thanks. Sorry, I forgot." She snatched the cup away, spilling near-boiling coffee on his jeans. Lucky he wasn't wearing shorts. She dumped some coffee in the sink. "You still take milk?"

"Yeah. Thanks." There was something dishonest about this implication of shared domestic routines. They'd lived together a while, but it had never gone without saying. And yet he'd loved her enough to want to spare her the misery of him. If that had been love.

She made fidgety small talk about the band, then mentioned Sophie.

"I don't think that's going anywhere. I . . ." Why tell her? So she could relish his failure? "So, trying to make it look like I killed July: prank or a serious effort to ruin my life?"

"Is your life ruined?"

"No. But I'm not laughing, either. I don't even wanna know what conspiracy theories are going around."

"You're overestimating how much people care."

That hurt. But she meant it to, so he focused on his coffee and relaxing his facial muscles. She was still pretty, but more ragged now, like a fancy dress with loose threads. She or some other layperson had cut her hair. Losing weight didn't suit her. There was a musty smell in the apartment he hoped wasn't coming from her, something like a bouquet of flowers left out too long. The faint reminder of lost fragrance, the acrid dustiness of the petals and the swollen, fetid stems. "Honestly, it looks like *you* care too much. And you were at my show."

She said what he expected: "Let's not forget it would be my band if you hadn't cast me off."

"You left."

"Yeah, the band."

"I'm not here to argue. I fucked up, but it's been a long time and you weren't wholly innocent, either." The courage to say so was new, but regrettable, because it sucked him deeper into the quicksand of this irrelevant topic.

"What did I do again? Flake out when it got serious? Get addicted to drugs? Cheat? Make it so uncomfortable you had to change bands? Oops, no, that was you." She was warming to the subject, her low voice hard and abrupt as a dropped pan.

"Cheat" was rich. By the end, he'd been courting affection or attention wherever he could get it, but too depressed to sleep with her, let alone anyone else. His faithfulness hadn't been virtue but should still count.

"You're right," he said. "But I thought we wanted to move on."

"Yeah, water under the bridge. Just months and months of my life wasted."

So he'd been a waste. "Sorry, I didn't mean to be dismissive." Deep breath, consider every word. Like chess: Once you made your move, you couldn't take it back, so you had to hover with your rook in the air until you were sure. As if you ever could be. The clock cuckooed, though it couldn't have been a round hour. "I was in a bad place, but for the record, I never betrayed you, except maybe emotionally."

She stared at him. "What other way is there?"

He tried again. "I messed up my life at least as much as yours." Tact and efficiency demanded that he not mention her messing up his. "Which is why I respect you wanting to clear the air."

Rather than pursuing the topic, she said, "I'm sorry about the paper. I was having coffee and saw you go into the station. I thought, no way, Simon's a good boy. I was planning to send you the picture as a joke. But then it felt weird, like you'd think I was waiting around to see you. Like July."

"I wouldn't have thought that. I hope she's okay."

"She's fascinating, but hard to observe without getting caught in her stickiness."

"I guess."

"I'm sure she's alive. Or was."

It wasn't funny, but he felt obliged to say, "We all know she *was* alive."

"More recently than you think."

He listened to his pulse beating faster and faster, tensed his muscles as if he could harden himself against hope. She knew something. He was afraid to blink, afraid the slightest movement would cause her to say it was only a joke, like tipping off that tabloid.

"You won't be angry, will you?"

"Nope," he croaked.

"You flatter yourself I went to Amsterdam to see you, when I could do that here anytime. We were touring there. When I saw you were, too, I got a ticket. It was a good show."

"Thanks. Did you go to the party?"

"After? I got a drink with my drummer and called it a night."

"So you only saw July at the show?"

"Nope." She smiled like a child who knows something the adults don't. When Simon was little, his parents had gotten so engrossed in a fight that they'd forgotten Franzi at a rest stop. He'd pretended to sleep while savoring the importance of his knowledge, but of course once he told them, it hadn't been about him anymore, or even Franzi, but which parent's fault it was. He could see why Nadine wanted to prolong the moment. "I saw her at *my* show the next night. We got to talking, and man did she have some stories about you. She was broke and less annoying than I remembered—at first, anyway—so we let her sleep in our bus."

He felt something exploding in his brain. He couldn't tell whether it was bright and happy like fireworks, or more like a nuclear power plant going up in flames. The last person to see July hadn't been him, or even Tanja. "Is she here? Does she know the police are looking for her?"

"Not so fast. She only spent a few nights with us. Let's say we had some personal differences. I can only take her in small doses."

"Where'd you last see her?"

"Autobahn outside Bremen. She was going to Hamburg or Hannover or something. I can ask the guys if you're that interested."

"That interested? She might be dead."

Her hands fluttered on either side of her face. "She's fine. Look, I'm texting Benno."

"Have you told the police?" he asked for the second time in twenty-four hours.

"I'm telling you, she's fine. Fine, fine, fine. I only told you because I know what a worrier you are. She'll turn up. If not, nothing happened on our watch."

"What did she tell you?"

"You mean about your imaginary girlfriend and you groping her?"

"No, after that." A serious conversation with Nadine was like trying to walk a cat on a leash. She was only interested in going places that had nothing to do with the direction they needed to move in. He'd forgotten that about her and didn't miss it.

"She said you hired someone to be your fake girlfriend, then went home with that stand-in. Then got falling-down drunk at a party July invited you to. When she tried to listen to your problems, you made a pass at her, said the girlfriend was bogus, clung to her leg and cried until she took you home. You've really matured."

The frustrating thing was knowing how good Nadine's intentions must've been. She didn't have to tell him about July. But she always needed her little triumphs, and why let such good weapons go to waste?

"I wasn't drunk. Someone drugged me."

"Really?" She still sounded snarky, but her eyes were wide with concern. "July?"

"Did she say so?"

"No, but who else would?"

He left the last sip of coffee in his cup so she wouldn't refill it. She must've put the filter in wrong because it had a sandy texture. Nadine hadn't been a good roommate and wasn't a great hostess. "I was thinking whoever drugged me did something to her. But you're saying she was okay that night."

She sighed and brought her hands to a rest on the tabletop. "She said she left something in your room but couldn't get back in. Tanja chased her off and she left with some British guy to avoid this creep who was on her case." Barer wanting his money, or another creep? "She wanted to call you but couldn't find her phone, and I didn't have your number anymore."

There was no point bringing up the fact that she could've gotten his number whenever she wanted, like she had today. She probably thought she'd done him a favor by not giving it to July. He felt like she was hiding something else, holding it back to savor another big reveal. But maybe it was just frustrating not to be able to ask the one person who knew what had happened. "About this creep, did she mention any names?"

"What're you, a detective?" She fumbled in all her pockets before turning up some rolling paper and a pouch of tobacco. "She said, this creep won't move on and leave me alone. Why're you so obsessed? In your place, I'd be glad she was leaving *me* alone."

"She might be dead."

"Yeah, you said that." She licked her thumb and index finger and started rolling. "A lot of people are dead and yeah, it's sad. But look on the bright side. Maybe she was planning to murder you."

"Obviously not, because I was unconscious and she didn't." There was the cat wandering off the sidewalk again, distracted by the glint of sunlight on broken glass, wind rustling a patch of weeds. "Anyway, that's not the point."

"What is?" She lit up and clamped the cigarette in her bared teeth as she stretched her arms over her head. Her bones cracked, and the cuckoo called again. She'd be insulted if he checked the time.

"I just wanna make sure she's okay."

"You can't if she's dead."

"Yep." He'd expected to come here and remember why she'd been so hard to get over, but all he was remembering was why they'd broken up.

"I'm sorry; I'm being insensitive. Let me see if Benno . . . Yeah, it was Hamburg. She was gonna hitch."

"That's reassuring." He started to get up, then sat again. He felt the wicker pattern of the chair carved into his back. "You need to tell the police."

"Nope. Busy." She took a long drag. "See, they actually wanted to talk to me, and I considered the possibility but, uh . . ." Her hands flitted through the air, conjuring up the words. "Knowing I couldn't be of real help, I . . . didn't wanna subject myself to the negativity of that encounter."

"You do know you have to go sooner or later, right?"

Her glance skittered across his face, from there to her ashing cigarette and the black-and-white flakes gathering on her lap. She swept them aside along with his words. "Sadly, I had to cancel my last appointment because . . . something suddenly came up. And something else might come up next time. I have to respect my own boundaries and protect my peace."

He wasn't up for arguing. "Fine, whatever." Tanja's secret was a moot point now. He thought of Weinert's pet theory about Nadine or her ilk wanting to get back at him. "Anyway, when did you redecorate?" A few questions later, he felt comfortable asking for a grand tour.

"It won't be very grand. I haven't changed much."

"Still. I'm looking for a new place and I've been off the market a while."

"The housing market, anyway." She got up to show him the plastic lion claws she'd glued onto her tub, the bedroom, which still had no other furniture in it, and the equally spare living room where they'd played together so often, the same old beanbag chairs and coffee table, only the candles and dried flowers on it changed. It looked like it always had, but felt different. He had to remind himself that he wasn't here to reminisce. The bed was too low to hide a body under, and the only piece of furniture big enough to conceal one.

"I'd love to catch up more." She glanced at the off-kilter clock, her thoughts already beyond this visit. "But my boyfriend's coming over. I wouldn't mind you meeting him, but he'd be weird about it, and you might, too."

"You have a boyfriend?" He did her the favor of reacting. "Is that going well?"

"You could say so."

"Great." He wasn't sure which question she was answering. "I'll head out then." He crossed two streets before calling Weinert.

~~~

Afterward, he was too keyed up to get the train, so he wandered cobbled side streets past construction sites overtaken by weeds, and front doors with the broken glass taped over. He realized he wasn't far from Barer's apartment. That visit seemed so long ago, especially considering everything he'd found out in the meantime. Was he any closer to finding July or even a plausible suspect than he'd been that night? At least he was further from being a suspect himself.

It looked good that he'd called the police and bad that Nadine hadn't turned up for questioning. He couldn't believe she'd done anything to July, couldn't help trying to. Had July been too pally-pally, or had Nadine gotten sick of her obsession with him? Either way, they'd left her to fend for herself. Had Hamburg been a stop on her way home, or where she was headed?

Against his better judgment, he messaged Soledad to ask what she was doing after work.

"Adam's having a wrap party. I'd invite you but it's cast and crew only."

The pity in her last sentence was like the brief firm clutch of a hand on his gut, and he regretted not following Tanja's advice. What did it matter, if she was seeing someone else? Had she and Adam finished an even more intimate shoot? But that was insulting, making her career about involvement with men. And making that involvement about himself. He'd misinterpreted, wanted to misinterpret, her friendliness. Not replying would look like the sulky reaction he was actually having, which was the last thing he wanted to convey. He was typing "Have fun" when she wrote that she'd be at work another hour if he wanted to stop by.

He decided to catch a train after all.

~~~

The few customers were of the lingering variety, their tables covered with crumbs, laptops, newspapers and empty dishes. Soledad was nowhere in sight, but he could hear running water and smell the floor cleaner that always reminded him of indoor pools. She came out with the mop.

"Can I give you a hand?"

"That's okay. What's new?"

He told her while tiptoeing along her mopping route to avoid leaving shoe-prints. "Was it back-stabby to call Weinert?"

"A little, but totally justified."

Waiting for her to elaborate, he noticed she had her hair piled up more tidily than usual, revealing dangly earrings with strings of colorful beads. The bold design made her face and throat look delicate, vulnerable even. Was that a normal fashion observation, or what a murderer would think? Maybe that was the look, encouraging the right fingers to play with the dangling baubles, slide down her throat. But they weren't for him, and neither was whatever dark stuff made her brown eyes stand out even more than usual.

"So what are you thinking?" he asked at last.

"I think the odds of her being alive just got higher. At first, I was thinking, how's she getting around without her wallet or phone? But now we know she was with Apathy Collective for a while." He wondered whether she knew the name of Nadine's band because of him, or if she was a fan. She stepped into the bathroom to finish mopping, then opened the toilet with the tip of her shoe and dumped out the dirty water. "But we should at least consider the possibility that Nadine did something."

"I don't think she did, but I checked her apartment." He followed her into the fluorescent brightness of the kitchen, where she washed her hands and pumped a few shots of disinfectant into a plastic tub.

"I'm just saying she was the last to see July and it's suspicious that she kept it secret."

"Speaking of, Tanja told me she saw July trying to get into my room that night and chased her off." That reminded him of other things Tanja had said, and he wondered what he was doing watching Soledad wipe down the countertops, not helping, not necessary, just there. His role in general. He felt like everyone knew more than he did, about the case and everything else. He was only half-joking when he said, "You're not hiding anything about July, are you?"

Her earrings grazed her shoulders when she laughed. "What do I have to do with her?"

"What's Nadine got to do with her?"

"You."

So Soledad didn't have anything to do with him. "Nadine said I should be happy she's not bothering me. July, I mean."

"Even annoying people deserve to get found."

"I know, right?" There was something more he wanted to say, or at least think, but he couldn't quite get it to surface.

"Don't worry. I'll be thinking about what we should do."

We was something to take home with him.

~~~

However hard she was thinking, it was days before he heard more from Soledad than what shifts he could have, starting with the morning after the party. He made a conscious decision not to think about what had kept her up so late. Other than that, he listened to music, read, talked to Farid and practiced his latest songs alone and with the band, reminding himself that the lyrics were only metaphors, not an indication of what he was capable of.

At rehearsals, he tried to get along with Micha and not sound jealous or wonder whether he'd killed July. Why should he? Mina came to pick him up from almost every practice session, sporting apartment listings and healthful smoothies in a revolting shade of green. Simon talked about what a good couple they made, something they liked to hear. He'd liked hearing that, too. Then he realized the last person to say that had been July, not so long ago, about him and Mei. Either way, Micha wasn't acting like someone with a body in his cellar.

On the weekend, the happy couple deigned to get pizza with Simon and Tanja, and Simon tried for a healthy balance of likable and enjoying himself. "I guess Tanja told you about Sophie?"

Micha nodded. Mina made the "aw" noise people use for puppies and bad news.

"It didn't work out between me and Lara, either. But here's to trying."

"To trying," everyone chimed in, clinking three half-liter glasses of beer and Mina's little cup of sparkling juice.

"At least Sophie came to Berlin." He didn't feel that she was in quite the same category of failure as some random hookup Tanja had never seen again.

"It's not nice to jerk you around like that, though," Mina ventured in her soft voice.

Simon swallowed down the anger rising into the back of his throat. After all, she was right. It was what he'd realized about Nadine, that there was something missing, something he felt foolish using big words like "compassion" to describe. Something *not nice*. He had a type, and that was it. What could be safer than someone even less emotionally available than he was? "I'm tired of games," he said, because people always said that, and he was, but mostly because he always lost.

His phone buzzed, and Mina murmured, "Speak of the devil."

Soledad had written: "Friends & I going to silent film festival in Hburg. Dorky but thought you might wanna check on the 2 elusive women in your life." It took him a second to get which ones she meant. The rest was about a hostel and renting a car. Didn't she know he wasn't supposed to travel? Still, it wasn't far. If Weinert needed to see him, he could hurry back, pretend he'd had an appointment or something. Who said he had to be available round the clock? Besides, as long as his name wasn't on any reservations, who was to know? He took his own remarkable lack of compunctions as a sign.

"Micha, can I borrow the van?" He could tell by the startled silence that he'd interrupted someone. "Some friends are going to Hamburg. It could be a chance to get some closure."

"Closure's very important," Mina said. He was glad she was there so Micha and Tanja wouldn't ask, what friends?

"There'll be a licensed driver, right?"

"Of course: Soledad."

"Are you sure that's a good idea?" Tanja asked.

Micha, who didn't know why it wouldn't be, repeated, "Closure's very important."

Six

Simon set out bright and early, leaving a note for Farid, who was still asleep. He felt bad for not inviting him, but the trip already had too many angles, and he didn't want to feel responsible. He'd have his hands full figuring out Sophie and trying to pick up July's trail. Good as he felt about tutoring Farid, it took a lot of energy.

Soledad and her friends were waiting by the van, and Adam wasn't with them. There was a blonde woman with the plump cheeks and overbite of a cartoon rabbit, and an Asian one in a ruffly black-and-white dress and a lot of black eye makeup.

"We got you a coffee." The goth proffered a cardboard tray.

"Thanks. I'm Simon. Hey." He handed Soledad the keys.

"Anita," the rabbit-faced woman said. She looked like one of those shy girls who always knew the answer but never raised her hand.

"Chrissi."

"You're awfully bright-eyed and bushy-tailed." Soledad said. "You can sit shotgun, since it's almost your car."

Her friends had seen even more silent films than he had, so he announced a ban on spoilers. Soledad wasn't saying much, but then she was driving.

They stopped halfway for a bathroom, more coffee and snacks. Soledad's friends offered to pay since she and Simon had provided transportation.

"You're thoughtful today," Soledad said as they waited out front, smokers without cigarettes.

"I was thinking the same thing about you. But you've got the road as an excuse."

"What's yours? Brooding about Sophie or July?"

"Not really. It's hard to brood when you don't know what to expect."

"That's the spirit!" She clapped him on the shoulder, saw him wince and patted the spot as if brushing off dust. It hadn't hurt but reminded him of July in a similar gesture, laughing because Tanja had asked about her past, and she thought he was in on it. He wished he had their whole bizarre relationship on tape so he could rewind to the important parts and have more to go on than stray flashbacks to his own stupidity. "Sorry, I don't know my own strength," Soledad said. "Anyway, I took the liberty of looking up the addresses of everybody in Hamburg who bought tickets to both shows."

"Great, I didn't think of that." He was having trouble thinking of it even now. Trying to get back into a state of mind where he believed he and his Watson could track down the perpetrator(s) was like trying to find his way back into a dream he'd woken from. He was in the wrong reality. Also, who was he kidding, she was definitely the Holmes.

"What would you do without me?"

"Good question."

"Which of you had the latte?" Chrissi asked.

"Me," they both said.

"That's the joke."

Anita, sidling up behind her, rolled her eyes.

Soledad clapped her hands. "Let's get this show on the road."

~~~

They left their luggage in lockers next to colorful bunk beds that looked like they were made of Legos, only less stable. Simon had his for the next couple days in case Sophie didn't ask him over. It felt presumptuous to assume a standing invitation, even if she had in Berlin.

He hadn't had time to shower before leaving, so he left the others poring over the festival program and slipped into the bathroom. When he came out, Soledad was folding a stack of papers into her purse. She smiled and handed him a couple business cards.

"The girls went to stand in line for tickets, but some might sell out. Wanna ask Sophie which films she wants to see? I mean . . ." She glanced away as if she'd heard a noise. "If you're coming?" She used the singular you.

"I'll call her." He knew that dreaded feeling of inviting someone and getting turned down. No matter the reason, it sucked, and he didn't want her to have it. Plus, the festival gave him an excuse for being here. Better than anything Sophie had come up with.

He let it ring until Soledad said, "Never mind; we'll scalp them if you can't come."

"Okay." He felt left out, as if his tenuous association with Sophie barred him from the reindeer games. It was just a matter of time before he'd have to find a new confidante. The thought left a lump bobbing in his throat like a buoy. Silly to get upset. This new intensity of their friendship was as sudden and heated as an affair. He shouldn't expect it to last.

"Since you're brooding anyway, take a look at this." She handed him her phone.

"First-Class Auto Shop?"

"It's Barer's home page, remember?" She tapped "Services" and then "Interiors." Dozens of before and after pictures. "If he wasn't in his own car . . ."

He put his hand over hers to scroll down. His heart stopped when he saw an interior missing the driver's-side headrest, but it was leather. It beat all the harder when he saw one like he remembered—with a column shift and dark blue fabric—but that one was missing both headrests, and one like it in black wasn't missing either. He regretted leaving his notes in Berlin, even if there was nothing in them he didn't know by heart.

"Just take it. You're breaking my hand."

"Sorry." He hadn't realized how hard he was gripping her phone. By the time he got to the bottom, he'd seen at least ten cars he could've been in. But did he really recognize them, or was he overwriting his memory with new images? What did it say that there were so many possible matches? He checked the bottom of the page: last updated June 30. Barer might not even have had all these cars in the shop when July went missing. He could've deleted the car or fixed it beyond recognition. Or he had nothing to hide and wouldn't have bothered.

"It might've been one of them, but I can't tell for sure." He was sweating so hard he could've used another shower. That was what he got for still expecting an easy fix, a smoking gun in somebody's red hands. She'd only been showing him a possibility.

"Think it over while we hit the streets."

~~~

Aslan Özer's apartment was the closest. They had their cards and explanations ready, but the chubby Turkish guy in his early twenties didn't ask.

"No way! Holy shit, Babe, Simon from Hare vs. Hedgehog is here!"

A frail brunette with acne sprinkled between her wide eyes and timid smile slipped under Aslan's waiting arm, as if that were her default position. "Is this a charity thing? You're our favorite band."

"Did we win something?" Aslan asked.

"Mind if we come in?" Soledad stepped past them.

Simon was flattered and embarrassed to recognize his own first album playing in the cramped apartment, which smelled pleasantly of baking.

"My mom's coming over but hang for a bit," Aslan said. "Babe, would you—?" He went into the kitchen, and Babe, who was too awestruck to provide any other name, led them to a sofa almost as small as an armchair and sat down in a folding chair opposite it.

"Wow, so, um." Her gaze moved back and forth between them like the eyes of a Kit-Cat clock.

Soledad said, "You might've read that one of Hare vs. Hedgehog's fans is missing. We're asking everybody who attended the concerts in Hamburg and Amsterdam for information."

"*Missing* missing?"

"Yes," Soledad said as Simon wondered what other kind there was. "What did you do after the one in Amsterdam?"

"We got a cab because the show went a little longer than we expected—we couldn't leave before the encores—and only just made our train."

"Do you know what time it was?" Soledad asked. "We're trying to figure out exactly when the show ended."

"Umm . . . Let me see. Babe," she addressed Aslan, who'd come in with a tray of coffee, glasses and water. "Do we still have the tickets?"

"One sec." He must've heard from the kitchen because he didn't seem surprised. After setting the tray on the coffee table, he shuffled through the pile of papers and receipts in a box next to the sofa. "Here."

"Thanks, that's great." Simon wrote down the time, but the main thing was the conductor's stamp, meaning they'd really been on that train. Did it matter, now that they knew July had been with Nadine? He didn't know what else to ask. Even if July's supposed friend in Hamburg was a different one than in Amsterdam, someone who'd brought his own date didn't fit the bill.

"Her name's July. Did you see her?" Soledad showed them a printout from July's website.

They took long, obedient looks, but shook their heads.

"We didn't really talk to anyone," Aslan said. "The second show was a little stressful because of the train, but it was worth it, right, Babe?"

"It was a birthday present," she murmured.

"Sorry we didn't pay more attention." His apology was as sincere as if they'd been hired to examine the guests.

"Thanks anyway," Simon said. He and Soledad hadn't touched the drinks, so it was easy to stand up.

"Um, sorry, before you go?" Aslan asked. "I know that's not why you're here, but could we take a picture?"

"Sure." Simon put an arm around his shoulders.

"Let's get one of all of us." Aslan crowded everyone together. "Like we're all hanging out, right?"

Simon laughed. "Right."

"Thanks so much," Soledad said after Aslan had taken a few selfies.

"Thank *you*," the couple murmured in sync.

"See you at the next show," Simon said over his shoulder as he and Soledad slipped past a plump woman in her fifties carrying an armload of Tupperware.

"Case closed. They did it," Soledad said. They spent the walk to the next apartment trying to come up with motives. "It's always the ones you least suspect," was her most convincing argument.

~~~

Soledad suggested that she go in alone because it was a woman, and he might seem menacing if Anja Keller didn't recognize him.

"Menacing?"

"Because you're a man. Not because you're particularly menacing."

"Okay, I'll be down here, frightening passersby."

He got restless waiting. Sophie hadn't called back, so he texted her about the festival. "We can just hang out if you're not a silent movie fan," he added in a second text that sounded a little desperate once he'd hit Send.

To avoid the appearance of lurking, he strolled up and down the block until he remembered Franzi, and that was one more personal failing, forgetting to tell her he was coming. He texted that it was a last-minute trip, so he understood if she was busy. He didn't mention Sophie or July. She could come to her own conclusions.

"Dying to catch up! How long you here for?"

"Until you have time."

In typical Franzi fashion, she didn't reply. Neither had Sophie by the time Soledad came downstairs.

"She was a little weirded out, but also the most average, not-murderer type imaginable. She stayed with friends in Amsterdam after the show, and July was on the road with Nadine by then. So we're down to Ruben Janssen."

~~~

They decided to take the subway rather than risk missing their first film. The thought of the approaching evening made Simon check his phone, but he had no new messages. If Soledad noticed him brooding again, she kept it to herself.

"I'll come with you this time. It's boring to wait." He didn't want to sound uptight, but this neighborhood was different from the one they'd just left. Empty shopfronts, less graffiti than in Berlin but a lot for Hamburg. Waterlogged armchairs, bits of pressboard furniture strewn like some giant had torn them apart in a rage, broken glass, dog shit. He hoped it was from a dog. The sun was low and hot, steaming the filth into a fine vapor that hung in the air.

"We've still got a ways to go." She consulted a map she'd marked with Xs.

"Do you honestly think it's possible . . ." They parted to let a stumbling drunk pass, then moved closer together. ". . . that she's okay?"

"Anything's possible."

He was tired of hearing that, sure she was spreading it like a white sheet over her real thoughts, but suddenly aware that he didn't know her all that well. Were they close enough to fight? He took a deep breath. "How likely do you think it is?"

"Like forty percent? We know she was fine at first, but the longer she's missing, the less likely it gets. Maybe thirty."

"Only thirty?"

"You wanted an honest answer."

They walked in silence interrupted only by her checking street signs against the map. The neighborhood was still dirty, but getting trendier, the first craft beer bars looming on the horizon.

"Don't get defensive, because it's perfectly normal to want to find her," she said, "but I've been wanting to ask why it's so important to you. Suppose she *is* fine."

"Suppose she isn't?" Silly as their detective work had seemed a couple hours before, pointless as their questions had felt, he was reluctant to stop now, afraid of ending up like one of those cartoon characters who run off the edge of a cliff but don't fall until they look down. "What if she's in trouble?"

"And nobody else is looking?"

"Who would?"

"Her parents, Barer, friends, this so-called cousin we may be about to meet?"

"Yeah . . ." She was right on both counts: July didn't exist in a vacuum, and the 'cousin' was probably no more related to her than Simon was. For all they knew, he could even be that affair she'd mentioned who—inexplicably—wanted to keep in touch.

"It might be a stretch," Soledad was saying, "but I looked through July's Facebook friends and figured 'Jans Ruby' could be the Ruben Janssen who bought the ticket and—"

"Hey!" Simon called to the guy who was just entering a nearby building riddled with anarchy symbols and hearts. "Wait up!"

Dreadlocks stopped and looked around like he might need to call for help.

Simon jogged over. "Ruben, right? We're friends of July's. We met in Amsterdam, remember? Got a minute?"

He hesitated. "Of course."

Simon hurried after him, picturing him whirling around with a knife or gun, Simon the hero between Soledad and danger. But that was just adrenaline. His heart was pounding and stalling out like his mom's ancient alarm clock whose morning routine involved hitting the floor, freezing and then going off twice as loud. He couldn't make out the individual beats. Finally, someone who had something to do with July.

"After you." Ruben opened the door, and Simon's anxious brain, allowed neither fight nor flight, produced more flashes of danger: him locking them in with gangsters, a tiger, carbon monoxide . . .

"Go ahead and leave them on," Ruben said to Soledad. Simon hadn't even thought to take off his shoes. "My roommate never cleans, but it's his place. Can I get you a drink?" He was talking too fast, but who wouldn't be nervous, letting in two virtual strangers whose only link to you is a missing person? For all they knew, Ruben had been conducting his own investigations and appointed Simon chief suspect.

"No thanks." Simon hadn't noticed Ruben's slight accent at the party. Was he the friend July had said was between Germany and the Netherlands? And something about her Dutch getting rusty. They must've been pretty close for her to learn it, and drifted pretty far apart for her to start forgetting.

Soledad said, "Water would be great, thanks."

Ruben led them to the kitchen and opened a window to dispel the sickly smell of a garbage bag that had needed changing last week. He filled a glass from the tap and set it on the table.

"Just a second." He left, and Simon heard a door close. He was either using the bathroom, or getting his chloroform rag or whatever his set used nowadays. Or doing what Simon did when he had unwanted guests—grasping the last opportunity for a moment alone.

Soledad took a sip of water and sighed. "What a fail. If I passed out, we'd know it's him. But he didn't have the chance to drug me." Simon wasn't sure if he was supposed to laugh. "Anyway, what I was saying before is he's not registered here. I got the address from a party he and some Hans hosted."

"Well done. I recognized him right away."

"Don't you—"

The floorboards creaked as Ruben came back. He pulled up a stool and sat towering over their chairs.

"So you and July go way back?" Simon asked.

"You're that band guy, right? Help me out here . . ." Ruben squinted and pinched the bridge of his crooked nose between his thumb and forefinger. "Samson?"

"Simon."

"Soledad." She bubbled away about how worried they were. "And the police have been all over us."

"It even looked like I was a suspect. Luckily, someone roofied me at that party."

"Luckily?" Was his surprise genuine?

Simon faked a laugh. If Ruben had done it, mentioning it put them in an awkward position. Or had he stumbled into a clever interrogation technique? "Luckily for not being a suspect. Unluckily because I can't remember what happened."

"That bad, huh?"

Was he making sure? "I remember being in a car with July and some guy, her speaking Dutch, but that's it."

"Not much to go on, seeing as you were in the Netherlands."

"Yeah." Simon could see nothing to lose by laying their cards on the table. If Ruben was guilty, he'd know they weren't onto him. If not, he might share whatever information he had. "Some guy with short hair was driving, her ex-husband I think." He thought back to those cars he'd half-recognized on Barer's website and his breath went short with the feeling of something left undone.

Should he have looked more closely? If Barer had done more than give him a ride to his hotel, they were wasting precious time.

"That bum," Ruben said. His hand, resting on one knee, became a fist.

"He said she owed him money?" Soledad's glass was nearly empty, and she was still conscious. He appreciated her willingness to be a canary in the mine for him. If it was for him. She'd asked him, but he hadn't had the chance to ask her, why they needed to look so hard for July.

"Nonsense." Ruben seemed to search for words. "She was unemployed after rehab, but she sorted things out."

"She's so motivated," Soledad said. "Hard to picture her with Thomas."

"She wasn't always like that." Simon hoped Ruben would take over and get a little more concrete about his own relationship to July.

"You mean when you met her at rehab?"

"Met is a stretch. She was a mess."

"Young people are self-destructive. Just depends what opportunities they get to destroy themselves. And someone as brutal as Thomas . . ."

". . . was a good opportunity?" Soledad asked.

Simon thought of Barer's flimsy excuse for July's battered face. There probably hadn't even been a fight for her to get in the middle of, just the violent lowlife she was with. He felt, all at once, worse about the odds that she was okay. Like every bad thing that had ever happened to her made further harm more likely.

"Sure," Ruben was saying. "She was inexperienced, and then this charming older guy—I've never seen it, but she says he can be charming—comes along and totally turns her head." He tapped his feet against the legs of his stool as they waited for him to go on. "Says she's gorgeous and he wants to help with her career."

"Career?" Soledad asked.

"It turned out he meant . . . pornography. She was very young and impressionable."

"How young?" Soledad must've been thinking what Simon was: unsavory or illegal?

"Still in school."

"She said she barely knew anyone when she came to Berlin." Soledad's performance was so convincing Simon almost believed she knew July.

"She'd just graduated and didn't have a job. Where was she supposed to meet anybody?"

"Where'd she meet you?"

"Didn't she say?"

"She never told me much about her past." Without knowing it, Soledad was onto something. Simon had always assumed July's vague references to exes were a play for attention. She'd never mentioned their names or even that she'd been married. Which one had she said was not only crazy about her, but actually crazy?

"So I'm the past?" Ruben seemed to be asking himself more than Soledad. He pursed his lips and exhaled through his nose. His eyes were so pale it was hard to tell if they were teary or only reflecting the overhead light.

What had July said that day in the park about leaving the past behind? He'd been distracted, busy thinking about how to get away. Probably a false lead anyway, one of those empty things you fill with meaning after the fact. The dream that becomes clairvoyant because there happens to be a disaster the next day.

"So, about all that money she was carrying..." Soledad prompted Ruben.

Simon thought back to the cash in July's abandoned wallet. If she planned to use it to pay off her debt to Barer, why hadn't she given it to him right away?

"Money? Oh, right. It was for... me, but Barer must've intercepted her."

"What for?" Simon asked as Soledad was saying, "How much?"

"Uh... ten-thousand. For, um, a down payment on an apartment."

"She had that much lying around?" Then again, what did July spend money on, other than concert tickets? Was the apartment for her and Ruben? He didn't know how to ask without giving away how little he knew.

Ruben shrugged. "She works hard."

While Soledad told some made-up anecdote about July's work, Simon tried to put the pieces together. Barer and Ruben said July had been carrying a lot of money, but Nadine said she was broke. Had she left it all in her wallet? That stack of bills was thick, but not ten-grand thick. For an old debt or a new home? Or something else? Both men had hesitated when asked about the money.

"Simon? You okay?" Soledad asked, and he thought this would be the horror-movie moment where Ruben took off his mask, revealed everything, the monster only there when you peeked out from under the covers, but Ruben just looked puzzled.

"Sure, what were you saying?"

"What you think happened." He couldn't tell whether her over-articulated speech indicated annoyance or concern.

"She was fine as long as she was on tour with Nadine."

"She was what?"

Soledad stomped on his foot, but he didn't see the harm. If Ruben had something to do with July's disappearance, he already knew. Ignoring what felt like a hammer being pressed onto his toes, he explained about her leaving with Apathy Collective and then hitchhiking.

"So she's here?"

"It's where she was headed."

"Maybe it wasn't about money," Soledad suggested. "Something personal?"

"Like someone she was involved with?" Simon was half thinking aloud, half hoping Ruben would chime in. "Let's see, first came Thomas, then . . ."

Ruben sighed. "Me. Then you."

"What about that waiter from the tapas place?" Soledad asked.

"Diego?" Ruben shrugged. "He's gay."

Simon was impressed by her power of recall but more interested in clearing up Ruben's misunderstanding. "July and I never . . ."

Ruben cut in: "You're such a big deal for her. She said at rehab everybody else just talked shit, but you were playing your guitar and *getting* it. I could never tell which she wanted more: to be with you or to *be* you."

Simon's face went hot. Had he given her a false impression, made her fall for some fake idea of him? "I just talk shit, too. I didn't have the same kind of problems other people there did."

Before Simon could decide how much to explain, Ruben said, "Oh, I know all about that. I used to hear about how perfectly you put it behind you. Then it was how you never had a bad problem to begin with. Like you were too good for something like that to happen to you. It was hard to believe, but you really don't seem like the kind of guy who has real problems."

"Um, I . . ." Did he mean real drug problems or problems in general? Maybe he saw Simon as one of those infuriating coasters who glide through life, getting whatever they want without any friction or effort. It seemed unfair for even a chance acquaintance to believe that. "It's not like I went there for fun. Besides, weren't you together back then?"

Ruben took a ragged breath, wiped his eyes and spoke through his fist. "Sorry. I've been so worried. We were never long-term. I don't know how serious she was, but I knew I wanted to be with her from the moment we met." Simon remembered Edeltraut talking about how devoted July's supposed cousin was, and felt sure Soledad was right. "I thought if I stuck around, things would work themselves out. Thomas, the drugs she was getting from him . . ."

Hard as it was to picture anyone having an immediate attraction to July, Simon had to feel for Ruben. Hadn't he also met someone he thought could be the one, only to find out Sophie was a kind of mirage, moving a little further away with every step he took toward her? And he must've been an equally elusive vision for July, appearing when she most needed a hopeful sign, tossing her a few words at each show but keeping the merch table between them; getting dinner with her, going to that party and even kissing her, but never real, nothing she could grasp and hold. Hadn't he felt the suffocating pressure of her attempts? He told himself he hadn't been like that with Sophie, had kept himself within bounds. And Ruben? Was still talking, and Simon should be paying attention instead of daydreaming about the fata morgana of a committed relationship.

"We got together before she went to rehab," Ruben was saying, "but obviously that was a bad time for her. When she got out, she wanted to start over, be a new person and have nothing to do with her old life. You really inspired her, not just by getting clean so fast, but because you didn't throw away your time there; you made something of it. She used to hide in the bushes and watch you play."

Was that what she'd wanted from him, inspiration? Maybe some of his discomfort around her had been the inverse of what she felt: a reminder of how low he could sink, so faint he was only aware of the dread it provoked.

"But you stayed friends?" Soledad asked when Simon found himself unable to speak.

"Yeah, just friends. Not for lack of trying." Ruben smiled as if summoning up a fond memory. "Maybe she's waiting for Simon."

Simon hated to think how much they must've talked about him. Usually, the thought of being discussed sickened him with the dread of negative opinions, some even worse than he really was, but the cringing shame of this moment was different. He hated how much she would've praised him to someone who was in love with her; hated himself for allowing her to develop such a false impression, and for what Ruben must've thought, must still think: that he believed himself worthy of adoration, July's or anyone's. He was about to say something, anything to change the subject when his phone buzzed.

"Go ahead," Ruben said. "I have to head out."

"It's not important." He got the feeling it might be, or would've been not too long ago. But considering how much he'd misjudged everything else, he couldn't be sure.

"I do need to get ready, though."

"Can I use your bathroom?" Soledad asked. "It's a long way to the film festival."

"Is that what you're here for?"

Simon launched into excessive description of the films, recycling opinions stolen from Chrissi and Anita to distract Ruben from Soledad searching his apartment.

"You really know your stuff. You know Murnau was going to catch a ship right before he died because a fortuneteller warned him not to travel by land?"

"What happened again?"

"He died in a car accident on the way."

"Life writes the best stories." It was a saying Simon rarely used, maybe because, until this summer, his life had never been stranger than fiction. How would it feel to go back to that now, like waking from a bad dream? Other than whatever had happened to July, this dream wasn't half bad. It felt wrong that harm to someone else had, however incidentally, changed his life for the better. He couldn't even say how it had.

Soledad came back. "Give us your number; we may have extra tickets."

Ruben wrote it on a napkin of dubious cleanliness.

Simon's phone buzzed again in the stairs.

"You're *impossible* to reach," Sophie said. "I called a million times."

"Glad you caught me the million-and-first time." There was nothing to gain by saying he'd called first.

"Were you at the movies?"

"No, we're going now." He trailed behind Soledad, stopping when she did, letting her check for cars. "Can you come?"

"Who's 'we'?"

"Me and a friend. She's been helping me with some witnesses." Making Sophie jealous wasn't at all like he'd thought. Just queasy dread in the pit of his stomach like when his parents had wanted him to take sides.

"Witnesses?! Why are you *still* doing that? Also, ditch her and come to my work. I'm bored, and we seriously need to talk."

Did she think finding a missing person was a hobby you picked up and dropped again just like that? He checked the time. "Where's your work?"

Soledad was mouthing something. He shook his head and looked away.

"Right at the central station. You walk out the main entrance and see these big, tacky neon lights. I'm here another hour and I'm not waiting around."

"I wouldn't expect you to." He hung up. "It was Sophie," he said with false cheer. "She says we need to talk."

"Isn't she coming?"

The queasiness was squirming around his abdomen like a restive animal. He wished they'd figure this out without him. He wasn't what he wanted to be, and couldn't be what anyone else wanted, either. "No, sorry, I don't think . . ."

She held up one hand. "Why don't you see if Franzi and Christian want tickets?" If she was mad, she was doing a great job hiding it. "We can meet for drinks after. Depending."

"Cool, great idea. Send me the details, and I'll pass them along." That would shift the responsibility to Franzi, at least.

"You know, I kind of get what July saw in Ruben, even if he's not about to win any beauty pageants. He's got that tough, brooding vibe. He seems intense below the surface."

Was she saying that to shed light on the case or to hurt him for ditching her? He couldn't think how to respond.

"Don't worry. Not everybody's looking for some macho."

"Thanks." Was that even a compliment? But he sensed that she meant well, and that was always something.

In the station, they realized they needed two different lines.

"Good luck." She gave him a little push in the direction he needed to go.

He leaned in, caught himself and gave her an awkward one-armed hug.

~~~

The internet café was as glaring as Sophie had said, wedged between a kebab stand and a sex shop. A newsticker announced: "Copy! Print! Surf the web! Cheap international calls!" but the interior was surprisingly sober: a few shelves of snacks and office supplies, printers and copiers in the front and computers in a dim backroom. He had to smile when he remembered telling his mom about Sophie's job.

"What're you smirking about?" she called from behind the counter.

"Nothing, just happy to finally see your headquarters."

"Ha, ha." Her beauty stood out from the dull backdrop of stacked printer paper but felt impersonal, like the china his grandmom kept in a cabinet to be admired, not used.

"Did you do something with your hair?"

"It's only like, ten centimeters shorter." She ran blue-nailed fingers through one side. She was wearing cutoff jeans and a t-shirt, but perfectly put together, like a model for casual wear. He wondered whether he'd bought her the shirt.

"Looks good."

"Catch the killer yet?" She sounded bored, he hoped with her job and not him. In the computer room, a twitchy gamer was hammering away at the keyboard, some violent fantasy on-screen. Out front, a bald man rested his hand on a creaking printer as if soothing a skittish horse.

"No, but we made some progress."

"Do tell." Now she was holding in laughter like when they first met.

He hadn't had time to sort through the facts. "July's ex-boyfriend says her ex-husband put her in pornos and hit her up for money after he got out of jail."

"Fascinatingly sordid. Look . . . Right here, Sir. Number sixteen?"

Simon stepped aside to let her ring up the bald man, whose stack of printouts reached almost to his elbows.

"Promise you won't hate me?" she said after.

She had a boyfriend. A husband. Kids? "You couldn't have said on the phone?"

"Man, you already hate me. I'm off in fifteen if . . . ?"

"I'll take a walk."

He didn't know what he felt. He should've let—or made—her say what it was. Because the second he stepped out into the garish street, he started to hope. He was jumping to conclusions. She might say something harmless. So harmless she thought he'd hate her? He needed perspective and got out his phone to call someone, anyone. Franzi had texted back.

"Hey weirdo who sets me up with random people instead of meeting me! Going to movie with your friends. Hope to see you after! Unless that siren snares you."

"Enjoy! Mixed signals from S. Will report back." He was surprised by a sudden, physical sadness that took his breath away. He felt like he was missing something terribly important. Because Sophie wasn't turning out to be the love of his life? Or, even more ridiculous, because he wasn't going to the movie?

~~~

Sophie was sitting in front of the kebab shop with two cups of Turkish tea and some baklava. His stomach growled in appreciation. Maybe it was all low blood sugar and not existential dread.

"I'm sorry I didn't tell you—"

"Tell me what?" he snapped. But that's what she was trying to do. "Sorry. Go on."

"July's in Berlin."

"What?!"

"Okay, so." She took a deep breath. "Like the week after you told me she was missing, this girl comes in looking rough, like she hasn't showered in days. That's not unusual among our clientele, but I'm like, where do I know her from? She's counting out all this small change, and I'm like, 'July, it's me, Sophie. Don't worry about it.' I was so surprised to see her I totally spaced out the whole Mei-thing. So she's startled and then she's all, 'Thanks, *Sophie*,' making this big deal about my name, and I'm like, yep, pretty much."

Simon, chewing a sticky coconut sweet, put one hand over his mouth. "She had internet access and couldn't be bothered to contact anyone?"

"I'm sure she did, just not you. Anyhow, she was a walking crisis, so I was like, I'll take five and you tell me what's wrong. It was this huge sob story that was *way* more than I had time for, so I was like, whatever, you can stay at mine tonight."

He burned his tongue on the bitter tea, then dumped in too much sugar. July was home laughing at melodramatic tabloids and letting him choke on anxiety after not giving a shit about her. And Sophie? She'd known for ages, even at brunch when she joked about reading his lyrics. He'd convinced himself he was imagining it, because that made more sense than what must actually have happened: Sophie blurting out something July had told her. "You knew I was sick with worry and being questioned by the police, and you didn't tell me?" He hadn't realized how angry he was. A husband and ten kids were nothing to this.

"Why do you think I'm telling you? I *tried* to tell you in Berlin."

"Not very hard."

"Would you let me explain? So she stayed over, then she was off with that guy she picked up at your show. Then she bounces back going on about what you and I supposedly put her through, but obviously trying to guilt me into letting her stay again. It was a huge mistake to invite her in the first place. I was like, ugh, how do I get this person out of my life?"

He stirred his sickly-sweet tea and waited, anger giving way to confusion. He'd been picturing the two of them cracking jokes at his expense. He watched Sophie cut the remaining baklava with the handle of her spoon. She looked sulky, like a normal girlfriend in a normal fight about normal things. Was she capable of harming someone? He couldn't believe it. Then again, he wouldn't have believed the rest. Just because she was gorgeous and had slept with him a couple times didn't mean she was a good person. It didn't seem to mean anything at all.

"So?" If she had harmed July—if she meant: *July's in Berlin . . . in a shallow grave*—he wanted her to finish confessing. After all, why keep the whole thing secret if she had nothing to hide? He watched his own calm at a deadening remove, surprised not to feel more.

"I just wanted her to leave me—us alone, okay? You're mad I didn't tell you, but, hello, *she* knew where she was. She must've left her wallet in your room to make sure you got in trouble."

"Did she say so?"

"No, but I could totally see her doing it."

He could see anyone doing anything at this point. It was like some over-the-top Agatha Christie mystery, a wild train ride through his life, everyone he knew aboard and guilty. But he was getting ahead of himself. "What did you do?"

"First, I listened to her go on and on about the sleazy guy from your show who only wanted her there as long as his wife was away, then about her scary ex and, sob, she never would've left with Nadine if it weren't for Simon. She had a *lot* to say about you."

He refused to care how much of his lovelorn ramblings July had repeated to Sophie. She was waiting for him to ask something, probably what July had accused him of, but he knew what he'd done—at least most of it. He wanted to know what *she'd* done. Both shes: Sophie and July.

She sighed and continued, "So the next day I realized on my way to work that July couldn't let herself out without the key, but I was already running late and I figured, she wanted to stay; let her stay. Like, there was food. Then I ended up staying with a friend. I felt bad, but I also didn't, know what I mean?"

"Mm." Part of him had snagged on "staying with a friend" like a loose thread on a splinter. He took a deep breath and pulled himself free.

"She was all weird when I got back. Like when you come home and the cat's stalking around and glaring at you?"

"I don't have a cat."

"Me neither; it died. But I was kind of over July's attitude. So when my friend came by later—" There was that friend again, with his glaring masculine article and familiarity with her apartment—"I had him wear this creepy mask and I pretended to get like, knocked aside when he burst in. July was scared shitless, like losing her mind about it. I know it sounds bad, but you had to be there. It was actually super funny." She had the defiant air of a kid whose prank turns out less harmless than she planned, beginning to realize she can expect detention instead of laughter.

"I bet." The night they met, and ever since, he'd thought of her playing Mei as a favor to him. Protecting him from July because she cared. But she hadn't known him, let alone July, when she signed on. He saw now that she'd done it for the same reason she did anything: her own amusement. It had only been another lark, like scaring July with some silly mask.

"Once she saw me cracking up, she was like, oh okay. As soon as he took off the mask, she started going on about how I had another boyfriend."

It wasn't worth asking whether she did. The hurt of it would only distract him.

"So there's this big blowup and of course I was pissed. She says she's sorry and then she's back to her sob story about how she's scared of her ex and we have to swear not to tell *anybody* where she is; it's sooo important."

"Ex-husband or ex-boyfriend?"

"Does it matter? Some super jealous type, apparently. Something like they were gonna get back together, then she wasn't sure, and he went ape-shit. She was being a drama queen, and like, why am *I* the person she goes to with this? She doesn't know me. I could be in a satanic cult. She got all teary and said he might kill her. I was all, okay, this sounds like an actual problem, but what am I, a women's shelter? Hello, call the cops! But she said that would make him extra mad and he'd just get away with it again."

"Again?"

Sophie shrugged. "Who knows. She was all over the place. Next thing, she's saying he'll come after *you* if she makes him too mad."

Another thing it would've been nice to know.

"I'm all, relax, there's this whole missing-person thing. Your apartment's totally safe, and how would this dude even know where Simon lives? So she said she'd go call the cops."

"Did she?" Wouldn't they have called off the search? Maybe she hadn't had the chance. Thinking back to those marks on July's throat, he had a pretty good idea what her ex had gotten away with before, even if he wasn't sure which ex.

Sophie shrugged. "Supposedly? But she literally went out to a phone booth, so it's not like I was there. She was loving the drama. As soon as she got back, she was all, 'Don't you wanna see Simon?' and my friend just peaced out at that point. I said, 'I'm sure as hell not taking you now,' but of course I did a couple days later, mostly to get rid of her but also because I did wanna see you."

"Right." Something was rising to the surface of his anger. Several some-things. Nadine had mentioned July avoiding some creep, and Sophie said she was afraid of an ex. At least two of them had been in Amsterdam. If she was avoiding Ruben, why come to Hamburg? She'd seen that balding guy from the show again. But she hadn't realized he was married, so he couldn't have been more than a brief fling. No one who'd known her long enough to want to kill her. Not that it took very long. He was horrified with himself for thinking that.

"Hello? Are you even listening?"

"I'm a little taken aback."

"Yeah, I can tell. But July and I are cool. I drove her back and even distracted this super heinous drunk lady who lives downstairs so she could sneak in. Then I had to wait while she checked for murderers or whatever. And she let me crash there when I couldn't reach you, not that I was dying for another slumber party. Even though she told me a billion times to keep it secret, I totally meant to tell you because you were upset."

She patted his knee, and he felt himself tense and grimace, as if he could close himself to her touch. "But after I spent ages thinking about how to tell you, I called and called and couldn't reach you. What was I supposed to do, leave a voicemail? By the next day, I was like, wait, July will obviously tell him herself so she can milk it for attention. Why should *I* have to? I didn't ask to be involved in her crazy shit! I was planning to stay longer but then I figured I better leave before she tells you because I *knew* you'd be mad, like right now. Totally what I was trying to avoid, especially with you springing that family visit on me. You were supposed to be over it by the next time we saw each other."

"But she *didn't* tell me."

"Well, that's on her."

She didn't even seem sorry. All she'd cared about was getting rid of July and avoiding a scene. And why *hadn't* July contacted him? Maybe Sophie was still lying, even now. What if she hadn't taken July home? The drunk neighbor sounded like Frau Heimstett, but July could just as easily have told Sophie about her. He needed to check Sophie's apartment. When he was little and his mom was afraid other kids would pressure him into getting in trouble, she'd said to fake sick if he felt uncomfortable. This qualified, even if he was trying to get into Sophie's place instead of out. "Do you live near here? I'm not feeling great and it would be cool if I could lie down. My hostel's far away."

"Your hostel? What are you, on a class trip?"

He thought of saying something snide about all the money he'd spent on her, but that had been his own stupidity and wasn't worth admitting to. He really did feel like he needed to lie down. Or run, very far and very fast, until he got somewhere he could breathe. He felt for his pulse. Her beauty was more irrelevant than ever, an ad on a billboard he could pass without a second glance. Almost. He couldn't help taking a last look at her perfectly manicured hands resting on the smooth skin below her frayed shorts. They were never really together, but he'd believed it for a little while.

"I don't think that's a great idea."

Because her boyfriend or July was there? "I don't think *that's* a good idea, either. I just wanna talk."

"So let's talk."

"Fine." He was bored, tired, anxious, aware of a hangnail on his thumb, wounded but unable to tend to it with her looking. He had a craving stronger than hunger or thirst to go into a room, any room, and lock the door. To be alone, with no one looking at him. The strain of being here, acting normal, was almost unbearable. He wanted to call Franzi like she was his mom, say he wasn't feeling well and could she come get him? But she was at the movie he'd looked forward to seeing. For a moment, he couldn't remember why he wasn't with her.

"As you may have gathered, there's this guy I'm seeing."

"I don't care."

"That's great, because, to be honest? I feel like you're too much. I thought, cool, fun times, hooking up with this singer the girls line up for, and then you're calling me all the time like I'm your wife."

"Why give me your number if you didn't want me to call?" He meant to sound sarcastic, but even he could hear the naivete in his voice.

"Because that's what people do, Simon. You sleep with someone and then you act like you're gonna be in touch. I'm sure you've done that before."

"All the time." He wasn't proud of it, but her thinking he took that kind of thing seriously made him want to dig up every scrawled morning-after note he'd ever tossed without calling, play back all his sleepy mumbles about not remembering his new number. He didn't want to be the person he'd have to be for her to respect him, but he wanted her respect.

"I did want you to call. I wanted to be hanging with friends and say, oh, it's the lead singer of Hare vs. Hedgehog. Then the July thing happened, and I got so fascinated by how obsessed she was, and what if you *had* killed her, that I couldn't look away."

"I'm glad I could entertain you." Forget fascinated: She'd *made* the situation. He tried to focus on whether there was any information left to glean from this encounter. He knew he should search her place, but felt queasy thinking of how they might run out of things to say and feel obligated to hook up one last time, then go back to resenting each other. Assuming she could be bothered to resent him.

"It was hard to tell you because I *do* like you. You're cute and talented, and definitely my type. But setting aside the fact that you live in Berlin, we aren't looking for the same things. I'm turning thirty, but I still want a life. Is that so wrong?"

"Of course not." Her voice had cracked on thirty, and he was sorry he wasn't sorry for her.

"I want to want the things you do, but I don't. Does that make me a bad person?" She was turning on the charm now, eyes big and lips pouting, leaning in. He wanted to protect her from feeling bad, but another part of him standing further off was telling him not to be a sucker.

"No." But it did and would make her bad for him. Suddenly, from this dream of endless corridors, he saw a way out. He didn't need to search her apartment. He'd tell the police. "I'm glad we had this talk." He pushed his glass of sugary sludge into the middle of the table. "Have a nice life."

"Wait." She got up so fast he had to catch her falling chair. "Don't go like that."

"Like what?"

"Like you hate me."

"I have a film to catch."

"I thought you missed it."

"The one after."

"At least let me walk you to the station."

It was a ridiculous thing to say, because they were across the street from it, but she didn't laugh until he did. And his might just have been primeval laughter, the cackling call of danger averted. She went in for a kiss, but he turned and gave her the other half of Soledad's hug. He didn't have a ticket or any idea where to go, but a train pulled in just in time for him to run and catch it.

<center>~~~</center>

He got out one stop later and bought a ticket. Weinert didn't pick up, so he called the police station and tried to explain things to that clerk Tanja had offended a million years ago.

"Sophie—that woman I was seeing?—just told me July stayed with her for a few days." He paced the platform, looking down at dark blotches of chewing gum and piss, dodging people who had somewhere to be. "She says July's back in Berlin, but I'm not sure that's true. Maybe someone could check Sophie's apartment?" he ended on a weak note.

"Are you with her right now?"

"No." He wasn't supposed to leave Berlin. Could he pretend it had been a phone call?

"What's her address?"

Another speedbump. "You tell me. She came in, remember? Her last name's Müller."

"Regardless of the circumstances, we can't give you her address. If she wanted—"

He didn't have time for this. "I don't want her address! I don't ever wanna see her again. I want someone to search her apartment!" Try not to sound hysterical. Too late. He wondered whether they got that a lot, people pissed off at their exes and trying to sic the police on them.

"Okay, I'll pass that along."

"What about July's apartment?"

"It's been searched."

"Oh." Since July got back? *If* she got back. Was Sophie's story a ruse, telling enough of the truth to be believable but not enough to get caught? She'd been dishonest about so many things that it was hard to trust even today's confession. Or had she only been complicit in the lies he told himself about her? Maybe all she was guilty of was a mean-spirited prank and looking for an easy way out from under everything he'd projected onto her. Not being Mei didn't make her a murderer. Already, he regretted calling the police before sifting through what she'd told him.

"Herr Kemper?"

Time to scrounge up what else he had to offer. "I also spoke to Ruben Janssen . . ." But nothing he said sounded like evidence.

The clerk interrupted, "You're not in Hamburg, are you?"

A train squealed and roared into the station, and he blew into the microphone to amplify the noise before hanging up. One more installment in his lifetime series of not being taken seriously. If Sophie had July, she could do anything to her by the time someone checked. No, that was only the upset talking. *Name your demons.* He felt rejected and made a fool of. Ashamed of being nothing but a joke and an inconvenience to someone who'd meant so much to him. Of having let a few daydreams and a virtual stranger mean that much in the first place.

But if he'd meant little to Sophie, July meant even less. Harming July and covering for it wouldn't have been entertaining like observing his anguish over the case had. It would only have been an extension of July's unwanted presence in her life. Like a relationship with Simon, killing July simply wouldn't have been worth her while.

Which meant she had no reason to lie about taking July home. Which meant there had to be another reason why no one—not him or July's friend or neighbors, not even the police—had heard a word since.

~~~

He called Franzi, who said they'd left the theater and were getting drinks. He didn't want to repeat everything when he got there, so he just said he was coming and Sophie wasn't; what train should he take. But he messaged Soledad: "Sophie had July but supposedly doesn't now. Says July was scared of jealous ex!" Alone, once again, in the midst of people who weren't, he felt a craving for sympathy squeezing his guts like hunger pangs. He added, "July was worried he might come after me next," even though the threat was abstract as a ghost story, and all the least relevant parts of his talk with Sophie still foremost in his mind. Only after hitting Send did he stop to wonder whether July was right.

Forget all the ways he'd turned off Sophie, all the embarrassing things July might've said about him. After days without any sign of her, Sophie's, Nadine's, Tanja's encounters were all outdated, and Ruben's even more so. But some of the last things she'd told them were that her creepy ex wouldn't leave her alone, that she was afraid he'd kill her and come after Simon, and that she'd called the police.

Only one of those things couldn't be true.

Soledad's response, all exclamation points and question marks, pretty much summed up how he felt. That, and a longing to be with the others that was now less about loneliness and more about safety in numbers. He'd told Soledad he was in danger *next*, like July was ahead of him in line. Like nothing bad could happen to him until some gristly reveal about why she'd come home but never reemerged. But someone could've been after him all along. Someone like Barer, who almost seemed to recognize him, or some other, more recent and angrier ex, lurking in the crowds at concerts, waiting for his chance. Ruben lived in another city and wouldn't know about everyone July got involved with—especially if it was someone she wanted out of her life. Was Barer really brutal like Ruben said? Maybe that was July's type. He tried to picture a sinister version of Barer, one who looked more capable of violence. But was that something you could tell by looking, what one person might do to another?

Leaning into one corner of the train, he watched for a sign of danger, not knowing what that would look like, either. He reminded himself that, whether July was home or had since been weighted down and dumped in the Spree, he was okay and could keep breathing. He kept thinking back to that night he and Soledad went to Barer's apartment, the way she talked him through every worry, her only concern their lack of toy guns to bluff with. But he'd need a lot more than that to feel safe now.

~~~

Christian was out front having a cigarette, and Simon's first irrelevant thought was, aha, Mr. Perfect smokes. But no one had said Christian was perfect. He was just a do-gooder. And descended from an Allied soldier, so he only had to feel bad about one Nazi grandfather instead of two like everybody else. Simon thought of something too ridiculous for a second thought and too worth it not to try.

"Can I talk to you?" He put a hand on the back of Christian's t-shirt to guide him away from the bar. He could feel the globe logo of some charitable organization and how ridiculous he must seem.

"Hey, you made it. I'm sorry Sophie—"

"I need to ask you something."

"Ask away."

"Could you lend me a gun?"

"Whoa, is this some kind of joke?"

"I might need it, and you're the only person I can think to ask."

"Because I'm Black? Listen, it's not like minorities get handed guns the moment—"

Simon held up his hands. "No, no, I meant your grandfather's. You said the army never collected it." He was only taking Soledad's suggestion of a toy gun to the next level.

"What're you gonna do, hold up a sock hop? That pistol hasn't been used in decades. You ever read *The Sorrows of Young Werther*?"

"Sure, but that was way earlier." He wasn't the one being extreme. Everyone around him was crazy or criminal. When they went in, Soledad would probably mention in passing that she'd murdered July. That, or July was fine, with a great explanation for why she was letting the police keep looking, and none of her exes wanted her or Simon dead. But he wasn't taking any chances.

"You think I don't know Goethe was before World War II? I'm trying to get you to think. Werther got hung up on a girl he couldn't have and then?"

"Shot himself."

"Yeah, but he didn't do it right and suffered for ages. Ever fired a gun?"

"At the fair when we were kids . . ." He saw what Christian was getting at. "I'm not planning on shooting myself. Or anyone. It's only in case Soledad and I are in danger." He remembered Soledad saying it would be great to find July tied up at Barer's, even if that put them at risk, because then they'd know where she was.

"What's she got to do with this?"

"Hopefully nothing. Long story short, my ex, Tanja and Sophie confessed to seeing July after she disappeared and not telling the police. She told all the last people she talked to that she was scared of some ex. Sophie said July was afraid he'd kill her. Or come after me," he added, a little ashamed of how fast fear for himself was eclipsing concern about July. But, even before today, looking for July had never been all about her safety. He'd made her disappearance about him, the way her presence had always seemed to be. Finding her had become so intertwined with finding success, love, ways to feel good about himself, that he could no longer picture any kind of good life where he didn't know what had happened to her. "It's all so mixed up I even used to consider myself a suspect, even though I blacked out."

"Technically, you could've done something and then forgotten. I saw it on *Tatort*."

"This isn't a detective show, and lots of people saw her since then," he snapped, impatient with anyone who couldn't follow the details of a case that still had his mind reeling. "The point is, you know whether you're capable of harming someone, and I'm not." It felt good to say, almost as good as knowing it.

"Says the guy asking for a gun."

"I'm worried we'll run into someone dangerous. I don't wanna fire it or anything, just use it to cover us long enough to get away." He had no clear image of what danger they'd encounter or flee from, only a suffocating sense of urgency sitting on his chest like a sleep demon, unsettling and paralyzing him at once.

"Who's dangerous?"

"I wish I knew." Would it help to write it all down? There wasn't time. He needed Soledad.

"I do wanna help . . . You're not just upset about Sophie and making up the rest?"

"I only saw her three times."

"I know, I know. But I don't wanna regret anything later. I know you were thinking she was someone you could commit to, start a family and all."

"Hm." That was definitely not something Simon had told him. He felt ashamed of his stupid fantasies, angry at Franzi for sharing them, and jealous that other people had partners close enough to tell things like that.

"You won't shoot Sophie?"

"Only in self-defense, and she's really far down on my list of suspects."

Christian laughed. "I'm sorry if . . . I don't know you very well, but I care about you. We could end up brothers if everything goes okay."

Brothers-in-law, Simon thought, but he didn't want to ruin the moment by being pedantic. "That means a lot to me." It didn't right now, when there was only space in his head for what bad things might've happened and whether worse could be prevented, but it would later. He didn't have a lot of friends, let alone brothers. "When you say, 'if everything goes okay,' do you mean between you and Franzi, or if I don't die?"

"Both. I need to give this some thou—"

"Simon!" Franzi pounced on him for a hug. "What're you doing out here?"

"Bonding. Aren't you thrilled?"

"Totally. Come on. Soledad needs to tell you something, and then you can spill the gory details."

What else could he do? He felt that time was of the essence, that terrible things were happening outside the exposed-brick walls of this subterranean bar, but he didn't know how to stop them. At least Chrissi and Anita were at another film so he didn't have to start from the very beginning.

"You go first," he said to Soledad. The idea that she might make some emotional declaration sparked in his mind like a dropped lightbulb, but logic was against it. Why now, in front of everyone?

"Barer left a message saying he decided to go with another collection agency. And asking me out."

"Charming. Do we believe him?"

"To me, 'another agency' means taking care of it himself."

"Meaning he figured out where she is."

Franzi and Christian didn't interrupt with questions, so Soledad must've filled them in. Simon told them what Sophie had said, leaving out the part about him being clingy.

"So July's last known location was Berlin, where Barer just decided to collect his own debt. What now?" Soledad asked.

"I have to know." He wasn't sure what that entailed, but saw everyone exchanging worried glances.

"It's different now," Soledad said. "We have to be careful. Who knows, asking me out could be him looking for a chance to get rid of me. I know we talked to him before, but, if he has July, he'll know who you are. And he might think we know more than we do."

"Simple Simon, I'm not sure this is your brightest idea." Franzi was looking at Soledad instead of him. "Drugs, illegal pornography, beating up his wife . . . Everything you've told me makes this guy sound dangerous. If he *is* holding July against her will, or if he . . . hurt her, he might do anything to keep from getting caught."

"That's why I wanted a—" He stopped himself. They needed to figure things out first. "It might not even be him. She's mentioned other guys. It could be a totally different one she's afraid of."

"Oh, that's *way* better," Franzi said. "Multiple scary men with grudges against you. I'm sure you have a brilliant plan?"

"I . . ." He hadn't made it that far, but he walked himself through it. "If I checked July's apartment, I'd know . . ." Whether she was there, and if so, dead or alive, alone or at the mercy of some faceless captor. Someone who, according to Sophie, had hurt July before and gotten away with it. It could be Barer or any ex, even some nobody like her hookup from the Hamburg show. Obsession wasn't logical. Just ask July. All he knew about this shadowy person was that they were jealous, prone to violence, and the reason July was off the radar. Because if she'd used her bank account, talked to her neighbors, ordered takeout, if she'd so much as made a call on her landline, the police wouldn't still be looking. "I'd at least know where I stand."

"What if you walk in on someone stabbing her or something?" Christian wanted to know.

Simon shrugged. They were talking in circles, letting more and more time pass.

"Aren't we forgetting a little someone known as the police?" Franzi asked. "Why don't we call and let them in on the action?"

"And tell them what? *Someone told me someone told them someone's after me, but I don't know who?* It sounds like some kind of delusion. Anyway, I already tried calling."

"You all figure this out, and I'll get that equipment we talked about." Christian sighed. "My mom's gonna be so pissed if she ever finds out."

"Are we talking about a gun here?" Franzi asked.

"I love how intuitive you are, dear. Your brother convinced me he isn't a hazard to himself or others. And you have until I get back to talk him out of it."

"I do trust your judgment . . . Step into my office." She drew Christian outside.

Watching the doorway for their return, Simon felt a fierce stab of envy. Because, even wanting to discuss her concerns, Franzi already sounded more than half convinced, simply because Christian was. What must it feel like to trust and be trusted like that? But now wasn't the time for petty jealousy.

"Looks good," Soledad murmured when Franzi came back in alone.

"Are you for real? I can't believe you asked my boyfriend for a gun."

"So you're official? Congrats."

"This is no laughing matter. And you—" Franzi turned to Soledad. "You seemed so nice and normal after all the flakes he's been involved with. *You* think this is a good idea?"

"I don't think it's a *bad* idea, per se. It doesn't make sense for July to go that long without telling the police she's okay, unless she isn't. At the very least, wouldn't she want her phone and wallet back? Then there's all her talk about a scary ex . . ."

"And you're not sure which ex, oh brother of mine?"

"No, but it's fishy that Barer went to Amsterdam in someone else's car. Money isn't a big enough motive—he could've just robbed her—but what Ruben told us about pornos might be. What if she's blackmailing him?"

"What can I get you?" The waitress was like some random figure popping up in a dream.

"A beer." She started to ask what kind, but he'd already turned back to Soledad.

"It didn't seem like she was strapped for cash," she was saying. "I'm still betting this is about jealousy."

"You're right. Sophie said the ex flipped out because July didn't wanna get back together. And maybe the apartment Ruben mentioned was for him and July, and that set someone off?"

"Except he said they were just friends. Are we ruling him out? He may be the only one the police haven't talked to."

"I'm not saying I'm not impressed with your Facebook stalking, but maybe the police did the same thing?" He nodded his thanks to the waitress, who'd brought him half a liter of light beer he didn't usually drink but couldn't care less about now.

"Ruben didn't mention being questioned, even though we did. But he *did* seem surprised about July having left with Nadine. Barer's in Berlin; any other ex she had in the meantime probably would be, too. And that's her last known location if we believe Sophie."

"Do we?" asked Franzi, who'd been turning her head back and forth like a spectator at a tennis match.

"Yeah," said Soledad as Simon said, "I guess."

"She had nothing to gain by telling you. Nobody knew she'd seen July except her boyfriend, and why would he turn her in?"

"Because July snitched on her for seeing me on the side?" Simon suggested.

"Sorry for getting you involved with her!" Franzi's mind went the same place his had right after Sophie's confession: "What if she killed July and made up a less incriminating story because she's worried about forensics? I mean, even like in a freak accident."

"I asked the police to check her place, but they didn't seem convinced."

"How about Christian and I stop by?" He sensed her eagerness to help and, despite the grim scenario she'd brought up, her hope of an easy answer. "We could take her if she turns out to be dangerous."

Hearing someone else say it made him sure she wasn't, but he'd already spent most of the day finding out how many things he'd been wrong about. It was worth a try.

"I don't have her address," he said, "but her last name is Müller."

"I'll ask at the copy shop. They're open twenty-four hours."

"Are you doing this tonight?"

"Shouldn't we? Where will you and your lethal weapon be in the meantime?"

"Don't call me a lethal weapon," Soledad said, and they all laughed in spite of everything. He clenched his teeth to keep them from chattering.

"Wait," Franzi said, "Are we forgetting Nadine?"

Soledad and Simon talked over each other again, saying, "Sophie saw her after," and "Nadine was before Sophie."

"Sorry, I'm new to the case. Before I let you out of my sight, Simple Simon, I need to know what you plan to do."

"When I get to July's?" Saying it aloud made everything he imagined seeing behind her door both more real and less likely. "It depends what I find."

"What *we* find."

There was such comfort in Soledad correcting him that, for a moment, he couldn't speak. "If she's there and she's okay," he said at last, "we'll tell the police. If there's someone she needs help getting away from, we'll get out and then call the police."

"Calling the police or calling the police: That's what I like to hear! Remind me what part of that requires a pistol from last century?"

"I think the idea is we point it at someone to keep them from attacking us while we run away?"

Simon nodded at Soledad. She was the one who'd said it would be good to make Barer think they had guns. But that was back when they were playing pretend, no matter how serious it had felt at the time, and how much more surreal tonight was.

"What if no one's there?" Franzi brought up the possibility he'd given the least thought, because it inspired neither hope nor fear.

He waited to see if Soledad had an answer, then said, "That could mean Sophie was lying or someone took July somewhere else in the meantime."

"Which would mean . . . ?" Franzi prompted him.

"I don't know," he had to admit. "I guess we'd wait for Weinert to call back."

"Police again. I love what I'm hearing." But Franzi wasn't smiling. "Are you sure you have to do this?"

Simon knew this question was for him and not Soledad. "You know when something feels so important that you absolutely have to take action?" Not for one moment of his life had he felt the kind of conviction and messianic zeal she brought to all her good causes. If she had any idea how conflicted and afraid he was, she'd never let him go. But somehow or other, this had become his mission, and he was going to see it through. Franzi was nodding, and he knew he'd found the right words.

Through hazy visions of shootouts and kicking down doors, he had a distant flashback to real life. "What about the girls?"

"What girls?"

"Your friends? Soledad, you stay here. I don't wanna ruin the festival for you."

"Are you kidding me? Besides, we only have tickets for tomorrow evening. We'll have long since solved the case by then." She patted his knee, and he felt her touch with the precision of infrared, a flash of warm colors in a world of blue-green tension. "Let's take the train and come back for the van after. I'm too nervous and tipsy to drive."

"That inspires a lot of confidence in your decisions," Franzi said.

A tote bag hit their table with a thud that shook the glasses, and they looked up to see Christian. "The . . ." He lowered his voice. ". . . bullets are in the inner pocket."

"Objection!" Franzi grabbed the bag. "Why are there bullets? I thought the party line was *not* shooting people."

"Better safe than sorry, dear. What if they need to signal for help or something? Anyway, the bullets are separate so there won't be any accidents."

Franzi's sigh of resignation reminded Simon of their mom, but he knew better than to say so.

"Okay, fine." She handed him the bag. "If, and only if, you need to signal for help or some other *not* crazy, violent thing, are you to shoot the gun, understood?"

Simon and Soledad nodded like good children.

"I labeled it 'Attn: German Historical Museum.' Not that that would be much help if you got caught." Christian looked at Franzi. "So you didn't talk them out of anything?"

"It would seem not. You guys heading out?"

"I think we better," Soledad said.

"Hang on. It's an M1911. Promise me you'll google it before you try any vigilante stuff. Think about what always happens in the movies: The good guy's gonna save the day, but the safety's on."

"Thanks, brother-in-law."

Franzi rolled her eyes, but said, "Please be so careful. If you don't check in afterward, I may have to murder you. Oh, and let's never tell Mom."

Simon pantomimed putting the parental filter over his mouth. "Dad would like it, though. Appeal to his sense of rugged masculinity."

"Don't do anything stupid. Either of you."

"Anything else stupid, you mean." Soledad took Simon by one trembling elbow to lead him outside.

<center>~~~</center>

There was a long wait for the next train. Soledad texted the girls from the platform.

"Should we tell Ruben?" Simon asked. "He's so into her, he must be going crazy worrying." It was hard being too much for someone who was only luke-warm about you—even when she wasn't a missing person.

"Sure, I'll go get us something to eat. Pay attention to how he reacts."

He let it ring for ages. It wasn't so much the importance of the call as the need to feel like he was doing something, not trapped here boiling over inside. He could just as easily have called in the morning when they knew more. At least, he hoped they would.

"Sorry if I woke you," he said when Ruben finally picked up. "It's Simon. I wanted to let you know we're finding out about July."

"Finding out?"

"I'll know more in a couple hours."

"Anything I can do to help? I could come meet you."

"That's okay." He waited through a blaring announcement that the cars on their train were hooked up in reverse order. As if they cared where they sat. "I have a train to catch in . . ." He checked the display and sighed. ". . . thirty-seven minutes. But I'll keep you posted."

"Okay, thanks so much, bye."

"Well?" Soledad asked when she came back with trail mix and buttered pretzels. "How'd he sound?"

"Concerned? Then I think he wanted to go back to bed." He laughed, hooking one finger into the collar of his shirt, but it was anxiety and not amusement shortening his breath. "Guess he's not losing much sleep over her."

She raised her eyebrows and stuck out her chin, thinking. It was the first time he'd consciously noticed this expression, but it had great familiarity, like a sign he walked past every day. Half of him said, *oh, this again*, recognizing the usual signs of budding intimacy, learning the language of another face, while the other half added a *not*. Was there any way he could keep from messing this up? But they had enough to deal with right now.

"He must be relieved," she said at last. "What I wonder is . . ."

"Hmm?" He'd taken advantage of her preoccupation to shove half a soft pretzel into his tense jaws.

"Why aren't they together?"

He put one hand in front of his bulging cheeks. "Why's anybody not together? It sounded like they broke up but stayed friends. Maybe it's kind of on-again-off-again? He definitely still has a thing for her, but she referred to him as her friend."

"You're sure she meant him?"

"I don't think she knew Barer would be there."

"She must've known he was after her. He turns up in Amsterdam and she takes off." She paused to munch a handful of trail mix. "Then she tells Sophie her ex is after her, goes back to where he lives and, poof, she's gone again."

"We should've listened to what people kept saying: It's always the ex."

"Makes me not wanna date anymore."

"Or at least not break up." He thought about her scene in Adam's film, wanted to say something but couldn't. There was no good segue.

It was cool on the platform, vast swaths of empty air between isolated passengers, and their laughter subsided into shivering.

~~~

He never imagined he'd be able to sleep, but he was out like a light as soon as their train left the station. His body must've known, he thought when he woke up in Brandenburg, that this was the last refuge before the big . . . what? "Battle" sounded melodramatic, "adventure" frivolous. The big thing that was happening. Soledad was asleep with her chin almost on her breastbone. Just looking at her made his neck ache.

He squeezed past her to the dining car and came back with two double espressos. When he tapped her shoulder, she snapped her head back, immediately alert. "Are we there?"

"Almost. Coffee?"

"More than anything in the world."

There was something feline about the way she closed her eyes as she drank, like a cat luxuriating in sun. He resisted the urge to stroke her head.

"I've been thinking," she said, as if she'd been hard at work the whole ride. "How do we get in?"

"Ring the doorbell?" Like July would answer. And he might as well plan on flying in through the window as breaking down the door. He'd wake all her neighbors before he got it open. Wait. "Oh! You're July; you don't have many friends—who do you give your spare key to?"

"The adoring old lady downstairs who's home twenty-four seven?"

"Exactly."

"Good thinking. By the way." She handed him her phone with a diagram on the screen. "The bullets go in here," she whispered, "and then we snap that part in here like this. Here's the safety on, and here it is off."

Once again, he felt like calling his mom, Franzi, even Soledad next to him to say he wasn't feeling well and wanted to go home. But it was too late now, already the middle of the night and in up to his neck.

Seven

Their cab had sped off by the time they remembered Edeltraut's last name and rang. Simon had time to wonder whether she took her hearing aid out at night or had died in her sleep before a fuzzy voice asked who was there.

"Sorry to bother you so late," Soledad said. "It's July's friends again. July said she'd be up to let us in, but she's not answering."

They repeated their story through her open door.

"I'm so glad she's alright," Edeltraut said. In his euphoria at solving the key problem, he'd forgotten she knew July was missing.

"Yeah, it was all a mix-up," Soledad said.

"I know. I think her buzzer is broken, because I already had to lend the key to that man I mentioned." She wrinkled her nose—because she disapproved of Barer, or because people kept waking her up? It didn't matter. Her key was gone. "I don't know if they're still up. Not getting much rest myself. Of course, I'm happy that—"

"Thanks!" Soledad yelled as they ran upstairs.

"Do remind him about my key!" she called after them.

Simon tried to focus, but each step took his thoughts somewhere else. How would they get in? When had Barer arrived? Was July alive? Better to knock and feign ignorance, or break in? People in movies shot through the doorknob. Or the bolt? That would be loud. How did people break in? So many burglaries, must not be that hard. Not like they went to burglar school. Or better to knock?

The police tape was torn, and he could see light through the peephole. He reached into the tote bag for the gun and tried to remember if the diagram had been from the shooter's perspective or a mirror image. Every second counted. He motioned for Soledad to get out of the way. Shooting the lock open would let him know whether the safety was on.

She shook her head and pressed down the handle of the door. He wanted to laugh, but instead watched it swing open. Then he pushed past her. Not being sexist, just have the gun.

The first thing he saw was July sitting at a small table facing them, as if she were onstage. One of her eyes was swollen shut, the other closed, and there was a bridge of blood from one cheek to the other. Her head seemed too heavy for her neck. Broken? After all this time and effort, he was back where he started: a corpse, not bogged down in a canal, not a pool of blood spilling over his floor, but a nightmare all the same. His heart crashed into something hard when Soledad said "July?" but that was nothing to the dizzying shock of the corpse righting its head as one dead eye flickered open. He grabbed Soledad with one hand, still pointing the gun with the other.

Then, a heartbeat later, relief: She was alive. The nightmare was ending. It was that moment when, still asleep, you realize it was all just a dream. When bad things keep happening, but don't matter anymore. Aside from July, the apartment was perfectly ordinary, with the pastel furnishings and clever use of space of an Ikea catalog. He heard a washing machine running, which seemed strange but also reassuring.

"Siiimon," July slurred like a drunk. "Knew you'd come."

There it was again: that claiming, wanting to own him. He was here and she was lucky and had no right to expect it. To expect anything from him. He imagined pulling the trigger. Putting an end to everything she'd put him through, forever. And she saw what he was thinking, couldn't help but see. When her head pitched forward, he thought he *had* pulled it, some primal instinct taking over. As Soledad ran to July, so much faster than his thoughts, he realized he hadn't heard a bang.

"Help me, you idiot!" For some incomprehensible reason, she was dragging July's body—why dead if there hadn't been a bang?—onto the floor. "An ambulance, call an ambulance," she was saying as she jammed her fingers into July's mouth. Ambulance? He strained his memory like the word was some cartoon he'd seen as a child and wanted to recall in detail. Then awareness shone through the fog of his thoughts and he dialed emergency services, gave them July's address and said she'd been poisoned, but only after Soledad told him to.

Poisoned. He watched July's throat twitch as Soledad choked her—why choke a dead person?—and slapped her face with the hand that wasn't down her throat, said her name over and over. Finally, he caught hold of the elusive thought that had been darting out of reach for what, five minutes? Five years? I didn't do this. Couldn't have. Was out of town.

With that out of the way, his mind was clear enough to notice two things: July's door had been unlocked—why?—and there was a hot, stomach-turning smell rising from the floor. Now that he'd gotten started, there were all kinds of things to notice. The note on the table in loopy purple handwriting—purple for a suicide note? "I can't live with Simon's rejection anymore. Thomas Barer kidnapped me and beat me up. Goodbye." A little impersonal. More like an anonymous tip-off than a final farewell.

"It says Barer did it." He left out the part about himself, unwilling to admit to the crushing defeat of learning that it was, in spite of everything, about him again.

Soledad didn't respond. In silence broken only by the hiccuppy sound of vomiting, he heard the washing machine stop, no more running water. What had she been washing before killing herself? When did she plan to dry it? She must've put it in before Barer beat her up. Where was he, anyway? Not here, or he would've stopped July, if not from poisoning herself then at least from writing the note.

Gun still attached to one hand like some grotesque prosthesis, he dropped the tote bag on the floor and knelt opposite Soledad to raise July's head above the spreading pool of vomit. "I'm not sure you're supposed to make her puke," he recalled. "At rehab, they said—" Had he heard a door, or was he just suddenly aware of someone else in the room? He stood up too fast and hit his head on the table. Pain resounded in his skull like church bells, blurring the shape of a man.

"Ruben?" he said when it settled. He glanced at July and saw that she was alone. Had Soledad left? No, she must be under the table. Now it looked like he was the hero making July puke up whatever.

He wanted to tell Soledad to come out and take credit, but Ruben, eyes red and snot running down his face, was stammering, "Made good time, didn't you? I . . . got here just in time to save her from Barer. But he attacked her. I was so worried about her!"

Not worried enough for an ambulance? But Simon wouldn't have thought to call one if it weren't for Soledad. One of Ruben's hands was wrapped in toilet paper and bleeding through. Simon wished he'd use it to wipe his nose.

"She's so upset." Ruben glanced at the table. "Oh no, I was worried she'd harm herself! Good thing you're here. Be careful with that antique there. I'll go get help." He sounded as scattered as Simon felt, unable to grasp that July had pulled one over on them again, completed her disappearing act. "She must've done it while I was getting cleaned up. Barer cut me when I tried to stop him." He was taking a step toward the door with each word, and Simon was having trouble processing his speech and movement at the same time. But he noticed one more thing.

"Purple." Moving between Ruben and the door, he pointed to the ink-stained fingertips protruding from the makeshift bandage. It felt like a riddle he'd solved, seeing through the magician's act, and he was as surprised to see Ruben lunge at him as he was by the hot, sharp stab of the door handle against his ribs while Ruben pummeled him.

Gasping with shock and pain, he tried for a warning shot, tried to aim for Ruben's legs, but nothing happened. He swung the useless gun at Ruben's face, but his blow was tentative, a pacifist's play-fighting, and he dropped it when Ruben knocked him into the table, making his head ring from the other side this time. He heard a shot or the gun hitting the floor, or was that his skull? He couldn't see straight. Everything was ringing with pain and noise, blending with the smell of vomit and something weighing him down, Barer, no Ruben on him, bleeding onto him or was that his blood, choking him like July was choking but he couldn't see her because it was dark and there was something he'd meant to but what and he was just for now—

A louder bang blasted the lights back on and left him weightless. No, a load had fallen off. Taking deep gulps of air that burned going in, he turned to see Ruben clutching his bleeding thigh. But Ruben wasn't looking at him.

"Didn't see you there," he said to Soledad, who was crouched beside July with the gun in her hands and her mouth open. Clenching his teeth, Ruben seemed to be grinning like she was an old friend he'd run into, but his voice was plaintive, like she hadn't played fair.

He struggled a little when she tied his wrists together with a frosting-pink apron from July's kitchen, but his face had gone greenish and his heart wasn't in it. She handed Simon a dishtowel to press onto Ruben's hot, sopping wound while she called Weinert. Then followed an eternity of blank space in which Simon belatedly realized why Soledad had ducked under the table. And that he'd been crazy to get in Ruben's way. He could've let him walk out and then called the cops. But that was in the past, a lifetime ago. Now they all lay panting on the floor, bleeding and dying or close enough that it didn't matter who was whose enemy.

The paramedics put July and Ruben in the same ambulance, which seemed wrong, a faux pas like seating a divorced couple next to each other, but then they were the most urgent. Simon insisted he didn't need an ambulance, but the harried mother across from July had called one when she heard the shot, so he and Soledad got in. Which was probably for the best because everything hurt and most of the blood on him seemed to be his own.

~~~

At the hospital, Soledad gripped Simon's hand, making alternately sympathetic and horrified faces about the stitches going into the sheared back of his head. He wasn't as upset as she seemed. What were a few stitches, a couple cracked ribs? July hadn't written that note, and it wasn't his fault. Ruben must've planned to leave before they arrived. Well, that would teach him to dawdle at the scene of the crime. Good thing they'd taken a cab from the station. Simon smiled through his tears. He wasn't crying; it just hurt like hell.

~~~

In the common room afterward, Simon felt extraneous, aware of drafts on parts of his scalp he didn't usually feel. Weinert had said to wait while he spoke to the doctors, so here he was waiting, no longer a patient and not visiting anyone. At least Soledad was equally out of place. It was like being one of two classmates invited to a friend's family dinner, looking to the other guest for cues. But she wasn't looking to him. He couldn't even tell whether her eyes were open. She had her elbow on the table, head on her fist, hair all over the place. He'd traded his gruesome t-shirt for a thin hospital gown, but there was still vomit and blood—his?—on her clothes. Visiting hours hadn't started yet, and the only other person there was a girl with a comic book open on her plaster-cast leg, dozing in a wheelchair. What else did they need to do? Soledad had given Weinert the gist. Was July well enough to explain the rest? Assuming she'd survived. He didn't have the energy for any other outcome, so he told himself someone would've let them know if not.

Sunlight was pouring through the flimsy white sunshade, and he had the absurd feeling that there hadn't been any night at all. Like at the North Pole: one long day.

"Land of the midnight sun."

"What?" She came to life with a start.

"Should I get coffee?"

"I guess."

"Can I ask you something?" Not because it mattered now, but because this was the first opportunity, here in this sleepy space outside of time.

She just looked at him.

"What's with you and that director guy?"

She yawned, apparently too tired to care why he was asking. "Adam? We met at school, dated for a while . . ." Her eyelids fluttered with the effort of staying awake. "I'm not a huge fan of his work and he's a little full of himself, but we're still friends. When it suits him. Some people need someone to pat them on the head and say, 'Good job.'"

"Yeah." He couldn't bring himself to ask whether she was doing the same for him.

Her yawn was epic, but she seemed to know what he was thinking. "The difference is, what you make is good."

"Thanks." He didn't want to press her and risk disrupting the vague, buzzing happiness of that statement, so he went out to the vending machine.

A haggard-looking Weinert approached him. "It could've gone either way, but she's okay. He is, too, if you're wondering."

"I wasn't. About him, I mean."

"Those are some nasty bruises." Weinert pointed to Simon's throat. "Looks like Herr Janssen wasn't planning on letting go."

Simon pressed the cappuccino button twice and fumbled in his pockets for change, but kept coming up with two-cent pieces. "He wasn't. I was blacking out by the time Soledad shot him." That sounded false, like an excuse he'd come up with. Or maybe it was finally sinking in, how close to death not only July, but he himself had been. What if he'd been alone, panicked and shut down like he had, gotten attacked like he had? Soledad had saved his life.

"Huh?"

"I got it," Weinert repeated. "Make it three."

He stopped searching his pockets and pressed the button. "Thanks."

"We had an eye on him, you know. If we'd known about Frau Tappet's movements sooner . . . Your girlfriend certainly messed things up for us. Didn't say a word about it down here and refused to talk to our colleague in Hamburg last night. She can expect to hear from us about impeding this investigation."

It took him a second to understand. "Sophie and I broke up." There was no pleasure or pity in having gotten her in trouble; he simply didn't care.

"Ah. Too bad." Weinert didn't seem to think it was, and neither did Simon. "On the plus side, it'll be easier when he goes to trial since you more or less caught him red-handed." *Purple*-handed, thought Simon, boy detective. "Speaking of which, it's up to you whether you want to make your statements now or tomorrow. Or later today, I mean."

"I'll ask Soledad." He felt exhausted, but not sleepy. Had it all been for nothing? But if he hadn't given away where July was, what would they have arrested Ruben for? July would've at least had to prove he was stalking her. Like when he'd called the police on her from Brussels. Except that July had been in real danger. And he'd rushed in like some vigilante instead of talking the police into it. But that wasn't all he'd done wrong.

"Are we in trouble about the gun?"

"To be honest, I think we'll confiscate it and leave it at that. Just promise you'll never meddle in another investigation."

"Gladly."

"Where'd you get it, by the way?"

No use getting Christian in trouble. "I found it at a friend's. I didn't plan to use it, but I was worried whoever had July would be armed. I don't think my friend will notice. It was in the cellar where nobody's been in decades." Did that sound plausible? What if Christian didn't have a cellar? But no one was recording this. More importantly, Simon was finally innocent, beyond the shadow of a doubt, with two witnesses to prove it. Not counting Ruben.

"Anyway." Weinert sighed. "Thanks for your help. It was really stupid, but kind of brave."

"I just wanted things wrapped up."

"You know what Herr Janssen said when we arrested him for attempted murder?"

"No idea."

"'Just attempted?' Then he cried like a baby. Of course, he'll be singing a different tune in court. Looking at your throat, I think it'll be two counts."

Simon laughed, but recalled that blink of an eye when he'd pointed the gun at July and thought about firing. Had Ruben cried because he hadn't killed her, or because he almost had? Simon felt like he'd swallowed ice, but the chill in his gut was too big to fit down his throat. Ruben was sick, a monster, but Simon had been wrong when he told Christian you knew what you were capable of. No matter how brief the moment, how faint her consciousness, July had seen him think about killing instead of saving her, and they'd both have to remember that forever. Or until they could persuade themselves it had been an illusion, momentary panic. Mixing up the victim with the perpetrator. Yeah, he could do that. Even if it took a while. He had one advantage over July, at least. He had someone to tell.

"In all seriousness," Weinert went on, "Frau Tappet's very lucky you arrived when you did. She won't make her official statement until she's discharged, but she says he gave her one last chance to take him back. Since he came prepared to poison her, he must've expected her to say no. Apparently, he was planning to drug himself and pretend she'd done that so she could commit suicide. Knowing she might've drugged you in Amsterdam would make that plausible for us. The idea was for you to arrive and find him unconscious and her dead. And she would've been if she hadn't bought time by biting him so hard."

"Biting?" Simon remembered the bloody toilet paper around Ruben's hand. And telling Ruben it was lucky he'd gotten drugged, because that made him not a suspect. Then telling him they were going to see about July and mentioning their exact departure time. Looking up their destination would've been a matter of minutes even if Ruben hadn't heard that announcement blaring in the background. Simon might as well have been Ruben's accomplice; every word out of his mouth had helped him.

"When he was trying to poison her. Really twisted guy. He's got a bit of a record, but this is the first thing that'll really put him away."

Simon nodded, each movement of his head putting that much more distance between him and Ruben. He hadn't meant to give July away or give Ruben any ideas. He reminded himself that Ruben would've wanted to kill her anyway, that it had nothing to do with him. At least nothing he could help. He remembered feeling sorry for Ruben, thinking Ruben wanted July like July wanted him and he wanted Sophie. But none of that lined up. July had never harmed him, no matter how much he rejected her, and all he felt for Sophie was some vestige of yesterday's annoyance.

Weinert added, "You would've been in trouble if we'd found her body in Amsterdam, you know. Being there that night, having a history with her—not like she gave you much choice. But now that we know you're innocent, can I just say I *love* your band? Once I realized who you were, I was really rooting for you not to be a murderer. I'll have to try and make a show one of these days."

"Thanks." For the first time, Simon had a clear view of the tattoo on Weinert's arm: a fox, not a hare. Nothing to do with the band, even if he was a fan. Not about him. Even July didn't have an H vs. H tattoo. He hoped. But all that was over now; it had to be. Everything else was.

"If you two do decide to give your statement, we'll arrange a ride for you. Just let one of the guards outside Herr Janssen's room know."

~~~

Soledad had her head on the table, hair spread in all directions like some fairy-tale princess deep in enchanted slumber on the forest floor. There was a dark smudge of oil or soot where she must've rubbed her eye. Something he'd still been choking on dissolved, and he was filled with tenderness that brought tears to his eyes. He needed to talk to someone, but didn't want to wake her, so he left her coffee, downed his and asked at the nurse's station whether he could see July.

"Technically no." The older woman's uniform was spotless and wrinkle-free, and she looked much too alert for the time of day. "But I'll make an exception since you saved her life."

It wasn't me, he wanted to say. I was just there. But then she might not let him in.

~~~

July was in bed, watching a muted TV. Her face had gone from pale to yellowish, a lemon tart with raspberries of contusions. The sickly color of her lips wasn't far off from her usual choice of lipstick, though.

"Hello." Her voice was formal. "How are you?"

"Could be worse."

"You look awful." A poor imitation of her usual teasing tone.

"I guess you don't have a mirror in here."

"Simon?" For once, she didn't drag out his name.

"What?"

"Thanks."

"Of course," he said, although nothing about it went without saying. "Anyway, it was Soledad who saved you."

"Saved me," she echoed in a dreamy way that made him wonder what they had her on. "I don't know how he got in."

"I'm sorry. I shouldn't have called him. When we saw him in Hamburg, he seemed so concerned. Maybe have a word with Edeltraut about handing out your key."

"He never could let go. And this is me saying that." She opened one eye a little wider. "What were you doing in Hamburg?"

"Sorting things out with Sophie." As long as she didn't think it was about her. Even if it had been, as long as she was gone. "I recognized Ruben."

"Sophie's a bad person. Not as bad as him, though."

"We were actually expecting Barer."

"That old teddy bear? He was an awful husband, but we're friends. You know he helped me set up my business after we got divorced? Said he owed me for ruining my life."

The words had a familiar ring to them. "So you weren't blackmailing him?"

"For what?"

"About . . ." He cleared his throat. ". . . illegal pornography?"

"What pornography? All he ever did was sell low-end drugs and fix cars."

"Never mind." What a fool he'd been, believing everything everyone told him. Ruben had played them in more ways than he could count. But he was going to jail. "Did he beat you? At rehab you were all . . . messed up."

"You did remember me!" There was an unpleasant, familiar gleam of triumph in her open eye. "I was never sure. You acted so weird whenever I tried to bring it up."

"No." He took a slight malicious pleasure in disillusioning her. "The police told me." Then he realized that this conversation was something like his childhood vision of heaven, where all your questions were answered, whether you asked how many grains of sand were on the beach, what T-rexes did with their tiny arms or what the hell this had all been about.

"Thomas never hit me. That was from when he caught me with Ruben and I tried to break up their fight. Which Ruben started, even if the police believed him and not Thomas. The two of them were so aggressive I didn't know who to stick up for. I wished the police would take them both, but all they cared about was how many grams Thomas was carrying. Ruben was only ever an escape for me, but what good is getting away to somewhere worse?"

She paused for so long he almost thought she expected an answer, but she was only catching her breath. "I got married too young, and Thomas is so . . . practical. You know he never once got me flowers? And that's when he was still interested."

"Hm." He was noncommittal, waiting for more interesting information.

"Thomas wanted to get married just like that." She snapped her fingers without making a sound. "He got bored of it just as fast. Having me around got in the way of his usual sleazy crowd. He was out all the time, never saying where he'd been. When he *was* home, I could feel the resentment. Then I met Ruben. I don't know if I even really liked him, but he made me feel like I existed again, the way he looked at me. He'd write me love letters, show up and surprise me . . . But sometimes he'd get so . . ." She shrugged one shoulder. "He's always had a problem with his temper. A real problem. We kept in touch but I hadn't seen him in ages. Then he said he'd been to therapy, gotten a place in Hamburg, could I come visit. After you told me you had a girlfriend, I was feeling . . . I wanted someone to take to your show. We spent the day together and it was great. We talked about getting a place together, giving it another try. But the way he was acting at the concert . . . Well, I said I wasn't sure. He got pissed and left, so I ended up staying with this guy I met."

"What was . . . never mind." He didn't want to hear that the fight had been about him.

"I heard Thomas was in Amsterdam so I invited him to your concert, but he couldn't get a ticket. Anyway, Ruben apologized and offered to drive me there. He really did seem sorry. Besides, I'd already invited you to his friends' party and didn't wanna miss the chance . . . didn't wanna disappoint you guys. I figured, what can he do with all these people around? He seemed relaxed, even around you. When I found out later you'd been drugged, I got really scared. Remember how he bought us drinks?"

Simon nodded.

"He called when we were on the way to your hotel, begging me to meet him, offering to come pick me up, then threatening me. He thought you and I . . . Anyway, Thomas and I brought you upstairs, then I figured leaving my wallet was a mistake, but you were passed out. Tanja said she'd call the cops if I didn't leave. Thomas was supposed to be downstairs, but I saw Ruben instead. He must've followed us. I waited until he looked the other way so I could duck into this bachelor party they were breaking up, then went up to this drunk British guy's room."

Like he cared about some British bachelor. "Fair enough, but why leave your wallet in the first place?"

A splotchy blush joined the other unappetizing colors on her face. "So I'd see you again. You know, like that one *Seinfeld* episode?" He still didn't, but he got the idea. "I know it sounds weird, but I was drunk, and it seemed like a great idea. Until I realized I should've taken some cash. I was planning to call and say, hey, I forgot my wallet. I even thought you'd take me to Brussels."

Neither of them mentioned why she might've thought that, after the only time he'd ever given her any hope. "You couldn't. You didn't have your phone."

"Yeah, but I didn't notice until Jack wanted my number the next day. I asked at the front desk but no one had turned it in, which really sucked, because I had barely any cash on me and tons in my wallet. I was planning to go on tour . . . or, well, on vacation." She sighed in creaking stages that sounded like someone trying to start up an old appliance.

He tried to think what else to ask, but he was drawing a blank. All his questions, all the agonizing, and the answers were so ordinary, things he could've thought of himself. Then he remembered what Sophie had said, that July had been perfectly fine and let him suffer. And what Sophie couldn't have known: She'd even made him doubt himself. "Why didn't you say where you were? Didn't you realize people would worry?"

"I don't have that many people to worry about me." It was hard to tell if her swollen face was smiling or wincing. "I certainly didn't think *you'd* notice."

"The police told me when I reported you."

"For what?"

"I thought you drugged me."

She hacked up a laugh. "Why would I do that?"

"You seemed like the most likely person. I mean, why would anyone?"

"I guess either Ruben was jealous or our drinks got mixed up." *I guess this, I guess that.* He couldn't help relishing this brief lapse in her unflappable assurance. "When we were fighting, I said I'd rather die than live with him. I never thought he'd be so . . . literal. But I didn't realize anyone was looking for me until Sophie told me. I thought it was a great chance to get Ruben to back off."

"How?" His head ached, and not just from the stitches and exhaustion.

"I called the police and said I'd seen him with me that night. I figured they'd question him—which is more than they'd do if I weren't missing—and he wouldn't take any risks. I told Thomas, of course."

"You did?" So Barer had lied about trying to track her down? He must've thought they were friends of Ruben's and not hers. Not that they were friends of hers.

She nodded. "I would've felt better staying with him, but he said some people had come around looking for me so I should lie low. After Nadine ditched me, I stopped in Hamburg just to be somewhere I knew my way around. It felt weird being there without seeing Ruben, but safe, like it was the last place he'd look. I'm really sorry I didn't let you know. When Sophie told me, my first thought was, serves Simon right. I got over that, but I wanted to leave you out of it, not get Ruben on your case. I didn't realize how . . . worried you'd be. I hope you're not mad." She was trying to pout.

"Listen, July." Finally, after all this time, it was the right moment for Dr. F's speech. "I'm not mad. I don't feel anything toward you, except relief that you're alive. Not because we're friends or there's any special connection between us, but because you're a human being. We're not soulmates or anything."

"Okay." Another jagged sigh. "It sounds weird, but it was never about you personally. I know it's hard to think of yourself as a symbol, but . . . I got married to stick it to my parents or I don't know, and then I was selling drugs, taking drugs, no friends, no future, Thomas already tired of me. I was such a bright kid. And then Ruben! At rehab, you were so . . . *pure*. Everyone was twitching and cursing, and you were playing your guitar and above it all. But you knew about all the ugliness, because why else were you there? I loved listening to your songs later, knowing where they were coming from, or . . . I thought I did. You showed me what it could be like to have a good life."

She was blushing so hard her bruises looked less severe. "I even used to think

I was in love with you. You were never distant like Thomas or aggressive like Ruben. You were always the same, because you weren't real. Somehow I thought if I waited around long enough, you'd love me back. When you finally kissed me, I was so put off. I couldn't believe my big pure symbol wanted to use me. I knew you slept around, but that wasn't about me. I had the usual silly fantasy you have about bad guys, that you'll be the one to reform them."

"But I never really was a bad guy."

"It was just a daydream. Once we actually spent time together..." She seemed out of breath, and he wondered if it was bad for her to talk so much, but there was no point stopping her now. Let the hospital figure it out. "It wasn't like I expected. Don't take this personally, but it ruined it for me. I'd had all these thoughts about you and your music, and you had no idea. It was like finding out Santa's your parents. You were just some guy."

What was he now, her tarnished symbol or just some guy who, for once, was listening? He took a deep breath. It was harder to say in the face of such little resistance. "I'm glad to hear that. To be very clear: I wish you a great life. I hope you'll be safe and happy. But there's nothing between us, and there never will be. We can say hi to each other at shows, and that's it."

"I understand and . . . think that's for the best." She took a ragged breath, and he noticed the sweat pearling along her hairline. "Who are you, anyway?"

He thought she was asking him something existential, then followed her eyes over his shoulder. He had no idea how long Soledad had been standing there.

"I'm with him," Soledad said.

"I can live with that."

"You're gonna have to," she said.

~~~

Soledad insisted she was up for giving her statement, so they wandered the ward until they found the room with two police officers outside. Fifteen minutes later, they were asleep in the back of a car like children on the way home from a long outing.

After taking turns dozing in the waiting room and answering questions, they stood blinking in the sunlight outside. It was like leaving a club with someone, each of you waiting for the other to suggest going home together or changing venues. She reminded him of that old song about someone you could steal horses with. Not only because she'd go through with something that crazy, but because he could count on her absolutely, even with his life. It was a new feeling and confusing. He was wondering how to make a cab to his place sound as innocent as he meant it, getting some sleep before they figured things out, when she said, "I'm going back to Hamburg, but I understand if you wanna stay here. In fact, I think you should."

It was the last thing he'd expected, even though it was what they'd planned the night before. That felt like another lifetime whose plans were irrelevant in this one. At their feet, a few sparrows were taking a dust bath in the hollow left by stolen cobblestones. He couldn't quite look at her.

"This has been . . . what should I say? An unforgettable experience. Probably great for my work, right?" Her laugh sounded exhausted. "But I need to clear my head. You know, I *shot* someone. And I'd already picked out the frying pan to bash his head in with if *that* didn't work. He could be dead right now, and I'd have to live with that."

He wanted to indicate that he understood and it was okay, to sound less gutted than he was, but he was having enough trouble breathing, standing and keeping his bodily functions going. All he could come up with was, "I'm so tired."

"I know. Me, too." She put a hand on his shoulder. "Let's talk later. I'll leave your stuff in the van and see you at the show, okay?"

"What show?" His weary mind couldn't decide whether she really wanted to talk or that was some consolation prize.

"Just the one you're playing. Go home and get some rest. I told Franzi we're okay."

"There are still things we don't know." Whatever questions he'd forgotten to ask July, that window had now closed for good. He wouldn't speak to her again.

"Yeah. But I think that's okay." Soledad's smile was sad and happy at once. Like everything.

He caught her by the arm. "One more thing." Only as he continued speaking did he realize she might've expected him to do something normal like kiss her. "Can we not tell Christian I messed up about the safety?"

This time, she laughed loud enough to startle all but the fattest and boldest sparrow into flight. "Oh, you did that part right. You just forgot to put the bullets in."

That seemed typical of him, in a way he was too tired to think about.

~~~

Getting out of the cab, he remembered Farid and felt relieved. He had that confused dread that comes with lack of sleep, the sense of dark powers hovering over him. It was good to have someone there to take care of things, whatever things there were.

Farid was skyping his wife and didn't notice Simon slipping into his room, where he closed the door, took off his shoes and lay down. The room was spinning again, or his head. But it had to be the room, because there was a wonderful new stillness within him. He pulled the covers over his face and lay a long time without thinking. Sometimes a scene from the night before, or the weeks before that, would play on the blank screen of his mind, but it went dark after each clip. At some point, it stayed that way.

He woke suffocated by the blanket, knowing it was daytime by the nauseous taste in his mouth. And his stupid toothbrush was in Hamburg! That tangential thought brought back the rest, and he felt a satisfaction like having played a good show. He'd get brunch—or whatever meal it was time for—with Farid, call Franzi, pick up some ibuprofen.

Finding an outfit was exhausting. His head throbbed, and when he tried to massage the base of his skull, he felt stubble and the bandage over his stitches. Shouldn't touch them. Risk of infection. He heard voices through the door and wondered whether Farid had put his wife on speakerphone. But they were speaking German. Did Farid have friends over?

He came out with his clothes under one arm, ready to nod a quick hello and bolt for the bathroom, then saw Cindi and froze. After his eyes adjusted to her platinum blonde hair and leopard-print dress, he saw his dad in the chair next to her, Farid on the edge of his mattress. They were having coffee and a perfectly natural conversation, like random figures thrown together in a dream who take no exception at never having met.

"Hi, Dad, Cindi. Hi, Farid."

"My boy's up at last! Let's see the damage." He was already squeezing past the mattress and reaching for Simon's head. "You're really okay? I couldn't believe what Franzi said. You should've told me; I would've . . ."

"I'm okay, Dad. Thanks."

"We didn't mean to barge in. But after talking to Franzi, I was a bit concerned about not being able to reach you. She managed to track down this fellow's number"—He nodded at Farid—"and he was nice enough to check and say, yessir, he's back and fast asleep. He said he'd take care of you, but Cindi and I had been meaning to come, and we thought, no time like the present."

"I did want to call first," Cindi said.

"We did call; we couldn't reach him. Oh, Cindi picked up an icepack for you. It's in the freezer. Not much space in that tiny fridge."

"Your father bring me also wonderful gift." Farid held up two glossy books: *Learn German Fast* and *Getting Ahead in Your Career.* "Thank you, Sir."

"Go ahead and call me Wolfgang." To Simon, he said, "The career one's for both of you. After all, music's a business, too."

"Thanks." He was touched that his dad had brought something for Farid and acknowledged his career probably for the first time ever. More than that, he was touched that he'd been worried enough to drive to Berlin and sit here making conversation with someone he'd branded a terrorist not long before. Of course, you could question Franzi's good sense in telling him everything. So much for the parental filter. "I'll get dressed and we can get something to eat?"

"Take your time. Cindi and I need to check into our hotel." He paused at the door. "Farid says you've got a show coming up. We'd like to come."

To his surprise, he didn't even mind saying, "Please do."

At dinner, Farid helped buffer the invasiveness of their questions. Thankfully, his German wasn't idiomatic enough to understand Simon's dad's racist jokes.

Cindi still tried to get in a few hits. "Managing to hold onto a girl these days? I hear there's a new flavor of the week." Another one of her wannabe-edgy questions that only made her sound like a "cool" mom using dated slang and her kids' friends' nicknames. Was she even old enough for that? Now that would be an edgy question.

But he reminded himself that she'd brought him an icepack and that he could've, but hadn't, died the night before. Besides, for once he had a comeback. "Actually I am seeing someone, but she's out of town."

"Something with S, wasn't it?"

"Soledad." He could count on his dad to have forgotten Sophie's name. It would be another story with his mom, who had the strange habit of taking notes while on the phone. Every time he visited, he found scrawled names of venues and people she didn't know. Then again, she and Soledad had gotten along so well, she probably wouldn't mind.

"How . . . exotic," Cindi said.

"Yes." His dad's smirk warned him to expect a tasteless remark. "Your friends are so *colorful.*"

"Soledad's nice. She and Simon are good friends," Farid offered.

"You're getting on in years," his dad said. "Glad to hear you're settling down."

"We're not holding our breath, though." Cindi couldn't help herself, so he chose to ignore her. She turned to Farid. "What about you?"

He glanced at Simon, uncertain what he was being asked.

"Farid's wife is in Syria. He's doing all he can to get her here."

At first, Cindi's face only registered a kind of disgusted horror, as if Farid's wife had some gruesome disease. But when she composed her features and said, "That must be so hard," it almost sounded like a normal human response.

Luckily, telling the whole July story—or as much as he could without mentioning Sophie—took up the rest of the evening, and he had a good excuse to go home and nurse his pounding head. Farid went upstairs, but Simon felt obligated to wait with Cindi and his dad. As their cab pulled up, his dad said, "I'm sorry for what I said about Farid. I didn't think he'd be, you know . . ."

"What, a person?" But he laughed to keep them from fighting. He was too aware of his headache, his dad's good intentions and his own good fortune. On his way upstairs, he called Franzi, who couldn't talk but wrote that she was sorry, she'd missed a few calls from their dad and used July as an excuse; she'd tried to talk him out of coming but Simon knew how he was. His next call, Soledad, was on her way into a movie but promised to call back soon.

~~~

Much as he dreaded their interaction, he had to invite his mom and Reinhardt to the benefit concert now that his dad and Cindi were coming. If only Franzi would commit so he could assign her one set of parents. To make matters worse, or better, depending on whether you were Simon or his label, the same tabloid that had called him a suspect ran a longer piece the day before the concert: "Rock Star Helps Rescue Abducted Fan."

At least it didn't make the front page, which showed Germans giving flowers and bottles of water to refugees arriving in Munich Central Station. Despite Franzi's doubts about how long this immigrant-friendly *Willkommenskultur* would last, the thought of so much welcome by a country that had once been the most racist on Earth made Simon's eyes go damp. The suddenly tolerant slant conservative tabloids were taking was the only reason he hadn't hung up when they called about July.

"I can't believe the press found out so fast," Soledad said when she called from a rest stop.

He was waiting outside their rehearsal space while Micha picked up lunch. Aside from getting ready for the show, spending all day rehearsing was a great way to both avoid his dad and convince him that being a musician was a real job. Which wasn't to say they weren't getting along. Having decided Farid was "one of the good ones"—another comment Simon could only respond to with a pained smile—his dad had offered to help find an apartment for him and, hopefully, his wife. Knowing his dad, that might entail bribing the property company, but so what? Everyone had their own way of trying to be good.

Farid's papers had come through, but, even after paying for an appointment on the black market, his wife had to wait two more months to be seen at the German embassy in Beirut. Simon was happy but still nervous for Farid, grateful for his dad's attempts to make up for any number of things. Helping Simon's friend because he knew Simon didn't want his help. Although getting Farid out of his kitchen would be helping Simon, too, now that he didn't have any stalkers or murderers to worry about and wanted his space again. Cindi, for her part, was spending a lot of time in boutiques on Ku'damm. They were getting along better than they had in years, so he didn't want to risk spending too much time with them.

"I can't believe that tabloid called me a rock star. But I bet Nadine sent them the lead as a way of making amends." Much like her offer to play a song in their set. She'd come by earlier that week to practice, and stayed to listen to his story, which seemed more like a movie plot he was spoiling every time he told it. "You're coming tonight, right? You won't be too tired?"

"I'll nap. I wouldn't miss it for anything."

He took a deep breath and looked up at the darkening clouds, felt that cool sigh before the storm that exposes the silver underbellies of leaves. "You know, I think I kind of miss you a little."

She laughed like there was nothing huge or world-changing about what he'd gotten himself to say. "Likewise."

"I hope it won't be boring now that we're done sleuthing." He said it like a joke, but was insecure enough to mean it.

"Yeah, what'll we do when we hang out?"

At least that meant they'd keep hanging out. "I haven't been to the movies in a while."

"Me, neither. Not to a talky, I mean. A movie sounds good. And boring sounds really, really good."

~~~

It felt funny to be onstage with Nadine again, funny how normal it felt. Not because he'd played with her so many times before, but because there was no tension left between them. She'd given up some moral high ground in telling him about July, or he'd gained it in finding her. Or they'd both realized how much time had passed. At the end of the day, they were two people who'd been very close and very wrong for each other, noticed before it was too late, and forgiven each other.

After a fifty-fifty split between their self-titled and *Georg's Friend*, they were playing a new song with the old lineup. Everything slowed down so he could take it in: Tanja sitting on an amp, nodding to the rhythm; Micha grinning and pouring sweat like he always did, even on mellow beats; Nadine ethereal and peaceful; the audience swaying, Soledad in the front, widening her smile when their eyes met, helping Franzi, Christian and Farid form a barrier between his two sets of proud parents. He felt like crying in a way he hadn't allowed himself since puberty, because there was too much life within and around him to put into words.

How rare that was, remembering why you'd become what you had, without feeling like you'd betrayed your younger self. He couldn't see July, but she was out there somewhere, alive and not his problem. What more could he ask of her?

~~~

"That last song's the one I want in my movie," Soledad said backstage. "I love that twist with the bed and the grave. You were amazing." Everybody else said so, too, and he had that feeling again, that stirring and growing of something larger than he was. He was crying as he hugged everyone, even Nadine, but sweating almost as much as Micha, so who could tell?

"Let's hit the bar," Tanja said. "I'm burning up."

"I'm okay," he heard himself say, and watched the others drift away until there was only one shadowy figure left.

"*Solo con Soledad.*" She laughed.

"What?"

"Alone with loneliness. Or with me."

"I've never been less . . ." Lonely, he wanted to say, but he knew how much like a line that or anything would sound, so he ran his hand over her hair, felt the ridges of curls and her warmth through them.

"I feel like we got close very quickly," she said. "Like people in a slasher movie."

"I feel like we understand each other." That was the biggest thing he could say, bigger than all his fears of failing her or himself, losing faith in what they could have.

When he squeezed past the crowd to get behind the merch table, she stood off to the side with his family and Farid, framing snapshots of him, the band and Nadine, who eventually drifted away like the dandelion seed she was. And he could think that about her, and not love or hate her at all.

He didn't spot July right away, because she wasn't sidling up like she belonged there, or craning over the table. He hadn't heard from her since the hospital, and she was a new person now that the cloud of dread surrounding her had dissipated. The bad lighting was kind to her bruises. Their eyes met, and he thought she'd shout or mouth something to bridge the crowd between them, but she just raised one hand in a shy little wave, and was gone.

Acknowledgments

Many thanks to my family and friends for their interest, help and encouragement, in some cases over the course of decades, and especially to my husband Sergej for being supportive, trying not to make noise when I'm working and bringing me hundreds (thousands?) of coffees. And to Emma, who's a dog and can't read but is very encouraging and one of my biggest fans.

Thank you to everyone who read early versions or sections of *What I Know About July*, especially Louis Fantini for beta reading and my former agent Devon for many rounds of edits. And of course to Tricia and everyone at Meerkat Press for all the editorial discussions and support on this and my last book.

Thank you to all my writing professors and teachers over the years, from school through NYU and FDU, especially my thesis mentor and fellow writer Ellen Akins, and to all the members of creative writing workshops I attended over the years. And to all the wonderful authors who make me fall in love with books again and again, and have taught me so much about writing and life.

Thank you to all the neurotic indie musicians and creatives out there for character inspiration, and to Berlin, my *Wahlheimat* and so often character in its own right—messy, changeable yet so insistently itself.

Finally, thank you to everyone who read this far, especially if you saw a little of yourself in this book.

About the Author

Originally from Virginia, Kat Hausler is a graduate of New York University and holds an M.F.A. in Fiction from Fairleigh Dickinson University, where she was the recipient of a Baumeister Fellowship. She is the author of *Retrograde* and *What I Know About July*, as well as many shorter pieces. Her work has appeared in *Hawaii Pacific Review, 34th Parallel, Inkspill Magazine, The Sunlight Press, The Dalloway, Rozlyn Press, Porridge Magazine, LitReactor, BlazeVOX, failbetter, Rathalla Review* and *The Airgonaut*, among others. She lives in Berlin and is also a translator.

Did you enjoy this book?

If so, word-of-mouth recommendations and online reviews are critical to the success of any book, so we hope you'll tell your friends about it and consider leaving a review at your favorite bookseller's or library's website.

Visit us at www.meerkatpress.com for our full catalog.

Meerkat Press
Asheville